Mu Gia Pass
Between North Vietnam and Laos

Green jungle, reddish-brown roadways, and thousands of bomb craters rushed by in a spiraling blur. Mitch's eyes jittered, trying to find something stationary in the spinning world. A terrifying realization jolted him. The O-1 was spinning—and upside down.

Panic seized him. He'd never been in an inverted spin—and he'd never talked to anyone who had.

In the twirling scene below, he saw more flashes. His mind was too overloaded to sense which guns were firing, competing for the second kill of the morning.

Ignoring tracers, Mitch pushed the left rudder pedal against the stop. The spin accelerated—wrong rudder. He jammed his right foot against the other pedal. Spinning seemed to slow, but he wasn't certain. Cramps stiffened his fingers, protesting against his death grip on the throttle and stick. One of J.D.'s silly sayings flashed to mind: "If it's inevitable, relax. No sense dyin' all tensed up."

"We gonna bail out, Lieutenant?"

Ellison sounded less frightened than Mitch expected. "Negative!" He concealed the conclusion reached with a glance at the altimeter—they were too low for both to jump clear and deploy good chutes before slamming into the ground.

Without warning, the lawnmower-like sound of the engine ceased. The propeller began winding down.

A Certain Brotherhood

A Certain Brotherhood

"Sensations I haven't felt for nearly thirty years held me hostage from beginning to end—I couldn't put it down. The sights, sounds, and even the smells are so vividly painted that I found myself reliving the rush of our aerial combat adventures over the Ho Chi Minh Trail. If someone asks what it was like to have 'been there—done that,' all I have to do is hand them this book. Thanks for the legacy."

—**Charles (Chic) Randow**, Nail 68

"*A Certain Brotherhood* captures the camaraderie, the loneliness, and the stark terror brought on by war. The flying scenes are both gripping and educational. Best of all, Jimmie Butler has created characters who are so real, I felt as if I knew them from my own service experience. I loved this book!"

—**James A. Davidson**
United States Naval Academy Class of 1969
Former Operations Officer on DE-Class Destroyers

"*A Certain Brotherhood* from a feminine point of view—I knew my brother flew tiny Cessnas without guns and his job was to set up bombing missions. I knew how interested he was in POW-MIA rescue activities. The blatant danger he was in was not brought home to me until my first trip to view The Wall in D.C. When I purchased three Kansas bracelets (all they had), I discovered the officers were *all* pilots lost over Laos. A few years later I bought two more from Kansas—two more pilots lost over Laos! Men reviewing this book understand; they were there. I've cried through it three times now—and hold him closer to me each time. If you loved someone who was there, YOU MUST READ THEIR STORY!!!"

—**Jacque Sue**—of the Sisterhood who Waited and Prayed

"The major characters are so well done you feel as if they're real people you've known for years. The action is continuous, heart-stopping, and so authentic you'll find yourself jinking to avoid the ground fire. This best-of-both-worlds combination of characterization and thunderous action makes the book impossible to put down. In the standard lingo of a book-reviewer, *A Certain Brotherhood* is a great read!"

—**Ivan Munninghoff**, Lt. Col., USAF Retired
United States Air Force Academy Class of 1967

A Certain Brotherhood

For as long as Mitch McCall could remember, he had wanted to follow in his father's footsteps as an Air Force pilot. In pilot training, Mitch nearly crashes a supersonic T-38. He walks away from the incident but can't shake off the resulting phobia about landings.

The Vietnam War escalates, and Mitch volunteers for combat as a forward air controller. FACs fly single-engine Cessnas over enemy territory and look for targets for armed fighter aircraft. Mitch accepts the new dangers in a make-or-break attempt to beat his fears.

In Thailand, he is teamed with Captain James D. (J.D.) Dalton. J.D. is a few years older than Mitch—but many years more experienced in almost everything. As a teenager, J.D. had idolized the ill-fated actor, James Dean. Now, almost a decade later, J.D. still lives by some of the actor's philosophies and flies his small Cessna as if this life were just a step toward whatever comes next.

In Hanoi, famed North Vietnamese General Vo Nguyen Giap is plotting a bold operation. If successful, his armies will overrun the U.S. Marines at Khe Sanh during the upcoming Tet offensive. His plan depends heavily on battle-hardened veteran Colonel Le Van Do. Le commands Battlefield C, North Vietnam's secret operations in Laos. Battlefield C contains much of the Ho Chi Minh Trail and is patrolled from the air almost every day by Mitch and J.D.

In late January 1968, the Communist forces launch a massive offensive during the Tet truce. The fate of thousands of American Marines at Khe Sanh depends on whether Mitch discovers the secret that Colonel Le Van Do has concealed beneath the 200-foot tall trees of the Laotian jungles.

★ ★ ★ ★ ★ ★ ★ ★ ★

A Certain Brotherhood tells of the courage, fears, motivations, and bonds of camaraderie shared by professional American fliers who flew in the Vietnam War.

OTHER BOOKS BY JIMMIE H. BUTLER

The Iskra Incident

Red Lightning—Black Thunder

A
Certain
Brotherhood

For S.E.A.'s FINEST FACs   CABLE: "CRICKET"

"HAVE WILLIE PETE, WILL TRAVEL"

FIRST LIEUTENANT MITCHELL L. MC CALL
UNITED STATES AIR FORCE

FLYING THE
O-1F
BIRD DOG, FASTEST
FIXED-GEAR FIGHTER
IN THE INVENTORY
SNEAKY &
UNDER-HANDED BUSINESS
CONDUCTED BY APPOINTMENT
ONLY.

SPECIALIZING IN:
ROAD, BRIDGE, TRUCK
& GUN DESTRUCTION;
HOT JEEPS & COLD SINGHA;
WOMEN, HOT OR COLD;
TERRORIZING NATIVES,
INSTRUCTOR PILOTS,
SAFETY OFFICERS, &
AIR COMMANDOS.

Jimmie H. Butler
Nav 12
30 Oct 2000

Colonel Jimmie H. Butler
USAF (Ret.)

CRICKET PRESS

CRICKET PRESS

Published by Cricket Press
6660 Delmonico Drive, D-215
Colorado Springs, CO 80919, U. S. A.

First Cricket Press Printing, November 1996

Cover based on an original painting by S. W. Ferguson of Colorado Springs, created especially for *A Certain Brotherhood*

Printed in the United States of America

The quotation on page 347 is from pages 90-91 of *The Electronic Battlefield*, by Paul Dickson, Indiana University Press, 1976.

This is a work of fiction. Names, characters, places, and incidents either are the product of the author's imagination or are used fictitiously.

This novel is primarily about FACs—Forward Air Controllers—
who flew small, unarmed observation aircraft against
the Ho Chi Minh Trail.
Day after day, FACs were in the middle of the action.
We witnessed the heroism. We knew the stories.

A Certain Brotherhood is respectfully dedicated to the memory of
Captain Dwight S. Campbell and Captain Robert L. Sholl
Det. 1, 603rd Air Commando Squadron
Nakhon Phanom Royal Thai Air Force Base, Thailand.
Flying an A-26 as Nimrod 36
in the pre-dawn darkness of 22 February 1967,
they gave their lives in the highest traditions of the brotherhood.
Too long has their story been known by too few.

Nimrod on the prowl: A-26 over Southeast Asia

★★★And to the rest of the members of that certain brotherhood.
You know who you are. ★★★

Acknowledgments

Writing novels is a solitary profession, but there are always people who are helpful and encouraging along the way. A number of people served that role during the more than a decade that *A Certain Brotherhood* was in the works.

Special thanks go to my sister, Jacque Sue. Without her support and encouragement, *A Certain Brotherhood* would not yet be in print.

Thanks to S. W. Ferguson, an aviation artist of extraordinary talent, who took my vision of a scene from *A Certain Brotherhood* and turned it into the dramatic cover on the novel.

Thanks to my friend, David Kuamoo, the most decorated hero I know from the Vietnam War. Dave's advice about North Vietnamese ground operations was extremely helpful in developing some scenes in *A Certain Brotherhood.*

Thanks, as always, to my friend and mentor, Paul Gillette (1938-1996), author of *Play Misty for Me, Carmela, 305 East*, and nearly a hundred other books. Paul taught me the things I needed to know to get my novels published. The writing community—particularly in Los Angeles and Colorado—lost a great teacher and friend when Paul passed away in January 1996. He is missed by many, many loyal friends.

Thanks to an unknown trio of U.S. Air Force fighter pilots of the 12th TAC Fighter Wing, Cam Ranh Bay, South Vietnam in 1967. Their "Interview with a Shy, Unassuming Fighter Pilot" brought many laughs to us during our combat tours in 1967 and obviously served as the inspiration of the promotion party depicted in *A Certain Brotherhood.*

Thanks to the many friends in critique groups who reviewed pages of *A Certain Brotherhood* in various stages of its development. The earliest versions were critiqued in Paul Gillette's Writers Workshop in the 1980s and later versions were read by very dedicated members of my critique group here in Colorado. I appreciate their many suggestions that helped *A Certain Brotherhood* be a better novel than it would have been otherwise.

Thanks to my daughter, Kellie Kathleen, who understood why *A Certain Brotherhood* wasn't dedicated to her as *Red Lightning—Black Thunder* had been dedicated to her sister, Kami (1966-1994).

Common Terms and Jargon of
A Certain Brotherhood

To maintain authenticity, I have included many of the common terms and the jargon that were part of everyday life for Cricket FACs in the 1960s. The following summary includes how some of those terms are used in *A Certain Brotherhood*. Call signs for some flying units remained the same for months or years. Others changed almost daily and were specified in the orders sent down for the day's missions. I have grouped them into the two categories for call signs used in *A Certain Brotherhood*.

Aircraft Call Signs (Permanent)

Alley Cat: Airborne Battlefield Command & Control Center (C-130) for Steel Tiger/Night

Blindbat: Flare Aircraft (C-130)

Covey: FACs of the 20th TASS in I Corps of South Vietnam (O-1/O-2)

Cricket: Airborne Battlefield Command & Control Center (C-130) for Steel Tiger/Day

Crown: Airborne Rescue Coordination Center (HC-130)

Hillsboro: Airborne Battlefield Command & Control Center (C-130) for Tiger Hound/Day

Jolly Green: Air Rescue Helicopters (HH-3)

Nail: FACs of the 23rd TASS at Nakhon Phanom RTAFB, Thailand (O-1/O-2)

Nimrod: A-26 crews of Air Commandos at Nakhon Phanom RTAFB, Thailand

Sandy: Air Rescue Escort (A-1)

Zorro: T-28 crews of Air Commandos at Nakhon Phanom RTAFB, Thailand

Aircraft Call Signs (Changing)

Bear: F-105 Thunderchiefs	**Hot Dog:** F-105 Thunderchiefs
Boston: F-105 Thunderchiefs	**Kingfish:** F-105 Thunderchiefs
Cadillac: F-105 Thunderchiefs	**Laredo:** F-105 Thunderchiefs
Cobra: F-4 Phantoms	**Nathan:** F-105 Thunderchiefs
Crossbow: F-105 Thunderchiefs	**Packard:** F-4 Phantoms
Fearless: F-105 Thunderchiefs	**Redneck:** F-4 Phantoms
Flamingo: F-105 Thunderchiefs	**Stag:** T-38 Talon
Gunslinger: UH-1 Helicopter Gunships	**Venom:** F-105 Thunderchiefs
Honda: F-105 Thunderchiefs	

Geographical Locations/Identifiers

Alpha, Bravo, Charlie, Delta, Echo, Foxtrot, Golf, & Hotel: These designators were assigned in 1966 to major interdiction points in the road network in central Laos.

Ban Karai Pass: Route from North Vietnam into Laos. The North Vietnamese built Route 137/912 across the Ban Karai Pass in 1966.

Ban Laboy Ford: Major interdiction point where Route 912 crossed a canyon of the Nam Ta Le River near the border of North Vietnam and Laos.

Chokes: The grouping of Alpha, Bravo, and Charlie in central Laos. The FACs commonly called them the chokes.

Cricket: The nickname of the operational area patrolled by Cricket FACs in the northern part of Steel Tiger in central Laos. Also, the call sign of the airborne controllers for the area.

Dog House: Nickname for the first major valley south of the Mu Gia Pass.

Harley's Valley: A wide meadow that covered most of the area between the Ban Laboy Ford and the border with North Vietnam. The valley was named by Cricket FACs for Captain Lee D. Harley, who was shot down flying an O-1 over the valley in early 1966.

Khe Sanh: A U.S. Marine base in the northwest corner of South Vietnam.

Mu Gia Pass: A deep canyon through the Annamite Mountains on the Laos/North Vietnam border. Roads through Mu Gia were the major infiltration route from North Vietnam. Mu Gia was the most heavily defended target in Steel Tiger in 1967.

NKP: The most common nickname for Nakhon Phanom Royal Thai Air Force Base, which was the home of the Cricket FACs of the 23rd Tactical Air Support Squadron (TASS). The base's other major combat unit was the Air Commando detachments, which became the 56th Air Commando Wing in 1967. In addition, air rescue helicopters and fighters (Jolly Greens and Sandies) were on continuous alert at NKP.

Steel Tiger: The nickname for the operational area where the Ho Chi Minh Trail came through central Laos.

Tally Ho: The nickname for the operational area in the panhandle of North Vietnam.

Tiger Hound: The southern part of Steel Tiger, which was patrolled primarily by the Covey FACs of the 20th TASS headquartered at Danang Air Base, South Vietnam.

Tchepone: A small Laotian village on Route 9, Tchepone became a major transhipment point because of key roads coming in from the north and west and of roads leading out to the east and southeast. Tchepone was one of the most heavily defended areas in central Laos.

Miscellaneous Terms/Nicknames

AB Triple C: The airborne battlefield command & control centers that controlled and coordinated out-country air operations. Daytime controllers included Cricket and Hillsboro. Alley Cat was the night ABCCC for Steel Tiger.

Arc Light: Air strikes by B-52s flying at high altitude.

Beeper: The function of the emergency radios that broadcast a warbling tone on UHF frequency 243.0. The purpose was to draw attention to fliers who had bailed out or crash landed.

BDA (Bomb Damage Assessment): A check after a strike to evaluate any damage the target suffered.

CBU (Cluster Bomb Units): Bombs that scattered many bomblets when released.

Combat Skyspot: An air strike by aircraft that were guided over the target by ground-based radar.

Crossing the Fence: Term used by NKP-based aircraft for crossing the Mekong River between Thailand and Laos. Was used going to and from combat missions in Laos or North Vietnam.

FAC (Forward Air Controller): Pilots who flew unarmed Cessna O-1s and O-2s (and, later, OV-10s) over enemy territory to search out targets and to direct air strikes.

PSP (Perforated Steel Planking): Interlocking steel planks used to make runways and parking ramps at forward airfields.

SAM: Surface-to-air missile

Tet: The lunar new year celebrated beginning of the first full moon after January 20th.

Thud: The unofficial nickname for the F-105 Thunderchief.

Triple-A (Antiaircraft artillery): The larger caliber antiaircraft weapons. Normally the shells had a diameter of twenty-three millimeters or more.

Willie Pete: The nickname for white phosphorous, which burns fiercely and gives off considerable white smoke when exposed to air. The marking rockets carried by FACs had warheads filled with white phosphorous.

List of Maps and Illustrations

Most photos are from the U.S. Air Force and the author's collection. The O-2 on page 254 was provided by James Wilhelm. Thanks to other former Crickets including: Charles (Chic) Randow, Victor (Pappy) Yoakum, Robert Johnston, Craig D. Elliott, and Pat Sweeney. Over the years they provided other photos that have added to the authenticity of *A Certain Brotherhood*.

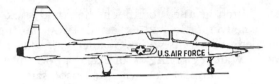

PROLOGUE

U.S. Air Force Pilot Training

April 1964

"Captain Walker's gonna put us through the wringer, Mitch."

Lieutenant Mitchell McCall heard the warning as he hurried toward the parachute shop. He stopped and turned. Two other student pilots were walking toward him, cutting across grass that separated the squadron headquarters from the parking ramp.

Waiting for his friends, Mitch looked at nearby rows of white T-38s. The midday sun glinted off canopies and caused a brilliant shimmering that made the jet trainers seem alive. He listened to the roar from afterburners on a T-38 streaking down a distant runway. Breathing in the familiar odor of jet fuel, he was eager to get airborne. Mitch smiled. He envied no one in the entire world.

Lieutenant Robbie Robinson's freckled face frowned even more than usual. He was the worrier among forty students remaining in their pilot training class. In the three months since the class became first to train in the new T-38s, Robbie's flying had gotten worse.

Strolling a few steps behind Robinson was Lieutenant Phil Schofield. Tall and lanky, he was as nonchalant as ever. Schofield was Mitch's best friend. For the last six months, they had ranked one-two in class standing. Who was number one on any particular day depended on scores on the latest check rides or academic tests.

When close enough for normal conversation, Robinson continued, "I overheard Captain Walker bragging to other instructors."

The threat didn't bother Mitch even though he soon would be racing in close formation with a T-38 flown by Robinson and Walker. Mitch smiled at the added challenge. "Don't look so worried. I'll keep up."

"I'm not worried about you," Robinson said, as the three lieutenants continued toward the building where flying gear was stored. "I'm worried about me."

"No sweat, tiger," Schofield said in his Texas drawl. "Just take two extra barf bags and call me in the mornin'."

"Easy for you to make jokes," Robinson said with a sharp edge in his voice. "You'll be flying nav training instead of rat racing with Captain W. screeching in your earphones. You saw how determined he was."

"Robbie's right." Schofield flashed a sly smile that seemed so natural on the laid-back Texan. "The words were 'I'm gonna have McCall's ass!'"

"We'll see." Mitch grinned, confident he could stick with the leader through any maneuvers. He had expected a routine flight to build up flying time needed to earn his wings. Walker's attitude added spice. "Just consider Captain Walker's giving us an extra opportunity to excel."

"I don't need special opportunities," Robinson said.

Mitch thought of his father, a combat pilot in two wars. "My dad always said you never know which mission'll be the biggest one of your life, so you'd better be ready for anything on every flight."

Robinson didn't look convinced. "I hope today isn't my big mission with everything downhill from here."

"You'll do fine."

After a few moments silence, Schofield asked Mitch, "Didn't they teach you zoomies anything practical in Colorado?"

"More than you learned in Aggieland," Mitch said, continuing their teasing rivalry between the Air Force Academy and Texas A&M.

Schofield sounded more serious than usual. "At least A&M taught strategy. It's not smart for a second lieutenant to clean-out his flight commander at poker."

Robinson nodded vigorously. "Especially when said flight commander has red hair and the temper to go with it."

"What could I do?" Mitch pictured Walker getting progressively drunker the previous evening in the stag bar at the officers club. "He kept throwing his money at me."

"You should've let the captains catch it. You were too big an accessory to his making a fool of himself. Near the end, you ran bluffs—"

"Poker's poker. If he couldn't see I was bluf—"

"Captain W. looks to be a poor loser," Robinson said. "We're in for it."

"If he doesn't learn drinking and poker don't mix, he'd better get used to being a loser."

Schofield shook his head. "Make that three extra barf bags, Robbie. Our friend looks to be a slow learner."

"Thanks, guys." Robinson grimaced as if facing an appointment with an executioner.

Mitch gave Robinson an encouraging tap on the shoulder. Exchanging glances, Mitch saw fear, undoubtedly due to problems Robinson had flying the high-performance jets in formation. "You'll do fine, Robbie."

Schofield gestured ahead. "Looks like a gathering of Mitch's *little* Vietnamese Air Force, with *little* being the operative term."

Mitch looked up. The flight-line shuttle had stopped at the parachute shop. Six Vietnamese student pilots got off. Mitch was uneasy with Schofield's teasing about their size, but he and the Texan were at least a head taller than the Vietnamese pilots. The visiting students appeared to be all baggy flight suits, helmets, parachutes, and boots.

As unofficial interpreter, Mitch had become acquainted with each one. He respected their dogged determination to learn to fly so they could fight the growing Communist insurgency in their homeland of South Vietnam.

When they saw Mitch, all six offered greetings in a cacophony of Vietnamese, French, and broken English.

Mitch returned the greeting in French and broken Vietnamese.

As everyone entered the parachute shop, Schofield said, "You bucking to be chief of staff of the Vietnamese Air Force?"

"Three days with Major Thao doesn't qualify me to take over."

Vietnamese officers understood more French than English, and Mitch had lived six years in France where his father was assigned after World War II. Mitch routinely helped the Vietnamese students. In addition, the base commander had picked Mitch to escort Vietnamese officers visiting the base.

Schofield lifted his parachute from a rack. "That was, what, your fourth time wining and dining VIPs?"

"Third." Still enthusiastic over last week's experience, Mitch began checking his parachute. "Major Thao told some great war stories."

"But," Schofield said, "helping whip the French at Dien Bien Phu makes him a little suspect."

"He also fought the Japanese while you were still in diapers." Mitch had been enthralled by the battle-scarred veteran's quiet stories of jungle fighting half a world away.

The Vietnamese pilots put away their flying gear, and all but one left.

As Mitch pulled his helmet from the rack, he noticed Lieutenant Tran Ngoc Nhu standing patiently alongside.

Flashing a smile trimmed in gold teeth, Lieutenant Nhu pointed at silver falcons on Mitch's helmet. In French, he said, "Your falcons are very magnificent. Would you please paint a dragon on my helmet?"

"Sure." Mitch had earned a reputation throughout the flying squadrons for his skill with a paint brush. He painted designs on so many helmets, he kept a set of paints in his class's flight room. He raised three fingers. "Bring your helmet to me in *three* hours."

"Thank you, Lieutenant Mitch," Nhu said in English. He picked up his helmet and clipboard and headed for the door. Using an idiom Mitch had taught the Vietnamese, Nhu said, "See you later, Lieutenant Mitch."

Before Mitch could respond, Schofield said, "Expedite. Expedite."

Nhu shook his head, flashing an embarrassed grin. "Me no expedite today, Lieutenant Phil."

"That's right," Mitch said in English. "You no expedite today."

Nhu nodded.

Two weeks earlier Mitch had translated *expedite* as meaning to do something as soon as possible. The following day Nhu had been late. When told to expedite his takeoff, he immediately took off from the taxiway. Mitch had been required to make one official explanation and scores of responses to teasing by Schofield and other classmates.

Gesturing at Schofield, Mitch said in French, "Water buffalo are smarter than Aggies."

Nhu laughed and went out through the door.

"I heard *Aggieee*," Schofield said, dragging out the final word in a Texas-drawl version of a French accent.

"If they taught Aggies to speak anything but Texan," Mitch said, "you might know what else I said."

Mitch led Robinson and Schofield outside into the bright afternoon sun. They separated and hurried across the parking ramp. The broad expanse of concrete magnified the oppressive heat, but Mitch hardly noticed. He shrugged off the heat as easily as the warnings about the upcoming flight.

His class standing in pilot training assured his choice of assignments on graduation day. Then, having earned his USAF pilot's wings, he expected to fly an F-105 in the greatest air force in the world. Not only did he fulfill his love of flying almost daily, but he also was married to a young woman who was beautiful, loving, and talented. He smiled at thoughts of Elizabeth and of their first child she carried within her.

Approaching his T-38, Mitch felt a deep-seated, almost religious, kinship with the sleek, needle-nosed craft. For the next hour-and-a-half, they would be a team—a team to teach Captain Walker that Mitch McCall was no easier to beat in the air than at poker.

Lieutenant Robinson's T-38, with Captain Walker in the back seat, taxied onto the runway. Mitch followed, stopping beyond the right wing and slightly behind. Robinson raised a gloved hand with its index finger pointing upward and made a circular motion. Mitch pressed harder on the brakes and pushed his throttles to military power.

Struggling to be unleashed, his T-38 leaned forward like a sprinter in the starting blocks.

Mitch loved the vibrations that carried the crackling roar into his body even though his padded helmet and earphones tried to keep the noise at bay. His senses were in tune with the aircraft. A glance at the instrument panel told him both engines were working perfectly. He tugged ritualistically on the ends of his lap belt, which already held him tightly to the ejection seat. Satisfied, he reached to the clock and put a finger on the timer button.

Robinson looked at Mitch.

Mitch nodded, signaling his readiness. His oxygen mask hid his smile of confidence and his eagerness to show what he could do.

Robinson tilted his head back, then nodded. Fiery cones of exhaust flashed from black tailpipes. The lead T-38 bounded forward.

Mitch punched the timer, released brakes, grabbed the control stick, and jammed his throttles into afterburner. Feeling the jolt from the burners, he glanced at the temperature gauges, which peaked out well below red-line. Satisfied, he returned his attention to the lead aircraft. He would have few chances to look into his cockpit while flying wing. Until his turn to lead the formation, his gaze would remain on the other T-38 only a few feet away.

In seconds, both aircraft accelerated through three hundred knots with gear and flaps retracted. Mitch watched for a signal Robbie was coming out of afterburner. Instead, the lead T-38 angled up sharply. Mitch followed, holding perfect position while both aircraft thundered into a steep climb.

Robinson turned his head, gazed at Mitch, and shrugged.

What's going on? Students leading a formation seldom watched the other T-38. Mitch decided Robinson was signaling that Walker had taken control. Now Mitch understood why they were still in afterburner even though Walker had not briefed a burner climb. Anger flared. Mitch believed in doing things by-the-book. Flying unbriefed maneuvers definitely was *not* by-the- book. His anger triggered new determination to surpass any trick Walker tried.

Peripheral vision showed the plains of Oklahoma falling away. The spinning altimeter reminded him of a clock in a time-travel movie. He'd made burner climbs before, but never beside an aircraft almost close enough to touch.

Seconds later the lead aircraft banked into a turn. Its nose lowered.

Letting his T-38 slide back a few feet, Mitch glanced at his instruments. In fewer than two minutes since brake release, he'd climbed nearly seven miles.

Walker raised a clenched fist, jerked it sideways, nodded, and retarded his throttles.

To avoid overrunning, Mitch yanked his throttles nearly to idle. He still coasted almost even with the leader before falling back.

"Stay awake out there," Walker growled.

"Stay awake?" Mitch blurted the words without transmitting. He glared behind his oxygen mask. Procedures called for a delay between the preparatory signal and the signal to execute. "Such stunts cause mid-airs." He vowed to be more professional than Walker. Seeing the lead T-38 pulling away, Mitch pushed the throttles to military power.

"I didn't signal you to fall back into trail," Walker said.

Mitch bristled at the sarcasm. He was a few feet out of position but still on the wing—certainly not close to trail formation behind the leader. He jammed his throttles into afterburner, held them there until he felt the boost, then pulled back to avoid overrunning.

A few calm minutes passed while the T-38s flew to the training area. Finally Robinson stared at Mitch, signaling Walker was in control again.

"Stag Three-nine Flight, go trail," Walker said coldly.

"Two," Mitch responded.

He let his T-38 slide behind to just below shimmering exhausts. Walker rolled left, entering a downward spiral. Mitch followed. His world seemed to exist only in relation to the other white trainer and to the blurry background of the reddish-browns and greens of Oklahoma. He couldn't risk a glance at the airspeed indicator. Nevertheless, the increasing roar of air rushing by told him they were approaching five hundred knots, normal speed for acrobatics.

After descending several thousand feet, Walker rolled out of the spiral and pulled up into a loop. Mitch followed. The dark background of the earth gave way to cerulean blue. Bladders in his G-suit filled, squeezing his legs to force blood upward. He tightened his stomach, grunting against pressures of his G-suit and of five Gs crushing him into the ejection seat. Exhilaration pushed aside his anger. He stared at the tail pipes and fought the pressures that could cause him to black out.

The next twenty minutes were a rat race of loops and rolls and Immelmanns and other maneuvers he'd seen only when instructors flew both aircraft. Mitch kept his eyes on the other white airplane. From one acrobatic maneuver to the next, the leading T-38 seemed frozen in place while a kaleidoscope of colors swirled in the background.

Mitch imagined combat with Walker trying to escape close-in pursuit. The more Walker seemed determined to shake Mitch's T-38, the more precisely Mitch held position. He moved throttles, stick, and rudder pedals as if he were as much a part of the aircraft as the U.S. Air Force emblems emblazoned on its white surfaces.

Knifing through a mile of sky every six seconds, the T-38s stayed together as if invisibly attached. During a sustained horizontal circle with both aircraft on their sides in wing formation, the nose of Mitch's T-38 was barely above the tip of Walker's wing.

"You're too close, tiger," Walker grunted.

"Roger!" *Getting to you, am I?* Smiling behind his oxygen mask, Mitch eased his aircraft up a couple of feet.

Moments later Walker rolled out of the turn, and the T-38s flew from the training area.

The turn toward the airfield surprised Mitch. A glance at the clock and fuel gauges answered his question. The burner climb and continuous maneuvering at high speed drained fuel more quickly than usual.

The G-forces and the tension of holding close formation left Mitch exhausted. Matching Walker's every maneuver left Mitch excited.

In those quiet minutes, however, Mitch got angry. He doubted his friend had flown any of the acrobatics. Robbie also had been cheated out of practice he needed flying on someone else's wing. Mitch seldom challenged authority, but Walker didn't deserve the authority he wielded. Mitch always became furious when justice didn't triumph.

When the two-ship formation crossed over the end of the runway at fifteen hundred feet, Robinson rolled sharply away to begin the racetrack pattern around to land. Mitch flew straight for four more seconds, then turned to chase the other T-38 from nearly a mile in trail.

Able to relax for the first time since brake release, Mitch stretched stiffness from his neck. He extended landing gear and flaps, then watched the leader's descending turn toward the runway. Determined to show the pressure hadn't fazed him, Mitch turned early as instructors sometimes did when showing off. He checked indicators for flaps and landing gear. "Stag Three-nine Two, gear check, touch-and-go."

"Continue," an instructor pilot said from a mobile control tower near the end of the runway.

The lead T-38 rolled out and lined up on final approach.

Watching Robinson seem to creep toward the runway, Mitch saw he'd narrowed the gap too much. He eased the throttles back to lose a few knots of airspeed. "Get it on the ground, Robbie," Mitch urged quietly. He couldn't land until the first aircraft was at least three thousand feet down the runway. The lead T-38 touched down just as Mitch aligned his aircraft with approach lights leading to the runway.

Mitch knew he'd cut it too close.

"Final, go around," the controller ordered.

"Three-nine Two's on the go." Mitch shoved his throttles forward, then flipped the gear handle upward in disgust. "Stag Three-nine Two request closed." He hoped the controller would let him stay in close instead of having to fly the larger rectangular traffic pattern.

"Negative, closed."

Disappointed, but not surprised, Mitch raised the flaps. Solo students seldom got to fly the shorter pattern. Throttling back to stay under three hundred knots, he watched the other T-38 lift off the runway.

Walker looked up at Mitch's aircraft thundering overhead, touched his fingers to his helmet, and waved his hand in a sloppy salute.

"Damn you," Mitch said without transmitting.

"Stag Three-nine One request closed," Walker said.

"Call downwind," the controller responded.

Mitch seethed while his T-38 soared to fifteen hundred feet. As an instructor, Walker was eligible to fly the shorter pattern while Mitch had to fly a ten-mile rectangle before his next chance to land. *Not fair, especially after Walker's unprofessional performance.*

A couple of minutes later, Mitch's T-38 returned to the runway heading. "Stag Three-nine Two, initial."

Before the controller responded, Walker said, "Stag Three-nine One request closed."

Mitch looked beyond the needle nose of his T-38 and saw the other aircraft on the runway. "Damn your hide!" Walker wasn't supposed to request a closed traffic pattern until airborne from his touch-and-go. His closed pattern would conflict with Mitch's overhead pattern.

"Uh, roger, uh," the controller said, then hesitated. "Stag Three-nine One, call downwind. Three-nine Two, take it around the pattern."

Mitch was livid. He discovered his fuel was near the minimum for solo students. His first landing would have to be a full stop. Walker had stolen Mitch's chance to practice even one touch-and-go. *No justice!*

"You copy, Three-niner Two?" The controller's voice was insistent.

"Stag Three-nine Two copied straight through on initial."

Get with it, dummy! Mitch chided himself for allowing his anger to get in the way. Thinking about the wrong things was a good way to get killed, so he concentrated on flying around the pattern.

He forced his thoughts from Walker until in the final turn, toward the runway. "Stag Three-nine Two, gear checked, full-stop."

"Cleared to land, Three-niner Two."

Mitch aligned his T-38 with the approach lights and wondered if he could conceal his anger during the debriefing. Contrary to what Phil had inferred in his Texas drawl, Mitch learned plenty of practical lessons at the Academy. He knew who'd lose if a second lieutenant displayed anger at his flight commander. But anger burned within.

Mitch was absorbed in those thoughts when his T-38 swooped over the dividing line between the asphalt overrun and the concrete runway. He sensed something was different an instant before the aircraft seemed to take over. Instead of gliding the last few feet to the concrete, his T-38 soared skyward in unseen currents of air.

Reflexes triggered. Mitch clamped tighter on the stick and pushed to force the aircraft toward the runway. A glance at the instruments revealed nothing about what had happened but gave a stark warning. Airspeed was bleeding away rapidly. His eyes flashed up for another quick look outside. He was at least thirty feet above the runway. If the T-38 stalled and fell, the impact would drive the gear through the wings.

His left fist shot forward with the throttles as if delivering a jab in boxing class

The wings wobbled. The aircraft faltered.

Fearing he'd reacted too late, Mitch froze, sure he was going to die in a flaming crash. He thought of Elizabeth and of their unborn child he would never see. He remembered the look on his mother's face nine years earlier when she was told an airplane had killed his father.

Afterburners lit off, jolting him as if rear-ended by a Mack truck. No longer falling like a bomb, the T-38 shot forward like a bullet. When he risked another look inside, the airspeed was thirty knots faster. "Three-nine Two's on the go!" His throat was so dry the words hurt.

Reflexes conditioned by months of training responded even though the aftershock of what just happened threatened to overwhelm him. As his thoughts caught up, he saw he'd retracted the gear and flaps and was rocketing beyond the far end of the runway. A feeling of something overlooked nagged him. His eyes were drawn to the fuel gauges. "Stag Three-nine Two'll be minimum fuel on this landing."

"Copied."

Mitch held his breath to stop hyperventilating. Letting the T-38 coast up to traffic-pattern altitude, he blocked out worries about fuel. Minimums were set to give a reserve for unexpected problems.

For a couple of minutes, Mitch flew through peaceful skies above wheat fields and pastures. However, fright rushed at him like hurricane-driven waves pounding a beach. In that terrifying instant above the runway, his youthful feelings of invincibility had given way to an unwanted realization—an airplane could kill him at a time of its choosing, no matter how good a pilot he might be.

When his T-38 swooped above the overrun for the second time, the engines were running smoothly—without indications of fuel starvation. Black asphalt gave way to concrete, and Mitch exhaled a sigh of relief. He hadn't run out of fuel.

The aircraft ballooned skyward again, but this time two things were different. Mitch immediately jammed the throttles into afterburner—and even less fuel remained.

"Three-nine Two's on the go. Emergency fuel!" The words spewed forth in a steady stream. The tone was noticeably higher than Mitch had ever heard himself speak.

Walker asked, "How much fuel do you have, McCall?"

"Enough for less than two times around the pattern, sir."

His glance dropped to his parachute's D-ring to verify the zero-delay lanyard was clipped to the shiny ring of metal. The lanyard would deploy his parachute seconds after he ejected—if forced to eject. Obviously some of his senses believed he wouldn't get his aircraft onto the runway.

"Give him a closed pattern, Charlie," Walker said.

"Roger," the controller said. "Break. Stag Three-niner Two's cleared closed traffic. Report downwind."

Reprieve! Mitch pulled into a climbing turn. The close-in traffic pattern might give him two more chances—if the fuel gauges were accurate. He rolled out parallel to the runway. "Stag Three-nine Two's closed downwind, emergency fuel, full stop."

Rushed by the need to reconfigure and complete landing checks, Mitch extended gear and flaps. Flashing red lights on the parking ramp distracted him. In a slow-motion race to the runway, three fire trucks and an ambulance moved between rows of parked jets. Chills flashed through his shoulders and arms. The emergency vehicles were for him.

He extended the downwind leg to have a longer final approach. Suddenly the term *final approach* bothered him. He stiffened his legs against the rudder pedals, strengthening his resolve to make sure this wasn't *his* final approach. He tugged the ends of the lap belt and rolled into the final turn. "Stag Three-nine Two is gear checked, full-stop."

"Cleared to land, Three-niner Two."

"Carry extra power to touchdown, Two." Walker sounded strained but more supportive than his usual tone in giving orders.

Mitch nodded. He pointed the needle nose beyond the big one-eight on the runway. Silently he mouthed words from the 23rd Psalm.

His T-38 glided, its wheels reaching earthward like an eagle's talons.

He kept the throttles above idle and was thirty feet higher than usual when he crossed from the asphalt to the concrete. The aircraft bucked, but Mitch maintained control. He held the glide angle until the tires were just above the runway. The T-38 floated a few more seconds. He pulled the throttles to idle, and the aircraft returned to earth.

While coasting more than a mile, Mitch felt drained of strength. For the first time he noticed sweat edging down around his eyes. He tightened his grip on the throttles and stick to control trembling that threatened to inundate him. He didn't know what had happened, but he felt somehow betrayed by his aircraft. The earlier kinship evaporated.

Mitch taxied off the runway and stopped on the adjacent apron. As he completed post-flight checks, a fire truck rumbled by. He took a moment to settle down, then followed the truck to the parking ramp.

He wished he'd never learned to play poker.

As Mitch taxied into the parking spot designated by the ground crew, he saw Walker and Robinson standing nearby.

Walker was waiting when Mitch climbed down from the cockpit. "You're no longer cleared to fly solo, McCall. You and I'll go up first period, tomorrow afternoon."

"Yes, sir," Mitch said, glad a day of flying remained before the weekend. He felt relieved he wouldn't be alone on his next flight, then was bothered that he felt relief.

Walker turned and headed for his office.

Robinson looked sympathetically at Mitch and shrugged.

Normally, such an announcement in front of the maintenance crew and a classmate would've humiliated Mitch. Now, just being alive overshadowed the embarrassment. He wasn't the first student in his class to suffer a bad flight and have to prove himself again before flying solo. Still, Mitch never had imagined it could happen to him.

His parachute and helmet seemed heavier than ever before. His legs felt weak, and he feared he would have to drop to a knee until his strength returned. He leaned against the aircraft as he signed the forms, then hurried toward the parachute shop.

Robinson got in step alongside. "You flew better formation today than I've ever seen, even by instructors."

"Yeah." Mitch appreciated the attempt to cheer him.

They walked in silence to the edge of the parking ramp.

Robinson said quietly, "I think you scared Captain Walker at the—"

"Scared Walker?" Mitch almost blurted out the utter fear he'd faced when death seemed certain—but no one openly discussed fears.

"Captain Walker was getting pretty nervous," Robinson continued. "I think he'll take it easy on you."

"We'll see."

Would Walker be vindictive enough to push Mitch toward elimination? It wouldn't be the first time an instructor had ended a student's flying career. Mitch was determined that that wouldn't happen, even if Walker tried.

"Once you get another flight under your belt, everything'll be okay."

"Right." Mitch shrugged.

He hoped getting over the fright would be that simple. Surging waves of remembered fear made him skeptical. Nine years earlier, he'd vowed to become an Air Force pilot while four jet fighters—flown by his father's friends—had thundered overhead in a missing-man formation. He'd always blocked out images of what his father had faced in his final seconds of flight. Now those thoughts raced at Mitch, giving his father's death an even more haunting dimension. And, for the first time in his life, Mitch realized he could fail to become an Air Force pilot.

Could he keep Elizabeth from discovering how frightened he had been—and still was? He sighed noticeably, knowing he must get that next flight behind him as soon as possible.

On Friday, high winds and thunderstorms grounded all training flights. In the intervening days, Mitch reminded himself he was a good pilot and one scary incident shouldn't change that. By the time he got airborne on the following Monday, however, Mitch McCall knew claws of fear had taken hold deep within him—and he couldn't pull free.

PART ONE

The Vietnam War

Nakhon Phanom Royal Thai Air Force Base, Thailand

February 1967

The Countries of Southeast Asia   1967

O-1F Bird Dog—fastest fixed-gear fighter in the inventory

23rd TASS Cricket

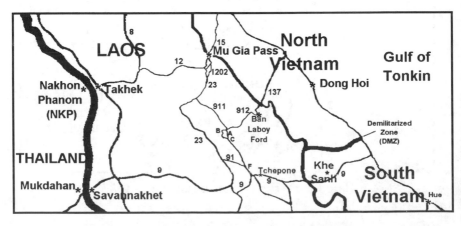

Major routes of the Ho Chi Minh Trail through central Laos

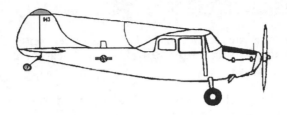

Chapter 1

"Three hundred five!"

The words rushed unbidden from First Lieutenant Mitch McCall. He looked around, relieved he was still alone in the administrative room of the Tactical Unit Operations Center. Pushing away a notebook of classified messages he was reviewing, he grabbed his cup and went to the coffee pot.

At four thirty-two in the morning, the nerve center for the base's combat operations was calm. Mitch heard a clattering teletype machine, which was linked to Seventh Air Force Headquarters in Saigon. Beyond the coffee pot, a hallway led to offices and to the briefing room for the forward air controllers, commonly known as FACs. Mitch was a FAC, trained to fly single-engine Cessnas to search out the enemy trucks and guns in Laos. Soon, he'd be in that room briefing for a mission more dangerous than any of his nearly fifty over the Ho Chi Minh Trail.

Sipping hot coffee, he stared with tired eyes. His surroundings had the drab sameness of many Air Force offices he'd seen in his three and a half years of flying. Tables, chairs, filing cabinets, and four-drawer safes in government-issue gray predominated.

Returning to the notebook, he felt uneasy. The secret message pushed aside earlier reported 305 antiaircraft artillery sites guarded Mu Gia Pass on the border between Laos and North Vietnam. In three hours he'd be over Mu Gia in an unarmed Cessna.

He twisted the left tip of his handlebar mustache—the only thing non-regulation about Mitch McCall.

"Settle down," he whispered, reminding himself the North Vietnamese didn't have enough guns for every emplacement. *Right, right, right!* He formed words but didn't utter them. Maybe *only* thirty to fifty guns awaited him. He held the cup for another sip, but thoughts remained on antiaircraft artillery, commonly referred to as triple-A. Three guns could fire hundreds of shells capable of blowing the wing off his O-1 Bird Dog. Tiny ripples on the coffee reflected overhead lights and exposed the fear he struggled against.

He had come early to prepare for the mission. The additional study wasn't making him feel braver, so he regretted not staying in bed.

Mitch heard boots thudding down the hall. He hoped they signaled the arrival of his roommate, Captain James Dalton. J.D. was to fly on the first of the squadron's sixteen missions. That briefing should've started five minutes earlier. Looking for J.D.'s mischievous grin, Mitch instead saw the scowl of Captain Pete Jansen, the other pilot on the first mission.

Jansen had the muscular build of a linebacker. Like Mitch, Jansen wore a flight suit adorned only with rank and a leather name tag. Pilots flying in the unacknowledged war in Laos didn't wear colorful patches identifying their units.

"Where the hell's J.D.?" Jansen stood with hands on hips.

Mitch scrambled to his feet. "I'm not sure, sir. He should be alo—"

"You didn't leave him asleep, did you?"

Mitch hesitated.

Jansen rolled his eyes upward. "Did he spend the night downtown with a *tealock*?"

Mitch winced, feeling somehow responsible. "He was gone when I returned from chapel last night, sir, and he wasn't back when I woke up. He doesn't stay in town often."

"Damned well better not when he's on dawn patrol. Had he seen today's schedule?" In addition to flying, Jansen scheduled pilots.

"I assume so, sir." Hoping to lighten Jansen's mood, Mitch said, "Last time Colonel Morton asked what J.D. was up to, I said I could either fly combat or try to keep up with J.D., but both are full-time jobs."

"Roger that." Jansen filled a paper cup with coffee.

"He should be along any minute, sir."

J.D. wasn't always on time, but he'd never missed a mission. Mitch hoped J.D. hadn't wrecked his motorcycle returning to the base.

"I'll give him five minutes." Jansen glanced at his watch. "Why're you here so early?"

"Thought I'd get a little more familiar with Mu Gia."

"That's right. We scheduled your first trip to the pass, didn't we?"

"Yes, sir." He'd flown enough missions over other sectors to be eligible for the region's most dangerous target.

"Mu Gia's a bitch." Jansen sounded matter-of-fact as he headed into the hallway to the briefing room.

Mitch slumped into his chair and returned to the messages. Several were OPREPs, the detailed operational reports pieced together after aircraft were lost. Most messages reported jet fighters shot down by Mu Gia's gunners.

Gazing at his coffee, he knew he might've died in one of those F-105 Thunderchiefs—if he'd finished pilot training with enough confidence to chose a fighter. His best friend, Lieutenant Phil Schofield, had gotten Mitch's F-105. Guilt mingled with fear as Mitch clenched his fist to steady the coffee cup. Gunners near Hanoi had downed Phil Schofield on his sixty-seventh mission. Phil had been missing in action since the week before Christmas, and Mitch felt somehow responsible.

He scanned the next message without concentrating. His two years as a copilot on long-range jet transports had kept him alive. And 305 AAA sites around Mu Gia were few compared to guns and missiles he would have faced over Hanoi.

But Mu Gia was still Mu Gia—with massed guns that could destroy

F-105s and F-4 Phantoms streaking overhead at five hundred knots. What chance did he have flying a propeller-driven Cessna at eighty knots? Seven months earlier he'd volunteered to go to war as a FAC. That decision now seemed one of the worst he'd ever made.

Mitch noticed his fingers held the left tip of his mustache. He yanked his hand down, and his fist slammed the table. Since learning he was scheduled for Mu Gia, he'd twisted his mustache innumerable times. He hated the habit, which surfaced when he was fearful.

The next message reviewed 37mm antiaircraft artillery. The Soviet-built AAA were low-tech guns in a high-tech war of surface-to-air missiles and supersonic fighters. Nevertheless, the World War II-vintage guns were the most dangerous threat in Laos. North Vietnamese gunners clustered four guns to blast coordinated volleys of sixty shells. Each explosive slug could down a Cessna.

He sighed a sound seemingly amplified in the early morning quiet. The numbers were depressing enough, but he was haunted because he hadn't seen a single round fired. Ground fire loomed like the bogeyman in childhood tales—a specter of evil all the more threatening because it was never seen. What he hadn't seen *could* kill him. Eight FACs in his squadron had been lost, most knocked down by the first volley from well-camouflaged guns.

Pounding boots provided a welcome interruption. He hoped J.D. was trying for coffee before slipping into the briefing.

Jansen stomped in and flung his crumpled cup at the wastebasket. "Can't keep waiting, so I've switched you. Maybe J.D.'ll have his ass here in time for your mission."

"Yes, sir."

Mitch felt relieved. Jansen's mission had to be safer than Mu Gia. Immediately a voice within taunted Mitch for being chicken. He returned the notebook to a sergeant and followed Jansen. "Where we going, sir?"

"Ban Laboy. Weather's good. Winds ten to fifteen knots from the south."

Mitch absentmindedly noted the winds. Instead of Mu Gia, he'd fly over the Ban Laboy Ford, one of the three most heavily defended targets in central Laos. "Are you low man, sir?"

"Right."

Mitch nodded, pleased Jansen would be leading. FACs flew in pairs over Laos because of the dangers in flying single-engine O-1s deep into enemy territory. As high man, Mitch would fly five-hundred feet above Jansen and watch for ground fire.

The FACs' small briefing room had a pockmarked table and two chairs. A discolored ashtray of heavy glass was empty except for a leftover dusting of gray. The ashtray shared the table with Jansen's maps and two mission kits, tattered brown portfolios containing maps.

Nakhon Phanom-based FACs were nicknamed Crickets, and a wooden plaque of the squadron patch hung by the door. Suspended from a purple umbrella with a two-way radio in its handle, Jiminy Cricket floated through blue skies and searched for trucks on the Ho Chi Minh Trail.

The intelligence briefer, Second Lieutenant Terry Winters, stood near the front wall. He never flew combat, so he wore starched fatigues. His face showed youthful enthusiasm, but his eyes hinted at exhaustion from long hours. He seemed to take a special obligation to ensure every flier received the latest information. Mitch liked that. He wondered if some of the weariness in Winters's eyes was due to his giving too many pilots their final briefings.

The wall behind Winters was covered by detailed maps of central Laos, with a little of Thailand on the left and some of North Vietnam on the right. The region of Laos patrolled by the Crickets was labeled Steel Tiger North. Black lines divided Steel Tiger into sectors and depicted roads snaking toward South Vietnam.

Mitch sat and pulled out his map for Sector 12.

Winters reported nighttime truck sightings and several AAA firings from around the Ban Laboy Ford.

Using a black grease pencil, Mitch marked an X on his acetate-covered map for each active gun site. In a small notebook, he wrote the coordinates of potential truck-parks. Mitch knew that flying Sector 12 in a Cessna was no milk run. He sat a little straighter. In spite of his fears, he was determined to be worthy of the heritage of the Cricket FACs.

When Winters finished, he asked, "Any questions, sir?"

Jansen stuffed his map into the portfolio. Referring to the upcoming lunar new year, he asked, "Anything firm on a truce for Tet?"

Mitch listened with anticipation. Every day—whether the enemy was shooting or not—brought him closer to November 24th, the end of his one-year combat tour.

"Nothing new, sir. We expect a bombing halt over North Vietnam."

Mitch asked, "But business as usual in Laos?"

"I'm afraid so, sir. It's hard to have a truce in a war neither side admits to?"

Jansen stood. "Triple-A can kill you just as dead while everyone else is celebrating."

As the two pilots walked into the hallway, Winters asked Jansen a scheduling question.

Mitch stepped onto the small porch of the Tactical Unit Operations Center, which pilots called the TUOC, pronounced like to walk without a pause between the words. He listened for J.D.'s prized motorcycle, a 1939 Harley-Davidson purchased from a merchant seaman in Bangkok. J.D. often bragged about buying the classic for two thousand baht, five bottles of Jack Daniel's, two cartons of Winstons, and a Christmas issue of Playboy. Instead of the motorcycle's roar, Mitch heard only the drone of electrical generators and aircraft engines in the distance.

Maybe J.D. was in an accident. Ten miles of road with maybe ten thousand potholes linked the town of Nakhon Phanom to the base. Hair rose on Mitch's arms as he recalled returning to the base on the Harley instead of waiting for the bus. J.D. had raced over the rough road at speeds faster than Mitch normally flew his Cessna. Mitch's death grip had torn a belt loop from J.D.'s jeans. J.D. had laughed most of the way.

A grassy quadrangle to Mitch's right was outlined by a three-rail, white wooden fence. Atop tall poles, bare light bulbs seemed to cast more shadows than light. Two flagpoles on the south perimeter stood bare, awaiting dawn and the raising of Thai and American flags. The sky showed no signs of sunrise. He looked west and saw the dimly lit flight line stretching toward blue-lighted taxiways and the runway in the darkness beyond.

Two green-and-tan helicopters—Jolly Green Giants—sat barely a stone's throw away. Four heavily armed A-1 Skyraiders were nearby. Crews for this air-rescue team slept in the adjacent alert shack, awaiting the next shrill warbling of the klaxons.

On three other days, Mitch had stood nearby when the klaxons had sounded. His blood had run cold as he'd watched those emergency scrambles of Jolly Greens and the Skyraiders that escorted the helicopters on rescues of downed fliers. His skin had tingled as he listened to the whine of turbines and the sounds of rotors beating the air. He knew the extraordinary feelings of such moments could never be appreciated by anyone who hadn't squinted against the swirling dust. The thunderous throbbing of the air left unforgettable images he sensed even now in the quiet loneliness of preparing to risk his life once again.

He heard the distant roar of a motorcycle.

Captain Jansen stepped outside.

Mitch nodded toward the road. "The lost sheep returneth, sir."

"Better never than late!" Jansen bounded down the steps and pushed open the gate in the barbed-wire-topped fence around the TUOC.

Mitch and Jansen stepped into the street. A bouncing headlight obscured a dark shape racing at them. The motorcycle was seconds away when the noise of its engine decreased. With the screech of tires on gravel and asphalt, the vehicle lurched sideways into a skidding stop. Jansen jumped back and stumbled against the fence. Mitch had seen the performance before, so he stood his ground. Watching the motorcycle, he tensed, ready to leap aside.

The breeze dissipated red dust that engulfed the motorcycle. Captain J.D. Dalton shut down the engine, parked in the street, and swung a leg up alongside the gearshift mounted on the gas tank of the vintage Harley. He smoothed the curled-up tips of his handlebar mustache, which was the best in the squadron.

J.D. was five feet, six inches tall, but Mitch decided long ago J.D. lived life much taller. Over his flight suit J.D. wore his riding outfit—a soft leather helmet with goggles in the style worn by aviators in the 1930s and a brown leather jacket with a faded patch of the U.S. Army Air Forces of World War II. J.D. draped his helmet over the headlight. He pulled out a comb and restyled his thick black hair, which was longer than regulations allowed.

Jansen strode over. "Forget your friggin' alarm clock?"

J.D. pulled out a pack of Winstons. "I've probably been awake longer than you, Pete." He lifted the pack to his lips and removed a cigarette.

Jansen's eyes narrowed. "The briefing was at four-thirty. Your butt should've been holding down a chair in there thirty minutes ago!"

J.D. pulled the unlit cigarette from his mouth and grinned. "I can't help it if Daeng turned out to be a morning person."

"Bullshit!"

Imitating Groucho Marx flicking ashes from a cigar, J.D. continued a realistic impersonation, "Can I help it if she also was an evening person and a midnight person?" He stretched and yawned as if needing sleep.

"Damn you, J.D. When you show for a mission, you'd better be ready to fly."

J.D. flashed a look of icy determination. "I'm here, and I *am* ready to fly."

Jansen shrugged and turned toward the helicopters.

J.D. lit his cigarette, glanced at Mitch, and winked.

Mitch averted his gaze to the star-filled sky to hide his amusement from Jansen.

Jansen turned to face J.D. "You're a hell of a pain in the ass."

J.D. grinned as if he'd received a well-deserved compliment. "Where we going?"

The cigarette bounced between J.D.'s lips. That was the instant, Mitch decided, a newcomer would've made an unexpected connection. Except for the handlebar mustache, J.D. had an amazing resemblance to the ill-fated actor, James Dean. The likeness became obvious once the mustache was ignored. The hair rising high above his forehead, the full lower lip, the strong line of the jaw, the way he held the cigarette, the protruding rounded chin, and the intensity in the eyes all contributed. Mitch had seen other similarities, including Dean's shuffling stride, which J.D. had down cold.

"*Mitch* and I are headed for Ban Laboy."

J.D. folded the helmet and slipped it inside his jacket. "I'm here with plenty of time left."

Jansen checked his watch. "It's too late to get you up to speed and pick up our gear."

"What's to get up to speed on? I flew Ban Laboy Saturday."

"But you missed the briefing."

"How many times do I have to be briefed on Sector 12?" Arrogance rang in J.D.'s voice. He pointed at Mitch's mission kit. "Einstein's got a black X on his map for each triple-A firing, and his notebook has winds, fighters if we have any, and target coordinates."

Mitch smiled at the accuracy. "I didn't write down the winds. They're—"

"From the south at fifteen knots."

"Ten to fifteen," Jansen corrected but seemed impressed.

"It's all a guess," J.D. said. "Only difference is the weatherman sits in his hole reading teletype messages, and I've fought the breeze on ten miles of bad road."

Jansen seemed to waver.

J.D. patted the motorcycle. "Hop on. We can save five minutes picking up our gear."

Jansen shrugged. "I'd hate to be a woman wanting to turn you down for anything."

"Not to worry." J.D.'s grin became more devilish. "If you were a woman, you'd never want to turn me down."

"Christ." Jansen shook his head. "It's Mitch's call. He's the one jacked around."

Mitch started to answer.

J.D. was quicker. "I'm sure he doesn't want to postpone his cherry ride to Mu Gia."

Mitch was pleased J.D. knew the significance of the original assignment.

J.D. said, "Besides, roomie, maybe today fate's scheduled you for that big mission. You wouldn't want to be circling Ban Laboy when fate's waitin' for you at Mu Gia."

Mitch believed less in fate than J.D. did, but they'd spent hours talking about preparing for the big mission. "I don't have a problem taking another briefing, sir."

Jansen frowned sternly. "You're damned lucky Mitch was here."

Mitch gazed sheepishly at his boots. "I wanted extra time to study Mu Gia."

J.D. shook his head. "Lieutenant Prudence probably goes to the dentist's office an hour early to look over the drills."

"Two hours for dentists. One hour for Mu Gia," Mitch said.

J.D. straddled the motorcycle. "You know what they say, kiddo. Another day, another two dollars and thirty-two cents."

Mitch smiled. He'd already heard J.D.'s line.

Jansen bit. "What the hell are you talking about?"

"February! Best month in the war. Don't you just love it?"

Jansen looked confused. "What in the—"

"Combat pay." J.D. acted serious. "February's only got twenty-eight days, but Uncle Sugar still gives us the whole sixty-five-dollar bonus. So Mitch'll earn an extra two bucks and thirty-two cents for hanging his ass out over Mu Gia. In January, you and I did it for two bucks and a dime."

"The extra twenty-two cents makes me feel much better," Mitch said, handing over his mission kit and a page from his notebook.

"Don't spend it all in one place." J.D. stuffed the paper into a pocket and handed the kit to Jansen. "Hop on."

As Jansen swung on behind J.D., Mitch suppressed a smile. *Good luck, Pete.*

J.D. started the Harley and turned to Mitch. "The mailman come?"

Mitch, who always checked before a mission, shouted above the noise, "Not since yesterday afternoon."

J.D. frowned. He twisted his jacket, showing an envelope in an inner pocket.

Mitch assumed it was a letter received the day before. He wondered if the letter had motivated J.D.'s all-night venture in town.

"Too damned late for a mail run," Jansen yelled.

J.D. grinned at Mitch and gunned the engine. "Not to worry, Petey Boy. We're about to make up for lost time."

"You damned well better start worrying, Jimmy D. If Colonel Morton finds out you missed a briefing, he'll have your ass."

"Won't be the first time." J.D. shrugged his James Dean-shrug and winked. With the cigarette dangling from his lips, he added, "What else can Mighty Mort do to me—make me a forward air controller, give me an O-1, and send me to Vietnam?"

J.D. unleashed his Harley. Spewing gravel and dust, the motorcycle accelerated while Jansen frantically clutched J.D. and the mission kits.

Mitch turned toward the TUOC. A small longing deep within wished someone would send him to Vietnam to fly his final 284 days against machine guns and automatic weapons instead of the AAA in Steel Tiger. A more determined voice told him to press on with his first mission to Mu Gia. He stepped through the gate and slammed it with a clang that reverberated across the flight line.

Cricket flight line at NKP

Chapter 2

Mitch checked his wristwatch: five twenty-eight.

Waiting in the briefing room, he gazed at the wall map and tried to avoid thinking of Mu Gia. Intersecting circles overlaid main roads, reminding Mitch of big caterpillars munching their way south. Each circle represented 37mm guns that had fired or had been identified in combat photography. Those guns were a threat to FACs flying within the circles. After losing two O-1s in January, Seventh Air Force restricted FACs to six thousand feet over those circles. Mitch glanced at Mu Gia, then looked away. Mu Gia was covered with black circles.

His engineering background caused him to seek comfort in numbers. He looked at the day's flying schedule posted by the door. A typical month included five hundred FAC missions, and maybe ten reported ground fire. He tried to feel reassurance in the averages but couldn't—two of January's ten had blown away O-1s.

Captain Robert Goodwin strolled in, and Mitch stood.

Goodwin crushed out a cigarette in the ashtray. "Looks like a good day for it, Mitch." He was tall and spindly with thinning brown hair combed across the bald crown of his head.

Ashes usually adorned whatever Goodwin wore, so Mitch's private nickname for the captain was *the Ashman*.

Goodwin plopped down in the other chair. He opened his mission kit and selected the map for Sector 6. After propping the map between his lap and the table, Goodwin pulled out a pack of Camels and a Zippo lighter. "I love these early morning flights."

Mitch settled into his chair. "I do better nearer noon, sir. Shorter shadows help me recognize what I'm seeing."

Goodwin lit up and took a long drag. "Landing at nine-thirty leaves the rest of the day to sleep. I sleep better with a Singha or two in me."

A Singha or two. Mitch wondered why Goodwin's conspicuous consumption of Thailand's famous brew hadn't left a beer gut. Mitch often saw Goodwin asleep in the shade of a tree with empty bottles scattered beneath his folding lounge chair. Goodwin was there so often, Mitch and J.D. called the tree *Goodwin's Tree*. Goodwin didn't maintain the professional image Mitch looked for in officers, but the Ashman had been businesslike on the two missions they'd flown together.

Goodwin scanned the map. "When do you make captain, Mitch?"

"Next month, sir." Mitch answered the unexpected question, then thought about adding, "If I last that long."

"I look forward to swigging a few Singhas at your promotion party. Being a captain's a lot better'n being a lieutenant." Goodwin continued innocuous small talk.

Mitch marveled at the ritual. He wanted to ask, "Doesn't going to Mu Gia scare the crap out of you?" But he didn't. Talking about fear wasn't part of the ritual.

Lieutenant Winters rushed in and took a questioning look at Mitch. "You again, sir?"

Mitch smiled. "You were so good, I decided to come back for more."

Winters turned to Goodwin. "Sorry to delay you, sir, but I was checking ground fire reports from a bird that just returned from Sector Six. Before I forget, we added the alert photographer. He'll meet you on the flight line."

Goodwin pointed with his cigarette at Mitch and referred to Mitch's personal call sign, Nail Fifty-nine. "Send him to Five-nine's bird."

Mitch agreed Goodwin should fly the lighter airplane. The flight leader had the most demanding mission, and O-1s were underpowered with only a pilot aboard.

After a sergeant briefed the weather, Winters said, "We have three requirements today, sir. You'll have Laredo, four Thuds who's target's the ford at Tango-Nineteen, here in the Doghouse." Winters touched his pointer to the network of roads snaking south out of Mu Gia.

Mitch wondered how the valley had earned the nickname. Perhaps it was because the north end narrowed like a pitched roof on a doghouse. Or the valley might have been so named for a more somber reason—the first Bird Dog shot down by the gunners of Steel Tiger was somewhere in that valley. In any case, being in the doghouse meant being in trouble.

Winters read coordinates for Tango-Nineteen and the scheduled time-over-target, then glanced at a note calling for a bomb-damage assessment. "Seventh has requested you BDA a pair of Combat Skyspots."

Mitch recognized the code name for air strikes directed by radar. FACs often checked afterward for damage because targets weren't seen by pilots who dropped the bombs or by the radar controllers. He wrote down the coordinates and drew a circle on Route 15 just above the border in North Vietnam.

"And," Winters said, "we need pictures of anything you find of six trucks Nimrod Three-two killed this morning." He read coordinates reported by the A-26 crew.

Mitch thought about the terminology. Those who knew the air war best—fliers and intel briefers—talked of killing trucks and guns. They seldom mentioned the men who manned them. So far, air strikes he'd directed hadn't killed trucks, guns, or men. However, he was more comfortable with destroying implements of war than killing people.

Winters touched his pointer to the map. "Near this intersection." Winters listed locations of guns that had fired at Nimrod Three-two.

Mitch copied the coordinates and put more black Xs on his map.

"Gentlemen," Winters said, "you're reminded all roads in Sector Six are in a high-threat area. Your minimum altitude in those areas is six thousand feet above the terrain."

Mitch nodded. He didn't need a reminder to stay high over Mu Gia.

Goodwin asked for news about Tet and received the answer given earlier. When there were no more questions, Winters left.

Goodwin stuffed his map into his mission kit. "I'll look for Nimrod's trucks, then check the road north through the pass. We'll have plenty of time to BDA the Skyspots and return to the Doghouse for Laredo."

"Anything special you want me to do, sir?"

Goodwin crushed out his fourth cigarette. "Just keep your beady little eyeballs on me every second I'm over the canyon."

"I've studied the maps and—"

"You ain't been to Mu Gia?"

"That's right, sir."

Goodwin nibbled on his lip as if trying to decide how much more to explain. "Gotta be a first time for all of us."

Mitch nodded.

Goodwin lit another Camel, took a long drag, and exhaled a series of smoke rings. "Today I'll spend quite a while over the guns, so . . . . Anyway stay over the plateau, or cross to the mountains on the east, if the sun gives you problems keeping me in sight."

"Yes, sir."

"When you cross that canyon, keep your nose moving."

"I never fly more than ten seconds in a straight line over the Trail." Frequent turns made a slow O-1 a more difficult target.

"Over Mu Gia, I wouldn't give 'em more than five seconds straight." Goodwin stood and brushed ashes off his flight suit. "Keep your eyeballs peeled so neither of us ends up touring that valley on foot."

"I'll do my best, sir."

"Don't get so worried that you choke when I'm hanging my bird out over the canyon."

"I didn't say I was worried, sir," Mitch shot back.

Goodwin shrugged. "Being worried's a given in an Bird Dog over Mu Gia." He added with a grin, "Besides, your mustache gives you away."

Embarrassed, Mitch tried to straighten the left tip, which he had twisted frequently since learning he was scheduled for Mu Gia.

Stepping beyond the windowless operations center, Mitch found a scene markedly different than before. More noise and people signaled the awakening of the base. The eastern sky promised daylight was returning to Southeast Asia.

Walking to the flight line, the FACs met two sergeants, who rendered crisp salutes. Goodwin's response reminded Mitch of a Hollywood actor playing soldier. Mitch snapped a salute as precise as demanded in his first year at the Air Force Academy. Most men at the base never experienced the dangers of the war beyond the Mekong River, so their salutes to fliers carried a message of respect instead of obligation. Mitch liked that. His pride in being a combat pilot helped keep his fears in check.

Passing the officers club, Mitch smelled coffee, eggs, and greasy bacon. Earlier he was too nervous to be hungry, and eating wasn't part of his pre-mission ritual. Now, hunger stirred, but he couldn't do anything about it for at least four hours.

Ahead Mitch saw the squadron's parking ramp. Interlocking planks of perforated steel, which everyone called PSP, looked like a wide, metal street. Instead of cars parked along curbs, more than twenty O-1 Bird Dogs were aligned wingtip-to-wingtip along the sides. The O-1s looked almost as innocent as Cessnas and Piper Cubs on hundreds of hometown airstrips. Four rockets beneath the high wing, however, suggested each aircraft was different from those flown by thousands of aspiring aviators. Definitely not for beginners, Mitch thought, knowing these small aircraft sometimes took experienced pilots on their final flights.

The PSP gave a sense of immediacy, of being on the front lines. "I'm glad we're not at some headquarters base with concrete runways."

Goodwin glanced at Mitch. "And all the comforts of home."

"Right."

"You're kind of weird sometimes, Mitch." He crushed out his cigarette on a plank at the edge of the parking ramp. He strode toward the airplanes, howled, and shouted, "Good mornin', Bird Doggies."

"You call me weird, sir?"

Goodwin winked. "So we're at war. That doesn't mean we shouldn't have some fun."

"You sound like my roommate."

"I learned that from J.D."

"That figures."

Walking between the rows of O-1s, Mitch and Goodwin passed five open-ended hangars on the west edge of the parking ramp. Mitch liked the way signs on the hangars humanized the maintenance areas. An official sign proclaimed proudly the area belonged to the 23rd Tactical Air Support Squadron. Jiminy Cricket flanked each side of the sign.

The cricket spirit was all pervasive. Maintenance men had stenciled a cricket on the cowling of every O-1. The result looked more like a black grasshopper than a cricket, but that didn't matter to anyone.

A less-official-looking sign declared the parking ramp was the home of TWA. Smaller lettering explained this TWA represented not Trans World Airlines, but Teenie Weenie Airlines. Mitch had admired the enthusiasm of the maintenance troops from the first day he'd climbed aboard one of the Bird Dogs they maintained with such dedication.

At the far end of the flight line, Mitch and Goodwin got into a pickup used for a half-mile trip to a building where flying gear was stored.

Minutes later, Mitch trudged to his O-1. He wore his flak vest, survival vest, pistol, canteen, hunting knife, and an M-16 rifle slung over his shoulder. One hand carried his helmet, decorated with silver falcons outlined in black like those on his helmet in pilot training. The other hand held his clipboard, binoculars, and what he referred to as his little bag of bullets. The bag was heavier than usual. He'd added four extra M-16 clips in deference to Mu Gia's 305 AAA sites.

Mitch was greeted by the ground crew and Sergeant Ellison, who carried an M-16 rifle and a camera. Mitch outlined requirements for photography and told Ellison to get aboard.

They followed Goodwin into the run-up area at the north end of the runway. Mitch swung his O-1 into the wind and began final checks. Advancing the throttle, he said, "My lawn mower sounded more powerful than this beast."

"I know one thing, sir," Ellison said. "The Pontiac I left on blocks in Jersey has more horses under its hood than're turning that prop."

Maybe twice as many, Mitch thought, as he double-checked the setup of his three radios. The FM radio was set to the interplane frequency he and Goodwin used like a private line. The UHF was set to the tower at Nakhon Phanom. He set the VHF to a frequency for Cricket, controllers in a EC-130 transport that served as the airborne battlefield command and control center for Steel Tiger. He set switches to listen to all three radios, but the microphone switch on the throttle could transmit on only one radio at a time. He also had an intercom switch to talk to Sergeant Ellison in the back seat.

Ordnance specialists had followed in a blue pickup. When Mitch signaled he'd finished his run-up checks, a young airman raced over. Both side windows were open, and Mitch rested his hands on the frames to show he wasn't touching any switches.

The airman checked rockets beneath one wing, then pulled safing pins with their red streamers from the back of the rocket tubes. After repeating the procedure for rockets under the other wing, he handed the pins to Mitch. "See you later, sir," he shouted, flashing a quick salute.

"Count on it." Mitch returned the salute before the airman ran to the other O-1. On intercom, he asked, "All set, sarge?"

"Whenever you are, sir. Would you mind closing the windows?"

"Sure." Mitch reached out to a window, which was held up by a latch on the underside of the wing. He grabbed the handle, rotated the window down, and latched it flush against the fuselage. After doing the same on the other side, he was fully enclosed in the cockpit—as in every other military airplane he'd ever flown. He smiled at the paradox of his country sending him to fight a 1960s' war in an airplane that could fly with windows open and always had its landing gear extended.

The airman continued checking Goodwin's O-1, so Mitch relaxed and enjoyed the peace of the moment. The engine's hum sent soothing vibrations through the cockpit. He glanced at the clock—six-thirty Monday morning in Thailand and six-thirty Sunday evening in Washington D.C. Elizabeth would be in church with her parents and his daughter, Mandy, who was nearly three. Mitch breathed deeply, trying to feel strength from Elizabeth's prayers. He felt only the calming reassurance of the machine surrounding him.

Goodwin exaggerated his drawl. "Ready to go do it, Five-niner?"

"Roger that, sir."

Goodwin's O-1 rolled forward. "NKP tower," he said, using initials by which Americans referred to the isolated base, "Nails Four-two and Five-niner are ready for takeoff."

"Roger, Nails. Winds are one-eight-zero at twelve knots. You're cleared for takeoff on Runway One-five. Have a good flight."

Goodwin guided his O-1 beyond the runway's centerline and braked to a stop. He paused long enough for Mitch to taxi into position. "Off we go, into the wild blue yonder," he warbled off-key on interplane.

Mitch smiled and whispered, "Bless us, Lord."

Chapter 3

"You still with me, Five-niner?"

"Roger, Four-two," Mitch said on the radio to Goodwin. "Got you in sight."

In the forty-five minutes since takeoff, Mitch had trailed loosely behind. For the last twenty miles, they'd flown along the southern face of the Nape Plateau, which had grown from a gentle ridge to a sheer cliff towering three thousand feet above the valley floor. The O-1s had reached Phou Vout, a peak at the southeast corner of the plateau. The valley beyond was the Doghouse.

Goodwin maneuvered aggressively as he left the skies above Nape and ventured over the heavily defended valley. "I'll take a few minutes to look for Nimrod's trucks."

"Roger that. I'll keep an eye on you."

Mitch looked beyond the other O-1 and saw main roads, bypasses, and spur roads crisscrossing the five-mile-wide valley. Two main roads snaked across and disappeared through a cut in the ridge at the southern end. A third road led toward Thailand along the south face of Nape. All three roads converged into Mu Gia's deep canyon. In addition, he saw the Doghouse's other distinctive feature: thousands of craters.

A mountain on the east side impressed Mitch. Phou Chuang towered four thousand feet above the pockmarked valley. Looking beyond Phou Chuang he saw miles of rugged peaks known as karst, the most fascinating geological phenomenon he'd ever seen. Sheer cliffs of limestone, hundreds and even thousands of feet tall, were common wherever karst jutted from the jungles. Mitch glanced at his map. Contour lines east of Mu Gia looked like swirls of a giant's fingerprints.

Joining Goodwin above the Doghouse, Mitch rolled from side to side every few seconds. Starting with his map and the coordinates Winters had given during the briefing, Mitch matched hills, streams, and an L-shaped meadow. Within seconds he located the reported position. He rolled the O-1, pointed, and said on intercom, "The coordinates for the truck kill are in that sloping meadow."

"I don't see any road, sir," Ellison said.

"There isn't one within several hundred meters." Mitch imagined flying through the darkness in a twin-engine A-26. "It's got to be tough to estimate coordinates when your only light comes from burning trucks, parachute flares, and antiaircraft fire."

"I'm glad I only take pictures in daylight."

"I'm not finding shit, Five-niner," Goodwin said.

"Roger that." Mitch wanted to scan the next closest road. "Give me a circle or two, and I'll take a quick look at the first bypass east."

"Don't waste too much time. We got places to go and people to see."

"Copied."

Using binoculars, Mitch studied a road winding through intermittent jungle. In two places, blackened foliage suggested recent fires, but he saw no burned-out hulks. Mitch pointed. "Nimrod probably got his trucks on that stretch of road. Get pictures from that ford to that S-shaped bend."

"Yes, sir."

Mitch was impressed by the dedication, discipline, and brute force of the North Vietnamese salvagers. Even when napalm gutted trucks, they usually disappeared by the time FACs flew overhead. "Can you imagine moving a truck on tires burned down to the steel rims?"

"No, sir."

"Me, neither."

Ellison asked, "Have you ever seen people along the Trail, sir?"

Mitch shook his head. "I saw more Vietnamese in Oklahoma than in Steel Tiger."

"Oklahoma?"

Mitch told of serving as unofficial interpreter for the South Vietnamese students.

"I hope you won't need to interpret for anyone today, sir."

"Right."

Turning north to catch Goodwin, Mitch said on interplane, "I couldn't find any trucks, sir."

In a bunker near Mu Gia's west wall, North Vietnamese Colonel Le Van Do listened through a dust-covered loudspeaker. Hearing the FAC's assessment, Le nodded. Less than an hour earlier, he'd ridden over the road where the Nimrod had destroyed five trucks and damaged four. The road crews had been in the final clean-up stage, so he wasn't surprised the American FACs had found nothing.

Sitting on an empty ammunition crate, Le leaned against teak logs of the bunker's wall and waited to learn more from the Americans. He sipped tea, hoping the hot liquid would revitalize him from the lack of real sleep in the last thirty-six hours. A familiar throbbing seemed centered in the lobe of his left ear. Shrapnel had cut away the earlobe sixteen years earlier, but the phantom sensation reoccurred sometimes when he was extremely tired.

Putting his tea on a crate, Le massaged the scalp beneath thinning black hair. He was in his third year as the North Vietnamese commander of the Central Region of Laos, an area about a third the size of North Vietnam. In charge of Mu Gia Pass on both sides of the border, he commanded tens of thousands of troops and workers except during summer. Then, his forces abandoned Laos to the two meters of rain dumped by the southwest monsoon.

Each year, Hanoi sent more men, trucks, supplies and antiaircraft guns—and the Americans sent more aircraft. Each year, his enormous responsibilities grew more daunting.

He gazed around the room, one of five in the bunker. Four soldiers wearing headsets sat at makeshift tables with communications radios that monitored frequencies Americans used over the Central Region. Most radios were Russian-made. Two were American-made, captured in South Vietnam.

Two other soldiers monitored field telephones connected to wires strung along the roads. The telephones provided a rudimentary way for Le to communicate with troops along hundreds of kilometers of roads. Unfortunately, stray bombs that spared roads often cut nearby wires.

Le usually worked out of his headquarters near the Ban Laboy Ford, so he recognized only three men in the room. Sergeant Dinh and Private Kiet were in his three-man bodyguard and had accompanied him through the night on the 120-kilometer journey from his headquarters. Sergeant Dinh had been chief bodyguard since Le had returned to Hanoi nearly three years earlier. Dinh was near Le's age and had almost as much combat experience. Private Kiet was less than half Le's age and looked younger than his seventeen years. Kiet had been assigned a few days before Le returned to Laos.

Both bodyguards appeared tired, and Le knew why. He always traveled in his GAZ-69. The rugged four-by-four handled rough roads better than larger trucks but offered little room to stretch out.

The third person Le recognized was Major Huynh Van Tho, who commanded the sector including Mu Gia. Tho was bent over a map covering a table near the radio operators.

Le had come to Mu Gia to oversee preparations for the Tet truce and for the hundreds of truckloads of supplies coming south from Haiphong during the bombing halt. He expected little rest even if the two O-1s didn't venture into Mu Gia.

The voice of an American pilot said, "Wouldn't expect any thrillin' results from the Skyspots either."

The loudspeaker carried the *click-click* of a pilot pressing a microphone button twice.

Le recognized Skyspot as the term for radar-directed bombing. He'd listened to enough American conversations to know the double-click signaled agreement. He joined Tho at the map. "Where's their target?"

Tho pointed north of the border on the map. "About midnight, two high-altitude strikes dropped bombs fifteen-hundred meters apart. At one target, trucks could drive around the craters. Hits on the northern target required use of a bypass during the night. We'd nearly repaired the main road when we had to send the bulldozer to shelter."

"Is the bulldozer secure?" Le had only six in the Central Region, and he planned to keep this one busy strengthening roads north of the border during the truce.

"It should be, Colonel."

"It had better be."

"Yes, Colonel." Tho hurried to the telephones and asked about the bulldozer's location.

The loudspeaker sounded again. "Don't see no customs inspectors."

"Maybe there's not enough traffic, sir."

Le decided the FACs were at the border.

"And I suppose you believe in the tooth fairy, too."

Le didn't understand. Perhaps the tooth fairy was a spirit some Americans believed in and others didn't. He guessed the FACs were only minutes from where the bulldozer had been.

Goodwin flew over the heart of Mu Gia.

Mitch kept in relative safety over the Nape Plateau, which formed Mu Gia's west wall. He watched the other O-1 roll back and forth. The constant maneuvers were a chilling reminder that while no one else was visible, this remote part of the world was inhabited by more than fliers in small airplanes.

Mu Gia was more majestic than he'd imagined. The deep canyon was one to two miles wide. Where sunshine reached the steep west slope, many shades of green glistened brightly. The roads and the river that drained the canyon were in shadow. Where the Doghouse merged with Mu Gia, countless bombs had peeled away trees. The canyon floor was a mixture of jungle and corridors along the roads where the jungle had been blown away. Looking east beyond the canyon, he wondered how the terrain could be so different from the smooth plateau beneath him. Innumerable peaks of rugged karst sparkled in morning sun. They stretched in an irregular phalanx across twenty miles of North Vietnam.

Goodwin said, "Someone got lucky last night. A time-delay on a seven-fifty makes a helluva crater."

Mitch spotted five new craters. Two had hit the road almost dead-center. Time-delay fuses permitted bombs to penetrate before detonating. The results were craters across ninety percent of the two-lane road. "Those are the best two bombs I've ever seen."

"Yeah," Goodwin said, "but don't count on Uncle Ho getting any real heartburn. In a day or two, the detour'll look like it's the main road."

Mitch saw tracks around the craters. By tomorrow morning, he thought, hundreds of heavy trucks would've packed down the detour. Next week, the craters would look like thousands of other misses scarring the canyon. He pulled out a grease pencil and wrote the coordinates high on the window, which he used as a notepad while over the Trail.

"I see more fresh craters up the road," Goodwin said.

"Roger. We'll get a few pictures here."

Mitch flew over the canyon toward Goodwin's O-1, which meandered northward. "When we get over the road, I'll break left, then do a quick reverse. Your shot'll be out the right window."

"Right window, sir," Ellison confirmed.

Mitch pressed his helmet against the window to estimate when the O-1 would pass over the road. "You'll have fifteen seconds at most."

"Roger, sir."

"Here we go!" He whipped the stick against his leg, and the aircraft rolled onto its side. A glance ahead showed Goodwin a mile farther north. "Standby!" He rocked his O-1 the opposite direction. "You see the fresh dirt?"

"Uh—" Ellison hesitated.

"Just beyond that main bend." Mitch grabbed the handle on the window, gave a quick twist, and held back as airflow rotated the window up against the wing. He stiffened his arm against the wind and pointed. "Two road cuts, right there!"

"Roger, sir."

Goodwin said, "They've had a bulldozer out this morning."

Le stiffened. Bulldozers left an unmistakable trail unless crews obliterated the telltale tracks. The pilot had found signs, and Le couldn't gamble on whether the signs would be enough to lead to the bulldozer. "Cleared to fire."

A sergeant relayed the command into a field telephone.

Le turned to Major Tho. "Now's not the time to lose a bulldozer."

Tho nodded. "Yes, Colonel."

Le hoped his gunners would drive away the O-1s, which were such a daily nuisance. If one were shot down, Americans would swarm to Mu Gia to rescue the pilot. They might stay overhead throughout the day. He had several camps to visit, and a continuous American presence wouldn't allow him to use roads freely.

"I'll be outside." Le hurried out the door and bounded up the log steps, two at a time. Sergeant Dinh and Private Kiet followed. Trotting into a nearby clearing, Le heard the hum of two aircraft and the staccato rumble of antiaircraft guns.

Mitch said on intercom, "Finding a bulldozer would be great. They're a hundred times scarcer than trucks." And, in nearly two months, he'd seen three trucks east of the Mekong. Killing a bulldozer would be an accomplishment worthy of the risks.

"Ground fire!"

The tone was so shrill, Mitch didn't recognize the voice. He tried to decide which radio had brought the excited message.

"Jesus! You got me in sight, Five-niner?"

Banked away from the lead aircraft, Mitch couldn't see Goodwin.

"Let's get outta here," Ellison shouted.

A part of Mitch cried out: *Good idea!* Nevertheless, he turned his O-1 north. "I'm headed your way, Four-two."

Flashes twinkling high above grabbed his attention. Dozens flickered, looking more like glimmers of reflected lights than like antiaircraft shells fused to explode before returning to the ground. A puff of black smoke replaced each flash. The sight jarred him to reality. He'd seen such puffs before—not over Laos but in movies about World War II. Excitement raced through him. Now he'd seen *real* ground fire.

Mitch spotted tracers on shells racing upward against the green jungle. Goodwin had banked ninety degrees, maneuvering desperately to escape. The O-1's symmetrical outline appeared as if Mitch were looking down on it.

"I've got you." Mitch saw more flashes on the ground and more rising tracers. "Break east! Thirty-sevens fired just west of the road."

Mitch reached to the armament panel and moved a switch. A green light indicated the corresponding rocket was armed. He swung the nose sideways, pointing at a hill erupting with antiaircraft fire.

Tracers converged on Goodwin.

Mitch held his breath until the shells passed the other O-1. Glancing at the hill with the hidden AAA site, he squeezed the trigger on his stick.

Ka-bamm!

A rocket blasted away, sounding like a hammer slamming a tin roof. Trailing a shower of sparks, the rocket accelerated toward the hillside.

Mitch didn't bother watching. Instead he looked at the struggling O-1 and the tracers. He switched to the VHF frequency monitored by airborne controllers. "Cricket, Nail Four-two's taking heavy triple-A over Mu Gia."

Goodwin turned east as shells raced by.

Mitch saw a single flash. Black smoke swirled from Goodwin's aircraft. When Mitch saw the top of the O-1 again, he was horrified. Most of the right wing was missing.

"Nail aircraft calling Cricket, say again."

"Bail out, Four-two!" Mitch heard words, then realized *he* had said them—and said them on the wrong radio. He switched to interplane. "Bail out, Four-two!"

Goodwin's O-1 tumbled, then fell into a steep spin.

The controller called, "Is Nail Four-two calling Cri—"

A rescue controller in an HC-130 intruded, "Aircraft transmitting one twenty-eight decimal four, this is Crown. Say location of emergency."

Mitch recognized Crown as the airborne rescue coordination center responsible for scrambling rescue helicopters. Ignoring the call, Mitch maneuvered more radically. "Four-two, can you read Five-nine?"

Hoping to see Goodwin tumble free, Mitch watched the falling aircraft. All he saw above the O-1 was a misty, swirling stream of avgas.

Cricket and Crown broadcast additional requests for information but were garbled by mutual interference. Mitch silenced the VHF. Listening for Goodwin was more important.

Tall trees blocked any view of the aircraft, but Le heard the distant, muffled explosion. "Got him," he said to Sergeant Dinh.

Feeling exhilaration that surged when his gunners were successful, Le headed for the bunker. Dinh followed. When they reached the steps, Major Tho was in the doorway.

"An American reconnaissance plane is coming down, Colonel!"

"I know."

"Any instructions, Colonel?"

Downing an airplane always changed the encounter. By the time the Americans returned attention to the bulldozer, it would be safe in a cave and all telltale tracks obliterated. The pilot—if alive—became the prize to be captured, killed, or rescued. Le contemplated the morning's battle. Roaring airplanes would fill the sky, offering more targets and more danger. He lost more guns and gun crews during air rescue attempts than at any other time.

"Bring the sector defenses to level one," Le said. The order recalled all guns and crews to their nighttime state of readiness.

"Yes, Colonel." Tho turned and hurried into the bunker.

"We don't have the time for this."

Dinh nodded. "I'd hoped you might get sleep today, Colonel."

Le smiled, understanding the double message. Sergeant Dinh was probably the one person in the Central Region who got less sleep than Le. Dinh's snatches of sleep came when Le was sleeping and the other two bodyguards and other soldiers provided security. Gesturing at the sun above rugged peaks of the east wall, Le said, "This is becoming a very long night, Sergeant."

Dinh grinned. "Yes, Colonel. As usual."

A puff of white smoke billowed near the gun site. "Take that, damn you," Mitch said without transmitting. He assumed the gunners were celebrating their kill, and the bang of his rocket should've disrupted the celebration. Unfortunately his marker was only a bluff—for now.

Frantically, he watched the O-1 plunge closer to the jungle. "If you hear me, Four-two, bail out now!"

The aircraft spun lower. The radio remained silent. Mitch saw no parachute. A tightness in his gut said this was how it would end for the Ashman.

Jolly Green and Sandies

Chapter 4

Tall trees swallowed Goodwin's O-1 in a single bite.

Mitch stared, looking for something to confirm a brave pilot had died. Nothing even indicated an airplane had died. He expected a more spectacular finish; at least white smoke from broken warheads of the marking rockets. Only the dissipating smoke from his marker kept Mu Gia from looking as if the frantic action of the last few moments hadn't happened—as if Goodwin had never existed.

Mitch felt jittery, like waking from a dream after something awful occurred.

Ellison broke into Mitch's thoughts. "What're we gonna do, Lieutenant?"

"We've got to find Captain Goodwin." He searched for a parachute. "You see a chute?"

"Negative, sir. I can't see much back here. I did hear a story, once, about an O-1 that crashed in Nam. The FAC survived without a scratch because his airplane got tangled in the trees."

"That might happen." *But war was full of such stories.* Mitch's gut feeling said Goodwin hadn't survived. Nevertheless, Mitch knew he must do everything possible, just in case. Discipline and training pushed aside fear. "Listen up on Guard." Mitch rotated the selector on the UHF to a channel preset to 243.0, the emergency frequency known as Guard. The radio was silent. Mitch slumped into the seat.

"No beeper, huh, sir?"

Mitch shook his head. He'd hoped to hear the irritating warble of the emergency radio packed in the risers of Goodwin's parachute. The absence of a signal, which would've started automatically, suggested Goodwin hadn't used his parachute.

"Maybe the radio malfunctioned, sir." Ellison didn't sound optimistic.

"I don't think he bailed out. We have to pinpoint the crash site."

Mitch looked for landmarks. A karst outcropping jutted from jungle northwest of where he'd last seen the O-1. In the opposite direction, the road meandered in the shape of a dog's head. Mitch had one line of position, but he needed another. He picked a spot on the main road where a short bypass split off. The crash site was due west of that intersection.

He turned north over Nape. From above the edge, he could see into the canyon while flying beyond the effective range of its guns. He was encouraged by how well he was carrying on in spite of shock that made him feel more like an observer than a participant.

Winds had carried smoke from his rocket to the crash site. The smoke, now a misty image, told him the guns that hit Goodwin were close enough to shoot at rescue aircraft.

He looked where his rocket had detonated but saw no hint of guns. Photo interpreters might do better. He pointed. "Get me a picture of the hillside where my marker hit." He held the O-1 steady while Ellison took three pictures. "Keep looking for a chute until I get us over the wreckage." He grabbed his map to mark the guns.

A radio call blared into his earphones. "Nail Four-two or Nail Five-nine, Crown on Guard. If you read, come up on two forty-three decimal zero."

Little time had passed since he'd silenced his VHF. Nevertheless, Mitch felt guilty for keeping everyone in the dark. He switched to the previous VHF frequency, so Guard would be clear in case Goodwin whispered into a survival radio. "Crown and Cricket, Nail Five-nine's on one twenty-eight four. Four-two's down four miles north of the border."

Both controllers blocked each other until Cricket surrendered the frequency.

"Nail Five-nine, Crown," the rescue controller said. Asking for a direction and a distance reference from an American base, he added, "I need a radial and DME."

"Mu Gia!" *Figure it out yourself.* "Standby."

Calm down. Mitch reminded himself Crown was only doing his job—and a very important job. Mitch assumed Crown wanted to launch rescue helicopters upon hearing his plea for Goodwin to bail out. Crews sat alert at Danang in South Vietnam and at Udorn and NKP in Thailand. Crown needed a location before rescue machinery could swing into action.

The O-1 wasn't equipped with useful navigational radios, so Mitch had to rely on his area map. It was marked with a polar grid—lines radiating outward from Nakhon Phanom and crossing circles in ten-mile increments. He picked out Mu Gia Pass. "Try the zero-seven-three at sixty-five miles."

"From NKP?"

Of course! Everything in a Nail's world was measured from NKP. Nevertheless, that was more obvious in Mitch's slow O-1 than in Crown's four-engine aircraft that could fly thousands of miles. "Roger that."

"Have you sighted any chutes, Five-nine?"

"Negative. I'm a couple of minutes from being over the wreckage."

"Crown designates Nail Five-nine as on-scene commander."

"Copied," Mitch said without much thought since his was the only aircraft on-scene.

"Nail, Cricket, we've got Laredo coming to you. You're cleared to use them at your discretion. Expect additional ordnance shortly."

The words sent a shiver through Mitch. A fullness in his throat told him tears of pride would come if he let them. He always felt the same emotions whenever the radios told of a pilot being down—and of scores of other Americans rushing to risk their lives to save the one in danger.

The feeling of mutual loyalties was mystical. A special camaraderie united him with fliers he'd never met—but he knew they'd try to save him, and he'd try to save them. It was a certain brotherhood that draft evaders who fled to Canada would never experience. Mitch wasn't sure he could adequately describe the feeling, even to Elizabeth.

He cleared his throat and glanced at his map for a nearby location to keep the F-105s away from the guns until ready to strike. "Send Laredo to NKP's zero-seven-zero at sixty miles, and tell 'em to standby. I've got a gun position for them."

"Nail, Crown. Be cautious bombing near the crash until you locate survivors."

I'm not a friggin' rookie! This was his first rescue, but he knew how vulnerable helicopters would be hovering over the wreckage. "Roger, Crown. Be advised we're looking for one survivor, but those guns have to go before Jolly Greens can do any good."

"Understand, Nail," Crown said. "Keep us informed."

On intercom, Mitch said, "See that dog's-head bend in the—" He stopped when he discovered a thin, wispy curl of black smoke above the trees. Locating the crash wasn't a problem anymore. "See the smoke?"

"Roger, sir."

"Photograph the smoke with identifiable landmarks so intel can pinpoint the location."

Grabbing his map, Mitch estimated coordinates beneath the black smoke and those of the gun position, then wrote them on the left window. "Cricket, the thirty-seven millimeters that hit Four-two are at Whiskey Echo Eight-two-two-six-zero-zero." Suspecting the North Vietnamese monitored control frequencies, he avoided broadcasting the exact location of the O-1. "The crash site's several hundred meters north."

"Roger, Nail." Cricket repeated the coordinates, then added, "I'm sending Laredo now. Expect Venom and Kingfish in ten minutes. Each is a flight of four F-One-oh-fives. Use UHF Two-thirty-five decimal eight."

Mitch scribbled Venom, Kingfish, and the frequency on his window. "Negative on the frequency change. I'm keeping my UHF on Guard in case Four-two calls."

"Damned outdated radios," Mitch said on intercom. In every modern aircraft, the pilot could monitor the emergency frequency while using another UHF frequency. He cursed posturing politicians who noisily took credit for peacetime budget cuts.

"Nail Five-nine, Crown, air strikes on Guard will get confusing."

"I'll change when other aircraft are overhead. But Four-two's near the west wall in a steep part of the canyon. I may be the only one who can hear him."

"Roger." Referring to rescue aircraft, Crown said, "Sandies from NKP'll be with you in twenty minutes. Expect to move to the other frequency by the time they get on scene."

"Roger."

Mitch divided his attention between the black smoke and areas likely to conceal AAA. He hoped to see the wreckage before the gunners tried for their second kill. He was certain U.S. Air Force crews weren't the only people gearing up for a fight over Mu Gia.

"The trees are tall," Mitch said on intercom, "so I'll put you over the top, looking straight down. I'll do a triple break with pictures out the right window."

"Copied, sir."

Mitch yanked the ends of his lap belt that already held him tightly to the seat. His thoughts were interrupted by pilots of Laredo flight checking in on the UHF radio.

"Nail Five-nine," Cricket said on VHF, "be advised the Jolly Greens and Sandies from NKP have crossed the fence. Sandy One'll contact you shortly."

Mitch understood the rescue force had crossed the Mekong River into Laos. "Copied."

Too many disruptions. Nearing the karst outcropping a half mile from the crash site, Mitch said, "Here we go!" Banking toward the hill, he hoped to trick the gunners into holding fire until he flew over—which he wasn't going to do.

Nearing the smoke, Mitch leaned out the window. Stiffening his neck against the air blasting his helmet, he strained against his shoulder harness to see the wreckage. He saw flickering red flames. Trees obscured the fiery image almost as soon he saw it.

He started counting silently to ten to fly a few hundred feet before reversing course. However, each second brought him closer to the guns. His count reached eight. Fear overpowered planning. "Here's turn two!"

He slammed the stick against his leg, throwing the O-1 onto its left side. Turning from guns frightened him. He couldn't see the flashes if gunners fired while the bottom of the aircraft faced the hill. Nevertheless he wanted to watch the guns while Ellison took pictures. When the karst came into view beyond the propeller, he rolled the wings level.

"Standby, standby." Mitch leaned into the airstream. The hill with the guns looked as peaceful as before. While he scanned for tracers, he rocked the O-1 back and forth. His breathing quickened. He struggled to calm the pounding in his chest. "Three, two, one." He yanked the stick against his thigh and pointed the right wing at the jungle.

Mitch studied a small rip in the jungle a mile below. Black smoke obscured the wreckage. For an instant he saw twisted metal mingled with red tongues of fire. He wanted to deny gut feelings saying Captain Robert Goodwin was part of the fire. Mitch felt flushed, as if he'd finished a sprint and needed to walk to avoid vomiting.

As Ellison snapped pictures, Mitch turned away, looking for guns— for anything to blot out the image of raging flames.

Flashes erupted in a meadow beyond the road.

He stared at the blinking lights, but the flashes ceased as quickly as they started. Only the ghostly shimmer of tracers danced against the east wall's dark shadows. He sensed, more than saw, shells racing toward a spot just beneath his O-1.

Adrenaline kicked his senses up another level. He yanked the nose upward. Straining to keep the tracers in sight, he jammed the throttle forward and kicked the rudder against the stop. He wanted a few more feet between himself and the path of the lethal shells.

Ellison asked, "Can you hold steadier, sir?"

"Negative!" Other flashes seized his attention. Guns that had gotten

Goodwin opened up. Mitch shivered, even though sweat trickled down in his helmet.

The O-1 shuddered a warning—the airplane was climbing more steeply than the engine could support. Mitch centered the rudder. He eased the stick forward to delay a stall that could send the O-1 plunging toward the jungle. He needed to level the wings to fight the stall, but he wanted to keep the shells in sight.

Breath came in gasps.

A voice on the radio seemed far away. "Nail Five-niner. Laredo's with you on Guard."

Tracers shined brightly in contrast to the hazy background near the horizon. Four distinct follow-the-leader lines of glistening lights seemed near enough to touch. Close—but the shells would pass behind.

Pop-pa-pop-pa-pop-pop-pop.

The noises startled Mitch until he realized they weren't detonations. The popping stopped in seconds. The sixty explosive projectiles continued across the canyon.

Mitch would've felt ecstatic about evading the first volley if not for the second. He tried to look south but had trouble deciding which direction was south. The O-1 pointed skyward, as if in a much-too-slow loop. South was somewhere beyond windows in the ceiling. He snapped his head back to look—and was terrified. Four streams were close and seemed on a collision course with the O-1.

"Lead, Two," a voice on the radio said. "I've got flak at twelve o'clock."

Laredo One said, "Roger. Break. Nail, what's your position from the ground fire?"

Right in the friggin' middle! Mitch's mouth was too dry to speak. Kicking the left rudder pedal, he slammed the stick in the same direction.

Shuddering increased to jaw-jarring intensity.

The flight controls no longer were in enough air flow to have any effect. The O-1 hesitated, then tumbled backward.

Mitch felt himself fall as if on a carnival ride where one couldn't keep his eyes open. His closed. The seat belt and shoulder harness kept him from being thrown around the cockpit. Nevertheless, his helmet banged the left window, and his feet flailed away from the rudder pedals. One boot crashed against the side of the cockpit. Air swished in through the window, and something brushed his face.

His eyes sprang open. He saw his maps swirl in a reddish haze of dust sucked from the floor. Grabbing for the maps, he caught the edge of one. The other floated out the window. The tumbling O-1 threw him sideways. His hand slammed against the window frame, and he lost the second map, too.

Pop-pa-pa-pop-pa-pop-pop-pop.

Flashes of tracers were everywhere. His nostrils filled with the acrid odor of fireworks on the Fourth of July.

He saw a line of tracers just aft of the wing. Seemingly in slow motion, the O-1 cartwheeled around the glowing shells. He leaned away as if extra inches might protect him from shrapnel. The wing slashed into the deadly path an instant after the shells disappeared. The popping stopped.

"Nail Five-niner, Laredo Lead. Radio check, UHF."

The radio call hardly registered in Mitch's consciousness. The scene beyond the cockpit swirled, like during spins practiced in pilot training. In those flights, white clouds and blue sky seemed to race around his jet trainer. Now, green jungle, reddish-brown roadways, and thousands of bomb craters rushed by in a spiraling blur. His eyes jittered, trying to find something stationary in the spinning world. A terrifying realization jolted him. The O-1 was spinning—and upside down.

Panic seized Mitch. He'd never been in an inverted spin—and he'd never talked to anyone who had.

In the twirling scene below, he saw more flashes. His mind was too overloaded to sense which guns were firing, competing for the second kill of the morning.

Ignoring tracers, Mitch pushed the left rudder pedal against the stop. The spin accelerated—wrong rudder. He jammed his right foot against the other pedal. Spinning seemed to slow, but he wasn't certain. Cramps stiffened his fingers, protesting against his death grip on the throttle and stick. One of J.D.'s silly sayings flashed to mind: "If it's inevitable, relax. No sense dying all tensed up."

"We gonna bail out, Lieutenant?"

Ellison sounded less frightened than Mitch expected. "Negative!" He concealed the conclusion reached with a glance at the altimeter—they were too low for both to jump clear and deploy a good chute before slamming into the ground.

Without warning, the lawnmower-like sound of the engine ceased. The propeller began winding down.

Chapter 5

Ellison screeched, "What happened?"

Mitch looked at the fuel gauges. Both showed empty. "No fuel!" He realized the gauges were inaccurate with the aircraft upside down. "Fuel's not getting to the engine."

The aircraft stopped spinning. Mitch hung with his full weight on his shoulder straps and lap belt, while the O-1—in an inverted spiraling dive—rushed headlong at a jungle-covered ridge. He snapped the stick sideways until the O-1 was upright, then pulled back as much as he dared. The aircraft was so low he could see individual branches on trees and bushes. The O-1 had enough airspeed to fly, but he feared it wouldn't clear the ridge. Getting the engine going might help.

He flipped on the auxiliary fuel pump and rechecked the fuel gauges. Both needles bounced wildly. The engine backfired and grumbled to life. The propeller whirred into a blur.

"Love that sound," Ellison said.

"Nail Five-nine, Crown. Radio check, VHF. Do you copy?" Signals from the airborne rescue center were weak.

"Standby!" *Everyone's missing us.* As Mitch tried to ease his crushing death grip on the throttle and stick. He could not. He realized if he didn't push aside his fear and let discipline and training take over, he'd die on this sunny morning in Mu Gia.

When he saw the O-1 would clear trees towering above the ridge, he started thinking of the jungle as an ally.

"Shit," Ellison shouted. "They're still shootin'!"

"Where?"

"All over the place."

From at least four directions—sixteen guns, Mitch thought—tracers raced across the canyon. The closest were almost on the O-1 but high. Mitch scrunched lower in the seat.

Explosive slugs streaked overhead, slamming into the cliff beyond the wing. Chunks of limestone and splintered teak cascaded into the O-1's wake.

Mitch looked frantically for other shells. Two AAA sites had fired wildly. "Those two are no factor." He spotted the fourth cluster fired downward from a rock shelf on the opposite cliff. These shells appeared frozen in mid-air—an aviator's visual warning of a collision course. Fear tightened his chest. The shells and the O-1 were converging on the same point above the ridge.

He shoved the stick forward and aimed at a gap in the trees. Men scrambled among camouflaged huts on the ridge, which jutted from the west wall. A soldier knelt, and his AK-47 sparkled. The gunfire looked like Morse code flashed from a signal light.

Mitch heard the AK-47's *rat-a-tat-tat* as the O-1 swooped across the ridge. On each side, trees towered higher than twenty-story buildings. Antiaircraft shells streaked overhead and exploded in the trees. Shards of molten shrapnel showered onto the hidden camp, but the O-1 flew clear, diving toward treetops beyond.

"The Lord is my shepherd." Mitch rattled off the words, continuing the 23rd Psalm through the line modified as, "Yea though I *fly* through the valley of the shadow of death, I shall fear no evil." At the moment, his faith was less than his fear of the evil surrounding him.

Mitch scanned for shells but saw none. The road wasn't even in sight. He saw no evidence of the war and of the hundreds of trucks that regularly rumbled past a quarter of a mile east. Trees, streams, rocks, and trails rushed by. Mitch realized he'd never flown so low without a runway beneath him. At least, most guns were near the road, and gunners couldn't see the O-1 hugging treetops near the west wall.

"Laredo One, Crown. I've lost contact with Nail Five-nine. Do you have him visual?"

The transmission was broken, forcing Mitch to fill in missing words.

"Negative, Crown," Laredo One said, almost unreadable deep in Mu Gia's canyon. "We're a minute or so from the rendezvous, and we can't raise him."

Peering through overhead windows, Mitch had to look straight up to see the top of the cliff blocking the signals. Trees on Nape's summit were more than twice as far above him as the top of the Empire State Building had been one summer when he'd walked the streets of Manhattan. Claustrophobia squeezed at him.

The enormity of his predicament sank in—he was flying a Cessna in the bottom of Mu Gia with no idea how to get out alive. One of J.D.'s pronouncements came to mind. If you go low, stay right on the trees. Staying low gave gunners only seconds to swing weapons around and shoot before even an O-1 could escape behind other trees.

"Are you gonna climb, Lieutenant?"

"Negative. We'd need at least five minutes to climb out." Mitch fought the temptation to add that climbing into the gauntlet of AAA would be suicide. Just above the trees was an invisible blanket of sky J.D. called never-never air—never fly there or you'll never come back!

Mitch called, "Crown, this is Nail Five-nine on Guard. Do you read?" After a few seconds, he repeated his call.

No one answered.

Losing radio contact was chilling. Mitch realized he and Ellison alone—and maybe Goodwin—were pitted against hundreds of North Vietnamese in Mu Gia.

Le was surprised to hear the voice on the radio. "I thought both aircraft were down!"

Major Tho said, "The last reports were he crashed near the first. Obviously—"

"The reports were mistaken!" Le stared at the antiquated field telephones. He wished he could get information as quickly from his troops as from the Americans. He caught himself staring without focusing. "We don't have time for this."

Tho nodded.

"Do you have decoys deployed?"

"At four sites, Colonel." Tho leaned over the map and pointed to four triple-A sites.

Le noticed one was near coordinates the pilot had reported earlier. He tapped the map at that site. "Lead them here."

"Do you want to start now?"

"No. Wait until the rescue planes arrive."

"Yes, Colonel."

Le decided he might learn more by listening for aircraft and antiaircraft fire. "I'll be outside." He grabbed his AK-47 and hung his helmet by its strap over his holster. Hoping additional gunners would be ready before more aircraft arrived, he paused at the base of the steps. "Tell me when defenses reach level one."

"Yes, Colonel."

Nearly paralyzed by desperation, Mitch was doing little more than guide the O-1 over trees rushing by. When he imagined Elizabeth and Mandy in a casualty-notification scene, he knew he must find a way to survive.

"I thought for a minute you were gonna get me sick, sir," Ellison said with a tense laugh.

Mitch was so absorbed in hopelessness, the words hardly registered. "Say, again."

"That's the wildest maneuvering I've ever been in, sir, but I'm liable to get sick if you do that spin thing again."

"No more spins. Get pictures of people and structures. Watch out for ground fire from the left." He opened the left window so gunfire would be more noticeable.

Mitch saw ahead—not far ahead—the canyon widened. Jungle gave way to a wasteland pounded to dust by thousands of bombs. The sight was terrifying. In ninety seconds, the O-1 would fly at treetop level into the Doghouse—where no trees remained.

He searched desperately for another answer. Could he pull a quick U-turn and follow Mu Gia deeper into North Vietnam? He looked across the canyon to estimate how much a turn would expose his O-1 to gunners. Ahead, a small ridge led east toward the road. The ridge had trees, and those trees could provide seconds of cover from some guns. He glanced beyond the end of the ridge and noticed a break in the vertical barrier of Mu Gia's east wall.

"Of course!" He remembered the giant's swirling fingerprint east of Mu Gia. Those karst peaks were intermingled with hundreds of canyons. AAA wouldn't be wasted there.

This chance to escape demanded thirty seconds in the open while flying from the ridge to the east wall. With more time to consider the odds, he might've talked himself out of the risky flight. But time had run out.

"Hang on, Ellison." Mitch rolled hard.

The airplane skidded toward the ridge, but he didn't level the wings until the nose pointed at the rugged east wall. He dropped beside tall trees, and let them shield the O-1 from guns to the south. Mitch yanked the O-1 over a tall stand of trees, then dipped into a gap.

In a clearing below the bunker, Le stood relieving himself in the bushes. He heard the distant drone of jets, but surrounding trees made the direction difficult to determine. *The generator's whine is strange.* He glanced at the camouflage-covered generator near the bunker and realized the muffled whine came from elsewhere. Turning, he was startled to see a silver-gray O-1 burst from the treetops.

Breaking out over a small clearing, Mitch saw stacked logs forming the wall of a bunker imbedded in the hillside. "Pictures!"
Rat-a-tat-tat-tat.
An AK-47's chatter grabbed Mitch's attention. In a frenzied search for the gunner, his eyes met those of a slender bare-headed man dressed in jungle fatigues.

Le flinched, surprised by the nearness of the American plane. He got a glimpse of the pilot as the O-1 hurtled across the clearing.

Mitch passed the last stand of trees, swooping over what looked like underbrush. He realized the bushes were a trellised framework interlaced with fresh leaves. Spotting movement and metal, he was terrified. He was fewer than twenty feet above a pair of 37mm guns, with both barrels aligned north. He saw crewmen—with fresh vegetation woven into netting on their helmets—cranking mechanisms to turn the guns.

Le tried to appear calm, but his heart pounded. He looked around. Everyone's attention was on the fleeing aircraft, so no one seemed to notice his fright. A chorus of automatic-weapons fire drowned out the shouting.
His mind replayed the previous moments. He realized one man had held a camera. Le remembered silver birds on the pilot's helmet.
Watching the big guns swing east, Le wanted to claim another American aircraft. His eyes followed the O-1, and he sighed involuntarily. *What a display of courage!* As long as such Americans keep coming, this war could never be won. Raising his hands to protect his ears from the expected firing, he felt part of him cheer for the daring Americans to escape.
The antiaircraft guns let loose a thunderous barrage.
In that moment Le realized something was familiar about the silver birds on the helmet.

The O-1 flew exposed over pulverized ground for the next quarter of a mile. There were hardly enough fragments of wood to suggest trees had covered the canyon. Rusted metal littered craters. The size of some craters shocked Mitch. He flew across several that could entomb his O-1 deeper than in a six-foot grave.

Pop-pa-pop-pop-pop.

Mitch looked up as flashes streaked in from the north and passed a few feet beyond the propeller. The *boom-ba-boom* of explosions obliterated the popping of 37mm shells burning through the air. Geysers erupted beyond the right wing as shells detonated in the red dirt.

Mitch banked away from the explosions. He sensed shrapnel sprinkle the tail.

"You okay, Ellison?"

"Just holding on, sir."

"Get pictures. You'll never have another chance like this—not with me, anyway."

"Not with nobody, sir."

Mitch crossed the road before he recognized that the meandering trail of gravel crushed into the earth was the road. Slugs from the guns overflown seconds earlier swished by, passing a few feet left.

Mitch banked hard to the right. The steep bank reduced lift, and the O-1 dropped. A stab of fear jolted him. He yanked on the stick and kept the aircraft from cartwheeling into a glistening stream draining Mu Gia into the Doghouse.

The sudden fright made his heart pound—almost in time with the staccato detonations of thirty antiaircraft shells hitting the ground. He tried to will himself into control but couldn't force his hands to relax. His death grip on the throttle and stick remained rigid until the O-1 reached trees near the east wall.

Mitch flew into choppier air in the side canyon. Like flying into stormy weather, the O-1 went from bright sunshine into dark shadows of vertical cliffs.

The canyon likely contained camps for troops who worked in Mu Gia, so he kept near the trees for a half mile. Scattered blasts from AK-47s were barely audible above the engine's echoes off karst walls. The gunfire didn't sound close, so he ignored it.

Trails interlaced the canyon. Mitch saw several camouflaged buildings. Two footbridges made of rope and vines crossed a stream that rushed to Mu Gia. He mentally catalogued his discoveries to report at debriefing. When he realized what he was doing, he felt better. Part of him now anticipated getting to NKP.

A wall of karst blocked his path, and Mitch followed the canyon's abrupt turn. A steeper canyon confronted him. Winds accelerated between narrowing karst walls and made the jostling of turbulence more severe. The stream, now a jagged ribbon of white foam in the shadows, cascaded from one brief pool to the next. Fewer trees clung to rocky slopes and swayed erratically in gusty winds that pushed the O-1 forward.

"I don't think soldiers would climb this far." Mitch coasted well above the trees. He felt optimistic. In minutes, he should be safe above the karst.

Ahead, the canyon turned.

Rounding a jagged spire of karst, Mitch hoped to see a long canyon open into a high meadow. Instead a box canyon, with karst cliffs towering hundreds of feet high, confronted the O-1.

"Jesus."

The only escape was behind, but the narrow canyon prevented a U-turn. He looked for a place to safely crash land. None existed. The floor angled up steeply to meet limestone walls.

The wind pushing the O-1 would provide a helpful updraft near the cliff, so he considered a half loop to reverse direction. J.D. had bragged of flying loops in O-1s, but he'd always started after diving to build airspeed to over a hundred knots. With barely half that speed, Mitch knew he would stall and fall back well before the top of a loop. "Damned gutless airplane!" He spit out the words, just before his mind returned to the words: stall and fall back. They offered a faint glimmer of hope.

Ellison asked, "Where're we going, sir?"

Mitch pushed the controls on the throttle quadrant forward to prod full power from the engine. Watching the onrushing cliff, he tried to judge the right moment to pull the O-1 skyward. If he pulled too soon, the O-1 would miss the column of wind deflected up the karst. If he waited too long, the aircraft would glance off the cliff and lose momentum.

Ellison's voice was more frantic. "Turn us around, Lieutenant!"

"Hold on," Mitch shouted, yanking the stick back against the stop.

The O-1 pitched up, pointing at the patch of blue beyond the tops of the karst. Mitch experienced the sensation of landing on a rugged, vertical runway, and he fought to keep from drifting into the cliff. Although the propeller clawed the air, speed decreased rapidly.

The danger with power-on stalls, Mitch thought, was that aircraft responded unpredictably—such as inverted spins.

Coasting into bright sunlight near the top of the karst, the O-1 shuddered, then faltered. Mitch kicked the left rudder pedal to the stop. The O-1 hesitated. For a terrifying instant, he felt he was starting to tumble backward, an out-of-control maneuver guaranteed to fling the aircraft against the karst. He yanked the stick left and leaned against the side, trying to coax the airplane to fall toward the left wing.

The O-1 fell sideways. The maneuver was more abrupt than the stall over Mu Gia, but Mitch kept his eyes open. Falling almost straight down, the O-1's nose oscillated like a pendulum. Now the engine, which had slowed the loss of airspeed in the climb, accelerated the O-1 and dampened oscillations. The updraft slowed the descent and forced air across the wings, ailerons, and elevator. The O-1 started flying again, well above the sloping floor. Mitch pulled on the stick and skimmed above boulders and the spring-fed stream.

Mitch heard barfing behind him. He pitied Ellison. The only thing worse than the last few minutes in the front seat had to be riding out those same minutes in the back. Exhausted, Mitch wanted to call time-out. Unfortunately, Mu Gia was two minutes away.

The realization frightened him less than he thought. Surprise was on his side this time.

Turning toward the opening into Mu Gia, Mitch began jinking. In the thirty seconds required to reach the main canyon, he heard bursts from AK-47s. All sounded well behind.

Reentering Mu Gia, Mitch flew in the shadow of the east wall. He kept the stick and rudder pedals moving to be a more difficult target.

Mitch saw a steep mountain ahead. *Phou Chuang!* He finally had a plan offering hope.

He checked the instruments and found all readings normal. Looking through the windshield, he was reassured by the steady blur of the propeller. The airplane was performing better than he was. In a voice Ellison couldn't hear, Mitch spoke quietly to the airplane. "Sorry I called you gutless."

Thuds—F-105 Thunderchiefs

Chapter 6

"Laredo, Nail Five-nine on Guard. Do you copy?"

"Roger, Nail, Laredo Lead's got you loud and clear. Say location."

"I'm down in Mu Gia just south of the border."

"Understand you've crashed in Mu Gia."

"Negative. Not yet, anyway. Have you heard from Nail Four-two?"

"Negative. We're overhead at fourteen thou' and haven't raised him."

"No miracle," Mitch muttered on intercom.

Ahead he saw the desolation of the Doghouse west of Phou Chuang. The east side was more inviting. He turned into the slowly rising canyon, stayed on the trees another mile, then climbed in sunshine along the rugged northeast wall.

Mitch looked at the clock: eight-ten. "Damned clock stopped."

"Say again, sir," Ellison said.

Mitch checked his wristwatch: eight-ten. He couldn't believe fewer than twenty minutes had passed since Goodwin crashed. "Disregard."

Ellison asked, "What are we gonna do now, sir?"

Mitch's sense of duty pushed aside accumulated fear. "We need to put in an air strike. That's one of the rules of the game."

He'd been taught to respond to being fired on, even if only with a marking rocket at the end of the mission. The threat of retaliation was the FACs' main weapon in discouraging gunners. Mitch would use Laredo to deliver the message. He also hoped the fighters would be accurate enough to take out guns that could attack rescue forces if Goodwin came up on the radio.

"How much fuel do you have, Laredo?"

"We can give you fifteen minutes before we're bingo."

Plenty. Mitch closed the windows.

Le stared at the dusty loudspeaker. Were the spirits punishing him for not observing Tet? The new year was a time to return to the home village and honor one's family and the graves of one's ancestors. For several years, Le's military duties had kept him from fulfilling such obligations. This year he would be part of the biggest effort yet by the Ministry of Defense to take advantage of the enemy during the truce. Le was eager to drive the war to a conclusion, but he wished he and his men could observe Tet.

He recalled a story he planned to tell gatherings of troops over the next few days. Under the cover of Tet celebrations nearly two centuries earlier, Emperor Quang Trung had surprised and defeated a Chinese army occupying Hanoi. The spirits obviously had smiled on Emperor Trung in spite of violating the essence of Tet. Le hoped to receive similar understanding—but the airplanes made him feel uneasy.

"Nail Five-nine's approaching the target, so standby for the strike briefing."

"Nail Five-nine, Crown. If you're not in emergency conditions, could you move your strike off Guard?"

That made sense, Mitch thought, since Guard was like a big, party-line telephone every pilot was supposed to monitor. "Laredo, are you in position to hear Four-two?"

"Roger, we're monitoring. Kingfish is overhead at twenty, and Venom's at twenty-two."

Mitch looked at his notes on the window. The frequency Cricket had assigned was scrawled by the call signs. "Okay, Laredo, Kingfish, and Venom, let's go up two thirty-five decimal eight."

"Laredo."

"Kingfish."

"Venom."

"Nail Five-nine, Sandy One's about six minutes out."

Things are about to get busy. Mitch knew the four A-1s and two helicopters soon would join the twelve F-105s and his O-1.

Mitch switched to 235.8 and listened as eighteen pilots checked-in. A shiver pulsed through his neck and shoulders. The brotherhood was gathering—and armed with more than fifty-thousand pounds of bombs.

He learned Kingfish and Venom had enough fuel to stay overhead for thirty minutes, then looked for Laredo. "Nail Five-nine'll be over the target in about two minutes. Laredo, I need your numbers?"

"Laredo's four Thuds, each with six mark one-seventeens with standard fusing. We've also got twenty mike-mike."

On the window Mitch wrote six 750-pound bombs and 20mm guns. "I'll take your bombs in a single pass. I doubt we have time for guns."

"Laredo copied."

Mitch hoped to cover the standard items only once. "Everybody listen up. Laredo's target's an active thirty-seven-millimeter gun position that shot down my flight leader. Target elevation's about thirteen hundred feet. The winds in the canyon are southerly. The forecaster called for winds from one-eight-zero at ten to fifteen knots at two, five, and ten thousand." He paused to let everyone copy and to allow someone to interrupt, if necessary.

Mitch continued, with numbers remembered from his target study. "High terrain's in all quadrants. The highest within ten miles is northwest at about seventy-one hundred feet and about five thousand feet due south. All terrain should be visual. No friendlies are in the area except for the possibility of Nail Four-two. His aircraft crashed several hundred meters north-northwest of the target, so I'll restrict run-in headings." He doubted Goodwin survived, but Mitch would ensure long or short bombs wouldn't hit near the downed O-1.

"We're in an intense thirty-seven-millimeter environment. Expect ground fire from the target. Also there are occasional reports of radar-directed, fifty-seven-millimeters in Mu Gia. Sound-off if anyone detects signals on your radar-warning gear."

After another pause, he continued, "If anyone gets hit, turn west for immediate bailout over the Nape Plateau. The high karst east is okay if you can survive the landing. If you can keep things together a little longer, Thailand's sixty miles west."

Mitch concentrated on procedures J.D. called choreographing a five-hundred-knot ballet. As FAC, Mitch was in charge and responsible for preventing mid-air collisions. He had three flights of fighters above, and he assumed the six rescue aircraft were divided into two flights. Since F-105s attacked from nearly twenty thousand feet above the ground, he asked, "Laredo, can you stay below Kingfish at twenty?"

"Laredo won't go above eighteen for roll-in, Nail."

Good. Mitch counted on altitude separation to keep the F-105s apart. Approaching the target, he located the hill with the camouflaged guns that downed Goodwin. He looked farther northwest and saw a faint curl of smoke above the burning aircraft.

Mitch picked out two pairs of fighters in a left-hand orbit. "Laredo, are you headed south in two two-ships west of Mu Gia?"

"That's Laredo."

"Okay, Laredo, your target's east in the canyon. Do you see the oblong karst that juts up a couple of thousand feet from the floor?"

"I see a hell of a lot of karst, Nail, but I think I've got the one you mean. This karst is north-south with lots of craters alongside."

"Roger that. Your target's two miles north of that karst. I want a run-in heading of two-ten, that's from north-northeast to south-south-west, and break off to the west. The FAC'll hold at seven thousand over the karst to the east." Two months earlier Mitch had stumbled through such instructions. Now his firm voice communicated confidence along with his instructions.

"Laredo copied."

"I'll mark the target with a Willie Pete," Mitch continued using the jargon for a rocket with white phosphorous in the warhead. "Let's set up from this orbit if you can be ready."

"Roger that, Nail. Break. Laredo flight, spread it out. Green 'em up. Lead's going burner—Now!"

Mitch flew his O-1 to the roll-in point for his marking pass. To confirm the rescue aircraft were clear, he asked, "Sandy One, where are you?"

"Sandy's two A-Ones at five thousand on NKP's zero-seven-five at fifty-eight."

Mitch wished he had his map with its grid of radials and distances. He guessed the A-1s were five miles west. "Are you over Nape, Sandy?"

"Roger. Jolly Greens and two more Sandies are twenty miles in trail."

"Sandy, if you'll stay over Nape not above five thousand, I'll turn things over to you when Laredo finishes."

"Copied not above five thousand."

Mitch searched into the glare of the sun in the southeastern sky and picked out Laredo. They were higher and strung out in extended trail. Timing was critical, and everything seemed right.

"You ready, Sergeant Ellison?"

"I've already tossed out my barf bag, sir, so I'm ready as I'm gonna be."

"FAC's preparing to mark," Mitch said on the radio.

He took one more look at the fighters, then pulled back the throttle and the stick. While the nose rose well above the horizon, he looked out at the rockets to verify the empty tube. Reaching up, he armed a rocket, then slammed the stick against his knee and dropped into a steep dive. "FAC's in hot!" *The brotherhood's taking the offensive.*

Mitch aimed the nose well below the meadow, then let the nose drift higher as airspeed increased. He aligned the target with the O-1's rudimentary sights—a grease-pencil mark on the windshield and a piece of tubing that stuck straight up from the engine cowling. After holding the mark on the target a few seconds, he squeezed the trigger.

Ka-bamm!

The rocket roared from a tube beneath the wing.

"Mark's away!"

Mitch jammed the throttle forward, rolled into a tight turn, and started pulling out of the dive. He scanned for ground fire and listened for warnings.

Waiting for the rocket to explode, Mitch divided his attention between the canyon and looking for Laredo flight. A small speck high in the eastern sky probably was the leader, but Mitch wasn't certain. A flash on the hillside disappointed him. White smoke from his rocket billowed upward from the northern edge of the meadow instead of the center where the guns were located. "Didn't correct enough for the winds," he said on intercom. Nevertheless, the mark was close enough for a reference.

"Laredo's got the smoke. Am I cleared in, Nail?"

Mitch searched for the lead fighter and picked out a moving speck. "Roger, Laredo Lead's cleared in hot. Your target's one hundred and fifty meters south of the smoke, near the center of the meadow. *Do not*, repeat, *do not* drop north of the smoke!"

"Copied, Nail. I'll stay south. Lead's in hot."

Maneuvering above the karst, Mitch scanned northeast. The speck seemed to hesitate, then started descending. Mitch alternated his gaze between the fighter and the target. He turned toward the fighter, positioning his O-1 over the east wall of Mu Gia when the bombs separated from the F-105.

Laredo One began a high-G pullout with afterburner glowing.

Mitch studied the meadow and saw sparkles. "Ground fire! From the target!" He saw the tracers were well behind Laredo One. "No factor, Lead."

"Thanks!"

Moments later, forty-five-hundred pounds of bombs exploded. Six huge geysers of dirt erupted in the southern part of the meadow.

Laredo Two asked, "Where do you want Two's bombs, Nail?"

"Middle of the meadow on the guns. Lead's a hundred meters long."

"Middle of the meadow and on the ground fire," Laredo Two said in an excited voice.

"Two's cleared in hot." His white smoke was drifting north toward the crash site. "Stay well south of my smoke."

"Two's in!"

Pessimism filled Mitch. He assumed the best pilot led the flight, and the leader had missed. With ground fire confirmed, Mitch didn't expect accuracy to improve. Everyone—except perhaps J.D.—got more nervous when guns were active.

Two's bombs were closer but not close enough. Return fire was no more effective.

Ellison said, "At least the other guns aren't joining in."

"Probably waiting for the Jollies." Mitch cleared the next F-105.

Sandy One asked, "Where's the crash in relation to the guns you're attacking, Nail?"

Mitch looked across the canyon and saw two camouflaged A-1s above the west rim. "The O-1 went into the trees half a mile north-northwest. You may see smoke from the site."

"We'll take a look," Sandy One said.

Within a minute, Laredo Three and Four dropped bombs. Both missed by wide margins.

Mitch said on intercom, "Not much to show for eighteen-thousand pounds of bombs."

"Maybe Venom and Kingfish'll do better, sir."

"Maybe. At least, nobody was hit." Mitch compiled his post-strike report, using target coordinates scrawled on the window. "I've got your BDA, Laredo, when you're ready."

"Go, Nail."

Mitch gave coordinates, times on and off target, and his assessment of no damage. He sighed the pain he felt deep inside. "Thanks for your help, Laredo."

"Sorry we couldn't do better for your friend, Nail."

"Thanks."

"Nail Five-nine, Sandy One's taking on-scene command at this time."

"Understand." Mitch checked his fuel. "I can hang around another twenty minutes. Be advised more thirty-seven millimeters have been active than I could keep track of."

"Roger, Nail. Tell me everything you've learned this morning."

That could take the rest of the week. As Mitch told what had happened, he maneuvered across Mu Gia and joined the A-1s over Nape.

"Okay, Two, let's take a look."

"Gotcha covered," Sandy Two said.

Mitch watched the lead A-1 soar up a couple of thousand feet, do a wingover, and dive as if attacking the crash site. Sandy Two scissored back and forth behind his leader. Mitch stayed to the side and watched for ground fire. The A-1s dipped low over the wreckage, then pulled up and jinked back and forth until safe above karst on the east side.

Mitch was making notes on his kneeboard when a call on the radio sent a charge of adrenaline through him.

"Crown, Sandy One's receiving a beeper."

Maybe Goodwin was alive! Mitch selected Guard, and he heard the

Whoop-Whoop-Whoop of a survival radio. "A good, strong signal," Mitch said on intercom.

Ellison asked, "Why would Captain Goodwin have waited to set off his beeper, sir?"

"Maybe he's close to troops and didn't want them to know he'd survived until Sandies and Jolly Greens got here."

He wished his O-1 had a device to point to the signal's source. Nevertheless, the A-1s carried homing equipment, so he knew the beeper could be located quickly.

Mitch looked for the helicopters and the other two A-1s. He didn't see them, so he rolled toward the canyon and looked for Sandy One. The big fighter wasn't east of Goodwin's crash where Mitch expected, so he scanned a wider section of sky. Seconds later, an oil-stained apparition in tan, brown, and green camouflage caught his eye.

Sandy One skimmed beyond the karst's natural cover and into the unobstructed skies over Mu Gia. Sandy Two scissored close behind.

Mitch saw Sandy One was headed for the guns that had shot down Goodwin. "Sandy, you're too far south!"

"Negative, Nail. The beeper's right on my nose."

The beeper might be ahead of the A-1, Mitch thought, but Goodwin's parachute would've had to drift *into* the wind to be ahead of Sandy One.

"Break it off, Sandy!" Mitch's decisiveness surprised him. "That can't be Four-two's beeper. It's a—"

Before he could say trap, eight guns spit tracers at Sandy One.

Sandy Two yelled, "Ground fire!" He rolled level, released clusters of fragmentation bombs, and jinked wildly.

Fiery tracers converged on Sandy One. Most raced by, but Mitch saw the flicker of exploding shells. He also saw flashes from four more AAA sites. "You're picking up more fire, north and south, Sandy."

The A-1 climbed and began a slow barrel roll. "Sandy One's hit."

The pilot's tone—cool and professional—impressed Mitch. In contrast, he yelled on intercom, "Get as much of this on film as you can, Ellison!"

"Roger, sir."

Mitch turned parallel to Sandy One.

Crown interrupted, "Sandy One, Crown. Say your status."

"Stand by. Break. Two, stay clear. I've got to jettison ordnance."

"Two's clear."

Trailing dense black smoke, Sandy One coasted into the upper part of the barrel roll.

Mitch saw that a chunk of the wing was missing. While the A-1 was upright, numerous pieces fell away as the pilot released his bombs.

"Your left flap's gone, Harold," Sandy Two said, "and there's a hell of a fire in the bottom of the cowling."

"The engine's had it."

"Can you stay with her until you reach the plateau?"

"Roger."

The meadow erupted with scores of flashes as fragmentation bombs dropped by Sandy Two exploded near the AAA site.

Mitch watched the A-1 make two sweeping rolls that left a corkscrew trail of smoke.

The burning A-1 rolled upright above Nape.

Sandy One said, "Drinks are on me, but I'll need a ride to the bar."

Mitch saw the A-1's big canopy separate and tumble backward. Moments later a rocket hurtled upward and yanked the pilot from the cockpit. Mitch called, "Crown, Sandy One's ejected."

"Keep us advised. Break. Crown now designates Sandy Two the on-scene commander."

"Two, copied."

Mitch saw a parachute stream out above the plummeting pilot. The silky canopy blossomed, and Sandy One drifted northward over the plateau. Sandy Two skidded into a tight turn around the descending pilot.

"Crown, Sandy Two. One's got a good chute. Break. Jolly One, you have us in sight?"

"Roger," a voice from the helicopter said. "We've got the chute."

"Come to me, Jolly," Sandy Two said. "Watch out for One's bird coming down in your direction."

"We're well clear," Jolly One said.

Mitch watched in fascination. Gravity exaggerated the A-1's downward swings. Spirals of oily black smoke became less symmetrical.

South of the dark trail of smoke, the whirl of helicopter rotor blades blurred tiny patches of jungle. Mitch spotted camouflaged fuselages suspended beneath the blurs. Two more A-1s—Sandy Three and Four—crisscrossed above the helicopters. Much closer, Sandy One's parachute floated above a meadow.

The A-1 Skyraider that minutes earlier had been Sandy One crashed inverted and exploded in the trees at the edge of a wide meadow. Two minutes later, the pilot guided his parachute to a smooth landing in another meadow, and thirty seconds after that, Jolly One touched down nearby with all three A-1s circling menacingly overhead. In fewer than ninety more seconds, the helicopter lifted from the meadow.

"Jolly One's coming out. Harold's aboard with nothing more than bruises."

"Wahooo," Sandy Two said.

Everything had proceeded like a well-choreographed performance, contrasting in every way with Mitch's frantic struggles over Mu Gia. He felt like crying out, "What about Nail Four-two?" Feelings deep inside said the brotherhood could do nothing more for Robert Goodwin.

Jolly One asked, "What's next?"

Sandy Two answered, "Standby while we refigure the game plan."

"Nail Five-nine, Crown. What are the chances Four-two survived?"

Mitch had dreaded the question. If he said to keep trying, others might die in vain. If he recommended the rescue effort be stopped, he might be condemning Goodwin to death or to months of harsh captivity as a POW. Mitch was being asked to play God, and he wanted no part of it. His fingers twisted the left end of his mustache so hard, pain surprised him.

"Five-nine, did you copy Crown?"

"Roger." Mitch sighed deeply. "I hope I'm wrong, but I don't think Four-two survived."

"Sandy Two, what's your assessment?"

"I didn't see the FAC crash, but you can walk across Mu Gia on the flak."

Crown didn't answer immediately. Mitch turned toward Mu Gia even though his fuel gauges indicated he should head for NKP.

Moments later, Crown said, "Attention Sandy Two, Three, and Four, Jolly One and Two, Nail Five-nine, Kingfish, Venom, and Cricket. Crown suspends the active search for Nail Four-two at time zero-one-forty Zulu. Sandy Flight and Jolly Green Flight are directed to return to base with Sandy One. All other aircraft maintain listening watch on Guard. Advise Crown of any contact with Nail Four-two."

Mitch looked into Mu Gia's canyon and couldn't see any more smoke from the O-1. He turned toward the Mekong and watched the helicopters and A-1s pull farther ahead.

Even with Ellison along, Mitch felt more alone than at any time since leaving Elizabeth at the airport in California. He also felt guilty. Losing his flight leader seemed somehow his fault. He was haunted by the possibility his warning had caused Goodwin to fly into the path of the antiaircraft shells.

Mitch forced himself to return to tasks accomplished on return flights to NKP. He pulled out a pen, glanced at the window, and started to copy his notes. Everything caught up with him, and his hands shook uncontrollably. He was near the Mekong River before he could write legibly.

Nakhon Phanom RTAFB—NKP—Naked Phantom—Naked Fanny

Chapter 7

Five minutes after crossing into Thailand, Mitch turned into NKP's traffic pattern. With eyes hardly registering what they saw, he gazed at the jungle clearing with its metal runway and tin-roofed buildings of reddish brown. The parking ramp he'd left three hours earlier appeared busier than usual. Mitch felt he'd aged in those hours. Even his fear of landings, which had dogged him since that bad day in pilot training, paled to insignificance.

After one of his best landings in an O-1, Mitch stopped in the de-arming area. He hung his hands limply out the windows while an airman replaced safing pins for the rockets. When finished, the ordnance specialist looked around. Mitch turned away. He'd hoped the airman knew why only one O-1 had returned.

The airman ran to the cockpit. "Where's your wingman, sir?"

Mitch shrugged. "He's, uh—" His throat went dry.

The airman's eyes widened.

Damn it. If Mitch couldn't answer such a simple question, he couldn't face debriefings yet to come. "He's, uh— The airplane crashed. Captain Goodwin's not coming back today." Adding *today* seemed to soften the blow. He'd never been good at talking about death.

"That's kind of becoming a regular thing around here, isn't it, sir?" The airman seemed less surprised than Mitch had expected.

"Seems to be."

The airman saluted and hurried to the pickup.

When Mitch taxied across the main parking ramp, everything appeared routine except for the extra activity around the rescue aircraft. Maintenance and refueling crews were busy preparing the helicopters and fighters for their next scramble. Now there were only three A-1s to work on.

Mitch guided his O-1 along the path of PSP that led behind the hangars to the FACs' parking ramp. Rounding the corner, he saw the crowd he'd hoped wouldn't be there. Most stood beyond an empty parking spot. He saw the base chaplain beside Lieutenant Colonel Black, the commander of the 23rd TASS. Nearby were at least twenty pilots in flight suits, fifty maintenance men in fatigues, and a couple of dozen men in civilian clothes.

"The word spreads quickly when we lose an airplane," Mitch said.

"Yes, sir." Ellison sounded exhausted.

"I suppose the turnout would've been larger if Captain Goodwin had been on the Jolly Green." Now, however, instead of jubilation, a somber mood pervaded. There'd been a death in the family, and everyone had come to pay respects to the fallen brother.

The marshaler signaled the O-1 had taxied far enough. Mitch stopped and shut down the engine. When the propeller stopped, maintenance men swarmed forward. Everyone seemed to feel obliged to help push the O-1 into its parking spot. Before Mitch could finish his checks, the door opened. Eager hands removed his rifle and bag of bullets. Other men helped Ellison with his camera. Mitch sensed something missing amid the commotion. Glancing around, he saw hardly anyone was talking.

Someone yelled, "The tail's got holes in it!" The announcement drew several of the curious, but most waited for Mitch and Ellison to deplane.

Colonel Black was beyond the door. Salutes weren't required on the flight line, but Mitch saluted as he stepped to the ramp. "Good morning, sir." The words seemed out-of-place as soon as he said them.

Black returned the salute. "Welcome back. Any hope for Captain Goodwin?"

"I—I don't know, sir. I'd feel better if I'd seen a chute." Mitch shrugged as the crowd murmured at his lack of encouragement. "There was more flak than I've ever seen."

He chastised himself for such a dumb statement since he hadn't seen *any* antiaircraft fire before. Only J.D. knew that, so people looked impressed.

Captain Jansen asked, "What happened, Mitch?"

Mitch started to answer, and someone handed him a Singha. Mitch didn't like beer so he rubbed the cold bottle across his forehead. Explaining how Goodwin was shot down, he distanced himself from his words as if hearing the story for the first time. He didn't mention telling Goodwin to turn just before the flak hit. Mitch also didn't tell about his wild ride through the canyon. Those who understood Mu Gia would find the story improbable, and those who could only imagine Mu Gia's dangers wouldn't appreciate how frightening the flight had been.

As Mitch finished a brief summary, Chief Master Sergeant Underwood pushed into the front row. Underwood, the burly line chief who supervised the maintenance operations, held out a jagged piece of metal. "Here's a souvenir to remember the flight by, Lieutenant."

Mitch took the shrapnel but knew that enough images already were burned indelibly into his memory.

Black asked, "How much damage, Chief?"

"Half a dozen holes in the rudder and elevator, sir. My sheet-metal troops'll have her patched by this afternoon."

"Look her over good, Chief," Mitch said. "We went a little fast with the window open."

"Unless you fly straight down, Lieutenant," Underwood said, "you can't make a Bird Dog go fast enough to hurt itself."

"I know." Mitch followed Black to the tail.

Underwood pointed out five jagged holes and a round hole gouged by a bullet.

Mitch was surprised by how shiny-new the ripped edges looked. Studying the gleaming metal, he didn't want to think about what shrapnel did to flesh. Comparing a big hole in the rudder with the cockpit, Mitch estimated a jagged fragment had passed about fifteen feet behind him. "They missed me by a tenth of a second."

"That's because today wasn't your day, roomie."

Mitch turned and found himself face-to-face with J.D. "A tenth of a second makes it damned close."

"Not a chance." J.D. shook his head. "Fate. You can't fight it."

Mitch shrugged. They'd had the conversation several times, and he didn't feel like rehashing it.

J.D. said, "I wish you hadn't let me talk you out of Ban Laboy."

"Me, too." *Would Goodwin be alive if J.D. had gone to Mu Gia?*

"Come on, Lieutenant," Black said. "I'll give you a ride to the TUOC."

"Sir, I have to return my weapons—"

"That's taken care of. I want you debriefed while everything's fresh."

"Yes, sir." Mitch knew there were things he'd never forget.

In the TUOC Mitch and Black joined Lieutenant Winters and his commander. Mitch endured an extended version of the normal debriefing. He told of the inability to locate the Nimrod's trucks, then pinpointed every gun site and structure he remembered. Everyone seemed awestruck by his description of the flight through the canyons.

Black, with all his experience, seemed uncertain how to respond. "I'll tell Chief Underwood to take *another* good look at that airplane."

After answering all questions, Mitch was asked to write a summary.

The two intelligence officers left, and Black stood. "I have to take care of some things before I brief at thirteen hundred."

Mitch jumped to his feet. "Yes, sir." He glanced at his wristwatch and was shocked to find he'd been debriefing nearly three hours.

Black paused in the doorway. Using the term for compensatory time off, he said, "If you'd like, I'll start your CTO tomorrow."

Mitch felt confused. He believed he was two days short of the twenty-four duty days required to earn four days compensatory time off.

Black added, "We can even leave you off tomorrow's schedule."

Mitch realized Black proposed to give the next five days off. "Oh, no, sir!" The words were more forceful than intended. "I mean, sir, I'd feel better flying before my break."

Black placed a hand on Mitch's shoulder. "When you get thrown, it's best to get right back in the saddle. If you change your mind, tell the scheduler I said it was okay."

"Thank you, sir." Mitch remembered the delay in getting back into the air after the landing incident in pilot training. If he waited to fly, he might never have the courage to go over the Trail again.

Mitch left the TUOC at one o'clock. The sun was bright, and the heat oppressive. Above the quadrangle, flags at half staff whipped in the breeze. How much different everything was from when he'd headed for the flight line. His fears of the *unknown* about Mu Gia and ground fire were gone—replaced by frightening memories of the *known*.

He pushed through the gate and followed a wooden walkway into a cluster of buildings that included the mail room. At a wall of postal boxes, he knelt and found his empty. A sign near the door indicated the last distribution of mail had been the previous afternoon. Mitch was too exhausted to feel disappointed.

He stopped at the outdoor snack bar at the far end of the buildings. He hadn't eaten all day, so he was hungry. Looking over the menu, which had limited appeal even on a normal day, he realized he didn't feel like eating. Instead he trudged to the street and up the gentle slope toward the chapel and the barracks area on the hillside beyond.

Mitch had difficulty looking at the plain, wooden chapel, which had been a source of comfort every Sunday since he arrived. Now, however, the chapel reminded him how perilous his daily missions were. The chapel had been dedicated in the memory of Captain Karl Worst, the first Cricket FAC lost over the Trail. Worst's two-thousand-pound O-1 had disintegrated over a target when hit by a fifty-thousand-pound F-105.

Mitch walked down the eastern slope where sections of trees had been cleared a few months earlier. Passing the Harley-Smith-Wolfe amphitheater, he avoided looking at the peaceful scene where he often went to read or to write letters. The outdoor stage and wooden benches memorialized Captains Lee Harley, Warren Smith, and Thomas Wolfe. Gunners along Route 912 had shot down all three FACs.

He kicked a stone along the dusty path and hoped he could finish his combat tour without a building being named for him.

Entering the clearing where the FACs lived, he thought the reddish-brown buildings were more like a campsite for workers in a national forest than a fliers' sanctuary from the war. Two long buildings faced each other across a dusty yard. A wooden walkway ran the length of each building, connecting a community latrine and shower room in the middle with six two-man rooms on each side.

Mitch stared hardly more than a pace ahead when he rounded the corner. He climbed four steps to the walkway and was near his room when he heard a shout.

"Over here, Mitch!"

He saw J.D. and eight other FACs in the area beyond the yard. They were crowded in a pool of shade cast by Goodwin's Tree. With a trunk rising more than twenty feet before branching, the tree was like a tall sentinel guarding the north perimeter of the FACs' domain.

Most men wore flight suits and were seated in a cluster of dilapidated wicker chairs and faded lawn chairs. Mitch scanned the faces. He was hoping to somehow see Goodwin—with cigarette ashes all over him—dozing near a pile of empty bottles. Mitch scuffed the sole of his boot on the walkway. He'd never see Goodwin beneath the tree again.

"Come on, Mitch," J.D. yelled. Raising a Singha, he motioned for Mitch to join them.

Mitch didn't want to talk. He realized, however, that he didn't want to sit alone in his room. He jumped off the walkway and headed for Goodwin's Tree.

J.D.'s flight suit was unzipped down to his waist, with sleeves bunched above his elbows. An unlit cigarette dangled from his lips. In the hand without the beer, J.D. had a stick, which had been a fallen branch from the tree. With the stick now stripped of leaves and smaller branches, J.D. doodled in the dust.

Captain Jansen reached into an ice chest, retrieved a Singha, and tossed it to Mitch. "Start with this. There's more coming." Jansen stood and gestured at his lounge chair. "Here you go, Mitch."

Mitch hesitated. He wasn't used to sitting while captains stood.

"Go ahead." Jansen guided Mitch to the chair. "I've sat too long already."

Settling into the chair, Mitch saw liquor bottles and several empty beer bottles between his chair and J.D. Everyone waited. "It's been a hell of a day," Mitch said, sorry nothing better came to mind.

J.D. dropped his stick, grabbed Mitch's beer, removed the cap, and handed back the bottle. "We decided to remember Bob by doing what he'd be doing about now."

Mitch nodded but assumed Goodwin would be sleeping.

J.D. raised his bottle. Sounding philosophical, he said, "Death is truth. It's the only thing to respect. In death lies the only nobility for man."

Mitch gave J.D. a questioning look.

J.D. shrugged. "Jimmy Dean said something like that once. Seems fitting."

Jansen raised his beer. "To Bob."

Everyone joined the toast.

Distracted by memories of the morning's action, Mitch swallowed twice before remembering how much he disliked beer. Nevertheless, he kept sipping, hoping to delay having to tell his story.

J.D. finished his beer on the toast and fished another from the ice chest.

Each man seemed to study his own drink. The conversation stalled.

Jansen said, "A hooch-boy's getting more beer," then shrugged as if realizing he'd repeated himself.

J.D. pulled his damp T-shirt from his chest. "Don't you just love these muggy days?"

Avoiding eye contact and conversations about the weather, Mitch looked for something to take his thoughts from the morning. He saw Lieutenant Colonel Fred Sanders and Captain Sam Randolph come around the far corner of the quarters. Mitch wasn't surprised each man went to his own room instead of joining in. Seeing those two reminded Mitch of the most significant thing his father had said about flying in World War II. "The time to learn about a man is when he's pressured by fear. That's when you'll discover his true character."

Now, two wars later and on the opposite side of the world, Mitch finally appreciated how perceptive his father had been. Mitch had lived by his father's words and discovered more about some FACs than their wives would understand in a lifetime. Except for the captain and lieutenant who hadn't lived through January, Mitch had figured out most of the pilots.

He had nicknames for some. Lieutenant Colonel Sanders had become Return-to-Base Sanders, or "Ol' RTB" for short. He went through the motions when scheduled to fly, but he never flew over guns anymore. About forty minutes after takeoff, Ol' RTB always had a rough engine, a noisy propeller, or low oil pressure—something that *forced* him to return to base. Mitch understood why Sanders wouldn't face the group on this particular day.

Until three weeks ago, Mitch and Sam Randolph had played tennis several times a week. On that morning Sam had watched his wingman and another American pilot crash after their airplanes were hit by ground fire. Now "Silent Sam" stayed to himself, except for flying and for every chapel service scheduled for any denomination.

Mitch sipped his Singha and glanced at his roommate. Of all the Crickets, J.D. was the most enigmatic. In spite of weeks of close contact, Mitch didn't know how his roommate handled fear. Mitch wasn't certain J.D. was ever afraid.

Mitch had tagged J.D. as "the Iceman," a nickname for which no originality was claimed. He'd discovered the title when *The Hunters* had been shown in the movie theater at the Air Force Academy. Robert Mitchum was the Iceman, a larger-than-life fighter pilot marauding Korea's Mig Alley in his F-86 Sabre. That night, most cadets left the theater wanting to be the Iceman.

Staring at fluttering leaves, Mitch felt ashamed that the intervening years had taken him further from his goal of being as fearless as the Iceman. Now as he thought of Ol' RTB and Silent Sam, Mitch knew this day could take him beyond the point of no return—if he let it.

"You all didn't invite me here to talk about the weather," Mitch said, interrupting J.D.'s comments on the upcoming rainy season. Mitch shifted to the foot of his lounge chair and reached toward J.D. "Let me have your stick."

J.D. complied. The others gathered closer.

Mitch brushed his hand across the ground, smoothing pebbles from the red dust. He tossed aside a few sprigs of dead grass. Using the stick, he etched an inverted V in the dust and extended a wavy line from the apex. He pointed at the V. "Doghouse." He swished the stick along the upward line. "Mu Gia." He glanced at the faces. He'd said everything necessary to establish the setting.

Mitch retold his story. The other FACs hung on his words as if listening to plans for a war-winning strike against Hanoi. Mitch finished a second beer and switched to bourbon and Coke, a mixture he drank slightly more often than beer.

When he finished, the patch of dust and most of the audience were no longer in the shade. Warmed by sunlight that had forced the shade eastward, the drawing included a squiggly line where the side canyon branched from Mu Gia. Two Xs represented the Skyraider flown by Sandy One and Goodwin and his O-1.

Gazing at the Xs, Mitch recognized the irony. He mourned the airplanes with almost the same reverence as the loss of a pilot. Tapping the stick in the dust, he sighed, then said almost in a whisper, "I feel responsible."

The others shook their heads and muttered denials, with J.D.'s "No way," the loudest.

Mitch guzzled the rest of his drink. "I told him to turn and led him into the tracers." He scrutinized the drawing, then destroyed it with two quick sweeps of his boot.

"But that was seconds before Bob got hit," Jansen said, with the obvious implication that Mitch's call didn't have time to make any difference.

J.D. looked at Mitch. "You didn't intentionally turn him into the shells, did you?"

"Of course not!"

"Then, roomie," J.D. said in a matter-of-fact tone, "this morning was Goodwin's time. You had no part."

J.D. made Mitch's guilt seem as ridiculous as J.D.'s question. Mitch looked at the sweeping impressions his boot had made. He wished the guilt could be obliterated as easily as wiping out the dusty image of deadly combat.

J.D. took Mitch's glass. The only sounds were his groping in the ice chest and the quiet rustle of the leaves in the branches above. J.D. poured a drink. "Did I ever tell you guys about the time Crazy Bob and I wasted four flights of Thuds trying to blow up two barrels? I guess the gomers needed fresh gravel, so—"

Mitch had heard the story at least a half dozen times. Nevertheless, he preferred listening another dozen times to thinking about the story he'd just told. Accepting the drink, he realized how hot the afternoon had become. He tried to remember when he'd last eaten.

J.D. continued the long version of his story. Everyone but Mitch laughed politely at the funny parts. Hardly listening, Mitch sipped his drink and fought off mental glimpses of the crippled O-1 falling into Mu Gia. Striking the stick against his leg, his hand moved in time with a throbbing pain deep within his soul.

One after another, others told their favorite Goodwin stories, intermingled with epithets about North Vietnamese gunners and Washington bureaucrats. Over the next couple of hours, other Crickets joined the group. When anyone asked Mitch for more details, J.D. intervened. Mitch was satisfied to sit silently, holding onto his grief, his guilt, his fears, and his sense of failure.

Mitch lost track of time. Finally he decided he'd rather write than listen. "Need to write a letter." Mitch pushed himself to his feet. His head swirled. Stepping back to regain balance, he plopped into the chair.

"You're kind of *key-mao*." J.D. used the Thai term for very drunk.

"Just a little shit-faced." Mitch's choice of words surprised him.

After stopping at the latrine, he pushed unsteadily into the room shared with J.D. Furnishings included a government-issue desk with chair, a leatherette-covered love seat, a sink, a mirror by the door, and a small refrigerator, which J.D. had bought in Nakhon Phanom. A makeshift curtain hung between two large wardrobe lockers, which jutted out near the middle of the side walls and served as a room divider. Two beds, two chests of drawers, and a night stand were in the sleeping area beyond.

Mitch sat, and his hand rose to his face. As he curled the left tip of his mustache, his eyes roamed the room as if for the first time. He seemed to have come for a purpose but couldn't remember what. Turning to the desk, he saw a picture of Elizabeth and Mandy and recalled he'd intended to write a letter about Goodwin being shot down. Well, he thought blearily, not *exactly* about Goodwin being shot down.

He opened his box of stationery. His blue pilot's log, with embossed wings of silver on the cover, rested on the paper and envelopes. He opened the log to the current page, which he'd marked with one of his Cricket business cards between the pages. His eyes took a moment to focus. The card had been designed by an original Cricket, obviously a fan of the series "Have Gun, Will Travel." Mitch read the words above his name: *For S.E.A.'s Finest FACS, Cable: Cricket. Have Willie Pete, Will Travel.* He didn't feel like one of the finest FACs in Southeast Asia.

Putting the card aside, he stared at the log book. Routine columns listed information student pilots at hundreds of airports kept track of. In addition, his log included items few of those pilots would ever list. One column kept track of his combat sorties. In another, he listed the numbers and types of aircraft he'd directed in air strikes.

Mitch used a column to grade his landings. The *OK*s and *Good*s outnumbered the *Bouncy*s, *Lousy*s and *Ugh*s. He remembered his latest landing, the only beautiful thing in an ugly morning. He scrawled *Beautiful* in the column. Concluding he couldn't concentrate well enough to complete the day's entry, he decided to finish after a nap.

Tossing the log book aside, he wrote "Dearest Elizabeth" near the top of a piece of stationery. He gazed at the paper and tried to decide what to say on such a day.

She had never understood his decision to volunteer for the war before his turn. But he never had told her he'd volunteered in the hope of regaining confidence lost on one bad day in pilot training. His fears were a burden he carried alone.

Ten minutes later, staring at a sealed envelope in his hand, Mitch gave in to exhaustion. He walked with deliberate steps from the desk to the curtain to the bed. He flopped onto his bed and wanted to erase the morning's images from his mind. Pressing a cheek into his pillow, he envied Rip Van Winkle. Mitch closed his eyes and wished he could sleep through the months until his DEROS—Date Eligible for Return from Overseas.

Chapter 8

"Up and at 'em, roomie." J.D. shook Mitch's bed.

Startled, Mitch rolled over rapidly, then feared he'd vomit. He grabbed the frame and held on until dizziness faded. By the time Mitch could focus, J.D. had disappeared beyond the curtains. Mitch slowly sat up.

The two lockers extended almost to the ceiling, so the sleeping area was in semi-darkness. Mitch checked his watch. The glowing hands indicated nearly six-thirty, but he was unsure whether morning or evening. Noticing he wore his flight suit, boots, and a T-shirt smelling of beer, he decided it wasn't morning. He stood unsteadily, thought better of it when the room seemed to move, and sat on the bed. He tried to remember what had made him sick. He recalled holding a beer beneath a tree. Then he remembered Goodwin.

"Better get in gear," J.D. said. "The van for tonight's ROE is due in twenty minutes."

ROE? In a moment, Mitch recalled the monthly briefing on the rules of engagement was on the schedule. Taking a deep breath, he tried to decide how to overcome the first hangover of his twenty-six years. A hot shower seemed the place to start, so he stepped through the curtains.

J.D. sat at the desk. He wore jeans, a plain blue shirt of Thai silk, and cowboy boots. His attire was topped by his James Dean hat—a gray cowboy hat of the kind the actor had worn in the movie *Giant*. J.D. peeked from beneath the brim and laughed. "Your eyes are the color of the stripes on the flag."

Mitch nodded, and his head throbbed. "I don't suppose you mean the white stripes." A glance at the mirror confirmed the answer.

"You look like you need another Singha."

Mitch's stomach knotted, and he had to swallow hard. "No, thanks. Already had one." Wondering how many he'd had, he looked absentmindedly at the desk.

"If you're looking for your letter, I dropped it off at the post office."

"Letter?" Mitch had a hazy recollection of licking an envelope and cutting his mouth. He touched a finger to his lips and felt the sting of a recent cut.

"The letter to your wife. You left it in the middle of the desk."

"Thanks." Opening his locker, Mitch wondered what he'd written. He undressed, wrapped a towel around his waist, and headed for the shower room.

J.D. called after him, "If you're not back in ten minutes, I'll send in the Jolly Greens."

Mitch nodded and started along the walkway. J.D. routinely joked about sending in the Jolly Greens when someone in the bar headed for the latrine. This evening, Mitch thought, the joke had no humor. For the next few minutes he stood in the shower hoping blasts of warm water would restore life to mind and body.

In spite of his best efforts, he couldn't remember anything he had written in the letter J.D. had mailed.

A few minutes before seven p.m., a blue step-van stopped in front of the headquarters of the 23rd TASS. Twenty FACs piled out, though hardly a word was spoken.

Mitch trudged up the steps and held open the screen door. While others passed by, he thought about how this evening differed from the first pilots' meeting he'd attended. In December, he'd known few FACs. Their boisterous behavior had seemed an effort to show they were tough enough to be away from home and family during the holidays. Goodwin had been one of the rowdiest, encouraging a chorus of Christmas carols while the flight surgeon tried to discuss a new strain of VD. Now, seven weeks later, three carolers were missing over Laos, and there was no hint of a song on anyone's lips.

The room was crowded, and the chairs were filled when Mitch entered. About a third of the men wore flight suits or fatigues. The rest wore civvies, mostly jeans or shorts, with tops ranging from Green Bay Packers sweatshirts to Aloha shirts of wild Hawaiian prints. Joining J.D. at an empty spot along a wall, Mitch saw three unfamiliar faces.

"New meat," J.D. said.

The tone was so matter-of-fact Mitch wasn't sure the words were meant as sarcasm. He studied the newcomers. Judging their ages, he guessed at their ranks: two lieutenants and a major, perhaps even a lieutenant colonel.

J.D. said, "That lieutenant looks like he could play on the line for Notre Dame."

Mitch nodded, thinking the larger of the three newcomers would have to be shoe-horned into an O-1's narrow cockpit. "I don't envy them." Besides having a full tour remaining, they'd reached NKP on a day of sadness and anger.

Gazing around, he caught Lieutenant Colonel Sanders's eye a moment before Sanders looked away. *What did Ol' RTB feel on such a day? Relief? Dishonor? Guilt because he avoided missions another pilot died trying to complete?*

Mitch also noticed Major Vincent sprawled bleary-eyed on a chair in the corner. Mitch had never met anyone who could put away more beer. His nickname for Major Vincent was "the Keg." Within a few days of arriving in December, Mitch had characterized the major in fourteen words: when he wasn't flying, he was drinking; when he wasn't drinking, he was flying. Meetings were the only exception. Mitch felt it ironic he and Vincent both faced this meeting with a hangover.

Alternating his gaze between the Keg and Ol' RTB, Mitch mused about how the two experienced pilots handled their fears. Taking a deep breath, he vowed he wouldn't give into his fears in either of those ways.

Lieutenant Colonels Black and Morton walked in, followed by Lieutenant Winters. Everyone else came to attention.

"At ease." Black waited until the noise died down as everyone settled again. He'd been the squadron commander for seven months. His build was slender, and the flight suit, which hung loosely from his shoulders, hardly revealed anything of the body beneath. Black wore standard Air Force-issue glasses and looked as if he belonged in front of a high school civics class. Nevertheless, his words had a sense of authority no one challenged.

"I've got a couple of announcements before Colonel Morton covers the nuts and bolts." Black spoke about the day's loss and said nothing indicated Goodwin had survived. "I've had a long talk with the group commander, and we won't be taking O-Ones into Mu Gia for a while."

Good. Mitch saw many FACs nod their approval.

Black continued, "The commander agrees Mu Gia has become too dangerous for Bird Dogs. Also, Seventh has agreed to give priority for ordnance to any FAC under fire."

"Big deal," J.D. whispered.

Mitch doubted the change mattered. When FACs were shot at, they got fighters, if fighters were available—and if the FAC survived the attack.

Black opened a folder, selected three photographs, and dropped others onto a table beside Lieutenant Winters. "Lieutenant McCall brought back some intriguing photos. The lesson here is that seemingly insignificant observations can be significant. First is a rather insignificant-looking vehicle. Anyone have a guess about what it might be?" He held a photograph toward his audience.

J.D. offered, "This year's model of a Russian limousine, sir?"

"Not quite," Black said over the laughter.

Mitch stared at the picture. A camouflaged truck beneath an overhang of trees looked like an unstylish crossbreed of a jeep and an old three-quarter-ton truck. Standing by a fender, a soldier gawked wide-eyed at the camera. His AK-47 was almost unslung from his shoulder. Mitch couldn't remember seeing the ugly little truck, but he recalled being busy when flying by the North Vietnamese camps.

"It's a GAZ-Sixty-nine," Black said, "a light four-by-four in service throughout the Warsaw Pact and other countries supplied by the Soviet Union. We don't see many in this part of the world. Notice the guard?"

Major Lawson asked, "Would that make it a command vehicle, sir?"

"Right. Once Intel decided that, they put the eagle-eye on all the pictures." Black raised a photograph of a soldier in a clearing. "If the GAZ-Sixty-nine hadn't been nearby, Intel probably wouldn't have paid attention to this man with his AK slung over his shoulder."

As the picture flashed by, Mitch tried to recall where those pictures had been taken. He remembered locking eyes with a soldier.

Raising a third picture, Black continued, "In this enlargement, Intel picked out the insignia of a Senior Colonel and identified Le Van Do, who's responsible for the Trail in Steel Tiger."

Mitch was pleased he'd accomplished something special. While others murmured, he remembered a man in a clearing. Mitch strained to get a good look, but he barely glimpsed the enlargement as Black flashed it around, then dropped the pictures on the table.

"Without the GAZ, we'd have missed the rank. Senior officers, except for Le Van Do, don't carry AKs. Intel doesn't have much on his background, but he lives like a jungle fighter, probably based on experience against the French. Good job, McCall." Black nodded to Mitch, then gestured at the new men. "Finally, I want to introduce three new Crickets who arrived this afternoon. Captain Forrester and Lieutenants Pittman and O'Malley."

Each man nodded.

Forrester looked older than most FACs, and Mitch wondered why Forrester wasn't at least a major.

Black glanced around. "I expect you to teach them the tricks, ASAP."

Mitch understood. Two FACs lost recently were new guys.

"Questions, gentlemen?"

Captain Worley stood. "Is there truth to the rumor, sir, that President Johnson's been invited to Hanoi for a peace conference?"

"If you believe that," J.D. said to Mitch, "you believe rocks'll grow."

Black looked surprised by Worley's question. "The Tet truce may be extended a couple of days, but I haven't heard anything on the President going up North."

Major Lawson asked, "Will this truce halt air ops over Laos, sir?"

"Colonel Morton'll cover the truce."

Morton stepped forward. He held a clipboard with several teletype messages. As operations officer, Morton was responsible for matching FACs to the daily tasking orders from Seventh Air Force in Saigon. Being operations officer also meant that while the commander maintained the good-guy role with the men, Morton enforced the rules. He was taller than most FACs. Mitch wondered how Morton fit his long legs between the pilot's seat and rudder pedals. Morton's words came out in a Texas drawl Mitch always recognized on the radios.

"The four-day truce starts day after tomorrow at zero-six-hundred hours local." Glancing at Lawson, Morton said with a skewed smile, "You can't expect the North Vietnamese to discuss a truce in Laos when they don't have any troops there."

Groans filled the room.

J.D. leaned over to Mitch. "Are we fighting a war, or not? I'm soooo confused."

Mitch chewed softly on his lower lip. He could close his eyes and see Goodwin's O-1 falling toward the jungle to verify he was at war—whether anyone else in the world knew it, or not.

As the noise decreased, Morton raised the papers. "Seventh says we'll be open for business, launching thirty-two sorties a day. We can expect more fighters than usual since all offensive air ops over North Vietnam will be curtailed."

Muffled comments swept the room.

"Incongruous," Mitch whispered. Deaths in Vietnam would be on hold to celebrate a holiday he didn't understand. Yet the truce in Vietnam could increase casualties in Laos.

Someone asked, "So everything across the border is off limits, sir?"

"The message calls for intensified reconnaissance of North Vietnam, but I suspect jets'll handle that. All armed reconnaissance and air strikes in the North will be suspended, so you wouldn't want to get shot down over there."

Distracted by memories of the morning, Mitch blurted, "Then what did Captain Goodwin get shot down for over Mu Gia, sir?"

Everyone was silent. Morton looked compassionate but uneasy.

Embarrassed at having spoken so directly, Mitch looked at his boots. "I guess what I mean, sir, is Captain Goodwin followed orders to try to keep the North Vietnamese from sending supplies through Mu Gia. Now we're giving them control of that same bloody ground." He paused and looked at Black. "That seems like a sacrilege or something, sir."

"Each of our people is important," Black said, "but we have to trust that our leaders in Washington have a better grasp of the big picture."

"Lieutenant McCall," Morton said, "the President obviously sees this truce as a potential step to a speedy peace. If that comes to pass, our sacrifices will've been worth the price."

Mitch glanced around and sensed general agreement. However, expressions suggested most FACs hoped they wouldn't become part of that sacrifice as Goodwin had.

Morton said, "Seventh is serious about us testing a night program over Steel Tiger."

"Hot damn!" J.D. popped a clenched fist into the palm of his other hand. "Maybe we can do some good for a change."

A few other pilots were enthusiastic. Mitch sensed the remainder recognized the dangers worrying him—facing increased antiaircraft fire, avoiding mid-air collisions in the darkness, and getting lost in an airplane ill-equipped for finding its way even in the daytime.

"Our second black bird's ready," Morton continued, referring to an O-1 modified for night missions, "and Seventh is sending eight navigators on temporary duty from Vietnam. The navs will fly as scope operators." Most of the audience looked uncertain, so Morton added, "Starlight scopes—sniper scopes. Supposedly we can look through a scope and see trucks in the dark."

"Cool," J.D. whispered.

"Anyway, Seventh's adding a night mission or two next week. Volunteers give your names to Captain Jansen." Morton turned to the commander and began a short conversation.

"Let's do it." J.D. was more enthusiastic than usual. "Night flying's where the action is."

Mitch grimaced. "I've had enough action to last me a day or two."

"I didn't mean this morning was nothing," J.D. said with a consoling look. "But I didn't come here to play traffic cop on empty roads, and the roads aren't empty at night."

"It's probably good for you, but I'm not ready." Mitch chose his words to avoid admitting that thoughts of flying an O-1 through heavy AAA at night terrified him.

Turning to the group, Morton asked, "Any questions for me?"

J.D. raised a hand. "Sir, is anyone addressing the fact that we can't see anything they don't want us to see from the new altitudes?"

"We're checking into binoculars that're more powerful, if that's what you mean."

"Binoculars don't show what's under trees, sir. I think—"

"Seventh wants us over Steel Tiger, and if we're going to stay, we have to fly higher. We've already proven we can't stay at fifteen hundred and maintain an acceptable loss rate."

Mitch wondered how *acceptable* was defined. After the two Crickets were shot down in January, Seventh had raised the minimum altitudes for FACs in high-threat areas from fifteen hundred feet to six thousand.

"Seems to me, sir," J.D. continued, "there is another choice. Those trucks would be harder to hide if we fly right on the treetops."

Reactions throughout the room suggested little enthusiasm.

Morton looked impatient. "If we couldn't survive at fifteen hundred feet, we're not likely to do better at fifty."

J.D. gestured at Mitch. "Lieutenant McCall proved an O-1 can survive on the deck, and he didn't even have another FAC vectoring him away from open ground."

"Your idea has merit, Captain Dalton," Black said, "but the high FAC might become a sitting duck. He might fly predictably while keeping an eye on a FAC at treetop level."

"We wouldn't have to fly low all the time, sir. But if we stay in the stratosphere looking at trees with binoculars, we're just goosin' ghosts."

Time to shut up! Mitch tried to transmit the message mentally.

Frustration edged lines in Black's face.

Mitch wasn't sure if the commander was unhappy with J.D. or with the inability to find hidden trucks.

"We'll consider split altitudes at the next meeting of our tactics board," Black said. "I doubt Seventh will approve anything below fifteen hundred even if we want to fly that low."

J.D. nodded. After attention shifted away, he leaned toward Mitch and whispered, "No guts, no glory."

Lieutenant Winters stepped forward and opened a notebook of information on the rules of engagement. "There are no significant changes this month from the rules I briefed in January." In a sing-song voice, he read words regulations required him to repeat each month.

Mitch heard without really listening. The morning's terrors kept intruding. He realized afterward that J.D. had been reciting, almost verbatim, the rules as Winters read them.

Black stepped forward after Winters finished. "We've got to keep doing the mission, gentlemen, but don't take any unnecessary chances. I've had too much experience lately writing letters to next-of-kin. I'm not getting any better, and they aren't getting any easier."

Black turned and led Morton out the door. Major Lawson called the room to attention, and everyone stood. After Black and Morton left, most pilots clustered around Winters.

J.D. slipped a cigarette between his lips. "Flying this war according to everyone's rules is like milking a bull." He paused and lit the cigarette. "The bull may enjoy the fondling, but you don't get much to show for your efforts."

Mitch frowned. He wasn't in the mood for J.D.'s humor. Noticing the crowd with the pictures, Mitch remembered the North Vietnamese leader in the clearing, then the enlargement. "The hairline!"

"What?"

Mitch tried to visualize the face. "That guy looked familiar."

With an expression of disbelief, J.D. pushed his hat back. "I hate to break this to you, Sherlock, but these guys all look alike. You know, black hair, short—"

Mitch hurried across the room.

Captain Jansen held a picture that appeared shot from ground level on the main road in Mu Gia. "These are unbelievable, Mitch!"

Other pilots expressed similar awe while Mitch scanned pictures on the table.

Captain Forrester held a picture of soldiers scattering while antiaircraft shells exploded in the treetops. "Lieutenant McCall, you must have balls of solid brass."

"Not quite, sir." Mitch was embarrassed to be credited with bravery.

"You bet he does." When J.D. saw the pictures, he raised his eyebrows appreciatively. "Uh-huh!"

Mitch remained too preoccupied to appreciate J.D.'s support. "Where's that closeup?"

Winters handed the photograph to Mitch. "Great pictures."

Unbelievable. Mitch felt queasy as if shock were taking over. "I know him. He visited my house once."

Those who heard the comment looked incredulous.

Winters said, "There's gotta be a mistake, sir."

"All these guys look alike, roomie," J.D. repeated.

Mitch agreed he had to be mistaken—but he didn't think he was. He edged his finger along the line between the man's high forehead and thinning black hair. "This gouge in his hairline. He said the wound was from a French bullet at Dien Bien Phu."

Winters looked skeptical. "He's wearing a hat in the photograph we have in our files. This is the first I've seen with that scar."

Mitch tilted the picture to change the lighting. "Notice his left ear. Shrapnel from a grenade took most of the lobe."

Winters asked, "You're saying Le Van Do visited you in the states?"

"He was Major Thao, Major Hoang Thao. He visited Vietnamese pilots at my pilot training base. I escorted him three days, and we had a cookout for him and the pilots."

Jansen asked, "Why would a North Vietnamese visit your base?"

"He was a South Vietnamese logistician sent to observe maintenance operations in preparation for expanding the Vietnamese Air Force." Mitch paused, staring at the picture. "At least that's what he said."

Winters asked, "When was this?"

"Spring of sixty-four." Mitch felt tingly. "Elizabeth was pregnant.

Thao made predictions about Mandy, based on the Chinese horoscope."

J.D. asked, "Was he right?"

Mitch hadn't given the question much thought. "She's only two, but she does fit what he said. Thao also talked about how he and I were twelve Chinese years apart making us both born in the year of the dragon. He was born in late nineteen twenty-eight."

"I believe that's a couple of years after Le Van Do." Winters paused. "Of course these guys have four or five complete names and biographies. That is, I'm sure Colonel Do does."

Mitch tried to convince himself he was mistaken. Studying the picture, however, he was certain Thao and Le Van Do were one man.

Winters said, "I can ask if Seventh has more on him than we have in our files. Unfortunately we don't have much on most of these guys."

Mitch remembered a photo album Elizabeth had given him as a going-away present. Most were family pictures, but she'd included one from the cookout. "I have a picture in my room of Thao and me. Elizabeth surprised us when we were cooking."

"I'd like to have a look," Winters said.

Mitch closed his eyes and memories from the long-ago evening in Oklahoma began to flow. "That first shot was the only good picture we got of him. I never gave it a second thought, but he seemed to stay aware of the camera the rest of the evening."

Winters asked, "Could you get the picture for me?"

Twenty minutes later the young intelligence officer had the photo from Oklahoma. Mitch had convinced Winters that South Vietnamese Major Hoang Thao and North Vietnamese Colonel Le Van Do were the same man.

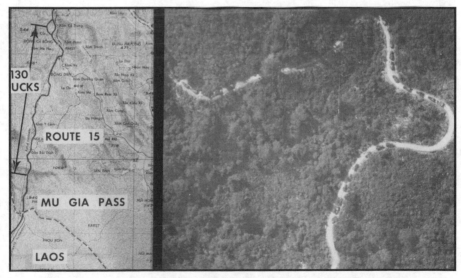

Trucks on the Road during the TET Truce—February 1967

Chapter 9

Mitch spent his four days off in Bangkok. He shopped for jewelry and toys—and tried to forget the war. Each night, however, dreams of Mu Gia interrupted his sleep. In the long quiet of trying to fall asleep again, he relived his Oklahoma encounter with the mysterious Vietnamese officer.

By the time Mitch returned to NKP, his curiosity had gotten the best of him. He hurried to the TUOC to find out what had been learned about Major Hoang Thao. Walking down the entry hall, Mitch spotted Lieutenant Winters with two FACs in the briefing room.

Winters's face brightened when he saw Mitch. "I need to see you, Lieutenant McCall. I'll be with you in a minute."

Mitch nodded, then went to the administrative room for coffee. He saw one of the new FACs seated at a table with pictures scattered over it.

Captain Ted Forrester stood and introduced himself. Forrester had a disarming smile like that of a favorite older brother. His friendliness put Mitch at ease.

Mitch guessed Forrester's black hair would've been curly if not cut so short. His sideburns were gray, and a patch of gray marked his black forelock. Mitch couldn't imagine why Forrester was only a captain. Pouring coffee, Mitch said, "I thought I was the only one who spent free time in the TUOC."

Forrester grinned. "Comes from years of flying bombers in SAC. Seems like I've spent most of my adult life in target study. I've been looking at pictures from this truce." He held one up.

Taken through a feathery-edged hole in clouds, the setting was like many Mitch had seen. A hard-packed ribbon of road ran along a shallow river. Splintered trees and craters were scattered through acres of pulverized dirt. He saw one difference. Seven large trucks were on the road.

"If I were a dog, I'd salivate." Mitch had daydreamed of surprising trucks in the open. "But, don't get your hopes up, sir. You're seeing more trucks than I've seen in fifty missions."

"Wait 'til you see the next one."

Mitch's mouth dropped open at the sight of more than thirty trucks spaced out along a dog's-head-shaped road. He noticed both pictures were labeled "Trucks Mu Gia Pass Area."

Winters burst into the room. "The whole Intel shop's been dying for you to return, sir! If you hadn't been due today, they might've recalled you."

Mitch's curiosity about the pictures faded. "What've you found out about Major Thao?"

"Colonel Le Van Do, probably!" Winters spun the dial on a four-drawer safe. "Seventh pooh-poohed us the first few days. Yesterday they sent a top-secret message and have made a half dozen calls since. They want to know everything you can tell us."

Opening a drawer, he removed a folder stamped top secret. He handed the cover sheet to Mitch and Forrester so they could sign that they'd had access to the top secret documents.

Winters pulled out the pictures taken in Mu Gia and the photo from Oklahoma. He also displayed a picture of a man in a uniform of the South Vietnamese Air Force.

The picture matched Mitch's memories of the man he'd met in Oklahoma. The hat in the picture obscured the hairline—and the scar Mitch remembered. "That's Major Thao."

Winters put the picture of Colonel Do alongside. "The wounds on the ears are similar."

"Looks like a match," Forrester said.

Mitch agreed. "There should be records of his visit to the states."

"Thao was on official travel from eight March through twenty April in nineteen sixty-four. He spent a couple of weeks at the Pentagon, and I beli—"

"He'd been there before coming to Oklahoma."

"Right," Winters said. "Then he visited seven bases, looking at aircraft maintenance equipment and procedures."

"What about since then?"

Winters smiled. "Four weeks after returning to Nam, he was reported killed in a guerilla ambush between Danang and Quang Tri. Yesterday, word came from the VNAF that Thao's body wasn't recovered."

Forrester said, "So the colonel went North almost three years ago."

Winters nodded. "And the sketchy profile Seventh's built indicates Le Van Do was sent to Laos in the fall of sixty-four, sir. He's considered General Giap's top operational logistician."

Grinning mischievously, Forrester said, "If Mitch had slipped a little rat poison in Thao's burger, the Ho Chi Minh Trail might still be a bunch of footpaths."

"He wasn't that kind of guy," Mitch said.

"He was a spy," Forrester said.

"It's going to take a while to think of him that way."

"Seventh wants to know what you remember," Winters said.

"I don't know what more I can offer."

"Identifying him ought to count for a helluva lot," Forrester said.

Winters nodded.

"I went to all his briefings and interpreted French when his English couldn't bridge the gaps. I remember thinking his English was better than he let on. I don't believe we covered anything helpful to him in Steel Tiger, but those meetings should be a matter of record."

"Seventh has sent inquiries to every base he visited."

"I hosted a welcoming party the first evening at my house. One night we were at the Officers Club, and we spent the other evening visiting a couple of watering holes downtown." Mitch paused to recall specific memories that had run through his mind during the last few days. "Mostly I remember personal things. His wife had died of some disease I thought didn't kill people anymore."

Winters scanned his notes. "Cholera. Nineteen sixty."

"He'd had two sons. I remember feeling sad for him because they'd been killed in a guerilla bombing of a bus near Saigon."

Winters shook his head. "Not likely. Now that Vietnamese intelligence is looking, they can't find a trace of his boys from about a year before he disappeared."

Mitch pictured recent headlines in *Pacific Stars and Stripes* declaring how the North Vietnamese had taken advantage of the ongoing Tet truce. "He talked about how important the Tet new year celebrations were. I guess that was a load of manure."

"According to those pictures," Forrester said, referring to the trucks, "they've had quite a celebration over the last four days."

"You can say that again," Winters said.

Mitch glanced at the thirty-truck picture. The label said 130 trucks had been spotted by the pilot of an RF-101 Voodoo in a single flight through Mu Gia Pass. Something drew Mitch to the road's distinctive bend. He rotated the picture, viewing it from different directions than the jet had been flying when the picture was taken. Suddenly he stopped as if the photo were a piece of a jigsaw puzzle now aligned to be dropped into place. He closed his eyes and saw the same dog's-head image without trucks. The road had been empty when he picked the distinctive bend to help locate Goodwin's crash site.

Mitch wanted to lash out at something. "How the hell can the people running this war let us die out there one day and let the NVA have the road for free the next?"

Winters looked surprised by the outburst. Forrester seemed to be sizing up Mitch.

Mitch's anger was pushed aside by embarrassment over the breach of his normally strict self-control. The truce had had the direct approval of the President. Mitch felt guilty. He'd never made a statement challenging lawful orders of his superiors. He pointed at the map alongside the truck-infested photo. "I lost my flight leader here last week."

Forrester nodded without showing emotion.

Mitch wondered if he'd been too blunt, especially to a new FAC who had yet to fly his first solo mission over the Trail.

Winters said, "You'll be even more upset by these shots of Quang Khe, sir."

"Don't count on it. I don't know where Quang Khe is, but Mu Gia's pretty personal."

Winters selected three pictures from those scattered on the table. The first, labeled "Quang Khe—29 January 1967," showed an abandoned dockside area prior to the truce. Bomb craters dotted the shore, evidence of the devastation of earlier air attacks.

Forrester asked, "Where is Quang Khe?"

"On the North Vietnamese coast fifty miles east of Mu Gia. Most traffic entering Steel Tiger on Route Nine-twelve is ferried across the river at Quang Khe. They slip supplies across a few loads at a time at night or when the weather's too bad for bombing." Winters dropped the other two pictures in front of Mitch and Forrester. "Unfortunately, there are truces."

The new pictures showed the same area on the second morning of the truce. Seven large ships were at anchor or along makeshift docks. The picture included at least one hundred small ships and sampans. A closeup of the shoreline, showed thousands of white bundles piled in clumps.

Mitch asked, "What are these?"

Winters shrugged. "Don't know, sir."

"Just the makings of war, I'd guess," Forrester said philosophically.

"Resupply's a hell of a lot easier when you don't have to worry about enemy air." Mitch paused. "I hope that message is getting relayed to the President."

Forrester nodded. "These pictures reveal something much more significant. They show a dangerous difference in how we view truces."

Mitch was surprised Forrester was making such an obvious point. "Well, Tet isn't our holiday."

"But we respect Tet, at least in Vietnam, but our enemy doesn't. The difference is even more basic." Forrester leaned back and brought his hands together, fingertip-to-fingertip, in front of him. "We observe truces hoping they'll lead to peace. The enemy uses truces to help win the war. I don't think McNamara and his whiz kids in the Pentagon have figured that out yet."

The directness of the criticism surprised Mitch although the words seemed without bitterness. Perhaps such bluntness, Mitch decided, was why Forrester was still a captain.

"I've seen top-secret messages backing you up, Captain," Winters said. Referring to the operational areas in the panhandle of North Vietnam, he added, "In the first three days of the truce, our birds spotted twenty-one hundred trucks in Route Pack One and Tally Ho."

An unintended whistle escaped Mitch's lips. "We've pounded North Vietnam for months. I can't believe they could put twenty-one hundred trucks on the road, even during a truce." With a sense of helplessness, he added, "And most of those supplies'll move into Steel Tiger beginning this evening when the truce ends."

"Washington extended the truce," Winters said. "We don't know when it ends."

Mitch asked, "Who's that supposed to help?"

"War fighters and politicians don't always see things the same," Forrester said. "I'd think twenty-one hundred trucks of supplies could keep a guerilla war going forever."

"Not forever, sir," Winters said, "but Intel at Seventh estimates that tonnage could support the Viet Cong four years if they can move those supplies the rest of the way."

Tossing the pictures of Quang Khe onto those of the trucks, Mitch fought off images of Goodwin's aircraft falling toward the jungle. "Makes a guy wonder why the hell we keep risking our lives." He couldn't imagine doing anything in an entire year of hazardous missions that would reverse the advantage given away during the truce. He thought of Elizabeth. He knew he couldn't look her in the eyes and justify why he'd volunteered to spend a whole year—and maybe the rest of his life—away from her and Mandy.

"All we can do," Forrester said, "is get out there and keep those twenty-one-hundred-trucks worth from making it the rest of the way."

"Right, sir," Mitch said with a frustrated sigh. "I was that optimistic once upon a time."

After a few more questions, Mitch said, "It's time for me to check the mail room and drag my bags down to the hooch."

"I'll give you a hand." Forrester gathered pictures. "The lieutenant's cheered me up enough for one day."

Leaving the TUOC, Mitch pushed aside his anger and tried to satisfy his curiosity about Forrester. "You say you came from SAC, sir?"

"I had a few years in B-Fifty-twos many moons ago. I was doing base-operations-type flying for the last two years before I became an O-One driver."

Strange background. Mitch had always heard the only quick ways out of B-52s were incompetence or suicide. Forrester's most recent flying—assigned to the miscellaneous transport aircraft of a base—often was done by older pilots serving out years remaining until mandatory retirement. Avoiding questions he wanted to ask, Mitch tried to make a connection with Forrester's background in bombers. "My dad flew B-Seventeens out of England in World War II."

"My dad was killed on a B-Twenty-four out of North Africa."

Mitch was aghast at the direction the conversation had taken. "I'm sorry."

Forrester shrugged. "That's why I chose bombers."

Then why aren't you still in B-52s? Mitch knew better than to be direct.

When they reached the wall of mailboxes, Mitch discovered several bright-colored envelopes crammed in his.

"Looks like you've got a bunch of admirers," Forrester said.

"I think my wife's gone a little overboard with the valentines." Mitch concealed how much he was pleased by her attention.

"As of this morning, I'd gotten four from my wife," Forrester said with a proud smile.

Mitch nodded, impressed by the sincere affection in Forrester's voice. Mitch was a bit surprised couples in their thirties still exchanged valentines.

Once Mitch was alone in his room, he settled at the desk. Ripping open the envelopes, he discovered seven valentines with letters or short notes. Two valentines were from Mandy, homemade creations of red construction paper, zigzag marks of crayon, and lots of glue and glitter. One by one, he stood the valentines on the desk. While rereading the letters, he heard J.D.'s familiar whistling accompanied by pounding boots on the walkway.

J.D. came in and stared at the colorful display on the desk. "I musta missed your visitor."

"Say again."

"Cupid." J.D. gestured at the valentines. "I'd expect him to personally deliver that haul."

Mitch smiled with pride. "Elizabeth's special."

J.D. reached for a handmade card. He sat on the edge of the desk, bumping hard enough to tip over most of the valentines. "Don't count on the honeymoon lasting forever, kiddo." He sounded indifferent. The look in his eyes wasn't.

Mitch gathered the fallen cards. He was determined not to allow J.D.'s bad mood to tarnish the good mood from Elizabeth's valentines. "How long the honeymoon lasts depends on how hard you work at it."

J.D.'s eyes became more alive. "Let yourself be a domesticated puddy cat on the ground and you won't be much of a tiger in the sky."

"Being married to the right woman isn't what keeps me from being a reckless tiger," Mitch blurted, then realized his words sounded like a challenge to J.D.'s marital situation—of which Mitch had learned little in the two months they'd shared a room.

Sliding his sunglasses down his nose, J.D. peered over them and exhaled a disappointed sound. He picked up the second homemade valentine. "Start crooning a Johnny Mathis love song, and I'm gonna demand a new roommate."

"You have a charming side, sir," Mitch said, relieved J.D. hadn't taken the comment personally, "but I'll save the love songs for Elizabeth."

J.D. nodded and turned his attention to the valentines he held. "These are the best kind." He went to his locker. Opening a door, he revealed two homemade valentines taped inside. "I don't want you thinking you're alone on Cupid's list."

Mitch moved his valentines nearer the wall. "There's plenty of room on the desk."

J.D. gave a you-should-know-better look. "Would Jimmy Dean show off his valentines on a desk? Next thing, you'll want me hanging pink curtains in the cockpit."

Mitch smiled, unwilling to be baited. For the first time in his weeks of envying J.D.'s skill and courage, Mitch realized he was envied. J.D. had the natural piloting skills Mitch longed to have back again, but Mitch was the one loved by a woman who sent five valentines. He grabbed his small calendar and crossed off the four days that had passed while he'd been in Bangkok. He thought longingly about Elizabeth and wished there weren't so many days remaining until August, when he planned to see her on R and R in Hawaii.

Chapter 10

Boom-boom-boom.

Dull thuds of distant explosions startled Le from a deep sleep. Darkness shrouded everything. Nevertheless, he heard the familiar gurgle of a nearby stream rushing over moss-covered rocks. The noise convinced him he was in the clearing where he usually slept. Trucks rumbled in the distance. The *pocketa-pocketa* chatter of antiaircraft guns confirmed his assumption. An American air strike had shattered the quiet.

Pushing aside the coverings of his jungle hammock, he looked toward the gunfire. The yellow flickering of a flare filtered through the foliage. The drone of a bomber came from the same direction. The Americans were attacking near the Ban Laboy Ford.

His wristwatch indicated eight-thirty. Le recalled collapsing into his bed at three-thirty in the afternoon after working thirty hours. He remembered nothing else afterward. Stiffness in his shoulders and back suggested he'd hardly moved. He located his AK-47 and field pack beside the entangled blanket within his hammock. Five hours was the most sleep he'd had at one time in the last week, maybe in the last month.

Sergeant Dinh called from the darkness, "You getting up, Colonel?"

"Yes."

Dinh roused the other two bodyguards.

Without light, Le completed routine chores to keep snakes and other animals out of his bed. He chose to sleep in the jungle most of the time though staying in the headquarters cave would be more convenient. In his years of jungle fighting, he'd seen too many men buried in caves that collapsed when bombs or artillery fire struck surrounding karst.

Minutes later Le entered his headquarters cave near the border of North Vietnam. The cave was in a jungle-covered karst south of the road between the border and the Ban Laboy Ford. Three seasons earlier he'd selected the cave, which stretched for hundreds of meters into the karst. Its main entrance was on the side away from the road. All approaches were in heavy jungle, so Le doubted American pilots would ever find his headquarters.

He trudged to his makeshift desk. When in the headquarters, he spent most of his time in his small office and in the communications room near the main entrance. He handed his AK-47 to Sergeant Dinh. "Tell Major Quan I'm here."

"Yes, Colonel."

Le was pleased he had a deputy such as Major Pham Duc Quan. Quan had a record of courage in combat. Wounds, however, had left him with a stiff leg. His limited mobility made him a perfect staff officer especially since Le preferred to get out of the headquarters to lead from along the roads.

Quan limped into Le's office. "You've just received a message from Hanoi, Colonel."

"What does it say?"

Quan shrugged. "The courier wouldn't give it to me."

Le's eyebrows lifted. "What could be that secret?"

Quan shrugged and called outside the office.

The soldier rushed in, saluted, and offered a coarse, brown envelope.

Le took the sealed dispatch from the courier, who looked younger than Le's twelve-year-old son. Turning to a lantern hanging from the wall by his desk, Le tore open the envelope. Positioning wire-rimmed glasses far down his nose, he squinted at the words. The primary message—Report to the Citadel in Hanoi—made him suck in his breath involuntarily. He checked the reporting date against the operations logs on his desk. Fewer than two days for the 650-kilometer trip was a tough challenge, even if he had no American bombers to worry about.

When he left Hanoi in late summer, he hadn't expected to return until the Laotian rainy season washed out the roads. A third of the dry season remained, so being recalled made no sense.

Perhaps, he thought rereading the message, they finally were going to purge him. Three political officers and fifteen other members of the party's Information-Liaison Groups had died in his Central Region during the current dry season. The two previous years had been little better. Fear flashed hot at the top of his spine and sizzled into his skull. Maybe he should've tried to ensure they didn't die from their stupidity—but he hadn't. He stiffened, and his resolve returned. "If that's what the party wants," he said quietly, "so be it."

Le handed the paper to Quan, then told the messenger to get something to eat.

Quan scanned the message. "Not much time."

"At least I'll have plenty of empty trucks to mingle with going north." Le knew the frantic days of the truce had brought most trucks in North Vietnam south to unload cargo in staging areas near the border.

Quan nodded. "Radios say the Americans haven't resumed bombing the fatherland yet."

"I hadn't heard." Le had expected the temporary truce to end earlier in the evening. His journey would be quicker and safer if trucks continued running openly in North Vietnam as they had during the truce.

Quan returned the paper. "There's so much for you to do here."

"Perhaps General Giap wants to give me a medal for our successes."

Quan looked as if he hadn't considered that possibility.

"More likely," Le continued, "it's because I failed in not attending enough self-criticism sessions." His confession sounded contrite, but he knew Quan understood the words mocked the party's requirement for weekly sessions. Working twenty-four-hours-a-day counted little if requirements of the party cadre weren't satisfied.

"And I failed," Quan said, sounding as serious, "because I didn't make sure you—"

"So," Le said with an enigmatic smile, "your punishment is to have my responsibilities for a few days. Tell Sergeant Dinh to have my GAZ ready in thirty minutes for a long trip."

Quan nodded.

Le extended the corner of the message into the lantern's flame. He watched the fire hesitate, then flare brightly and turn the paper to ash. *Would the upcoming days treat him as harshly?* Forcing happier thoughts, he pictured Kiem, his seventeen-year-old son who had started combat training several weeks earlier. "If I reach Hanoi in two days, maybe I'll see Kiem before his unit heads south."

Forty-one hours later, Le sat uncomfortably in the Citadel. He scanned the high-ceilinged conference room and its sparse furnishings, most of which dated from when the French ruled Hanoi. A North Vietnamese flag near the door and a mural on the back wall were of a more recent vintage. In the mural, a beneficent Ho Chi Minh smiled down in front of a large gold star. Between points of the star, red and gold scenes depicted successes of Ho's long career as a Vietnamese nationalist.

Le wore a hastily issued uniform, and he was surprised everything fit so well. Wearing uniforms with North Vietnamese markings was restricted to North Vietnam, so his uniforms had been stored before he left for Laos. He was intrigued that a better uniform mattered for whatever was about to happen. Finding his family waiting at the Citadel when he arrived had been a bigger surprise. Purges weren't conducted that way.

Le and his son, Kiem, sat by a massive table of teak. Kiem's uniform of the People's Army of Vietnam also was new and unadorned but for different reasons. Kiem's gaze darted around from the blank walls to the mural to the barren courtyard beyond open windows. He held a hand-carved flute, and his fingers danced across the openings as if playing a silent tune.

Recognizing Kiem's nervousness, Le had tried to draw him into quiet conversation. However, they had little to talk about. Le's far-flung duties had caused him to live apart from his sons much more than he'd lived with them. Le couldn't reveal he'd gone the last three autumns to Battlefield C, as Laos was called. Nor could they speculate that Kiem's unit, which had left Hanoi two days earlier, likely was en route to the war in South Vietnam. There were heavy penalties for openly acknowledging North Vietnamese troops were assigned in Laos and South Vietnam.

Chinh, Le's younger son, sat on a wooden bench beside Rieng, Le's sister-in-law. She'd raised the boys after their mother's death from cholera seven years earlier. Le smiled as he watched Chinh, who obviously was undaunted by the most important military headquarters in the country. Using a piece of charcoal, Chinh sketched on scrap paper found earlier.

Glancing up, Chinh grinned. "See, Father." He raised the drawing of a peaceful setting with a water buffalo and a rice field.

"Very good." Le added warmth to his smile. The picture was more detailed than he expected from a son not yet thirteen. Le wished the war would end so he could spend more time with his sons—and so they would be spared, as many in his family had not been.

Chinh's face brightened. "Bac Ho," he squealed.

Le was confused by Chinh's use of the endearing form of uncle with Ho Chi Minh's name. The president liked to be addressed that way by common people, but Chinh's words weren't directed at the mural. Chinh looked with sparkling eyes toward the door.

Le turned and adrenaline jolted him. Ho Chi Minh was walking gingerly across the wooden floor. General Vo Nguyen Giap stood in the doorway. His chubby face, shiny boots, and sharply creased, brown uniform contrasted with Ho's thin features, brown sandals, and Mao Tse-Tung suit of suntan cotton.

Le and Kiem jumped to attention. Scrambling to his feet, Chinh rushed with open arms toward Ho. Rieng stood, keeping her gaze on the floor.

"Chinh!" Le called out.

Chinh hesitated, but Ho bent over and embraced the youngster.

"Be at ease," General Giap said as he entered and motioned for an aide to follow.

Le relaxed some. Kiem remained rigid and wide-eyed.

Chinh offered his drawing. "This is for you, Bac Ho."

Ho greeted the others warmly, then put on plastic-framed glasses and bent over to admire the drawing.

Chinh beamed. Le looked on with pride.

Giap took a medal from his aide and plunked it clattering onto the table.

Le glanced at the medal, shocked his facetious remark to Quan had been accurate. Giap's smile gave the appearance of being painted on his round face, and Le decided the general was trying to hurry things along.

When Ho stood, Giap nodded to the aide, who read a citation.

Le stood at attention, stared at the mural, and listened. He heard glowing statements about his heroic actions in Quang Binh Province of North Vietnam, which was above the demilitarized zone separating the North and the South. He'd been to Quang Binh—but only to pass through en route between Hanoi and Laos. Nothing was said about Laos, where he'd fought against the American aviators and the Royal Laotian Army for three years. Le bit his lip and tried to look impassive. Deep inside, he was tiring of the constant deceptions.

Almost before Le realized it, Ho was before him pinning on the medal. Ho spoke in a fatherly tone about Le's great contributions to the just cause of the Vietnamese people. Le stood a little taller and took a moment to accept that his endless hours of moving supplies through Laos had contributed.

Even as Le savored the words, Ho turned to Kiem and Chinh. Ho spoke in enthusiastic terms about how the two young Vietnamese should be eager to follow their father's heroic example.

Chinh giggled a young-boy's giggle. Kiem's chest puffed out against his uniform as Ho mingled in words about imperialists, liberation, sacrifice, and American aggression.

Le hardened inside as he watched Kiem transforming from a terrified recruit to a young soldier ready to go forward for the greater glory of Vietnam. Le didn't want his sons sacrificed as his father and three brothers had been against the French.

Giap stepped forward. "You have a meeting, Comrade President."

Ho nodded, then bid farewell.

Le snapped to attention as Ho, Giap, and the aide walked to the door. Le was confused, unsure what the ceremony really had been about. Why had he been pulled from his nightly war to receive a medal for actions he hadn't done?

Giap hesitated in the doorway. "After your family leaves, Colonel Do, come to my office."

The painted-on smile remained. Nevertheless, the glint in the eyes was that of the warrior who'd humiliated the French at Dien Bien Phu.

Ten minutes later Le followed Giap into a small room off the general's main office. Green drapes covered the walls. Le assumed the drapes concealed war plans. A black cloth shrouded a table beneath a picture of Ho Chi Minh.

"The Ministry of Defense Party Committee has gotten complaints." Giap paused to light a cigarette.

Le shifted uneasily, knowing the Party Committee was where political directives were interposed over military operations. He chose to wait for Giap to reveal specific criticisms.

"Commissar Dung says you don't allow enough free time for party lectures. He fears an outbreak of deviationism, personalism, and liberalism."

"My men don't have time for deviationism, General." Le tried to speak in a tone that concealed his anger.

"The Party cadre addresses soldiers in the South every day."

"Armies in the South fight one day in twenty, General. We hardly sleep that often."

"Commissar Dung believes you need to make a more sincere effort."

Le's fingernails dug into the palms of his hands. "We can take more time every day for *kiem thao*, General." Le put bitter emphasis on the term for the self-criticism sessions he considered a humiliation forced on the army by the Party. "That'll give more time for the cadres in the South, too, General. If we don't repair roads, our armies in the South won't have enough supplies to fight even one day out of twenty."

Giap pursed his lips and nodded.

Le knew he hadn't said anything Giap didn't already understand.

Giap crushed out his cigarette. "I've just learned South Vietnam's trying to exhume Major Hoang Thao."

Le was confused by the unexpected change of subject, Giap's choice of phraseology, and by the alias Le hadn't thought of for months.

"They are suspicious," Giap continued, "that maybe he didn't die. Why would they connect you with Thao, now?"

Astounded, Le tried to think of an answer. "There's been no

connection since I left the South. Have there been defectors who would know the cover name?"

Giap shrugged. "That possibility hasn't been mentioned. Anyway, that's not what we're here to discuss." He stepped to the table and pulled away the cloth.

Le saw a montage of maps of North Vietnam, South Vietnam, Laos, Cambodia, and parts of Thailand. He recognized the maps as American in origin, like those his men recovered from downed aircraft.

Giap picked up a pointer and put the tip near Le's headquarters. "This area." He swept southeast to the tri-border region where Laos, North Vietnam, and South Vietnam met.

Le recognized the rugged area as the main infiltration route for tens of thousands of army troops walking to South Vietnam. His son, Kiem, would follow that route in the next two months. Nevertheless, Le's men moved trucks and supplies over roads well west of those mountains, so he couldn't imagine what the general wanted to know.

Giap tapped the pointer against his hand. "How long to build a new road there?"

Impossible! Le drew in a breath involuntarily and looked at Giap.

The general's eyes were fixed on Le.

Le gazed at the map, bending forward for a closer look and to stall for time. Tightly packed contour lines represented one steep ridge after another. He tried to conceal his misgivings. Perhaps Giap's years in Hanoi had caused him to forget what mountains were like. Le was unsure how to respond, but he assumed the general wasn't wanting a *No*. He glanced at Route 911, the main road seventy kilometers west of the mountains. "How far east of Route Nine-eleven, General?"

"As far as possible."

Le glanced at the general, hoping to detect a clue about how to answer. Giap was stoic, less emotional than Le remembered in earlier encounters. The painted-on smile was gone. "When we built Nine-eleven, General, we chose the best terrain. Moving very far—"

"How long, Colonel Do? You are our expert."

Le hesitated.

"At least thirty-five kilometers east. Fifty, if possible."

Le stood to his full height. "I don't believe we could build and maintain a road there. The monsoon rains would—"

"You're saying such a road can't be built, Colonel?"

"Yes, General."

Giap looked serious a moment, then the smile returned. "Good."

Le couldn't hide his confusion.

"If you don't believe it can be built, the Americans won't think so, either."

Le nodded. His relief lasted only an instant. Fooling the Americans didn't matter *unless the road existed*.

Giap continued, "The entire length would have to be concealed."

Le nodded. His men were masters at building bamboo trellises and interweaving vegetation to obscure what was beneath. "The concealment would be easier than building the road, General."

"We thought that last year." Giap's tone was accusatory.

During the previous dry season, Le's men had built Route 137/912, the road from the coastal town of Quang Khe across the Ban Karai pass into Laos. For more than a hundred kilometers, concealment had been perfect. Only days before the linkup would've been made with Route 911, a FAC had discovered the new road. Within days, defoliation aircraft had sprayed the road. Le pictured the O-1 he'd seen up close in Mu Gia. "And, General, fewer Americans aircraft were in the skies last year."

Giap tapped the map. "But there's more jungle for cover."

"And more rivers and mountains. The terrain's difficult for trails, impossible for roads."

"So were the mountains at Dien Bien Phu." Giap's expression broadened into a look of great pride. "But we moved two hundred artillery pieces in around the French, anyway."

Piece-by-piece! Le scanned the map again. "Are you talking about a road for trucks or for bicycles and pack animals?" Pack bicycles carried up to three hundred kilos, but he'd still have to transport them across the rivers.

"Trucks. Anything you handle now."

Impossible! "When do you—"

"I'm not asking for the road now—but I want you to think about it."

Le looked at the map and knew he didn't want to think about it.

Giap took the black cloth and covered the table. The room looked as before, with nothing to reveal that the out-of-the-way chunk of jungle was of special interest. "Now, the possibility of such a road exists only in your mind and mine."

Only in yours. Le was unable to accept the road was possible.

"Your son can ride with you as far south as Thanh Hoa where he can rejoin his unit."

"Thank you," Le said, pleased to have more time with Kiem.

"It'll be better if the Americans don't notice your absence from Laos."

Le nodded.

"You should be ready to leave Hanoi at dusk."

"This evening?" Le tried to hide his surprise.

Giap gave a curt nod. A hardness in his eyes said there was no room for compromise.

"Yes, General." Le was disappointed he wouldn't have more time with Chinh and Rieng. But, an afternoon was more than he'd thought possible two days ago.

Giap moved to the doorway. "You will not discuss this with anyone."

"Yes, General," Le said, following Giap.

"If I decide to have you scout the route, I'll send the message: 'The buffalo are thirsty'."

"Yes, General," Le said, hoping that day would never come.

Walking away from Giap's offices, Le felt dazed. Some of his mental confusion was from weariness—he'd slept little during his jarring hours of travel over bumpy roads. He went toward the exit nearest to where his family was waiting in a nearby park.

A thundering *ba-boom* shook the building. Dust puffed from seams in the walls and ceiling. Le lunged into a doorway and dropped to a knee. A shadow flashed over trees in the street. A second *ba-boom* was swallowed by the deep-throated roar of low-flying jets. He heard glass shatter.

Le remained tense and opened his mouth in anticipation of devastating explosions. When adrenaline forced aside mental exhaustion, he decided the noises were sonic booms. He glanced around and saw other soldiers—some smiling—resuming normal duties and showing none of the apprehension he felt. Embarrassment flushed Le's cheeks. These headquarters bureaucrats showed less panic than he felt as a war-hardened veteran.

He stood and brushed dust from his knee. *Damned American pilots!* He was angry that their audacious flying had unnerved him twice in a few days. As he stepped outside, a vision of the low-flying O-1 in Mu Gia flashed to mind. The image of birds on the pilot's helmet suddenly was more vivid than before—and that image matched birds on a helmet he'd seen in America three years earlier. And, a photographer had been in the back seat. Maybe, he realized, the connection to his earlier role as Major Hoang Thao hadn't come through a defector. Le whirled and hurried inside.

Once within a guarded vault, Le entered a hallway stacked with cartons of unsorted papers. He pulled a page from a box and scanned the typing. His English wasn't as good as when he'd served in South Vietnam and visited America. Nevertheless, he decided the form was from an American maintenance squadron at Danang Air Base. The page was creased and smudged. Le assumed it had been taken from the trash at the base. Pushing the paper into the box, he went to the nearest clerk.

In minutes the clerk produced a Special Order, which included a heading of the 23rd Tactical Air Support Squadron (PACAF).

"This is what I'm looking for."

Le scanned the list of pilots who flew the O-1s that dogged his men each day. Beside the names—numbers, mostly in the forties, fifties, sixties, and seventies—matched the Nail call signs used most often on the radios. Le sought out fifty-nine, the call sign of the pilot who'd startled him in Mu Gia. Le wasn't surprised by the name alongside: Mitchell L. McCall, 1LT, FR69928, Pilot "B" Flight.

Le pictured the American who'd befriended him for those few days. "So, Lieutenant Dragon, you've come to my homeland." Dragons were born under the sign of luck, Le thought, which partly explained how he'd survived so many close calls in the jungle. Now Le understood why luck had been with the pilot that day in Mu Gia.

Be careful, my friend. Not even a dragon's luck lasts forever.

Chapter 11

A week of routine missions helped Mitch distance himself from seeing Goodwin shot down. Hurrying to the TUOC for a 0900 briefing, Mitch saw men behind an ambulance parked by the dispensary. He slowed when he saw them removing a stretcher. The body was covered, and a queasy tightness wrenched Mitch's stomach. Above the adjacent quadrangle, the American and Thai flags flew at half staff—for the second time in February.

Four men carried the stretcher into the dispensary. A half dozen sergeants and airmen remained outside. When Mitch reached them, he mechanically returned their salutes. His eyes were drawn into the ambulance where another sheet-covered body waited.

Mitch felt warmer at his temples than the morning justified. He hated blunt reminders that flying was a dangerous profession. Perhaps, he'd jumped to the wrong conclusion. Flying wasn't the only way to die in northeast Thailand. Yet everyone at NKP understood that if death struck, the victim likely would fall from the minority who wore flight suits. Mitch turned away from the ambulance and glanced at the men who'd remained respectfully silent.

"Nimrods, sir," a sergeant responded somberly to Mitch's unasked question. In a tone of quiet reverence, he continued, "We lost two A-Twenty-sixes early—"

"Two?"

"Yes, sir. Between here and downtown NKP."

"On this side of the river?" The revelation surprised Mitch even more than learning two A-26s had been lost. Each night, Nimrods flew some of the most dangerous missions of the war. Losing two in Thailand suggested a mid-air. *What a waste. Come halfway around the world, take ground fire every night, then die in an accident.* "What happened?"

"Don't know for sure, Lieutenant. One crew survived, but I heard they were pretty banged up when the Jolly Greens brought them in."

Mitch wanted to stop himself, but he had to take one more glance into the ambulance. With a sigh, he said, "I wish they'd park these things somewhere else."

As if on mental autopilot, Mitch headed toward the TUOC. His anger tried to focus on something other than the direct evidence of dying. Two cumbersome ambulances routinely parked in front of the dispensary, up the street from the TUOC. That put them seconds from the flight line but on a direct path between the crew quarters and the briefing room. *Damned poor location!* Mitch tried to deny he was superstitious. The Thais had more than enough superstitions to cover everyone. Nevertheless, passing ambulances each day on the way to fly combat seemed akin to walking under ladders or behind a black cat.

He replayed the moments just shared with six men he didn't know about the deaths of two men he probably didn't know. He'd felt an unspoken sense of intimacy and brotherhood, as if everyone had lost members of his immediate family.

Mitch was in the TUOC pouring coffee when he realized he hadn't checked his mailbox. This was the first time he'd forgotten that step of his pre-mission ritual.

Lieutenant Winters walked in carrying his clipboard and an empty cup. In contrast to his usual hustle, he seemed dazed. "Hear about the Nimrods, sir?"

Mitch told of the encounter at the ambulance.

Winters shook his head. "That doesn't even hint at what happened."

"Really?" Mitch sat on the edge of a desk.

Winters filled his cup, then spoke in the hushed tone of a tribal elder passing on unwritten tales of heroes past. Just after midnight, Nimrod Three-five and Nimrod Three-six had teamed up against a convoy south of Mu Gia. During an attack, several ZPU machine guns shot at Nimrod Three-five. Fire spewed from the A-26, and the pilot turned toward NKP. Nimrod Three-six trailed closely behind, ready to shout a warning if the fire threatened fuel tanks.

Mitch pictured the darkness and the lead A-26 illuminated by uncontrolled flames. "It takes guts to fly tight formation on a burning aircraft."

Winters nodded, then continued. Nearing the airfield, Nimrod Three-five entered the landing pattern. Like a guardian angel, Nimrod Three-six continued in close trail, watching for indications that time was running out. When the pilot on Nimrod Three-five extended the landing gear, the airflow change pumped new fury into the flames.

Winters looked at a teletype message on his clipboard. Turning to the second page, he said, "Everyone monitoring the tower heard Three-six call, 'There it goes. Get out!' Three-Five responded immediately, 'Roger, we're bailing out.'

"Seconds later, Zorro Two-eight was landing his T-28. He reported a flash that changed the black sky into daylight. After a second flash, Zorro saw one fireball fall rapidly. Another veered into a shallow spiral and exploded on impact before completing the first circle." Winters stared at his coffee cup, which he rotated slowly in front of him. "Three-six either flew through debris, or there was a sympathetic detonation in his bombs."

Mitch winced; the second explosion—fuel tanks and bombs instead of fuel tanks alone—would've been more devastating than the first. "Who got out alive?"

Winters had trouble speaking. "Captain Campbell and Captain Sholl didn't make it."

"But which plane were they on?"

Winters tried to speak, then raised two fingers.

Mitch felt a chill. Men in the second A-26 had given their lives for those in the burning aircraft! Tears in his eyes reflected pride in being part of a brotherhood whose members put lives of others above their own.

"It's an eerie feeling," Winters said, his normally cherubic features now pale and lined. "As a career ground-pounder, I guess I never expected to get so close to such heroism."

"Guardian angels aren't supposed to die."

Winters nodded but didn't speak.

Mitch had trouble expressing the grief and the anger tearing at him. "What kind of war is this? Our finest young men die in the darkness while 'Hell no, we won't go!' echoes off monuments of American patriots." *Where was the justice he'd grown up to expect?*

The two lieutenants stood in silence until Winters was called away. Mitch refilled his cup, walked to the briefing room, and told Captain Jansen about the Nimrods. Recalling the details, Mitch knew he'd feel a special pride each time he shared the story. He assumed that in the years ahead, the tale of heroism would be repeated on many a Memorial Day or before thousands of fluttering flags on Fourths of July.

After the briefing, Mitch detoured by his mailbox. He was delighted to find a bright-colored envelope from Elizabeth. Receiving a letter boosted his spirits and helped offset his recurring memories of the scene behind the ambulance. He slipped the letter into a pocket and hurried to catch Jansen.

Cruising across the Laotian plain behind Jansen's O-1, Mitch pulled out the envelope. He noticed the light fragrance of perfumed powder Elizabeth often dusted her letters with. Mitch rubbed the envelope against his cheek. For a few moments he was with her as he savored memories triggered by the soft scent.

The first few lines of the letter were so distracting, he almost forgot where he was and where he was going. "How would you like visitors, darling? I've spent hours thinking and praying about your last letter, and I have decided Mandy and I are coming to Bangkok!"

Mitch reread the words, which were written with more flourishes than usual in her delicate script. He was thrilled with the possibility of seeing her sooner than August in Hawaii. Traveling from Washington, D.C. to Bangkok, however, required passports, visas, and more shots than she and Mandy would want.

Stop playing troubleshooter. He decided to read the rest of the letter before gathering reasons why a visit to Bangkok wouldn't be feasible.

"I know you're about to say vaccinations and passports and visas take time. I'm working on them. Please write today—this very moment—and tell me you want us to come and give me the schedule for your next CTO."

He smiled, marveling at how her determination and bubbly optimism could remain in an envelope a week, then leap off a piece of stationery and make him feel loved in his airplane high in the Laotian sky. He wanted to please her in return and to show her how much he loved her. Reaching to the pad on his kneeboard, Mitch lifted the first two pages to reveal a blank third page. In big letters he scrawled, "Yes!! I want you to come to Bangkok!!"

Mitch doubted he'd ever send the note. If he did, however, he could say he wrote it "this very moment." Nevertheless, *wanting* her to come and *letting* her come were two different matters. He checked Jansen's location, then read the rest of the letter. He reread the first paragraph, which had the only mention of the possible trip. She knew him too well to try to oversell him on a new idea until he got used to it.

He imagined four days together in Bangkok but wondered about tickets. He couldn't pay for the trip even with his forty-seven-dollar-a-month raise starting when he made captain. He assumed she was working the money problem with her father. *What if Mandy got dysentery or a hundred other diseases that kept many Asian children from reaching their third birthdays?* Of course, he countered, he and Elizabeth could take precautions to keep Mandy healthy.

Mitch recalled the horrifying scene outside the dispensary. Some morning, the body in the ambulance might be his. Or even worse, he might disappear into the Laotian jungles with little likelihood she would know whether he lived or died. If she ever were to get that telegram notifying her he was lost, Mitch wanted her home near her mother and father.

He couldn't let her come. Sadly, he replaced the letter into the envelope. He advanced the throttle to catch Jansen. A feeling of abject disappointment weighed on him as he tried to think about the mission. In the half hour necessary to reach the Trail, however, his thoughts kept returning to problems a Bangkok visit would entail.

Near Route 911, Mitch realized his main concern was that she'd arrive right after he was lost. But how likely was that? He might fly three missions between her departure from Washington, D.C., and his CTO. Three missions, he thought, out of a combat tour of up to three hundred.

"Damn!" He banged his fist against the door. Here he was ready to sacrifice four wonderful days against a one-in-a-hundred chance fate would pick him at the worst possible time. He began thinking of *when* rather than *if*. March was too close. She might get everything taken care of by early April. However, he wanted Mandy to have as much immunity as possible. He lifted the upper pages on his kneeboard and wrote MAY in big letters below his earlier note. May would evenly split his year away from home.

He yanked out the letter for another quick look. Now he paid more attention. Elizabeth apparently referred to the letter he wrote while drunk the day Goodwin was shot down. Mitch wondered what had been so convincing. Whatever it had been, he was glad he'd written it.

Chapter 12

Seventeen missions later, Mitch stopped on the taxiway and shutdown the engine. He removed his helmet while the ground crew pushed his O-1 into its parking spot. Grabbing his flight cap, he paused to admire the pair of silver bars pinned to the blue material. J.D. had left this set of captain bars on the desk, along with a "Congratulations, roomie" note. Mitch slipped the flight cap on, pleased to have completed his first combat mission as a captain.

Approaching his quarters an hour later, Mitch climbed the steps to the walkway and spotted J.D., Forrester, and Jansen sitting beneath Goodwin's Tree. When Mitch jumped from the walkway to join them, they noticed him.

"Go away, Junior Captain," J.D. shouted, making shooing motions.

Mitch was surprised, then noticed Jansen trying to conceal a portable tape recorder. Mitch suspected the trio was plotting something for his promotion party. "Better be good to me if you want free beer."

"Worry yourself not." A cigarette bounced between J.D.'s lips with each word. "We'll be there tonight to spend your new riches."

Jansen and Forrester smiled knowing smiles.

"Right." The party likely would consume at least two months' worth of his meager increase in pay.

No one budged to shake his hand, so Mitch went to his room. Periodically he peeked out and saw his three friends around the tape recorder. Usually J.D. was gesturing with his hands.

Following dinner, nearly forty Crickets took over the room that served as the lounge in the three-room officers club. The Singha and hard liquor flowed freely—at Mitch's expense.

After the drinking and story-telling had been in full swing for thirty minutes, Forrester burst in through a doorway leading from the kitchen. He'd changed from his flight suit to a set of fatigues without pilot wings. A cardboard sign proclaiming "Wing Information Officer" was pinned to the flap of the left pocket. On each shoulder, an oversized, hand-drawn eagle of cardboard implied the rank of colonel.

Forrester clanged a ladle against an empty lard can. "Hear, ye! Hear, ye! We have a special visitor this evening direct from the sandy beaches of the South China Sea. I'm the information officer from our Twelfth Tac Fighter Wing at Cam Ranh Bay, and it's my humble pleasure to introduce the notorious Captain Jett Jockey."

J.D. sauntered in. The sleeves of his flight suit were rolled up above his elbows, and his flight cap was tilted at a rakish angle. Beneath his chin a gold-and-black checkered scarf puffed out of his flight suit. Safety pins held cardboard campaign ribbons and a cardboard Captain Jett Jockey nametag above his left breast pocket. J.D. carried a swagger stick, wore his set of mirrored sunglasses, and had a big, unlit cigar clamped between his teeth.

He strutted around like General Patton looking over a new set of troops. He stopped in front of Mitch, inspecting him from head to foot with eyes hidden by the glasses. J.D. touched the swagger stick to the new rank on Mitch's shoulder. "Captain, huh? What's this man's Army coming to?" He shook his head, then turned and joined Forrester.

Forrester said, "The reason Captain Jockey is—"

"You can call me Captain Jock, for short."

Mitch couldn't see the eyes, but he detected the hint of a frown suggesting J.D. realized he'd left himself open. "Did you say to call you Captain Jockey Shorts?"

Everyone roared.

J.D. pointed his cigar threateningly at Mitch. "I'm doing the jokes, kid."

"Well, considering—" Mitch extended his arm, flattened his hand, and wiggled it as if specifying the height of something. Hoots and whistles augmented the laughter, since J.D. seldom put up with teasing about his height. Mitch lowered his hand a few inches. "Just seemed an appropriate nickname, Captain Jock."

J.D. waited for the uproar to subside. "Son, you're about to set a new mark for the shortest captaincy on record."

When the laughing and teasing waned, Forrester said, "Anyway, Captain Jock's here to be interviewed by—"

"Uh, Colonel," J.D. said in deference to Forrester's cardboard eagles. "Is that an Aggie class ring you're wearin'?"

Forrester looked surprised as if the question wasn't part of the skit. "Yes, Captain Jock. I am a proud graduate of Texas A&M."

That drew hoots, whistles, and a "Hook 'em, Horns" from Major Lawson.

"Really? You're the second Aggie I've met." J.D. appeared serious. "The first had both arms in slings."

Forrester crossed his arms and refused to bite.

J.D. cupped a hand to one ear and leaned toward the crowd. "How'd the Aggie manage to break both arms, you ask?"

Several FACs echoed, "How did he break both arms, J.D.?"

"Said he'd been raking leaves." J.D. paused, then added, "He fell out of the tree."

Forrester groaned, frowned a mock frown, and looked at his notes until the laughter died down. "Anyway, as I started to say before I was so rudely interrupted, Captain Jock is here to be interviewed by a famous news correspondent who's come all the way from the Land of the Big BX." Using the second most common nickname for Nakhon Phanom, he added, "Let's give a warm, Naked-Fanny welcome to Mister Headline Seeker."

Jansen pushed open the kitchen door and strolled through. He carried a tape recorder and microphone. Three cameras and a lei of flowers dangled around his neck. He wore red-plaid Bermuda shorts, an orange Denver Broncos shirt, and unmatching knee-length socks showing above his jungle boots. Rolled-up copies of *Pacific Stars and Stripes* stuck out of every pocket. Jansen wore an Air Commando hat with a PRESS card sticking out from the side where the brim was turned up.

"I hear there are headlines to be made here this evening." Jansen promenaded across the room with his head and shoulders bouncing to a rock-and-roll beat. He stopped in front of Mitch. "We moved our interview from Cam Ranh for one reason, Captain, and that's because we wanted to hear a few words from you on this momentous occasion." Jansen's hand shot out, pushing the microphone at Mitch's mustache.

Mitch stepped back to avoid being hit. He stammered, "Well, uh—"

"The few words we want to hear are 'You're buying the Singha'."

Mitch tried to keep a straight face. "You're buying the Singha."

"Not me, dummy. You!"

"True. I'm buying—"

"That's all we need from you, Captain." Jansen yanked the microphone away and allowed the cord to dangle, showing it wasn't hooked into the tape recorder. He pulled a newspaper from his back pocket. "Before we boarded the plane over in Veeet Nam"—Jansen's pronunciation sounded like President Johnson's way of saying the name—"today's *Stars and Stripes* was hot off the presses."

Jansen displayed the altered front page. Pasted in the center was a drawing of Alfred E. Newman from *Mad Magazine*. Red headlines proclaimed, "McCall Promoted to Captain." Black letters beneath the picture said, "Stock Market Takes Biggest Plunge Since 1929!!"

Jansen snapped a picture with Mitch holding his newspaper, then joined J.D. and Forrester. Jansen placed the recorder on a table and extended the microphone.

Forrester sounded dignified as he spoke into the microphone. "We'll let you Crickets witness this important interview, but you must show Mister Seeker and Captain Jock all the respect they deserve."

Whistles and catcalls erupted.

Forrester nodded. "I see we understand each other." He activated the tape player.

Forrester mouthed words matching an official-sounding voice on the tape. "The following statements were recorded when a civilian correspondent"—Forrester gestured to Jansen, who bowed—"interviewed a shy, unassuming Air Force Phantom jet fighter pilot."

Mitch recognized the words from a tape made by pilots in the 12th Tactical Fighter Wing at Cam Ranh Bay.

J.D. placed both hands on his hips in an I'm-ready-to-take-on-the-world stance. The crowd whistled, groaned, and hooted.

Mitch assumed the reactions were as much to the description as to J.D. Mitch had met many fighter pilots. Few were shy, even fewer were unassuming, and he'd never met one who was both.

The tape continued, "So the correspondent wouldn't misconstrue the pilot's replies, the wing information officer was on-hand"—Forrester placed a fist over his heart and beamed at the crowd—"as a monitor to make certain the real Air Force story would be told. The captain was first asked his opinion of the F-Four Phantom."

Maneuvering his hands wildly through the air, J.D. mouthed words in synch with a new voice on the tape. "It's so fuckin' maneuverable, you can fly up your own ass with it."

Amid the chuckles of the crowd, Forrester cleared his throat, then spoke in synch with an intentionally unemotional voice representing the wing information officer. "What the captain means is he has found the F-Four highly maneuverable at all altitudes, and he considers it an excellent aircraft for all missions assigned."

Jansen continued with the tape. "I suppose, Captain, you've flown a number of missions to North Vietnam. What did you think of the SAMs used by the North Vietnamese?"

J.D. nodded vigorously as his hands became imaginary fighters and surface-to-air missiles. "Why those bastards couldn't hit a bull in the ass with a bass fiddle. We faked the shit out of them. They were no sweat."

"What the captain means," Forrester said, "is surface-to-air missiles around Hanoi pose a serious problem to our air operations, and pilots have a healthy respect for them."

J.D. mugged throughout Forrester's explanation.

Jansen took a somewhat superior stance, the effects of which were negated by his outfit. "I understand, uh, no one in the Twelfth Tac Fighter Wing at Cam Ranh Bay has got a MiG yet. Uh, what seems to be the problem?"

J.D. reacted indignantly, grabbing the straps of Jansen's cameras. Jansen struggled and stuck out his tongue. Forrester interceded as if to prevent J.D. from strangling Jansen.

J.D. shouted words to match the tape. "Why you screwhead! If you knew anything about what you're talking about, the problem is MiGs. If we'd get fragged by those peckerheads at Seventh for those counters in MiG valley, you can bet your ass we'd get some of them mothers. Those glory-hounds at Ubon get all those frags while we settle for fightin' the friggin' war. Those mothers at Ubon are sittin' on their fat asses killin' MiGs, and we get stuck with bombing the damned cabbage patches."

Forrester finally got J.D.'s hands disentangled. "What the captain means is each element of the Seventh Air Force is responsible for doing its assigned job in the air war. Some units are assigned the job of neutralizing enemy air strength by hunting out MiGs, and other elements are assigned bombing missions and interdiction of enemy supply routes."

The mention of interdiction brought a mixture of cheers and boos.

Jansen feigned concern about keeping distance between himself and J.D. "Of all the targets you've hit in Vietnam, uh, which one was the most satisfying?"

"Ah, shit," J.D. moaned in a drawl overwhelming the voice on the tape. "Getting fragged for that friggin' suspected VC vegetable garden. I dropped napalm in the middle of the fuckin' rutabagas and cabbage, and my wingman splashed it real good with six of those seven-hundred-and-fifty-pound mothers and spread fire all the way to the friggin' beets and carrots."

J.D. reached into his flight suit and pulled out two blackened carrots with their leafy tops still attached. He took a big bite of a carrot, then frowned. "Yech! I need a Singha."

After J.D.'s thirst was satisfied and reasonable order was restored, Forrester reset the recorder. "We were discussing beets and carrots. What the captain means is the great variety of tactical targets available throughout Vietnam makes the F-Four the perfect aircraft to provide flexible response."

J.D. rolled his eyes toward the ceiling in a where'd-this-guy-come-from expression.

Jansen continued with inane questions—favorite ordnance, R and R trips to Hong Kong, and problems in taxiing on the metal matting—each of which drew a vociferous response from J.D., followed by Forrester's *What-the-captain-means* explanation. Finally Jansen began winding up the microphone cord. "Thank you for your time, Captain."

"Screw you! Why don't you bastards print the real story instead of all that crap?"

"What the captain means is he enjoyed the opportunity to discuss his tour with you."

Jansen tugged on one of his mismatched socks, then hesitated as if recalling something he'd missed. "Uh, one final, uh, question, uh, could you reduce your impression of the war into a simple phrase or a statement, Captain?"

"You bet your ass, I can," J.D. shouted. "It's a fucked-up war!"

Forrester chimed in, "What the captain means is *it's a fucked-up war!*"

Laughter and shouting continued for a couple of minutes. J.D., Jansen, and Forrester beamed at the adulation, and Mitch shared the limelight. Thinking about how naturally J.D. took to the fighter-pilot role, Mitch wondered again why J.D. wasn't piloting an F-105 or an F-4 instead of a Cessna.

Mitch was pleased his celebration had given everyone a respite from the war. He looked at smiling FACs and knew any of them might not survive the next day. Nevertheless, in these moments of camaraderie, concerns about the real dangers disappeared.

The tape was replayed several times before the crowd began thinning out. Some FACs needed sleep before morning missions, so they offered congratulations to Mitch, then excused themselves.

Mitch followed two out and went to the latrine. Returning, he saw Major Vincent passed out in a corner. Everyone but the Keg was crowded around a table. Mitch moved beside Forrester and discovered J.D. seated across from Major Van Sant, the senior of the eight navigators who'd joined the Crickets for night missions. J.D. and Van Sant each held a shot glass that Jansen filled from a bottle of Jack Daniel's.

Mitch asked Forrester, "What's happening, sir?"

"You can drop the sirs now, Mitch. From now on I'm Ted, at least until you make major, and then you can decide whatever you want to call me."

"Yes, si—Ted. This'll take some getting used to." Mitch felt very junior to Ted.

"You've earned it. Anyway, what we've got going here's a manhood check," Ted said with a sly grin. "They're drinking a shot of your whiskey once a minute until one of 'em gets full."

"I'm glad whiskey's cheap over here," Mitch said with mock concern.

Jansen looked at a stop watch Van Sant had placed on the table. "Five seconds."

J.D. raised his glass. "To Captain Mitch McCall!"

Van Sant nodded and clinked his glass against J.D.'s.

"Time," Jansen said.

J.D. and Van Sant drained their glasses with less of a grimace than Mitch made. J.D. spotted Mitch. "Don't worry, Mitch. Major Van Sant won't run up much of a bar bill."

Van Sant smiled. "We'll see who's bragging an hour from now."

Mitch sensed Van Sant had to concentrate to get the words out. "Anyone taking bets on who goes under the table last?"

"The major's bigger," Ted said, "but J.D.'s the sentimental favorite. Besides, J.D. didn't drink much until after the skit, so Van Sant had a big head start."

More toasts were offered and more whiskey was downed with each passing minute. J.D. remained rambunctious and almost as steady as at the start. Van Sant began to falter. J.D. kept stirring up the friendly rivalry between pilots and the outnumbered navigators. "Major V's gonna need someone ta navigate him home."

Someone near Mitch said, "Dalton's as much of a show-off jerk in the bar as in the airplane."

Mitch bristled. The speaker wore civilian clothes, but Mitch remembered him from an introduction as Captain Kirkland. "What kind of asinine crack is that?"

Kirkland looked blearily at Mitch. "What's it to you?"

"J.D.'s my roommate, and I'm paying for the beer you're drinking."

Kirkland shrugged. "So you want a medal for roomin' with him?"

The response caught Mitch off guard. "That's not the question."

"Flying with him's a lot tougher than putting up with him on the ground. He flies like he's all balls and no brains."

Ted smiled as if the assessment rang with truth.

Mitch remembered J.D. mentioning being teamed with Kirkland on night missions. J.D. piloted while Kirkland rode in back and used a starlight scope to locate trucks. "So he's aggressive."

"Aggressive?" Kirkland's tone was sarcastic. "He's fine if you wanna fly with someone who shoots from the hip."

"When it's kill or be killed," Ted said, "I always put my money on the guy who shoots from the hip."

"Yeah!" Mitch nodded vigorously. "The real question is, 'Are you killing any trucks?'"

"We're getting a few, but we—"

"J.D.'s claimed nine trucks destroyed in six nights."

Kirkland glared. "We could be going about it a whole lot smarter."

"When you've logged a hundred missions like J.D. has, maybe you'll be smart enough to tell him how to fly."

"If he doesn't stop flying under the damned flares, it won't matter, because I'll refuse to fly with him." Kirkland drained his beer. "He flies like he's got a fuckin' death wish!" Kirkland tossed the bottle into a garbage can and stomped out the door.

The final comment troubled Mitch.

Ted put a hand on Mitch's shoulder. "You're a good, loyal friend."

"Sounds like Lassie."

Ted grinned. "Lassie would've taken a bite out of Kirkland's ass."

Mitch smiled. "Kirkland deserves a little understanding. If they put me with J.D. at night after a few missions over the Trail, I wouldn't be able to speak coherent sentences."

At that moment, Van Sant was unable to swallow his whiskey. He stood, staggered to the door, and started vomiting before he got outside.

J.D. watched with childlike intensity. "He didn't even say, 'Thank you, Mitch'." J.D. grabbed the bottle from Jansen, held it high, and shouted, "Thank you, Captain Mitch, wherever you are."

As J.D. took a couple more swallows, Mitch said to Ted, "I've watched J.D. down quite a few, but I've never see him so drunk."

"We'd have a scoop if he weren't."

Later the crowd had dwindled to half a dozen. Mitch watched the Keg's roommate rouse Major Vincent. The Keg wanted another drink, but his roommate angled him to the door.

"Lucky for you Major Vincent didn't wake up fully," Ted said with a grin. "Could've cost you another month's pay."

Mitch nodded. "It's time to try to herd J.D. home." Mitch pulled his flight cap from his pocket, used his sleeve to buff the captain's bars, then put on the cap. Approaching J.D., Mitch said, "Time to call it a night."

J.D. screeched words slightly slurred, "Hat on in the bar! Ring the bell, somebody. Mitch has to buy a round."

Memories of Clark Air Base in the Philippines flashed through Mitch's mind causing him to reach automatically for his cap. He'd seen an unwary lieutenant wear a flight cap into the club's bar. Someone rang the bell, and the lieutenant bought nearly two hundred drinks.

Mitch kept his cap on. "There's no bell, this isn't a bar, and I've been buying all evening. Tonight I'll wear my cap wherever I want."

J.D. leaned against the wall and seemed to have difficulty interpreting the words. "Right. But you gotta always wear those captain bars with honor. They belonged to one of the best, most superior pilots ever in this man's Air Force."

Mitch rolled his eyes upward. "You're overstating by a few dozen superlatives."

J.D.'s composure changed from a friendly drunk to an angry drunk. "Watch what you say! You only got them bars cause I thought you'd be worthy."

Mitch yanked off his cap. "If there's a problem, you can sure as hell have 'em back." He started to remove the insignia.

Ted clamped a hand on a shoulder of each man. "Hold it, fellows. I don't know who's mixed up, but you aren't transmitting on the same freq."

Mitch glared at J.D. and waited for an explanation.

J.D. shook loose. "Keep 'em, but remember they belonged to a better man than any of the three of us'll ever be."

Mitch was more confused. "What are you talking about? Weren't they yours?"

J.D. stared at the insignia. "They were, but Major Johnny Ingersoll gave 'em ta me when I made captain."

"Who's he?"

"My pilot in Voodoos." J.D. pulled another Singha from a tub of ice water, then took a long drink. "I'm here 'cause a Johnny."

Ted asked, "Saved your life a time or two?"

"That, too." J.D. spoke deliberately, then looked as if checking his words to see if they'd make sense. "But I hadta volunteer for Nam ta help finish the job for Johnny."

Mitch still didn't understand.

J.D. continued, "Johnny went to Phantoms when I went to pilot training. Got killed last summer in a mid-air over Hanoi."

"That's a crying shame," Ted said.

Looking at the bars on his cap, Mitch felt cold inside—like he'd felt behind the ambulance. "It's hard to imagine a worse fate for a warrior than dying in an accident in wartime."

"Easy." J.D. seemed to study his beer a moment. "It's much badder if a warrior dies accidental-like in a war we *lose*."

Ted nodded. "Growing up without my dad would've been harder if he'd died in Korea, where we didn't win."

Mitch realized he would've felt worse if his father's accident had been in Korea during that war. He also was surprised that the conversation included more feelings about dying than he'd heard at NKP.

J.D. sounded philosophical. "I'da settled for my ol' man dying in Korea."

Mitch exchanged a questioning glance with Ted. "I think the Singha's shorted synapses between your brain and your mouth."

J.D. stared with eyes that seemed slow to focus. "Shot glasses are still there. Buy more Jack Daniel's, an' I'll drink your ass unner the table."

"Some other time. I've got to fly tomorrow."

Nodding, J.D. turned to Ted and seemed to study him. "You're okay, Captain Forest Man. I wish I'd brought my first lieutenant bars with me over here. I'd give ya a set."

Ted smiled. "Don't sweat it. I'd better not need single bars anymore."

"These were very special especially for a Texas Aggie like yourself." J.D. chugged the rest of his Singha. "Got promoted, an' the colonel turned my gold bars silver." J.D. giggled.

Mitch didn't get the point. "So? All first lieutenant bars are silver."

J.D. finally stopped giggling. "Colonel changed our gold ones inta silver by blessing them with a Texas Aggie magic wand."

J.D. cackled. Ted laughed, although Mitch suspected the laugh was more due to how much enjoyment J.D. had gotten from his joke.

"Get it, Forrest Man?"

"Sure, J.D. Aggie magic changed gold into silver."

Still laughing, J.D. tossed his bottle at the garbage can. As he started for the door, his humor turned off as with a mechanical switch. "Does matter how a warrior dies. I'm here so Johnny can't ever die in a war we lose."

Mitch didn't have any doubts about America winning the war, but he was bothered by Kirkland's accusation that J.D. had a death wish. "Then maybe you'd better be more careful about how you fly."

J.D. paused in the doorway. "Maybe we'd win this li'l shoot-em-up a li'l sooner, Junior Captain, if'n you were *less* careful about how you fly."

Maybe.

As Mitch and Ted shepherded J.D. to the quarters, J.D. sang several loud renditions of "There are no Fighter Pilots down in Hell." Once in the room, J.D. unzipped his boots and kicked them clattering against his locker. He pushed the curtain aside and did a belly-flop onto his bed. "Ya throw a helluva party, roomie."

"Thanks." After removing his boots, Mitch put them under his bed. He always kept them in the same place in case the base was attacked at night. He'd concluded long ago a terrorist attack against the barracks would be the most effective way to drive O-1s from the Trail. "Of course, if you'd been on CTO, my bar bill wouldn't have been half as much."

J.D. didn't open an eye. "Ya wouldn'ta had half the fun. I'm cheap at twice the price."

"You're right about the fun. So tell me more about Major Ingersoll."

"Long story." J.D. rolled onto his back and pulled his pillow over his eyes. "Met maybe four—maybe five years ago."

Mitch removed his flight suit and hung it in his locker. "Where was that?" He waited.

J.D.'s snoring broke the silence.

Mitch stepped through the curtain. "Don't you want to take off your flight suit?" J.D. didn't move. Mitch shook the bed. J.D. didn't even flinch.

Mitch turned off the light and slipped into bed. Too excited to be sleepy, he let his eyes get accustomed to the dark, and he listened to J.D.'s snoring.

Mitch was proud to be a captain in spite of his weaknesses as a pilot. He knew the bars on his flight cap had been worn by two brave members of the brotherhood. He worried about having enough courage to be worthy of J.D.'s confidence.

Mitch considered his progress since that scary day in Oklahoma. The flight through Mu Gia had been even more terrifying, but residual fear hadn't stopped him from doing his duty, day-after-day. He held himself to a higher standard and was pleased by how far he'd come. Those were among his last thoughts before he dropped off to sleep.

His next conscious thought was tremendous fright when a loud

"Hey!" awakened him. He jerked enough to bang his bed against the wall, then froze. While he listened in the darkness for clues about what was happening, shivers coursed through his body. He tried to reinterpret the sound. The exclamation was like a response to someone plunging a knife into J.D. Mitch held his breath and forced himself to lie even quieter, trying to hear anyone creeping around the room. He thought of the poorly guarded perimeter in the jungle beyond the next building. More than once, pilots jogging around the base had found Thai guards asleep.

Those concerns flashed through in milliseconds as he listened for clues. With one ear pressed against his pillow, he heard his thumping heartbeats as clearly as if his heart were beating on his eardrum. The thudding was so fast he had to concentrate to hear anything else. In the distance, an air conditioner hummed hot air out into the humid night. Closer, the quiet ticking of the alarm clock was noticeable for the first time in the three months Mitch had slept by it. For several seconds he heard nothing else. Rolling slowly onto his back, he tried to get a look at the center of the room.

"Hey!" Bed springs creaked and the bed frame scraped the wall. Items in J.D.'s flight suit clattered as he stood. "Where the hell are we?"

Mitch heard a fear in J.D.'s voice he'd never sensed before. "It's okay, J.D." He tried to sound comforting without his voice revealing his fright. "Mission's over."

J.D. grunted something.

"You're not flying anymore. Go back to sleep." Mitch wished he'd convinced J.D. to remove his flight suit.

J.D. stretched out on the bed. Moments later he was snoring.

"Thanks a lot," Mitch whispered while trying to slow the rapid thumping in his chest. He considered getting up to ensure the door was locked but knew the problem was J.D., not someone lurking on the walkway. He checked the clock: one forty-one. Mitch was wide awake and knew he would be for some time.

One long minute after another disappeared into the darkness. He concentrated on Elizabeth's visit to Bangkok. Nevertheless, he kept returning to J.D.'s dream of being lost in night skies. The longer Mitch remained awake, the more disconsolate he felt. Even with all the courage packed into J.D.'s small body and large soul, J.D. hadn't eliminated all his fears.

Mitch had been encouraged by how far he'd come in trying to be brave. Lying in the darkness, he realized how much further he had to go to become the man he wanted to be.

Four F-105s on a Combat Skyspot

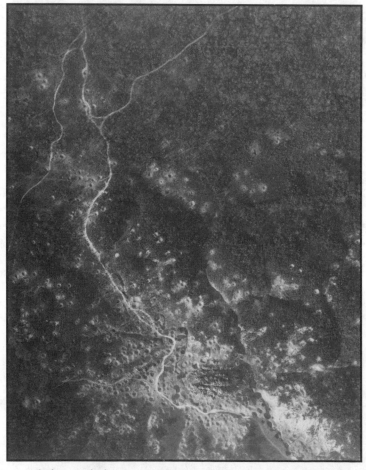

Alpha and the intersection of Routes 911 and 912

Chapter 13

"I don't like this at all," Mitch said on interplane.

He was flying over the area he considered the heart of Steel Tiger. Looking east across rolling hills, Mitch saw the intersection of Routes 911 and 912, the roads southbound from Mu Gia and Ban Laboy. South of the intersection was Alpha, a bombed-out interdiction point where the road wound around an out-of-place outcropping of karst. Alpha, along with Bravo and Charlie—the designations of two other vulnerable spots in nearby hills—had been original choke points when strategists believed traffic could be choked off in Laos. No one believed that anymore, but the FACs still referred to the area as the Chokes.

Mitch wished he were flying in sunshine instead of silhouetted a few feet below ragged gray clouds. Stirring restlessly against his shoulder harness, Mitch yanked the stick against his thigh. The heading changed abruptly for perhaps the hundredth time in the last ten minutes. He was uneasy because of the concentrations of guns deployed to defend the intersection and the Chokes. "They taught us from day one not to fly under overcasts."

"No guts, no glory, roomie," J.D. said from his O-1 maneuvering north of Alpha.

"Malarkey, *roomie*."

"Look on the bright side. Ground fire's gotta be easier to see."

"Thanks a lot, sunshine." Mitch wished he were at the Sunday chapel service rather than flying his nineteenth combat mission as a captain.

"Did I tell you how easy ground fire is to see at night?"

"Captain Kirkland said you made seeing triple-A easy."

"Kirkland's a pussy. He ought to be out here in the day time, and I should still be out there at night."

"Right." Mitch knew Kirkland's complaints had gotten J.D. yanked from the night program.

Mitch was staying well west of the guns around Alpha, and he wished J.D. would, too. Seeing the solitary karst, Mitch couldn't help thinking about another mission to Alpha early in the year. He knew almost as much about that fatal mission as if he'd been there instead of Silent Sam.

The overcast had been similar. That morning, ground fire rose without warning. The O-1 flown by Sam's wingman, Captain Greene, crashed in the first meadow southeast of Alpha. Minutes later, an armed T-28 from NKP swooped low over the wreckage, was hit by intense automatic weapons fire, and crashed in a vertical dive a half mile east. Mitch suspected those same gunners now were watching him and J.D.

Ten miles east on Route 912, Le was riding toward the intersection with Route 911. Beneath the overcast and a triple canopy of foliage, midday seemed like dusk. Ahead a soldier stepped from the roadside and displayed a signal flag indicating American aircraft were ahead. Corporal Cung braked the GAZ to a stop.

Le was surprised that Americans were present with clouds so low.

He'd hoped to make his eighty-kilometer trip without having to hide. He also was concerned about a southbound convoy of thirty trucks he'd passed a few minutes earlier. Le assumed the aircraft would be O-1s. "What kind of aircraft?"

"I don't know, Colonel."

Le nodded. His system of flags, signal lights, and rifle shots provided primitive warnings. The details he needed, however, usually were available only in his communications centers. He had little time to waste. Nevertheless, he needed to learn more before venturing into the open meadows where Route 912 neared Route 911.

"Stop the convoy behind us," Le said to the soldier, then looked ahead and recognized the next bend. In three years he'd come to know all his roads without needing a map. He tapped the barrel of his AK-47 against the dashboard. "Stop at Ban Topen."

Corporal Cung shifted the GAZ into gear, followed the road beyond the bend, and turned onto a spur road. For a couple of thousand meters, he steered through a green tunnel of foliage. Wherever the overhead canopy thinned, fresh cuttings were woven into trellises. In a few minutes, the vehicle entered an area of scattered bunkers, storage tunnels, and dugout shelters large enough to hold trucks. Cung parked by the command bunker of the major staging area near the abandoned village of Ban Topen.

Mitch reached up without thinking and curled the left end of his mustache. If flying under the overcast weren't enough of a worry, this mission brought its own special dangers. Somewhere above the clouds, four F-105s were streaking across central Laos toward Alpha. Lid, a controller at a radar on the hillside near the barracks at NKP, was directing the fighters. The procedures were similar to a radar-controlled approach to a runway. In this case, Mitch thought, the fighters were flying at eighteen thousand feet, but only their bombs would come in for a landing.

"Come over here," J.D. said, "and you can get a free plane wash."

"No, thanks."

Mitch looked beyond Alpha. A misty area of gray rain connected the clouds to the lush jungle. He spotted J.D.'s light-colored aircraft against the heavy rain. Mitch scanned in all directions. Several showers looked like columns keeping the clouds from falling on the jungle.

Mitch checked the time. Barely five minutes remained until the fighters would send twenty-four bombs screaming through the overcast.

Le entered the bunker and went to the intelligence section. He was told two O-1s were near the intersection, apparently awaiting a radar-directed strike.

"Good." Le now understood why the Americans had come beneath the clouds. "Perhaps they'll leave as soon as bombs are dropped."

One radio carried the radar controller's directions. Another radio crackled with a static-tinged voice, "Mother Monsoon's getting an early start with the old two-three-four punch."

Le watched the loudspeaker that often carried conversations between pilots of the O-1s.

"Say again, Three-six."

"The eighty inches of rain due to start next month. That's two inches of rain every three days for four months."

Le nodded. In a few weeks, prevailing winds would shift southwest and bring heavy rains daily to the jungles of Laos and the airfields in Thailand.

"Yeah, I've been thinking about problems the rains are going to cause."

Le thought the second voice sounded familiar.

"Roomie, you notice how often you think about a problem as if thinking about solving it was gonna solve it?"

"Just facing facts, *roomie*. Bird Dogs aren't equipped to fly in tropical downpours."

"So what if you're flying an airplane that can't go out and play in the rain? Be glad you're not carrying a shovel while eighty inches of rain beats on your helmet."

"Right."

Right. Le knew his men would abandon the roads and spend most of the rainy season working in North Vietnam. He turned to a soldier monitoring Cricket's frequency. "What are the call signs?"

The soldier looked at notes. "Nail Three-six and Five-nine, Colonel."

Le stared at the loudspeaker and pictured McCall's airplane rushing by in Mu Gia. *Be careful. There's peril for metal dragons beneath the clouds.* The other call sign seemed familiar. After a few moments he smiled. His radio monitors had complained that Nail Three-six was unpredictable and often spoke in code words that were undecipherable.

A sergeant monitoring the Vietnamese command radios asked, "Do you want to clear sector gunners to fire on the Americans, Colonel?"

Le paused, picturing the American lieutenant who'd befriended him. "No. Maybe they'll leave after the bombs are dropped. If we shoot one down, other aircraft will be overhead the rest of the day, and our convoys will be stalled until dark."

"Yes, Colonel."

Le turned to the loudspeaker. During the silence, his eyes focused on a dusty microphone hanging on a hook by the speaker. He thought about a dispatch he'd received two days earlier confirming South Vietnamese Intelligence now knew he'd been a spy in the South Vietnamese Army. His cover story no longer mattered. He reached for the microphone, paused a few moments, then pressed the button. "Go home, Metal Dragon. You do not belong here."

Mitch tried to replay the words that seemed spoken in a fake accent. He wondered what J.D. could be up to with a dragon analogy.

J.D. asked, "What the hell are you talking about? The Bird Dog's sure no metal dragon, and you need to work on that accent."

"Wasn't that you?"

"Negative." After a short pause, J.D. added, "You're a day late playing April Fool's."

Mitch recalled spending much of the previous day trying to avoid J.D.'s pranks. The speaker had to be J.D. No one else had used the frequency since takeoff.

"Flamingo Flight," Lid said on the strike frequency, "come left to zero-three-zero degrees. This is a dogleg to final. Accomplish pre-release checklists."

"Left to zero-three-zero," Flamingo One said. "Flamingo Flight, green 'em up."

Although still curious about what had just happened, Mitch focused on the mission at hand. Lid was guiding the fighters to the intersection. He and J.D. were supposed to be close enough to the target to report on the accuracy of the strike. *Close enough—but not too close.*

Mitch held well to the side, in case the bombs fell long or short. He was high-man, but he felt responsible for the assessment since he was more accurate with the maps than J.D. was.

"If you wanta talk metal dragons," J.D. said, "I'd go for the Thuds with their Gatling guns spitting fire."

"I wasn't talking dragons."

"Metal dragons you mentioned litter my country," Le said. "They should stay in America instead of invading where they don't belong."

A chill in the back of Mitch's neck spread downward as he recognized the term metal dragon. In Oklahoma, South Vietnamese Major Hoang Thao had said Mitch's birth date in January 1941 put him under the sign of the metal dragon in the Chinese horoscope. Mitch looked at the battle-scarred road as if it could help pinpoint the man now known as North Vietnamese Colonel Le Van Do. The feeling of being watched caused Mitch to roll into a hard turn and maneuver continuously.

J.D.'s voice was more insistent. "What the hell's going on, roomie?"

"Standby!" Mitch tried to decide how to respond in this unexpected game. He remembered Major Thao had claimed being born under the sign of the earth dragon.

"Flamingo Flight," Lid said on the strike frequency, "come farther left to zero-zero-five."

"Zero-zero-five, Flamingo."

"You, too, are far from home, Earth Dragon," Mitch said slowly and distinctly. "If you and those like you had stayed home, maybe I could have, too."

"This is my home, Metal Dragon."

Lid made additional corrections to the heading of the fighters, but Mitch hardly noticed.

"Laos instead of Hue?" Mitch pictured Major Thao talking of growing up in Hue, which had become part of South Vietnam after the French withdrew in 1954. Now, of course, Mitch assumed anything said in Oklahoma could be false.

"Dragons must do their duty. You know that."

Mitch nodded, reminded himself of his mission, and glanced at the clock. Less than a minute remained until the bombs were due to drop, so Mitch looked for J.D. The aircraft wasn't near the shower where Mitch had seen the O-1 earlier. Expanding his search, he was about to ask J.D. for his location when Mitch saw the other O-1 above the target.

Mitch screeched, "What are you doing?"

"Waiting. Are you going to tell me what that was all about?"

"Get the hell out of there!"

"Maybe I can tempt your dragon man to take a free shot. Then he'd be impressed by how fast I got bombs on him."

"If you don't pull back, I'll abort the mission." Mitch knew either FAC had the authority to cancel the bombing. Explaining the reason afterward would be a problem. "I've lost one flight leader, and I don't want that experience repeated!"

"Don't get your bowels in an uproar."

"Are you moving back? I'll abort, so help me!"

"Okay, okay, but we're missing a golden opportunity to teach them not to shoot at us under an overcast."

"Not while I'm with you, thank you." Mitch watched J.D. bank steeply and turn away from the road. "Even if the gunners didn't get you, the bombs might."

"Why are you so friggin' worried, Einstein? On a clear day when you can see all the way to the Mekong, Thuds hit the road two percent of the time. The safest place in the universe is right over the target."

"Just humor me, okay?"

Click-click. "Now you gonna tell me?"

"Not on this frequency."

"That was your buddy from Oklahoma. Right?"

"Un-huh."

"Strange."

"Un-huh." Mitch shivered at the realization that he'd talked with the commander of an enemy force Mitch had been sent half way around the world to defeat.

"Flamingo, come left to three-five-six," Lid said. "Fifteen seconds remaining. I'll begin a count at five."

Watching in silence while J.D. angled away from the intersection, Mitch wondered how close Le Van Do was to the target.

"Five. Four. Three. Two. One. Zero."

Mitch had no idea how many seconds a 750-pound bomb needed to fall seventeen thousand feet, so he kept his eyes on the target.

"Bombs are on their way," Flamingo One said.

"Flamingo Flight, come left to a heading of two-seven-zero. Climb to flight level two-four-zero."

"Left, two-seven-zero. Climbing to twenty-four."

Mitch hardly noticed the exchange between Lid and the fighters. Instead he concentrated on maneuvering and keeping the intersection in sight. His imagination pictured twenty-four bombs bursting out of clouds immediately above him. He watched and waited—and waited.

Numerous flashes erupted like a string of giant firecrackers, then were swallowed by geysers of dirt, rocks, trees, and smoke.

"Missed me," J.D. said.

"Thank God for small favors." Mitch was relieved both O-1s had been missed.

Mitch flew toward the target. While smoke drifted away, he located four clusters of fresh craters. The closest had missed the intersection by about fifty yards although two bombs had blasted a spur road leading into the jungle south of the target. "Damned little to show for the risks we've taken this morning."

"Don't forget the harassment value."

"Them or us? I felt pretty harassed those last few seconds." Mitch was eager to complete the assessment and get away from all the guns hidden along the Trail.

"I doubt if one Combat Skyspot out of a hundred closes a road more than thirty minutes."

"If we don't find a better way, this war could go on forever."

"You'd better spend chapel time praying the monsoon comes early."

"Right," Mitch said sarcastically, but conceded J.D.'s answer was as good as any. The monsoon would do what the Air Force and Navy pilots couldn't accomplish—close the Ho Chi Minh Trail in Laos.

Le stood watching the loudspeaker, second guessing himself and avoiding the questioning look of the soldier monitoring the FM radio. Le heard Nail Five-nine make the post-strike assessment and was pleased the bombs wouldn't delay any convoys.

Moments later, Le heard a pilot say, "Cricket, Nails Three-six and Five-nine are RTB."

"Good," Le said, encouraged the two O-1s were returning to base. Grabbing his AK-47, he hurried out, eager to continue to the headquarters of his southern sector. He settled into his GAZ as a truck stopped alongside. Le was surprised to see Major Quan get down from the cab.

"I'm glad I caught you, Colonel." Quan offered a quick salute. "A courier arrived and said he had a message that demanded your immediate attention."

Le frowned as he stepped out. He'd been encouraging Quan to take more initiative and act as commander during Le's absences. "What are you doing about it?"

Quan shrugged and offered an envelope with an end torn open. "I didn't understand the message, sir."

Le grabbed the envelope, grunted his frustration, and made a point of yanking out the single sheet of paper. He placed his glasses far down on his nose. For an instant the words made no more sense to him than they had to Quan. He reread "The buffalo are thirsty." Suddenly Le recognized the code words General Giap had given nearly two months earlier. A feeling of exhaustion swept over him, much as when malaria recurred. He settled onto the seat and leaned against the dashboard.

"Are you ill, Colonel?"

Le was too preoccupied for the words to sink in. Finally, he gazed up with vacant eyes. "You'll make the trip to Tchepone. Return to headquarters by noon tomorrow—and be ready to take command."

Crossing the Mekong, Mitch saw the road to the base glisten in a few patches of sunlight. Trucks, buses, and motorbikes bumped along at near-normal speeds, suggesting showers had done little more than settle the dust.

"The spirits must've washed the runway," J.D. said, turning into the traffic pattern.

"Spirits?" Mitch was still thinking of the discussion of dragons inspired by the Chinese horoscope. The metal runway looked wetter than the road.

"I've been reading one of Ted's Tom Dooley books."

"Tom Dooley?"

"Not the Kingston Trio's Tom Dooley. I'm talking about the Navy medic who spent a few years treating Laotians. He said people around here believe spirits control almost everything."

"Right," Mitch said facetiously while starting his pre-landing checks. In deference to the spirits and their damp runway, however, he extended his traffic pattern for extra spacing. J.D. was at the far end of the runway when Mitch flew across the threshold.

His O-1 was drifting slightly left when the tailwheel touched down, followed an instant later by both main wheels. *Not bad.*

Mitch noticed the airplane wanted to keep drifting. His right foot slid forward, applying rudder and tailwheel steering. He pushed lightly at first, then more aggressively.

The slide continued, triggering long-suppressed fears. Mitch's grip on the stick and throttle tightened. He jammed the rudder pedal to the stop and pressed hard on the top of the pedal, applying the brakes on the right wheel.

Momentum didn't change.

Brake failure!

The aircraft charged on.

He pumped the useless brake and leaned sideways as if body English might halt the skid.

With the engine in idle, the O-1 was rolling at thirty knots when the left wheel dropped off the runway. Mitch feared the mud would grab the wheel and pitch the O-1 forward onto its whirling propeller. He was reaching to shutdown the engine when the tailwheel dropped off the edge, and he regained control. The O-1 bumped forward, but the tailwheel steering allowed him to guide the aircraft to a stop with one wheel on the runway and two off.

Mitch took a deep breath and tried to calm his surging heartbeat. His grade for the landing changed from *Not Bad* to *Scary*.

"Nail Five-nine, Tower. Do you need assistance?"

"I don't think so, Tower." Mitch was embarrassed his predicament had come to anyone else's attention. He saw J.D.'s aircraft turn, giving J.D. a clear view from the far end of the runway. "A brake failed, but I can get the bird to the ramp."

Delayed fear settled in, shaking Mitch from the inside. Nevertheless, he forced the reaction aside and pushed the throttle. The O-1 hesitated, then edged forward. Pushing the right rudder pedal to turn the tailwheel, he guided the aircraft onto the metal planks. Other than the track of mud that persisted for several turns of the tires, the O-1 headed down the runway as if the unplanned excursion had never happened.

Mitch sighed. The fresh, red mud tracked onto the runway would dry up and blow away long before he'd shake the residue from his confidence.

He needed to report the brake failure, so he decided to check out the problem. He steered to the centerline, then watched the wheel when he pressed the brake. The wheel stopped, but the O-1 glided forward as if on ice. Two more tests convinced him the brakes were fine—the slick runway was the problem. Mitch slumped in the seat and brooded about two inches of rain every three days for four months.

After the O-1s were parked, J.D. ambled over. He waited while Mitch finished filling out the maintenance forms.

Walking to the pickup, J.D. said, "I think the spirits done come to live in you."

Mitch was too absorbed in reliving the landing to put up with J.D.'s horseplay. "What the hell are you talking about?"

"Your face. You give new meaning to the term *white man*."

Mitch turned away, embarrassed his fright was obvious. "I scared the hell out of myself. Is that okay?" He wanted to explain how much the thought of crashing on landing had haunted him for nearly three years, but he couldn't say the words. "I have this thing about landings."

"Landings are no big deal. Any landing you walk away from's a good one."

Mitch frowned his response. He didn't need clichés.

J.D. slid his sunglasses down his nose and looked above the frames. "You serious?"

"Damned straight." Mitch stomped to the pickup, tossed his gear into the back, and got into the passenger side of the cab.

J.D. got behind the wheel and drove to the main road before speaking. "The runway's a little slick this mor—"

"A little!" Mitch crossed his arms and exhaled loudly. "It's going to be that bad, or worse, until November."

"So? You can handle landings, roomie."

Mitch hesitated. "I've had trouble with landings for a long time. Today didn't help my confidence."

J.D. looked across, studying Mitch. "Landings are no big deal."

"They are for me."

"Come on. After what you face over the Trail, landings should be a piece of cake."

Should be—but they weren't. "As you pointed out this morning, I worry more than I should."

"Don't get a hernia over little problems. There are worse things than crashing and burning and getting killed."

"Like what?" Crashing on landing was a subject Mitch had thoroughly analyzed.

J.D. pulled into the parking lot in front of the building where the pilots' gear was stored. "Crashing and burning and not getting killed."

"Gee, thanks! That'll help me relax whenever I roll out on final."

"You've got to stop worrying about the wrong things, Mister Wizard." J.D. slapped Mitch reassuringly on the shoulder. "At least when you're landing, the mission's over, and no one's shooting at you."

That was the most logical argument J.D. had offered. Mitch stepped from the pickup and gathered his gear.

J.D. grabbed his M-16 and helmet, then hesitated. "I know a surefire way to get your mind off landings."

"What's that?"

"Before each mission, you stop and take a leak out in the quadrangle over by the TUOC."

Mitch stared in disbelief across the pickup bed. "What kind of a cockamamie idea is that?"

"It worked for Jimmy Dean when he was nervous about doing his first scene with Liz Taylor." J.D. paused as if he'd spoken heresy. "Even heroes can get a little nervous if the stakes are high enough. Anyway, before he went to join Liz, he just unzipped in front of thousands of people who'd come to watch the filming of *Giant*. After that, he figured he couldn't do anything more embarrassing with her."

Mitch studied J.D. and decided he was serious. "Well, I'm not a hero like James Dean. So I'll go to chapel tonight and pray it doesn't rain any more for a week." His CTO for April was scheduled to begin the following Sunday.

"And then?"

"I think I'll practice landings on my CTO. I was already planning to save money hanging around here instead of going to Bangkok."

J.D. acted disappointed. "I unselfishly offer the benefit of my vast experience, and you choose a logical solution instead."

Heading into the building, Mitch smiled, appreciative J.D. had helped put things into perspective. "I'll try my way first, thank you."

"You know what they say in Cajun country?"

Mitch held the door open, almost afraid to ask. "What?"

J.D. stopped. "You've got two choices in life, ace. Either you give up your dreams, or you have to pay for 'em."

Mitch was surprised to hear something so profound from J.D. "I've paid pretty damned heavy the last three years."

"And you haven't let go." Stepping by Mitch, J.D. added, "Jimmy Dean would've been proud of you."

Mitch assumed that was the highest praise he could ever hear from J.D. Mitch felt honored in the midst of his feelings of insecurity.

"Now, roomie, I want to hear about dragons."

Chapter 14

After a week of uneventful missions, Mitch practiced landings on two of his days off. Through thirty-seven landings on NKP's metal runway and the dirt of Downtown NKP International, Mitch felt most of his confidence return.

Nearing noon on his first day back on the schedule, Mitch was ready to head for the TUOC. A triple knock on his door was a short-long-short pattern—F in Morse Code—Ted Forrester's trademark. Mitch grabbed his flight cap and opened the door.

Forrester grinned broadly. "You get all the mud out of your hair?"

Smiling, Mitch nodded. Beyond Forrester, the open area separating the two buildings was a sea of drying mud. Earlier in the morning, J.D. had unleashed his special celebration of Songkran, the Thai New Year. With boxes of water balloons strategically placed and taking a water hose up on the roof, J.D. had brought the Thai tradition of water throwing to a new level. Most FACs had joined the water fight in a temporary respite from the war.

As Mitch and Ted started along the walkway, Mitch said, "I feel like I've still got mud in my ear. I'll be unhappy if J.D.'s rain dance gets us more than eighty inches of rain."

"We'll see," Ted said, "but that's why the Thais waste water when it's most scarce."

"Great!" Memories of sliding off the wet runway remained vivid. Walking up the hill, Mitch thought about their mission for the day. "You ever been to Sector Sixteen?"

"Negative."

Mitch recalled his one mission over the area most distant from NKP. "It's the only sector in Steel Tiger without roads. Seventh sends us out every three or four weeks to ensure the gomers aren't sneaking a road through. So far, there's no evidence the NVA's interested."

"So you're not expecting triple-A?"

"Maybe crossing Nine-eleven. J.D. calls this the 'R and R mission—almost.' Once we're across the road, we can descend to a couple of thousand feet above the terrain."

"That ought to be fun for a change."

"Right," Mitch said, realizing he'd never thought of any mission across the river as fun.

Mitch relaxed after following Ted across Route 911 and flying well east of the defenses. He checked peaks ahead against his map and picked the most prominent one at the far end of Sector Sixteen. When they reached that peak, they would be at the far side of Laos, within five miles of the demilitarized zone between North and South Vietnam. "Recommend we head for the tallest mountain there about eleven-thirty and make a general scan as we fly across."

"Sounds good to me." Ted began weaving in the general direction of the peak.

Mitch flew lazy S-turns over pristine hills that showed no signs that war was a nearby neighbor. He studied rolling ridges and looked for cuts that would allow north-south roads to pass through. Using binoculars to check out a jungle trail, he followed the meandering pathway until it spread to nothingness in the next meadow. Water buffalo might have used it, but no trucks or pack bicycles.

Ted said, "You know what the big difference I notice is?"

Mitch assumed the answer was obvious. "No big reddish-brown holes in the ground."

"Well, that too. I don't see a single, white parachute anywhere."

Mitch looked and didn't see any of the tiny parachutes that kept flares in the air as long as possible. So many parachutes dotted the trees along the main roads, Mitch no longer noticed them. "You've got new eyes. After a few months, you don't notice little things anymore."

"It's like we're in a part of the world no one else has ever been."

"If you see anyone, he may be pushing a bike. Intel says the North Vietnamese carry seven-hundred pounds on special bicycles."

"You're kidding."

"That's part of what makes this such a damned tough job. How do you stop men on bicycles when you can't find hidden trucks?"

"As long as Washington lets ships bring in everything the North Vietnamese need, you and I aren't going to win the war in a pair of Bird Dogs."

"You've got that right."

"If we ever send heavy bombers to Haiphong's harbor, it won't matter how many pack bicycles are in the trees, because they won't have anything to carry."

"Sounds like a former Buff-driver." Mitch agreed strikes against North Vietnam had too many restrictions favoring the enemy.

"Have you seen photos of Russian ships in Haiphong with decks crammed with trucks?"

"Roger that."

"Seems futile to try to kill a truck at a time when hundreds are kept off-limits in Haiphong."

"Roger." Mitch was glad Elizabeth wasn't listening in and hearing about how little he was accomplishing.

Le had pushed his weary team all morning. With a strong wind at his back, he hiked south in a narrow valley. His path was relatively clear, but almost in the shadow of the dense jungle towering above him on the steep western slope. He hoped this would be the last day of scouting before reaching a staging area along Route 9.

Listening to the rustle of wind in the treetops, the screech of birds, and the gurgle of the stream, he noticed a steady drone. The only engines he'd heard for twelve days were high-flying jets going to and from North Vietnam. Perhaps truck noise, his subconscious seemed to say, in an optimistic hope he was nearer his southern roads than the map suggested. Nevertheless, his eyes flashed upward an instant before an O-1 flew out from beyond the cover of the trees.

"Down," Le screamed, lunging toward a leafy cluster of banana trees beneath a tall durian tree. "Get under cover!"

Le's bandoleer of ammunition snagged a branch, throwing him off balance. He thudded into the dirt and rocks, clawed into the underbrush, and startled rats that scurried noisily away. The strong odor of bad-smelling cheese enveloped him. Le realized he'd split open one of several ripe durians scattered under the tree. He ignored the stench, rolled over for a better look, and tore at canvas straps on his pack. He edged beyond overhanging banana leaves, which were nearly ten feet long. He saw two O-1s—and a chill ran through him. A threat, but at least they were higher than when he was buzzed in Mu Gia.

The closest soldier shouted, "How did they know we were here?"

"They couldn't have." Le hadn't had radio contact since leaving his headquarters, and even he had never been certain where each day's trek would lead. He couldn't explain how the Americans had found his small group. He looked toward the soldiers who had been trailing him, and the sight jolted him. The two men behind had been carrying surveying gear beneath a bamboo pole. The gear in its protective crate was wrapped in netting of green camouflage. Now it lay abandoned—in stark contrast to the reddish brown earth beneath.

"Cover the crate!" Le yanked his knife from its sheath and hacked at the base of the nearest banana leaf.

"I think I saw troops," Ted shouted.

"Where?" Mitch looked for the other O-1 and discovered it flying a tight turn.

"The north-south valley below me. Five or six guys in the open, five-hundred yards north of where the stream jogs across to the east."

Mitch located the valley, then picked out the corresponding area on his map. As he marked with his grease pencil, a radio call from Cricket interrupted Mitch's concentration.

"Attention all Nail aircraft, this is Cricket with a weather advisory. NKP's forecasting thunderstorms within ten nautical miles of the field between thirteen hundred and sixteen hundred hours."

Mitch checked his wristwatch, which showed nearly half an hour into the forecast period. He looked around. Above the western horizon, blue and gray merged into an indistinct haze. Closer, a few puffy clouds of brilliant white floated in bright sunshine.

Ted said, "I don't recall the weather guesser mentioning thunder boomers."

"No sweat." Mitch switched the selector to transmit on the control frequency. "Cricket, Nail Five-nine. What's NKP's current weather?"

"Standby, Five-nine. I'll give 'em a call."

Mitch saw Ted reverse his turn and circle in the opposite direction. Mitch flew over, about five hundred feet above the other O-1. He clamped the stick between his knees and rolled into a steep bank as he focused binoculars on the valley.

"I'm getting a bit confused," Ted said. "A minute ago I thought I had a rectangular box in the middle of the trail. Now I can't find the sucker."

Mitch scanned over his binoculars. The valley, which was two to three miles long, was a mix of reddish-brown ground and many shades of green. The stream crossed in four places, so he didn't know which crossing Ted had referred to. He glanced at the two rockets hanging beneath his left wing and reminded himself that on missions to Sector Sixteen, FACs seldom used any rockets. "Why don't you put a couple of smokes where you think they were?"

"You don't think that's a problem?"

"Negative. We don't have friendlies out here, and this is generally the route North Vietnamese troops take on the walk south."

"I'll try, but I've lost my fix on where they were."

Mitch angled south so he'd have a good look up the valley when the rockets hit. He watched Ted's O-1 pitch up, roll, and drop toward the valley.

"Nail Six-six is in hot."

Le heard backfiring. Something had changed. He looked skyward and saw an O-1 circling south. The second aircraft wasn't obvious until it broke out of a dive. "They're marking us!"

Adrenaline roused him. He scrambled to the opposite side of the durian and braced against the trunk. He listened for fighters. The wind and his breathing kept him from determining if the O-1s were alone. Le wished he had a radio.

Bang. Bang.

Le heard rockets explode well north. He saw sparkling chunks of phosphorous arcing ahead of fuming white tails of smoke.

Like a dragon's breath from both nostrils. Even at two-hundred meters, the expanding puffs were the closest any had come to him in his years in Laos. Le wondered if the circling aircraft were from Khe Sanh, the base of O-1s that harassed his southern roads. Perhaps his tormentors had come from Thailand. "Is that you, Metal Dragon?"

Studying the area near the puffs of smoke, Mitch saw nothing of interest.

"Nail Five-nine, Cricket with your weather."

"Go, Cricket."

"Be advised NKP has a thunderstorm over the field at this time."

Ted said, "Maybe the weatherman can't detect a thunderstorm 'til rain beats his tin roof."

"That's a roger. What do you think, Six-six?" Mitch took hold of the left end of his mustache and curled the tip.

"I doubt we'll see the troops again. How's your gas?"

Glancing at the gauges, Mitch was surprised. "My bird's burning a little extra."

"Keep an eye on it. Running out of gas here isn't like being over a four-lane interstate."

"Roger that." Mitch knew a much different fate awaited pilots who ran out of fuel over central Laos. He recalled rumors about downed pilots being skinned alive—and worse. He pushed such thoughts aside and guessed at how much fuel would remain after the 110-mile flight home. "If a storm or two's around the field, I'd like to have gas left when we get home."

"Where'll we go if we can't land at NKP?"

"NKP International."

"I practiced landings there during my checkout," Ted said. "Might be okay if the weather scares away the water buffalo."

"Understand." Mitch pictured trails that crisscrossed the southern third of the dirt strip. "If the weather's bad at home, downtown won't be much better."

"If gas is tight, I don't think we oughta press."

"Not for a handful of soldiers in Sector Sixteen. If you're gonna buy the farm, it oughta be for something that matters."

Le saw both O-1s turn west and disappear. After a few moments, he stepped into the clearing. The acrid stench of burning phosphorous floated in with the misty, white smoke.

He noticed a stench far worse. Looking at his shirt, he discovered a mix of dirt and the insides of an overripe durian. He scooped a glob of creamy-yellow fruit from between his bandoleer and his shirt. Sucking the fruit from his fingers, he marveled at how something that smelled like decaying fish could taste like the richest butter, flavored with almonds.

Yanking off his shirt to wash away the stench, Le gazed west. He said quietly, "If that was you, Metal Dragon, I hope the spirits treat you as harshly."

After crossing Route 911, Mitch concentrated on the two remaining dangers—the weather and the jittering needles on the gas gauges. Noticing his fingers had returned to his mustache, he yanked his hand down.

"The weather's building in a hurry," Ted said.

Mitch nodded. Earlier clouds had looked like bulging white pillows scattered over the green-brown patchwork of the Laotian plain. In the last half hour, clouds had multiplied at least tenfold. "I understand how the weatherman might've been surprised by the first crash of thunder."

"J.D.'s ceremony may've been more effective than we guessed."

"Remind me to thank him appropriately!"

"Like with a little strychnine?"

Mitch laughed. "Something like that."

He watched clouds churn higher, like steam from a smokestack on a crisp, winter morning. A massive thunderstorm took the shape of a giant chariot glistening brilliant white in the sun. He could understand how the psalmist in the Holy Land might've concluded that such clouds reflected the radiance of God. On this afternoon centuries later, however, clouds seemed like enormous sentinels, scurrying to close ranks and block the path to NKP.

Ted said, "I think we're overmatched. Which way?"

Mitch estimated the white barrier already reached more than twice as high as his O-1 could fly. "Can't go over 'em. Let's go north a little ways."

"Roger."

Minutes later, they flew northwest into an aerial canyon of towering white. Mitch dashed back and forth between the wispy walls. When his O-1 slipped beyond the limits of the narrow canyon, clouds engulfed him in a dazzling whiteout. Guns, trucks, fighting, and dying seemed distant. The majestic purity of the clouds provided an exhilaration that kept his thoughts away from the slick wet runway ahead. "The Lord is my shepherd. I *shall* not want."

Ted asked, "You got any idea where we are?"

"No sweat. Keep pressin' on." A generally westerly heading would take the O-1s to the Mekong River, and turning north at the river would take them to the town of Nakhon Phanom.

The distance between the walls of clouds narrowed, blotting out more and more of the afternoon sunshine. Clouds, pure white minutes earlier, had transformed to dirty gray. Mitch looked over his shoulder. The canyon had closed behind them, barring sun from the deep pit. He gazed up through the overhead windows. The small patch of brilliant blue was like a last view of the world from the bottom of a grave.

"I don't think we can get through this crud ahead," Ted called.

"We'll have to go down." They were still well south of the karst ridges east of Thakhek, the border town across the Mekong from Nakhon Phanom "The clouds look at least a couple of thousand feet off the deck."

"Okay. I'm going underneath and turning west."

The view beneath contrasted with the bright sunshine in Sector Sixteen. Pillars of torrential rain linked clouds and jungle. Farther west, the ceiling was lower with fewer rainless patches. Lightning shimmered, sizzling static into Mitch's headset. Exhilaration was gone. He discovered his fingers twisting his mustache again.

When the first raindrops slapped the windshield, Mitch closed the windows. Soon there was no option other than fighting through heavy rain. He flew in under Ted's O-1, in loose formation behind the wing.

The deluge swallowed the struggling aircraft in a blurry grayness. Mitch could see fewer than two hundred yards in any direction. Ted's O-1 descended ever lower and became a fleeting apparition. Mitch fought to stay close enough to keep it in sight but far enough away to avoid being thrown together in a mid-air collision.

Torrents of water rushed across the windshield. Mitch felt as if he were flying through an endless waterfall. The steady assault on aluminum and Plexiglas merged with the drone of the engine. The roar overwhelmed the background noise from the radios he monitored— except for frequent crackles of lightning-induced static.

The noise and shuddering also masked normal clues of engine failure. The engine quit, but Mitch didn't immediately notice the loss of noise and vibration. When he realized the propeller was winding down, adrenaline brought every nerve to full alert.

He fought to suppress panic as his hand dropped to the throttle. He felt a pull on his mustache as it didn't completely unwrap in time. His head snapped up, and he looked at the fuel gauge for the right tank. The tank contained plenty of fuel. He looked to the other wing. The needle bounced below the big E at the edge of the red "NO TAKE-OFF" arc.

Mitch grabbed the fuel selector and twisted so hard he was surprised the handle didn't break. In a swirl of motion, he jammed the mixture and propeller controls full forward, pulled the throttle back, glanced at the ignition and battery switches, then yanked upward on the switch for the auxiliary fuel pump. He'd done all he could, except pray and look for a road or a meadow. Blurred images of trees grew larger.

He checked the altimeter. At four hundred feet above dikes around the rice fields, he was too low to bailout.

Barely visible, Ted's airplane was pulling away.

Mitch pressed the microphone button to call just as the windmilling propeller began spinning furiously. He pushed the throttle full forward, willing to sacrifice fuel to keep from being separated and alone.

When the distance to the other O-1 had narrowed, Mitch settled down. As tingling chills in his shoulders faded, he laughed at himself over the bad timing on what was a routine event on many missions. Cricket FACs used fuel from one tank for the first thirty minutes of flight, then switched to the other. Most FACs used from the second tank until it ran dry or they were headed home knowing the first tank had enough to land on. When he'd let the tank run dry before, the engine had quit at six thousand feet—not a few hundred above the ground.

Mitch asked, "You switched your fuel yet?"

"Good idea. This'd be a helluva time to run a tank dry."

Click-click.

Ted said, "I'm starting to doubt we'll run out of this weather before we get to NKP."

"Such powers of observation. They oughta make you a FAC and send you to Thailand."

"Be serious! I heard somebody slid off the side a week ago, and the runway was hardly wet."

"Two weeks ago, and that damned metal sure didn't look slick."

"Was that you?"

Click-click. "Anyway, that landing's old news."

Or, was it? Were there lessons he'd missed? During the skid, had he done nothing more because there was nothing else to do? Had he frozen at the controls? He'd relived the incident a hundred times trying to decide. It remained unfinished business, and he knew better than anyone else that unfinished business could haunt a flier for a long time.

The blurred image of the Mekong River appeared.

Flying beyond the Laotian bank, Mitch called, "Cricket, Nail

Five-nine and Six-six are crossing the fence."

"Roger. Contact NKP tower."

Evading the weather had kept the O-1s well south of the airfield, so they turned north.

Mitch switched frequencies and called, "NKP Tower, Nails Five-nine and Six-six are about twenty out. How's your weather?"

"Roger, Nail. NKP's three hundred feet overcast, visibility half to three quarters of a mile in heavy rain and thunderstorms. Winds are variable two hundred twenty degrees to two sixty degrees at eighteen, gust twenty-five knots. Say intentions."

"Shiiiit!" Ted said.

"We've gotta get on the ground, Tower. Are you expecting any improvement?"

"Negative, Nail. Radar shows thunderstorms in all quadrants. No change is predicted for a couple of hours."

Ted asked, "What do you think?"

"We'll never stay on that runway."

"NKP International?"

"That mudhole would have the crosswind, too."

Ted suggested, "Maybe we could put down on the road from town."

The road would be more aligned with the winds, but Mitch rejected that possibility. "I don't even like riding the bus over that collection of chuckholes."

NKP Tower said, "Be advised that Nail Three-six and Six-seven diverted to Mukdahan."

Mitch asked, "To where?"

"Mukdahan. A radar site fifty miles south."

Ted asked, "You have enough gas?"

"Maybe. Let me see if I can find the base on the map."

Mitch found the name Mukdahan beside a small circle, representing the approximate location of the airfield. That was barely enough information to find the runway on a clear day. "I'm going to be damned close on fuel. The quicker we turn, the better."

"You got it!" Ted turned south.

Mitch said, "Tower, we're gonna give this Mukdahan place a try."

"Roger Nail. Call Viking Control on two seventy-eight four."

"Switching." After setting in the new frequency, he said, "Viking control. This is Nail Five-nine. Do you copy?"

A deep voice responded, "Understand Nail Five-nine calling Viking."

"Nail Five-nine and Six-six are two Oscar-Ones out of NKP. We're about thirty-five miles north looking for a place to land. What's your weather?"

"Viking's got a big thunderstorm overhead, and we have others in all quadrants. Surface winds estimated twenty gust thirty."

"Where are your winds from, and what's your runway heading?"

"Winds are variable, generally out of the west. We don't have a runway. We've got a big grass field that favors landings to the northeast."

"Great," Mitch said on interplane. "Another damned buffalo pasture!

No wonder it barely shows on the map."

Ted said, "I haven't found it yet."

Mitch switched to Viking. "Your weather doesn't sound too pure, Viking. I think we'll head back to NKP."

"Copied, Nail. Give us a call if we can be of further assistance."

"Roger." Mitch added on interplane "Don't hold your breath."

The O-1s reversed course again and started up river.

Mitch switched to NKP. "NKP Tower, Nail Five-nine again. The weather at Mukdahan's bad, and we're headed your way."

"Roger, Five-niner. Our weather hasn't improved. Winds are varying from two thirty to two ninety degrees at twenty-five, gust thirty-seven, with occasional gusts to forty-two knots. The airfield's closed except to emergency traffic."

"We're sure as hell getting into an emergency."

"Understand, Nail Five-niner and Six-six are declaring emergency. Say intentions?"

"Damned if I know. Standby."

Ted said, "Guess I'd vote for trying that cow pasture at Mukdahan."

"Concur." Mitch knew he agreed more due to fear of NKP's slick runway than because he believed Mukdahan was a safe alternative. "Grass has to be better than slick metal." He switched radios. "NKP, Nail Five-nine. Tell Mukdahan we're coming their way."

The O-1s reversed course a third time. Mitch knew it was the last .

Viking tried to locate the tiny O-1s on radar but couldn't distinguish them beneath huge thunderstorms. "Okay, Nails, continue flying down river until you see buildings on the Laotian side. That'll be Savannakhet. Then, turn west and look for a lake with a big green field beside it."

Great! Mitch discovered his fingers intertwined in his mustache again. On interplane he said, "This operation needs a backup plan."

"If you spot a paved interstate," Ted said, "let me know."

Roads were quagmires. "I'd settle for a little pavement. Next time I volunteer to fly Bird Dogs, I'll tell 'em I want to fly where roads are paved." The rain was so heavy Mitch couldn't identify objects across the river. "I'm going to fly the east bank so we don't miss the buildings."

"I'll fly the center of the river."

"Good. Otherwise, I won't be able to keep you in sight."

Minutes passed in the blurry mid-afternoon darkness, punctuated every few seconds by jagged flashes of lightning. The intense rain robbed everything of natural color. Nothing beyond the windows seemed real. The only reality was the right fuel gauge. Bouncing in the small red arc, the gauge's needle was driving the flight to a conclusion.

"I never told anyone this before," Ted said, "but all my life, nothing's scared hell out of me more than lightning."

"Guess you're getting your fill. How you handling it?"

"I was so damned busy earlier, I didn't have time to notice all the lightning. Then, I figured I'd let the monsoon take its best shot. I didn't come half way around the world and fly fifty-one combat missions just to get zapped by weather."

"Was it that easy, to forget the lightning, I mean?"

"Woulda been easier with a few cold Singhas." Ted added with a teasing laugh, "I bet the left tip of your mustache has a helluva curl by now."

"I'll never tell." Mitch was embarrassed his nervous habit was such common knowledge.

Large images materialized in the blurry rain. *Buildings! Real buildings. Not tiny huts with tin roofs.* "Savannakhet! Eleven o'clock low—or almost level."

Ted banked toward Thailand. "If you see a big green field, give a yell."

"Viking, Nail Five-nine. We're turning inbound."

"Roger, Nail. Our spotters outside are gettin' wetter'n hell."

Mitch closed to within fifty yards of Ted as they left the certainty of the river. Everything had a blurry sameness after he left the Mekong behind. Part of his confidence disappeared along with the river. Mitch tried to remember if it was a green field and a lake or a green lake and a field. Nothing looked green. Everything was a soggy brown.

"Nail," Viking said, "our spotters hear aircraft to the north."

"There it is! Nine-thirty low," Ted shouted.

Mitch saw nothing hopeful, but Ted's tone was encouraging. A large blur formed into the surface of a windswept lake. A meadow sloping up from the water's edge showed no hints of green until he was overhead. He frantically scanned ahead and to his left for the other O-1. He wanted to stay within gliding range in case he ran out of gas. However, a tight landing pattern depended on how soon Ted turned.

Mitch spotted Ted's O-1 in a descending turn, so he rushed through the Before Landing Checklist. After locking his shoulder harness, he rocked forward a couple of times to test the mechanism. He smiled grimly, confident he would stay attached to the seat—not so confident the seat would remain fixed to the floor in a crash.

He set the flaps and turned, dropping the nose below the imaginary horizon. "Nail Five-nine's turning base for landing behind Six-six."

He watched Ted's airplane over the far edge of the lake. Ted's landing would confirm the field was safe—or so muddy it would flip the aircraft.

"Nail Six-six is on a low go," Ted said. "I dropped a smoke canister for a wind check."

Mitch watched the lead aircraft climb above the wet slope. Red smoke spewed from the can while it plunged to the ground and bounced three times in tall grass. The red haze rose a few feet and streamed away toward the Mekong.

Not good, but a quartering tailwind was better than running out of fuel circling to land toward the lake. Skimming above angry waves, he saw the field transform into lush green, still dulled by the water flooding across the windshield. Safe or not, he was going to land.

"He maketh me to lie down in green pastures. He leadeth me beside the still waters." *Green*, yes, *but still? Not by any stretch of the imagination.*

The shoreline slipped by. The green field, vivid even in the near darkness, sloped up to meet his craft. He kept extra power on until his wheels were almost in the grass.

Mitch repeated words that had comforted him in Mu Gia, "Yea, though I *fly* through the valley of the shadow of death, I shall fear no evil, for Thou art with me." He eased the throttle to idle, hesitated a couple of seconds, then pulled the stick back, stalling the O-1.

The tail wheel hit with a thud, and the main landing gear slammed into thick, wet grass. Mitch held the stick hard against the stop. The O-1 slowed quickly.

By God, I did it. Renewed confidence replaced tension.

He kept the aircraft moving to leave the area clear for Ted. Ahead he discovered large radar antennas and two O-1s nearby. He swung into the wind for after-landing checks.

Ted's light shimmered off the lake, then glimmered only in pouring rain after the O-1 crossed the shoreline. Just before touchdown, the tiny aircraft hovered like a duck reaching webbed feet for the first touch of water. The Bird Dog settled, bounced slightly, then clung to the earth.

"Nice landing," Mitch called.

"No sense getting killed unless it means something."

"Roger that!"

Mitch parked by the O-1s straining in the wind against their tie-down ropes. A half dozen airmen, with ponchos flapping furiously in the gale, scrambled around. In a few minutes both aircraft were secured. Mitch was given a poncho, but by the time he sprinted fifty yards to a building near the radar antenna, his boots and flight suit were soaked. He bounded up the steps and collided with J.D., who was standing on the porch. Ted was close behind and bumped into both of them.

J.D. grinned broadly. "Do I know how to make rain, or what?"

Mitch exchanged glances with Ted. They grabbed J.D., pushed him down the steps, and threatened to keep him in the downpour.

"Come on, guys. What's a foot of rain between friends?"

Finally Ted stepped back so J.D. could get out of the rain. "When this war's over, you ought to think about becoming a medicine man. Hire out to do rain dances."

"*Little* Chief Pain in the Grass," Mitch offered.

"Careful, roomie," J.D. said defensively, then switched to the offense. "Humidity seems to be affecting your mustache." J.D. paused, then added with a grin, "At least the left side."

"I know," Mitch said sheepishly. He reached to straighten the exaggerated curl.

J.D. reached up and ran his fingers along his own mustache. "Yours should be a sight to see by the time we've had eighty inches of rain."

"Don't count on it." Mitch already had decided to cut off the tips of his handlebar mustache as soon as he returned to NKP.

Chapter 15

After eluding the American O-1s, Le and his surveying team were slowed by the first heavy rain of the season. Six hours of hard hiking the following day brought Le to a staging area on Route 9. Twenty more hours were consumed—dodging nighttime air attacks and daytime aerial patrols—on the 110-kilometer trip to his headquarters.

Le sent Hanoi a message that he was back in command, then was briefed on what had happened while he was absent. Pleased that Major Quan had handled things well, Le hurried to his campsite, which his men set up during the briefing. Climbing into his jungle hammock, Le hoped he could sleep the rest of the day. He fell asleep immediately.

In less than an hour, his dreams were interrupted by persistent repetitions of "Colonel Do." Emerging from what felt like a drugged sleep, Le clawed aside mosquito netting.

Quan looked solemn. "We've received a coded message, Colonel."

"Handle it," Le growled, upset Quan could become dependent again in a couple of hours.

"You're to report to the headquarters at Quang Khe by dusk."

Le's thinking was sluggish as if mired in the red mud. "Dusk? What day?"

"Today, Colonel."

"What are those imbeciles thinking? Less than eight hours, all daylight, and sixty-five kilometers. Did they say what they want?"

"No, but the message was signed by General Giap."

Le slid weary legs over the bamboo frame. "Get my vehicle ready."

An hour after dark, Le dozed in his GAZ-69 parked near a bunker complex southwest of Quang Khe. A helicopter swooping low over the Song Giang River awakened him.

As the *whop-whop* roar increased, soldiers set torches afire at four corners of a nearby field. Flames brightened, then whipped crazily in the rotor downwash as the pilot hovered. When the helicopter landed, five men jumped to the ground, took gear that was handed down, and hurried away. The helicopter lifted off and disappeared in the black sky.

In fewer than ten minutes, Le was called into a room in an underground bunker. General Giap sat behind a table made from ammunition boxes. In battle fatigues, Giap looked much as Le remembered from thirteen years earlier at Dien Bien Phu. Instead of the tension of battle, Giap's face showed the painted-on smile displayed in their meeting in Hanoi. An empty chair was by the table. Tea brewed on another crate.

Giap nodded to his aide, who left and closed the door. "You're losing weight, Colonel."

"Much exercise and little sleep, General."

Giap nodded. "I brought three chickens you can take with you."

"Thank you, General." Le wished he could eat one immediately but knew Giap hadn't flown from Hanoi to deliver chickens.

Giap spread an American map on the table. "Tell me what you learned."

Le opened his dispatch case and removed notes he'd kept separate from maps. He stepped beside Giap and pointed. "General, the straight-line distance from my headquarters to this area southwest of the DMZ is about fifty-five kilometers. A road through those mountains would cover more than eighty. From there, it's twenty easy kilometers to link up with Route Nine."

"Easy?" Giap bent forward to study the map.

"In the dry season." Le recalled his hike through the mud. "Drive three trucks over the same tracks, and it'll pack down. Much of that area's in the open, so trellises wou—"

"You probably wouldn't connect with Route Nine."

Le was confused. "That's the way I scouted."

Giap looked disappointed. "I may want to parallel Route Nine in the next valley north."

Le scanned the area. "That should be almost as easy as cutting south if we were well into the dry season. More trellises would be necessary because that area's more open."

Giap nodded and tapped a finger halfway between the DMZ and Le's headquarters. "Can you build a road through those mountains?"

A road was possible—given enough time, an unlimited number of workers, and no American bombers. "Such a task would be difficult and time consuming."

"How long?"

"Last year," Le said, pointing at the road he'd traveled to Quang Khe, "we needed four months to build the road over the Ban Karai Pass."

"Yes, but the distance was a third longer."

"And, General," Le said, impressed with Giap's detailed knowledge, "most terrain was easier, and we had only four major river crossings. Here, we'd have to cross rivers eighteen times and ford thirty-five streams. We'd have to clear maybe fifty kilometers of jungle."

"Can you put trucks across the rivers on rafts?"

Le considered the five toughest crossings. All had dense jungle nearby, so logs were available for temporary bridges of rafts. He routinely lashed rafts together where American bombers kept him from building permanent bridges. "That's possible, General."

"Once you get orders, could you move trucks down the road in twenty-eight days?"

"Twent—" Le stopped himself, to keep his response from showing how ridiculous he thought the idea was. "No, General. I don't have enough men and equipment to keep open the roads we have now."

"What would you need besides men?"

Surprised, Le checked notes. "Fourteen places require major grading."

"Would two bulldozers and two graders be enough?"

"Perhaps," Le said, wishing he had the extra equipment for his everyday mission, "but seven cliffs would have to be blasted to—"

"We have explosives. What else?"

"To keep the road secret, General, seventy-two places require trellises. Maybe eighty if we run the road farther east."

"How long to build a trellis?"

Le reviewed what he's seen in the last two weeks. Some needed a few meters to hide approaches to fords. A couple of segments were hundreds of meters long. Le shrugged. "It depends on how many men I assign—"

"Say you had a hundred men to build a trellis. What's an average time?"

Le paused. He'd never had the luxury of assigning a hundred men to a single trellis. "With a hundred men to cut vegetation and build the framework, we'd probably need a day on the average."

Giap gestured to the chair by the table. "So, if I give you eight thousand men, the trellises would take a day."

Le's mouth dropped open as he realized the scale of Giap's vision. "We have to replace vegetation every few days."

"Could five men take care of a trellis?"

"On average. Some would require more."

Giap gazed at the mildewed ceiling. He spoke in a voice that seemed meant more for himself than for Le. "Five times eighty. Four hundred men for an average of three weeks."

"They'll be needed indefinitely to keep the road hidden."

Giap put his elbows on the table and rested his chin on pointed fingers. A twinkle in his eyes joined the painted-on smile. "Three weeks, Colonel. What else?"

Le was mystified that maintaining foliage for only three weeks could make sense. Still distracted, he said, "We'd need men and equipment to excavate truck shelters. I can't estimate how many at each stopover point until I know the size of the convoys."

"Easy." Giap took two teacups and put them on the table. "Zero."

"Zero trucks?" Le was confused.

"No." Giap looked as if perturbed by a foolish answer. "Zero truck shelters."

Le was more confused. Surely the general didn't believe the road could be traversed in one night. "In two sections trucks would do well to cover twenty-five kilometers in a night. Each convoy would require at least three nights."

"Three." Giap nodded. "I understand."

Le wondered if the general did understand. All truck parks Le commanded had shelters. Most were painstakingly carved—many by men using picks and shovels—into hillsides. Others were bunker-like structures of teak logs and dirt. Each shelter required many hours to build, and many had saved trucks from everything but a direct hit.

"From my experience, General, shelters are neces—"

"If your secret road remains secret, shelters aren't needed."

It's not my secret road. Le tried to hide his frustration. "We can't keep a road secret from the Americans indefinitely. They aren't the French with a handful of aircraft, General. If the road doesn't stay secret, lack of shelters will cost many trucks." Le's worst daytime losses came when too many trucks took refuge in truck parks with too few shelters.

Giap looked amused at the somewhat insubordinate response. He poured tea. "If you keep the road secret long enough, there'll be no need to keep it secret indefinitely."

"Only if the war ended before the camouflage turns brown, General." Le couldn't imagine a single road that significant.

Giap pushed a cup of tea toward Le. "What else will you need?"

The steady assault on top of two exhausting weeks had Le feeling overwhelmed. He took the tea, using the opportunity to think. Trying to recall what he had covered and to think of what remained, he took a gulp of tea and burned the roof of his mouth. After a few seconds to recover, he said, "Rafts take time, especially to support bulldozers."

Giap picked up his tea, leaned back, and lifted his feet onto the table. Cradling the cup in his hands, he stared at Le. "With ten thousand more men for a week, would that be enough for eighteen river crossings, thirty-five fords, and fifty kilometers of jungle?"

Le shrugged, realizing Giap was taking in everything. "I suppose so, General."

"So, what could possibly take four weeks?" Giap hesitated, then let out a hearty laugh.

"I have no idea, General." Le wondered, however, if he could count on receiving more than eighteen thousand new workers.

"We are about to speak of things you will not discuss with anyone else, Colonel."

"Yes, General." Le tried to imagine something more secret than the implausible scheme just covered.

Giap sipped his tea. "The American invasion of the South has been much larger than expected. The leadership in Hanoi grows impatient."

As well as the leadership in my headquarters. Le hid his frustration over the seemingly endless war.

"Le Duan and General Tran Van Tra are calling for a massive offensive in the South led by the People's Liberation Armed Forces. They believe the people will rise up in support and throw out the Americans."

"That would be welcome."

"I fear Duan and Tra have forgotten lessons the French taught us before we taught the French a lesson at Dien Bien Phu."

Le nodded. He'd barely survived two human-wave assaults in the Red River Delta. French firepower had decimated his unit both times.

"I'd prefer to give the Americans a Dien Bien Phu and count on people rising up in the streets of Washington as the people of Paris did."

Le focused on the map and saw the small circle representing the U.S. Marine base at Khe Sanh. Although much nearer the coast, the American base was almost as isolated as the French base had been.

"To assure success," Giap continued, "I'd need your road a few days."

"When would you need the road, General? The rainy season's upon us. Keeping such a road open, even a few days, would be impossible."

Giap shrugged. "Battles remain in Hanoi, and I may lose. In any case, it wouldn't be before your next dry season. Now, I want you to mark my map where I would need to position soldiers in the twenty-eight days before I would use the road."

Le put aside his tea. "You recall, General, when you first asked if such a road was possible, I said it was not?"

Giap nodded with his painted-on smile. "For three years, you've done the impossible in Battlefield C."

"Yes, General, but I believe it prudent to plan more time for something *this* impossible."

"Secrecy is critical. If Americans discover what you're doing, all could be lost. If we take little time, they will have little time to find out what's going on."

"So far, General, I don't even know what's going on."

Giap smiled.

Le turned to the beginning of his notes. "When we get bulldozers and graders across rivers determines when men will be needed at certain areas. Trellises on the north end will need to be maintained from the beginning, not for just three weeks."

"But those are decisions you know how to make."

Le nodded. "Yes, General, but it'll take a while to translate my notes to your maps."

Giap stood, and Le stood in response. "I leave for Hanoi in four hours."

"Yes, General."

Giap stopped by the door. "If you ever receive a message that says it's time to feed the buffalo, I'll need your road in twenty-eight days."

The lower end of Foxtrot early in the war

Chapter 16

Three weeks later Mitch returned to his room following an afternoon mission. He felt lost. Normally he would've used the time to write to Elizabeth. Now she was en route, so he'd see her before she could receive a letter. He pictured her entertaining Mandy on their flight to Hong Kong.

Two more missions, he thought, opening his locker and removing packets of jewelry and toys purchased in Bangkok. For the next half hour, he checked each item to ensure nothing was broken, then packed everything in a bag. He was putting the bag into his locker when he heard angry whistling accompanied by the thumping of boots on the walkway. The door swung open and hit the desk with a bang as J.D. charged in.

Mitch closed the door. "What's wrong?"

"Nothin' you can fix." J.D. crumpled an envelope and hurled it into the trash can.

Mitch watched. "I suppose this isn't a good time to invite you to chapel this evening."

"Won't fix it either! I'm goin' to town." J.D. yanked open his locker.

"Did you see our names on the schedule for dawn patrol tomorrow?"

"If I'm not there, you have my permission to leave without me." J.D. kicked his flight suit into the corner and grabbed his jeans.

"Colonel Morton wouldn't go for that."

"If he can't take a joke, screw him."

Mitch sat back and watched. Undoubtedly the wastebasket held the answer. While J.D. pulled on his cowboy boots, Mitch said, "How about dinner at the club and the movie?"

"Not tonight." J.D. crammed his flight suit, flying boots, shaving kit, and clean underwear into a bag, then grabbed his leather aviator's jacket and helmet.

"Fly safe." Mitch was glad he wasn't riding downtown with J.D.

In the doorway J.D. gave his James Dean shrug. "Don't bother waitin' up for me, mom."

Mitch listened to the receding thuds on the walkway. Moments later, he heard the engine of J.D.'s motorcycle roar to life, followed by the wail of the vehicle racing up the hill.

After waiting long enough for J.D. to travel well beyond the main gate, Mitch retrieved the letter from the wastebasket. Slumping into a chair, he put the crumpled envelope on the desk and smoothed the worst wrinkles. The letter was from J.D.'s sister in California.

Mitch turned the envelope over three times, producing ample opportunity for the contents to fall out. When that didn't happen, he tapped the envelope against his palm and tried to decide how he might help. J.D. was a danger to himself and the mission if personal problems distracted him when his concentration should be on flying. Still, J.D. hadn't requested help and likely would resent Mitch's reading the letter.

Mitch wadded the envelope into a ball, tossed it into the wastebasket, and picked up his Bible. Perhaps he would find an answer at the evening worship service. If not, the letter would be there when he returned.

"Damn you, J.D."

Mitch shouted his frustration into the early morning darkness as he approached the quadrangle in front of the dispensary. He hadn't seen J.D. in twelve hours, and the Harley wasn't parked in front of the TUOC. A few minutes remained until briefing time, but Mitch doubted those minutes would make any difference.

Stopping by the mail room, he found his box empty. He shrugged off the lack of mail. In thirty-six hours he'd be with Elizabeth for the first time in more than five months. No mail was preferable to the letter J.D. had received. That letter, which Mitch had returned to the wastebasket a second time, carried news that J.D.'s ex-wife was getting remarried. Mitch had been a little surprised that J.D. was divorced, since divorces were uncommon among Air Force officers. Nevertheless, Mitch was pleased J.D. wasn't being unfaithful to a faithful wife.

At the TUOC's gate, Mitch paused and listened for the distant scream of J.D.'s motorcycle. The deep-night quiet was broken only by the steady hum of portable generators, by hammering inside a hangar, and by the crowing of an early rooster.

Once inside the TUOC, he poured coffee, then scanned the latest Weekly Air Intelligence Summary from Seventh Air Force. The list of aircraft losses was depressingly long. He wondered if any of the missing pilots had been about to go home or to meet their wives on R and R in Hawaii. He felt guilty about his happiness while things were so tragic for others in the brotherhood.

Mitch settled into a chair in the briefing room and checked his wristwatch: four twenty-nine. In a minute, J.D. was going to be late—again.

Lieutenant Winters came in and dropped mission kits on the table. "We're diverting you to Foxtrot, sir. There's still lots of action, so I want to check the latest ground-fire reports."

Mitch nodded, and Winters hurried away. Good news and bad news, Mitch thought—good due to the short reprieve before J.D. would be missed officially; bad because the delay was due to excessive triple-A.

Mitch folded his sector map to display Foxtrot, where a road had been carved from a hillside above the Xe Namkok. He'd patrolled above Foxtrot once or twice a week for nearly five months.

He pictured the road, river, jungle, and pulverized no-man's land that had been jungle. The road ran along the river for more than three miles, but the last mile was the most dangerous for the truckers. In that stretch, the narrow road clung to the hillside a hundred feet above the river. All trees were long gone, and there was no place to hide. Foxtrot was heavily defended by 37mm AAA and ZPU machine guns camouflaged in hills above the road and in a large meadow across the river.

Winters returned. "Isn't Captain Dalton here yet?"

"Should be along any minute. I'm low man, so you can go ahead."

After a weather briefing, Winters pointed at the maze of roads on the wall map. "The North Vietnamese are pushing through as much as possible before the monsoon. Large convoys were sighted last night on all main roads." He swept his pointer between the Mu Gia and Ban Karai passes, then down through the Chokes to Foxtrot at the southern boundary of Steel Tiger North. Winters touched Charlie, twenty miles north of Foxtrot. "We're most interested in a sixty-truck convoy that passed through Charlie a little after midnight. Within an hour, we parked Blindbat Zero-three over Foxtrot, and he's been dropping flares ever since."

Mitch nodded. Blindbats were C-130 cargo planes that carried nearly three hundred flares to light the roads for strike aircraft. "Did Blindbat keep the trucks above Foxtrot?"

"Looks that way, sir. We want you to see if you can find them."

"Fat chance. There are hundreds of hiding places above Foxtrot."

"But if you find one that hasn't reached cover . . . ."

Mitch nodded. Some of the best truck kills had come after night attacks prevented convoys from reaching assigned hiding areas.

Winters continued, "We're scrambling a photographer, sir. We'll want pictures of likely truck parks and of remains of six trucks a Nimrod killed between Delta and Echo." Winters hurried through the reports of ground fire and sightings of several other convoys.

While Mitch copied information and marked his maps, he kept hoping J.D. would arrive.

Finally, Winters said, "Seventh requests you get airborne ASAP to relieve Blindbat before daylight."

Damn! Mitch suspected he and J.D. wouldn't be early. "Surely Seventh doesn't think they'd push through Foxtrot in the minutes between when Blindbat leaves and I arrive."

"Seventh diverted you so something like that can't happen, sir."

Mitch nodded. Gathering both mission kits, he wished J.D. hadn't picked this morning to be late. "Tell 'em we'll try to be there before Blindbat turns into a pumpkin."

Stepping out into the cool air, he was less confident than he'd sounded. He listened in vain for the distant roar of the Harley. "Damn you, J.D.," Mitch muttered as he pushed through the gate and slammed it with a *clang*.

When Mitch reached the parking ramp after picking up his flying gear, J.D. still was missing. Mitch had little time to decide what to do. He knew the squadron policy. FACs didn't fly single-ship missions over the Trail. But this was an important mission, and with luck, J.D. would catch up by the time the lead O-1 reached Foxtrot. If not, Mitch could stay safely over hills west of Foxtrot and ensure trucks didn't slip through.

The alternative was to report J.D. absent and cancel the mission. If J.D.'s failure to show for a combat mission was discovered officially, he could end up with an officer effectiveness report that would kill chances of ever being promoted to major.

Walking to his O-1, Mitch decided to go as far as possible without J.D. When Mitch reached his aircraft, he recognized Sergeant Ellison waiting with a camera.

Ellison flashed a weak smile. "This is the first time I've been called out from alert since February. No offense, sir, but I was kind of hoping it wouldn't be to fly with you."

Mitch grinned. "We survived Mu Gia, Sarge, so we can handle anything Foxtrot throws at us." Mitch preferred to put Ellison in the high aircraft but wasn't sure J.D. would get airborne. "Go ahead and get in. I need to drop things at the other bird."

Mitch went to the other airplane and explained that J.D. was running late. Mitch told the crew to protect the maps for an hour, then return them to the TUOC if J.D. didn't show.

When Mitch was in his O-1 and being pushed into the taxiway, he heard an approaching motorcycle.

J.D. skidded to a stop beneath the wing and rushed over.

Relief overwhelmed Mitch's anger. "Good morning, sunshine."

"Sorry," J.D. said with a sheepish look. "I celebrated too hard last night."

"Celebrated?" Mitch remembered J.D. bitterly throwing the letter into the wastebasket.

"Sure. Alimony payments are almost over."

"What?" Mitch acted surprised. "You never said you were divorced."

"You haven't had the *need to know*." J.D. dragged out the last phrase, which usually referred to whether someone should be given classified information. "Where we going?"

"Foxtrot." Mitch summarized Winters's briefing.

J.D. kicked the tire. "What are you waiting for? Get this little bird in the air." He whirled and hurried away. Moments later, he raced his motorcycle down the taxiway.

Mitch watched J.D. disappear around the corner on his way to the personal equipment building. *This morning was going to work out okay.* Mitch signaled he was ready to start the engine.

An hour and eight minutes later, Mitch was over hills west of Foxtrot, and J.D. was fewer than ten miles behind. Except for Mitch replacing the flare ship, the situation was unchanged. The large convoy that came through Charlie hadn't gotten through Foxtrot.

Using binoculars, Mitch studied the road stretching south on the hill above the Xe Namkok. Even bathed in the long, flat, rays of early morning sunshine, the road wasn't broken by a single shadow for more than a mile. On intercom, he said, "No trucks. No signposts. No workers with makeshift tools. If it weren't for that road, you wouldn't believe men even existed on the west side of the river."

"Yes, sir. It's spooky never seeing people."

Mitch nodded. But they were there by the thousands. He turned north and backtracked toward interdiction points where trucks had been seen.

During the next twenty minutes, Mitch confirmed some of Winters reports. On interplane, Mitch said, "The night fliers must've screwed up Uncle Ho's timetable."

"Didn't leave the gomers time to clean up the mess," J.D. answered.

Ellison photographed two burned-out trucks smoldering between Delta and Echo and the remains of a third, wheels-up in a ditch.

Mitch circled four times but saw no signs of the other three trucks. However, he did notice muddy patterns along the fords south of Charlie. The grades on the south side were very wet from water that dripped off southbound trucks. In places, dry dirt had been scattered on top of the fresh mud. On intercom, he said, "Obviously, heavy southbound traffic went through the fords. Get pictures, especially where the NVA tried to hide the evidence."

"Roger, sir," Ellison said.

Between Charlie and Foxtrot, Route 911 met Route 91, which came in through a valley stretching westward toward the Mekong. On the Foxtrot side of the intersection, the south sides of the fords were almost dry. Excitement surged. *Trucks had turned west on Route 91.*

Mitch asked, "You notice the fords, Three-six?"

"Roger that, buddy. The trucks turned off before Foxtrot. They won't waste Uncle Ho's petrol detouring far, so we oughta find them at the first Howard Johnson's on Ninety-one."

"My thoughts exactly."

Well, not *exactly*, Mitch decided, but he'd reached the same conclusion. Trucks would be sent only as far west as necessary to hide for the day. Drifting over Route 91, he studied every hint of a spur road that might lead into hills west to Foxtrot. Under his direction, Ellison took photos of the road for the first two miles west of the intersection. Of the thousands of hiding places, Mitch thought, hardly one could be spotted from six thousand feet.

Mitch noticed J.D. over the jungle-covered hills. "I didn't get a good look at what you were wearing this morning. It wasn't your outfit with the big S on the chest, was it?"

"Say again?"

"I hoped you were wearing your Superman costume. Without X-ray vision to see through the upper canopies, the Philistines are gonna win again."

"I tried to tell that to the powers-that-be. If we can't get a good look under those damned trees, we're just goosin' ghosts."

Mitch remembered J.D. making that comment the day Goodwin had died. "Maybe the pictures'll show something."

"When pigs fly! We might as well have slept in if all we can do is buzz around up here in the stratosphere."

"Another routine day at the office," Mitch said without hiding the frustration in his voice. "Only difference is this morning we could almost smell the exhaust fumes."

"Almost," J.D. said in a deliberate tone.

"What do you think?"

"I don't think. I react. Enough of this ring-around-the-rosie crap. I'm headin' home."

"What?" Mitch didn't understand the sudden shift. "You have an aircraft problem?"

"Sure, like Ol' RTB. Cough! Sounds like my engine's running a little rough. Cough!"

"We shouldn't split up. I'll follow you."

"Hold here west of Foxtrot," J.D. said firmly, "as you would if I hadn't graced you with my presence. If I need you, I'll call."

As mission commander, Mitch was responsible for both aircraft. He was reluctant to agree to an unbriefed scheme. "I don't know what to say."

"Try 'Sayonara,' then sit like a smiling Buddha."

Mitch wanted to say no. However, nothing in his 112 combat missions suggested an effective alternative to whatever J.D. was trying.

Near Tchepone, Le Van Do sat in an underground bunker, which was the headquarters of his southern sector. The night had been chaotic. He knew of losses totaling twenty-seven trucks. Still, between Tchepone and Mu Gia, more than six hundred trucks had reached cover for the day. Most gun crews had received the stand-down order and were moving their antiaircraft weapons into protected bunkers.

Now as he was beginning to relax, Nail Three-six had done something unpredictable. Le looked at the soldier monitoring the FM radios.

The soldier said, "They don't normally split up, Colonel."

"I know." Le listened another minute. Only static was on the frequency. He turned to the sergeant with the field telephones. "Get a visual report on what those aircraft are doing."

"Yes, Colonel."

Pessimistic about getting a quick answer, Le turned to the loudspeaker. He was fewer than ten kilometers from the intersection of Routes 91 and 911, so he considered going outside and trying to see for himself. However, the bunker was hidden in triple-canopied jungle, so he wouldn't see airplanes anyway. He had to depend on the Americans' lax communications security to get a picture of what was developing.

As the seconds of silence mounted, Le's uneasiness increased. *What are Metal Dragon and his crazy comrade up to?*

Mitch maneuvered as if checking hills west of Foxtrot. Instead, he watched the other O-1. After five minutes of trying to keep the small aircraft within the field of view of his binoculars, he began to suspect J.D. was doing what it looked like: going home.

"Five-nine, radio check," J.D. said.

"Loud and clear," Mitch answered.

"Remember the Alamo!"

Mitch saw the O-1 pull up, hover motionless a moment, then stall. He caught his breath in horror as J.D.'s O-1 plunged into a spin. He pressed the transmit button, then barely kept from asking about the

maneuver. "Are you doing okay?"
Click-click.

The soldier at the FM radio looked questioningly at Le. "I do not know what this Alamo thing is, Colonel."

"I don't know either." Turning to the duty officer, Le yelled, "Put Sectors Sixteen and Seventeen on full alert." He tried to picture what was happening in the skies above all the trucks he had hidden near Route 91. *Be very careful, Metal Dragon. The stakes are very high.* Le called out to the duty officer, "Sector commanders are cleared to fire."

Mitch steadied his binoculars and watched the spinning aircraft. Perhaps there were no words because J.D. was struggling to regain control--but Mitch didn't think so. He was convinced J.D. had picked the quickest way to the treetops- an unconventional descent that wouldn't tip off a vigilant, but unsophisticated, enemy. Anyone else who saw the falling aircraft shouldn't suspect the O-1 would be zooming low over the hills northwest of Foxtrot in five minutes. Mitch smiled in admiration.

Ellison asked, "What did that Alamo thing mean, sir?"

"It means you oughta thank your patron saint that you're not riding with Three-six."

After J.D. descended below the horizon, Mitch couldn't see the airplane against the jungle. He waited nervously until enough time had passed for an out-of-control O-1 to plunge to earth. Nothing suggested a crash. He pressed his microphone button twice.
Click-click.

A second later, a response sounded in Mitch's headset.
Click-click.

Mitch pulled on the ends of his lap belt. "Be sure your camera's ready, Sergeant Ellison. Things may get very busy."

Chapter 17

J.D. pointed his O-1 at the tallest tree on the next ridge. He held the stick fixed until instinct told him to raise the nose. The highest leaves seemed to duck below the propeller and pass between the tires.

Hearing Mitch's double click had pleased J.D. Mitch understood the game. Long explanations—that would alert eavesdroppers—weren't necessary.

Treetops looked like an undulating blanket of green. J.D. passed beside some trees and coasted over others. Most of the time, he flew so low he couldn't see beyond the next hill. He opened the windows. Air whooshing by was more noticeable—and so, too, would be sounds of ground fire.

Periodically he looked high beyond the windshield. Shortly after flying out of the spin, he saw Mitch. *Not an easy target for gunners.*

J.D. grabbed one of four smoke grenades held by a bungee cord along the side of the cockpit. The cylindrical canister was similar in size to a soft-drink can. He held the spoon-like safety handle against the canister so the handle wouldn't spring free when he pulled the safety pin. He yanked the pin, readying the grenade to spew red smoke upon release of the handle.

Four minutes after reversing course, he said, "Turn the hounds loose, roomie."

"Say again."

"Three-six is ready for the hunt. You have me in sight?"

"Roger that."

"Time to earn that extra two bucks and a dime Uncle Sugar's paying us. I want to run parallel to Ninety-one. Keep me far enough over hills so gunners in the valley can't pick me off."

"Roger. Come left thirty degrees."

"Left, thirty." J.D. turned to the new heading.

After a minute, Mitch said, "Come right twenty-five. You'll skirt south of open canopy."

"Right, twenty-five."

"You're in the ball park with four miles of jungle to Foxtrot."

J.D. completed the turn, then rolled back and forth, looking down out of one window after the other. "This jungle's triple-tiered. The second canopy looks more than a hundred feet above the ground."

Crossing ravines, J.D. could see to the side beneath the lush foliage. Those glimpses revealed streams and undergrowth not visible from six thousand feet.

"Come right another ten," Mitch said. "The jungle ahead thins out."

J.D. crossed three more ridges before reaching a wider gap. "I'm going to check out this little canyon." He banked hard, then rolled out on a southerly heading that led deeper into the hills.

"Good heading. Nothing ahead but jungle for five miles."

"If'n I had a big, ugly truck, this is where I'd hide it.

J.D. discovered a powdering of red dust on lower trees. An image of something else caught his attention. Whatever he saw reminded him of nets of canvas straps thrown over cargo on the C-130s. He swung his head for another look before the image fell too far behind. He need not have hurried. Bamboo-and-vine trellises stretched all along the hillside beyond his wing. Looking through the intertwined foliage, J.D. saw trucks, barrels, bunkers, and stacks of supplies.

"I've got trucks!"

High in a tree ahead, an AK-47 blinked. Tracers zinged just above the wing. J.D.'s breathing quickened. He rolled left and skimmed by the tree, passing the shooter at eye-level. Gunfire erupted all around, including the roaring chatter of machine guns higher on the hills.

"Ground fire! All around you!" Mitch sounded like a thirty-three-rpm record played at forty-five.

J.D. was bothered that his left hand wasn't free. Conscious thoughts skipped from ground fire to the smoke grenade. *Throw it, dummy!*

He hurled the grenade out the window.

Mitch concluded gunners would try to knock down both airplanes now that a real truck park had been found. Flashes from two hilltops nearer Route 91 spit tracers at him. He felt the rush that occurred when he saw tracers coming his way. "Ground fire! Toward the high FAC!"

Mitch rolled away from the rising shells. *Can't get shot down today!* He pictured Elizabeth en route to Thailand.

Steady streams of tracers rose faster than 37mm shells. "ZPU-Twos or ZPU-Fours," J.D. said, identifying the source as antiaircraft machine guns mounted in twos or fours.

Maneuvering away from the ZPUs, Mitch spotted more flashes along Route 91.

"They've got us in a cross fire, Captain," Ellison yelled.

A quick look told Mitch two 37mm sites had opened up. Rolling more violently, he tried to reassure himself his earlier maneuvering to escape the ZPUs spoiled the aim of gunners along the road. He was impressed with the discipline and coordination. Before, all had held their fire; now, the battle was joined.

Tracers crisscrossed above, below, and in front. J.D. heard Plexiglas in a back window shatter. He rolled hard, aiming into the first ravine branching to the side. Bullets from at least three gunners chased his aircraft, clipping off limbs from trees ahead of him. Moments later, he dropped beyond the next ridge.

"You have my smoke, Five-nine?"

Mitch rolled hard to see the jungle-covered hills. He raised his binoculars and scanned the winding, narrow valley where he'd last seen J.D. "Roger, roger. I've got red smoke!"

"My smoke's in a truck park. Figure the coordinates, Magellan, and get us ordnance."

"Get pictures around the smoke," Mitch shouted without using the interphone. "Cricket, Nail Five-nine and Three-six have trucks and guns. We need bombs, ASAP."

"Say location, Nail, and verify you have active guns."

"Affirmative!" Mitch grabbed his map. "Send fighters to NKP's one-thirteen at eight-five."

Cricket repeated the numbers and asked for the coordinates of the trucks.

"Standby." Mitch remembered he needed to watch out for J.D., who was wandering around without guidance. Spotting J.D. two hills to the south, he switched to interplane. "What do you want to do now?"

"Keep me close, but I've had enough of imitatin' a duck in their shooting gallery."

Mitch gave instructions to keep J.D. clear of the valley with the red smoke, then studied his map and identified the valley. Mitch directed Ellison to take photos covering the valley from Route 91 to more than a mile beyond the smoke. After writing the smoke's coordinates on the window, Mitch broadcast them to Cricket.

The buzz of voices and the reports of ground fire had told Le this morning was far from routine. Nevertheless, the pilot's coordinates were the first solid piece of information Le had. He hurried to American maps on a wall of the bunker. He put on his glasses, squinted at tiny numbers on the map, and narrowed in on hills south of Route 91.

"Damn!"

"Nail Five-nine, Cricket. Could you verify those coordinates? We don't show a motorable road within two hundred meters."

"Some rookie's worried about rules of engagement," Mitch said on intercom. Before he responded to Cricket, he heard J.D.

"Cricket, this is Nail Three-six. Unless they tote those mothers around under helicopters, the trucks I saw are within two hundred meters of a motorable road—by definition!"

"We're surprised by the coordinates. They're not where we expected a legal target."

"Trust me, Cricket," J.D. said, "and get us bombs!"

"We're working on diverts. Expect Hot Dog, four Thuds, in about ten minutes."

"Hot dog," J.D. answered drolly. "Be advised we need more than four."

"Copied."

On interplane, J.D. said, "While we're cooling our heels, buddy boy, let's probe the perimeter and see how big a target we have."

"Let's not take chances. We've got all day to roll back the jungle."

"You and I've got maybe forty minutes, Magellan, and you're the best in the squadron at getting coordinates right."

Mitch didn't think his kind of accuracy was critical. Once foliage was blown from the hidden road, ensuing strikes wouldn't depend on precise coordinates. FACs could follow the road and peel away cover in two-hundred-meter chunks.

Hoping to convince J.D. to return to a safer altitude, Mitch said, "It's about time for you to start playing high-man again. We don't need the license number of every truck."

"No sweatski. I've had my adrenaline fix for the day. I'll go in only far enough to see dust on the trees and toss a smoke for you."

Mitch assumed arguing was a waste of time. For the next few minutes, he guided J.D. into the upper ends of adjacent ravines. Twice J.D. discovered dust, dropped a smoke grenade, and withdrew.

When the F-105s arrived, J.D. gave the briefing and asked what they were carrying.

Hot Dog One said, "Everybody else has a standard load of six seven-fifties each. I'm carrying four seven-fifties and a thousand pounder with a VT fuse."

"Hot dog," J.D. said, this time with obvious enthusiasm.

"Perfect," Mitch said on intercom. The VT fuse would detonate the thousand-pound bomb above the ground. The trees would absorb much of the blow, but the bomb could scatter truck-killing shrapnel over a wide area.

J.D. continued, "Today we've finally got a real target. I hope you can give us some real bombing."

"Just mark it, Nail," Hot Dog One said. "I'll hit it."

J.D. finished briefing, then switched to interplane. "Go get 'em, tiger. This time we ain't just blowing away trees and monkeys."

"Make sure we don't blow away any stray O-1s."

"Not to worry, roomie."

Mitch rocked against the shoulder harnesses, waiting impatiently for Hot Dog One to get into position. Satisfied with the timing, Mitch pulled on the ends of his lap belt, then rolled into a dive. "FAC's in hot."

Mitch aimed well below the narrow valley where the red smoke had been. Ignoring thoughts of Elizabeth, he hurtled downward and downward, determined to make the mark as accurate as possible. He squeezed the trigger, and a rocket blasted away. Yanking the O-1 into a hard turn, Mitch saw twinkling flashes from a ZPU on the hill above his aim point. Tracers heightened the exhilaration that had covered his arms with goose bumps. Rising shells confirmed his rocket was screaming toward the right valley.

"Ground fire," J.D. called out on the strike frequency. "ZPU-Two toward the FAC."

The bottom of Mitch's aircraft faced the guns. He tried to get his mind off the scary feeling of being unable to see the tracers. He whipped the O-1 in the opposite direction. The tracers were well behind, so he climbed to regain altitude. Moments later his rocket exploded.

"Captain," Ellison asked on intercom, "how close do you have to be to see it's a ZPU-Two instead of a ZPU-Four?"

"Closer than you and I want to be."

"Lead has the smoke, Nail," Hot Dog One said.

"My mark's in with the trucks. Lead's cleared in hot. Put your thousand pounder about a hundred yards southeast of my smoke. That'll be in the truck park and might discourage the guys with the ZPU. I'll take your seven-fifties on a separate pass."

"Lead's in hot with the VT only."

Mitch watched the F-105 grow larger with each second that narrowed the separation between the two aircraft. He rolled toward the fighter as if planning to join his eighty-knot O-1 in formation with the five-hundred-knot fighter. Mitch saw the bomb separate. With afterburner glowing, the fighter rose abruptly into a climbing turn. Mitch followed the bomb. He was over the target at six thousand feet when the bomb detonated.

Mitch saw the flash and a circular shock wave racing outward. Foliage swayed. Branches were slashed from the upper canopy and plunged through lower canopies. "I'm afraid we wasted that one," Mitch said on intercom. For a sickening instant, he wondered if he'd put in the strike where there were no trucks or roads. He could see one jungle-covered hill after another. From six thousand feet, they looked pretty much alike.

A blinding flash drove a gigantic shock wave boiling outward. Chunks of swirling fire arced up, reminding Mitch of the finale at a fireworks display.

"Ammunition truck," Mitch said on intercom.

J.D. shouted, "Shiiiit!"

Ellison yelled, "I got it! I got it!"

Mitch scanned around the explosion and saw the O-1 beyond an adjacent hilltop, headed away from the target. "Get the hell out of there, J.D.!"

"Yes, sir."

The next pilot asked, "Where do you want Two's bombs, Nail?"

"Fifty meters north of the ammo truck. I want to work this valley back toward Route Ninety-one."

Mitch divided his attention between the fighter and the scene below. A hundred-foot crater had been gouged from the jungle floor, and splintered trees were smashed outward. Flames belched from two nearby trucks. Firecracker-like explosions sparkled on the hilltop where the ZPU had fired.

Mitch was enthralled. He'd never seen anything like it.

"Two's in."

Mitch made sure J.D. wasn't near the target. "Two's cleared in hot."

J.D. asked, "What the hell happened?"

"Weren't you close enough to see?"

"I missed it 'cause I'd bent over to kiss my ass goodbye."

Mitch laughed. "If you want to find out, you've gotta stay alive until debriefing."

"You're taking fire, Two," Hot Dog One said, "from the main valley north."

Mitch was banked toward the target, so the bottom of his O-1 faced that valley. He yanked the stick against his thigh and rattled off on the strike frequency, "We took thirty-sevens from there earlier."

The O-1 rolled into a sixty-degree bank away from the target, and Mitch scanned Route 91 and the sky above. Nothing indicated guns had hurtled shells at his aircraft or the fighter. He couldn't pick out tracers either. "See anything, Ellison?"

"Negative, sir, but I'm not sure where I'm looking."

"Forget it." Mitch rolled violently toward the target.

Reacquiring the diving F-105, he took a deep breath and hoped his maneuvering had thrown off the gunners' aim. Elizabeth and Mandy flashed through his mind, and he forced them aside. If shells were going to hit him, they were going to hit him. He watched six bombs separate from the fighter, then tracked them toward the target.

Hot Dog One said, "You're well clear of the ground fire, Two."

"Twinkle-twinkle little stars," J.D. said.

Mitch glanced up and saw dark puffs where the 37mm shells had detonated. He watched the bombs disappear into the trees. "Damn. He's long," Mitch said on intercom even before seeing the flashes. The bombs exploded a hundred yards farther up the valley than the first bomb. Geysers of dirt, smoke, and trees heaved skyward. "You're too long, Two. Three, I want you back from Lead's bombs. I want to work down the val—"

A brilliant yellowish-red flash burst from the jungle near where Two's bombs had struck.

"Wow!" Ellison yelled on intercom. "Hold her steady, please, sir. I want to get that."

"Just like the movies." Mitch was mesmerized by the napalm-like explosion. This wasn't napalm, however, since the F-105 had dropped iron bombs. The spectacular detonation was a fuel tanker or a storage tank. Black smoke churned skyward, fed by dancing plumes of red.

"Got it, sir," Ellison said. "Wow!"

"You sure hit something, Charlie," Hot Dog Three said. "Nail, is Three cleared hot?"

"Roger, but I want the bombs north of the black smoke even though Two got a tanker."

"Three's in hot."

"I had a feeling something was in that clump of trees," Hot Dog Two said.

"Bullshit," J.D. said on interplane. "The target's so big even a rookie can't miss."

"Nail Three-six, Cricket."

"Go, Cricket."

"Cricket's diverting Cadillac, Fearless, and Nathan. Cadillac's off the pre-strike tanker and should be to you in ten minutes."

"Okay, Cricket," J.D. said in his James Dean drawl, "tell them to turn right at the Mekong and fly to the bonfire."

"Uh, are you still at NKP's one-thirteen at eighty-five, Three-six?"

"Close enough. We're a little easier to find than we used to be."

Mitch checked the time and the fuel gauges. He'd been airborne an hour and forty-five minutes, so he would've been starting for NKP in another fifteen minutes. He wanted to stay as long as possible but knew he and J.D. would need to be replaced soon. "Cricket, Nail Five-nine. We can handle Cadillac, and maybe Fearless, but you'll need to send a couple more Nails down here."

"Cricket's diverting Three-three and Four-seven who crossed the fence a half hour ago. They should be there by the time you finish Cadillac."

"Copied."

Mitch watched Three's bombs plunge into the trees where he wanted them. Even while debris from the explosions hurtled skyward, three trucks burst into flames.

"Good bombs, Three." Mitch picked an offshoot of the main valley for his next target. "Break. Four, let's go about fifty meters east of Three's bombs."

"Roger, Nail, fifty east. I'm ready to roll in."

"Four's cleared in hot."

Once Mitch spotted the fourth F-105, he divided his attention between the aircraft and the growing conflagration in the valley. The tanker exploded again, spewing liquid flames onto nearby huts and bunkers. Camouflage, burning in the trees, spread the fire from one concealed truck to another. He saw eight rectangular fires, and each appeared to be a truck. In a narrow gully leading from the original explosion, Mitch saw secondary explosions—more than he could count. After so many missions when he'd accomplished nothing more than keep the enemy in hiding, he was thrilled by the spectacle.

Mitch asked on intercom, "You getting all this, Ellison?"

"As much as I've got film for. You fly interesting missions, sir."

"Occasionally." Mitch tried to locate J.D. "Three-six, you're missing a hell of a show. Isn't it time to get on the elevator and return to the top floor."

"Not to worry. I'm out of your way, and I'm getting a look at how these guys beat us."

"Stay out of the way of the bombs."

"That's a lesson I already learned today, boss."

Mitch checked the location of Hot Dog Four and banked to about forty degrees as if trying to intercept the big fighter-bomber over the target.

Six bombs separated, and Mitch watched them plummet.

"ZPU!" Mitch banked hard as he shouted the warning. Lines of red tracers were rising west. "He's firing at you, Four, but well behind."

"Copied. Thanks."

Mitch looked toward the source of the ground fire, trying to locate the active guns. Black smoke obscured hillsides and parts of the valley. Without muzzle flashes to pinpoint the ZPUs, Mitch could only guess where the gunners were concealed.

The bombs sailed into the jungle one hundred and fifty meters from the aim point. Studying through binoculars, Mitch saw nothing but splintered trees, geysers of dirt, and an expanding cloud of dust. He cleared Hot Dog One to drop his remaining bombs, which blew a truck on its side and set another on fire.

"Great job, Hot Dog," J.D. said on the strike frequency. "Standby to copy the numbers."

"Lead's ready to copy."

J.D. gave the target coordinates and the beginning and ending times of the strike.

Cadillac flight checked in on the frequency. The leader said, "Nail Three-six, Cadillac flight's inbound from the west at fifteen thousand."

"Continue. Lookout for Hot Dog on the egress."

"Hot Dog's on the rejoin five miles south of the smoke at twelve thousand."

"Cadillac copied."

J.D. continued, "We've got a real turkey shoot going here, Cadillac. These turkeys were imported from Russia, Czechoslovakia, and Poland."

Satisfied the inbound fighters could stay clear of those leaving, Mitch concentrated on the sight below. "As Three-six said, you've done a fantastic job, Hot Dog. I count eleven trucks burning, so I'll give you eleven destroy—No, twelve destroyed. There's not enough of the ammo truck left to burn. You've had at least fifty secondary explosions, and there're at least twenty secondary fires. I'm also pleased to give you destruction of an active ZPU-Two, which had been shooting at the FACs. I'll give you one-hundred percent of your ordnance in the target area. At this point we don't know what all we have, so I'll give you twenty-percent target coverage. Great working with you, Hot Dog."

"Thanks, Nail," Hot Dog One said. "Call us anytime you have a target like that. Break. Hot Dog, let's go button four."

"I guess you'll have to give them the rest of the BDA in the debriefing," J.D. said on interplane.

"The way the fires are spreading, they might get another truck or two. Once Cadillac mixes things up, it'll be hard to say who hit what."

"I'm not talking about trucks." J.D. added in a playful tone, "I'm talking about the three hundred monkeys Hot Dog Four blew away when he tossed his bombs into the next time zone."

"Get me a body count, and I'll include your number."

Cadillac's strike was a repeat of Hot Dog's, without the blazing fuel tanker and the ammunition truck. Ground fire was sporadic. The eighteen-thousand pounds of bombs Cadillac threw into the battle blew away more trellises and started more fires. Afterward Mitch saw eighteen trucks burning, the huge crater where the ammunition truck had been, and four storage areas blazing fiercely. Hardly a second passed without another explosion.

Fearless and Nathan were overhead, and the other two FACs were holding west of Echo. Mitch wanted to direct air strikes the rest of the day. However, fuel gauges dictated he must give the target and fighters to the other Nails. After a quick hand-over briefing, Mitch turned toward NKP with J.D. trailing somewhere below.

"I've got a cousin with the Marines down south," Ellison said. "One of those trucks might've had the bullet with his name on it."

"We saved more than a few Americans," Mitch said, swelling with pride. After five months of risks, he'd accomplished something that could help win the war. And, he thought, looking forward to Elizabeth's visit, he'd survived the most significant battle of his life. He felt more exhilaration than he could remember since early in pilot training. He asked J.D., "Is that the big mission we've been preparing for?"

"Let's hope it's practice for the really big one."

Mitch smiled, trying to imagine a mission to top what they'd just accomplished. He used the next twenty minutes to transfer notes scribbled on the windows. He was luxuriating in the morning's accomplishments when J.D.'s voice interrupted.

"Hey, Toro."

Afraid to imagine what J.D. might be up to, Mitch hoped he'd misunderstood. He scanned to one side, then the other until movement in a broad meadow caught his attention. A herd of water buffalo was stampeding in all directions. He looked closer and spotted an O-1 in the middle of the herd. Racing away from the sun, the O-1's shadow was barely ahead of the pursuing aircraft. The shadow and the airplane could hardly be closer unless the wheels were bouncing across the meadow.

Mitch said, "You've heard of the three things most useless to a pilot, haven't you?"

"I know. I know," J.D. said. "Runway behind you, altitude above you, and airspeed you don't have. I've spent this whole tour flying without airspeed I don't have."

Mitch agreed with J.D.'s view of the O-1's speed. "That's not what I'm talking about. I'm talking about all the altitude above you. Don't you think it's time you used some of it?"

"If the altitude above's useless, I don't see any sense flying around in that useless air."

Mitch knew he was wasting his time. "That's not what the saying means."

"Whatever."

A whirlwind of motion surrounded J.D. Huge beasts—most gray, a few tan—kicked dust into roiling clouds. He guessed some water buffalo outweighed his airplane. When a panicked animal blundered into his path, J.D. popped the stick back. He watched a tire pass inches above horns, which had a tip-to-tip span at least twice the width of his cockpit.

The stampeding buffalo reminded J.D. of his fifteenth summer, the first after he'd left home. For two of those months, he'd worked on a cattle ranch in Wyoming. On horseback he hadn't been closer to those Wyoming cattle than his mechanical steed was to the water buffalo. J.D. imagined an immense buffalo turning to fight, with horns arced up while hooves pawed the ground.

"You know, roomie," J.D. said, "Jimmy Dean was a aficionado of bull fighting."

"And your fascination with water buffalo's a warped reincarnation without the red cape?"

"Could be."

J.D. envisioned himself with Jimmy Dean, playing a scene only Hemingway could write.

Suddenly, his imagined sounds of matadors, bulls, and screaming admirers disappeared. The engine misfired twice, then quit. The unexpected hush was tempered by the swish of wind rushing past the windows, the thunder of crashing hooves, and the gentle hiss of the radios—and a guttural sound that escaped his throat.

In the instant he recognized the propeller had started winding down, a small part of him shrieked: *This is it! Let it happen.*

Other instincts were overpowering. J.D.'s gaze snapped to the fuel gauge in the left wing root: the needle was bouncing on E. His hand shot to the fuel selector and twisted the handle, connecting the engine to fuel in the other tank.

Even before he touched the handle, his eyes had darted to the view beyond the windshield. Ahead, the meadow was fairly level except for horns, heaving shoulders, and bouncing flanks. J.D. had no doubt he was going to land. Even if the buffalo stayed out of his way, he had another worry. *Would the engine restart quickly enough to clear trees beyond the meadow?*

He maneuvered the stick with one hand. His other moved automatically through items in the checklist for engine failure. Instead of using the last bit of extra airspeed to cling to the sky, J.D. landed hot. The main wheels hit solidly, causing the spring-steel struts to spread, then bounce the aircraft into the air. The O-1 touched down fifty feet farther across the meadow. He kept the tailwheel in the air, fearing if it touched the uneven ground, the O-1 might spin around out of control.

Mitch tried to identify the strange noise in his earphones moments earlier. It had sounded like an exclamation although he wasn't certain of the language. Listening for more, he looked behind the wing and located the buffalo. The O-1 was among them, racing across the meadow.

Underbrush grabbed at the tires, slowing the O-1 more rapidly than the metal runway ever did. Moments after the second touchdown, the engine sputtered, backfired, then resumed its steady hum. Eyeing the treeline, J.D. pushed the throttle and felt the reassuring pull of the propeller.

When the O-1 had almost enough speed to fly, a confused buffalo that should have gone left veered right—right in front of the propeller. J.D. yanked back instinctively. The O-1 staggered into the air, but he had to push the nose forward to avoid stalling. The propeller missed the horns, but J.D. sensed a wheel graze the shoulder of the frantic animal.

The O-1 dropped hard, bounced, dipped a wing toward the underbrush, and threatened to cartwheel. J.D. leveled the wings before the airplane touched down again. The O-1 was clear of the herd, but

J.D.'s stomach knotted instead of relaxed. He'd lost speed needed to clear the trees.

J.D. lifted the O-1 just above the underbrush. He held the airplane there, letting the airspeed build. Studying the treeline, he saw a single, narrow gap. The O-1 could pass through only if a wingtip were pointed at the ground—but he wouldn't have enough airspeed for such radical maneuvering. At the last possible moment, J.D. yanked the stick and rolled toward the break in the treeline.

Hundreds of birds were roosting in the trees. When the airplane hurtled into the treetops, an eruption of fluttering feathers and flapping wings enveloped the O-1 in a maelstrom of birds.

An unexpected thought blared into Mitch's consciousness: the shadow wasn't ahead of J.D.'s O-1! He searched for J.D. The O-1 and its shadow had climbed trees at the end of the meadow. He couldn't estimate the distance separating the O-1 from its shadowy image on the treetops. Both were intermingled with more birds than Mitch had ever seen.

A large vulture smashed into the metal brace in the center of the windshield, and J.D.'s eyes closed involuntarily. The windshield held, but J.D. felt the O-1 yaw. His eyes opened in time to see the wing strain against a dead, denuded bough, which had sliced into the wing inboard of the landing light. The bough shuddered, then snapped.

Mitch's excited voice came over the radio, "You okay down there?"

J.D. wasn't certain, but he was too busy to answer. The O-1 broke free and dipped toward the maze of trees beyond. J.D. kept the airplane flying even with a six-foot chunk of rotted wood embedded in the wing. Looking for signs the wing was about to fall off, he let the aircraft ease down nearer the next meadow. The sturdy little Cessna was holding together remarkably well. He checked for indications of engine damage and saw nothing out of the ordinary. His adrenaline rush began to subside. Other than the skid caused by the drag of the tree limb, the O-1 operated normally.

Ellison asked, "You see all those birds, sir?"

"You bet." Mitch was more interested in establishing contact with J.D. "Do you read me, Three-six?" Mitch's tone was more insistent, even though he could see the O-1.

"Loud and clear. Are you okay up there?"

"I'm doing fine." Mitch knew the question as an attention-diverting ploy J.D. often used to avoid answering.

Mitch looked closer. Something about the left wing seemed strange. He reached for his binoculars. By the time he was ready to look through them, J.D. had pulled in behind. Mitch twisted sideways but couldn't get a good look. Something had happened, but he didn't know what. "You get those birds on film, Sergeant Ellison?"

"Negative, sir. Used every shot I had over the target."

Good. Bringing home pictures of J.D. engulfed in a flock of birds at treetop level wasn't a good idea.

J.D. kept behind the higher O-1. He gingerly shook the control stick, trying to dislodge the wood. It didn't budge. He shimmied in his seat, pushing first on one rudder pedal, then the other. Still the debris clung to the wing. He considered a more violent attack with the ailerons and rudder but couldn't be sure hitting the tree hadn't weakened the joint where the wing was bolted to top of the cockpit.

He crossed his arms and stared at the wood, as if he could intimidate the branch into breaking free. In spite of his best effort, nothing happened. He lit up a cigarette. The problem had to be solved, he thought, before he taxied into the maintenance ramp. After a couple of moments, he decided a quick landing at the dirt strip downtown was the answer. Satisfied, J.D. luxuriated in the exhilaration of the last few minutes and wished he could relive the excitement. He could do without the limb in the wing, but he'd experienced nothing else in the world to compare with getting so close to the edge without going over. He raised a clenched fist toward the overhead windows. "Eat your heart out, Jimmy Dean—wherever you are!"

Trucks destroyed along the Ho Chi Minh Trail

Chapter 18

Flying across the Mekong, Mitch still couldn't see J.D. "You back there, Three-six?"

"Stickin' to you like cheap cologne, roomie."

Then fly where I can see you, roomie. Mitch said nothing, so Ellison wouldn't suspect anything was wrong.

"I'm going to shoot a landing or two at Downtown NKP."

"You're the biggest hero of the week, and you want to practice landings?" Mitch assumed an enthusiastic gathering would be waiting.

"You led the flight and directed the strike, ace. I was just the lowly scorekeeper."

"Right, Mister Humble."

"Take the spotlight. I'll slip in later to claim my little corner of the limelight."

Suspicion flooded over Mitch. "Keep an eye on your fuel."

"You can bank on it, roomie."

Instead of the control tower, Mitch selected the frequency for the radar that guided aircraft to NKP's runway. He requested a practice approach. The radar controller ordered a northwesterly heading that put Mitch a couple of miles closer to town than he would've flown in the visual traffic pattern.

He focused his binoculars on J.D.'s O-1 about to land on Nakhon Phanom's dirt strip. The aircraft looked normal touching down and rolling to a stop. Mitch nodded, convinced his suspicions were correct. Instead of practicing touch-and-gos, J.D. had stopped to fix something before returning the O-1 to the maintenance crews.

The radar controller guided Mitch's O-1 to the runway. When Mitch taxied from the de-arming area, he saw J.D. approaching from the east.

"Captain," Ellison said on intercom, "if you're ever gonna fly another mission like today, I'd be glad to take a wake-up call."

"But if it's gonna be one like February, you'd prefer I didn't call."

"No disrespect, sir, but for another flight like that, consider I've got an unlisted number."

Mitch raised his hand over his shoulder. "We make a hell of a team, Sergeant Ellison."

"Yes, sir." Ellison shook hands enthusiastically.

"Also, Sarge, we shouldn't volunteer how Captain Dalton found the trucks."

"About how he was flying so low, sir?"

"Roger, that. If he wants the credit, that's fine, but we'd better leave that to him."

"Understand, sir."

Mitch taxied around the hangars and discovered a large crowd. A couple of minutes later, Ellison was whisked away to the photo lab. Mitch stood within a sea of eager faces and described the burning truck park while he filled out the aircraft forms.

J.D.'s O-1 charged around from beyond the hangars, scattering people from the center of the taxiway. Shuddering to a stop in front of Mitch's aircraft, J.D. smiled at Mitch and popped a salute.

A sergeant shouted, "Wow!"

Similar exclamations rose in a disorganized chorus even before Mitch returned the salute. When he saw the shattered Plexiglas, he understood the commotion.

Swarming like a colony of olive-drab ants, airmen pushed J.D.'s O-1 into the parking spot facing Mitch.

Mitch saw a deep gouge in the wing. "Claim your little corner of the limelight," Mitch said to himself because no one else was nearby anymore. He tossed the forms into the seat and grabbed his gear. He had trouble getting closer than the centerline of the taxiway. Even from there, the damage was intriguing. Blood and feathers smeared the windshield and a wing strut. He edged closer and was studying the gouge when J.D. and his entourage crowded in front of the wing.

An airman with a southern accent said, "Somethin' big like a goose musta bashed this wing, sir."

"Well," J.D. said, sounding thoughtful, "there were an awful lot of birds."

Mitch caught Chief Underwood's eye. Grinning, the Chief looked skyward with an expression of disbelief. Mitch smiled. J.D. hadn't lied, but Mitch was sure neither J.D. nor Chief Underwood believed a bird strike had caused such a symmetrical gouge. Mitch was convinced J.D. had hit a tree in the midst of that *awful lot of birds.*

Someone pulled feathers from the gouge and offered them to J.D.

Mitch wondered if the stop downtown had been to put those feathers in place. He forced his way into the inner circle around J.D. "Hell of a job, partner."

J.D. raised a clenched fist. "We finally did it to 'em."

"You better be careful."

A flash of worry crossed J.D.'s eyes as if he feared what Mitch might blurt out. "We both have to be careful."

"I'm concerned about you." Mitch's grin broadened. "Any more exposure to the limelight, and you're risking a third-degree burn."

"Right." J.D. looked relieved. "Gentlemen, don't overlook Captain McCall. He's the Cricket who directed the strikes that blew all those trucks to smithereens."

A growling roar went up. Several hands patted Mitch's shoulders.

He blushed since he hadn't been trying to steal J.D.'s well-deserved plaudits. "It's a team effort, and Captain Dalton spotted the trucks. But," Mitch added, gesturing to those around him, "we couldn't have flown without two good airplanes. You all gave us these good birds, and the ammunition we blew up won't kill American soldiers."

A bigger roar engulfed the scene.

The smiles and looks of pride delighted Mitch.

J.D. took his M-16 and mission kit from a sergeant who was carrying them. "We need to debrief, and we'd better get goin' before Mister Lincoln, here, recites the Gettysburg Address."

Howls of laughter filled the air.

In the TUOC, Mitch was relieved the questions could be answered without revealing how J.D. found the trucks. By the time the briefing was over, reports indicated succeeding strikes had raised the toll of trucks above thirty-five.

The amazing results were the main topic of conversation in the Officers Club when Mitch and J.D. arrived. They were joined at lunch by at least a dozen other pilots. Afterward J.D. led the crowd into the bar and retold the story as more fliers drifted in.

About one-thirty, Captain Jansen brought a message. Lieutenant Colonel Morton wanted Mitch and J.D. at the squadron headquarters as soon as possible.

Mitch felt uneasy. "What do you suppose Colonel Morton wants?"

J.D. finished his beer. "Maybe he wants to pin a medal on us."

"Where do you suppose he's planning to pin it?"

"Not to worry."

"Maybe one of us better."

Once they reached the squadron, they were kept waiting. Mitch paced around the squadron's operations center while J.D. entertained the schedulers and radio operators with tales of burning trucks. After ten minutes, Mitch and J.D. were called into Colonel Black's office, the only room in the building with any privacy.

"Close the door," Morton said from behind Colonel Black's desk.

As J.D. took care of the door, Mitch noticed several eight-by-ten photographs on the desk. He also noticed Morton didn't say to sit or even to stand at ease.

Morton glanced from one to the other. "You gentlemen have anything to say about this morning's mission?"

Mitch deferred to J.D.

"Great, sir. If we had more like it, we might win this war sooner."

Morton looked at Mitch.

"I liked the feeling that we accomplished something, sir."

Morton nodded, his expression noncommittal. He swept his hand across the photos, spreading them toward Mitch and J.D. "You brought back some interesting pictures."

The tone triggered a sense of foreboding in Mitch. He stepped forward to see photographs Ellison had taken. Mangled trucks and churning smoke dominated most pictures. Mitch was so impressed, his worries subsided.

J.D. moved a couple of pictures to reveal those beneath.

As if Mitch had been told what to look for, his eyes were drawn to one object—the tiny outline of an O-1 above a jungle-covered ridge. He glanced up and found himself looking into Morton's cold, gray eyes.

"Some of your pictures are damned interesting, McCall. Who the hell do you suppose is flying that airplane in violation of Seventh Air Force regulations covering high-threat areas?"

"Actually, sir, the target wasn't in a high-threat area. We were—"

"I know damned well where you were!" Morton's eyes narrowed.

"Sir," J.D. said, "that's my aircraft."

"The same one that's grounded for a major structural check?"

J.D. shrugged. "Yes, sir."

Morton turned his angry eyes to Mitch. "I read your report, McCall. You didn't mention Dalton's gross violation of air discipline."

"No, sir."

"As mission commander, you're responsible for all pilots in your flight."

"Yes, sir."

"Then why'd you permit Captain Dalton to fly the way he did?"

"No excuse, sir."

Mitch's phrasing triggered anger he'd been suppressing. During his first day at the Air Force Academy, he'd been told there were four appropriate statements for a *doolie* to say to an upperclassman: Yes, sir; No, sir; No excuse, sir; and Sir, may I ask a question? He'd just given three of the four as if still a lowly doolie, instead of the captain who'd led the squadron's most successful mission of the year. He nearly blurted a more direct response.

J.D. spoke first. "Sir, I chose to go low on my own."

"You think I don't know that?" Morton's voice was filled with exasperation. He leaned back and crossed his arms. "We've never expected you to show a lot of air discipline, but I expected more out of Captain McCall as a flight leader."

Mitch was surprised at being the focus of Morton's criticism, and he didn't know how to respond. He hadn't experienced a chewing-out since his first year at the academy, and most of those had been part of the game. He stiffened—standing almost in a brace as when being berated by upperclassmen. He bit on his lower lip to trap insubordinate words struggling to get out.

Morton focused on J.D. "We assigned you two as roommates because we hoped McCall's spit-and-polish would rub off."

Jeez! Mitch tried to avoid an expression disrespectful of Morton's rank.

"Instead," Morton continued, "McCall's learning your bad habits."

There are worse pilots to learn from.

Morton turned to Mitch. "We'd hoped you might pick up some of Captain Dalton's aggressiveness, but we didn't expect you to stop using good judgment."

"Yes, sir."

"Do you know why Dalton's here?"

Because one of his best friends was killed over Hanoi. Mitch assumed Morton had his own answer. "No, sir."

"Because instructors in pilot training recommended he be assigned to cheap airplanes until he matured and learned air discipline." Morton grabbed a personnel folder from beneath other papers. Turning to J.D., he continued, "That's almost a direct quote from your training report, and it's damned obvious they were on target."

J.D. took a deep breath. "Yes, sir."

Mitch couldn't see J.D. but sensed the revelation had been a shock. Officers weren't allowed to review the official assessments written on them by senior officers, so Mitch assumed J.D. hadn't seen the report.

"And," Morton continued, "I heard about that haircut incident. You're damned lucky you don't have an Article Fifteen in here, too."

J.D. nodded.

Mitch wondered what had brought J.D. to the brink of an official reprimand. Mitch felt as bad for J.D. as he felt angry for himself. The mystery of why J.D. wasn't in fighters had been solved.

Mitch recognized a more ominous implication—the training report was part of J.D.'s promotion folder. Serious criticism in the training report could keep J.D. from being promoted to major. The best counter to such criticism would be an effectiveness report documenting bravery in combat. Mitch was afraid J.D. was going to lose there, too. "Sir, may I make a statement?"

Morton fixed a cold stare on him. "Go ahead, McCall."

"Sir, because of Captain Dalton's initiative this morning, he discovered a real truck—"

"Don't confuse initiative with irrationality, Captain."

"Sometimes, Colonel," J.D. said, seeming to recover his normal demeanor, "you have to be a little irrational if you're going to take the enemy by surprise."

"Don't give me that rubbish, Dalton."

J.D. shrugged. "It worked for the Japanese at Pearl Harbor."

"You know damned well that's not what we're talking about. Your obvious disregard for regulations resulted in a broken aircraft. You're a FAC at NKP because you were a problem in pilot training. When people become a problem to me, I become a problem to them." Morton grabbed up a page that had come from a teletype machine. "Group headquarters has tasked us to send two FACs to augment the Coveys of the 20th TASS. Guess who just volunteered?"

Mitch's stomach tightened. "How soon would we go to Vietnam, sir?"

"I expect to arrange transportation by day after tomorrow."

"I can't, sir." The words came out before Mitch could stop them. "I mean, sir, we're scheduled for CTO tomorrow, and—"

"Your CTO can be postponed."

"But, sir, my wife arrives in Bangkok tonight."

For the first time in the conversation, Morton was stopped. He raised a hand to his chin as if deep in thought. "She's coming over?"

"Just for this CTO, sir. All the way from Washington, D.C."

Morton looked at the tasking message. "Beginning tomorrow, huh?"

"Yes, sir. Captain Dalton and I are due back Saturday afternoon."

Morton exhaled what sounded like a sigh of exasperation. "I should be able to arrange transportation from Bangkok to Danang."

"Thank you, sir."

"Don't thank me. Your wife's why you're temporarily off the hook."

"Yes, sir."

Morton stacked up the photographs. "And tomorrow," he said, pausing to look into the eyes of each captain, "if either of you flies an inch lower than traffic-pattern altitude, except during takeoff and landing, I'll make you wish you'd defected to Hanoi! Have you got that?" Morton stared at J.D.

The silence stretched too long. Mitch said, "Yes, sir."

"Understood, sir," J.D. said.

Morton seemed satisfied. "Now get out of here before I get angry."

Mitch hurried through the door. J.D. followed out to the building's entryway at his James Dean pace. Before Mitch could exchange more than a glance with J.D., Major Reed Lawson bounded in from the porch, almost colliding with Mitch.

Smiling enthusiastically, Lawson said, "Way to blast them today, Mitch. You, too, J.D."

"The mission was a real kick-in-the-ass, sir," J.D. said.

If Mitch had felt like even smiling, he would've laughed at the double meaning.

"I talked to the commander after his pre-flight briefing," Lawson said. "He told me to write you two up for DFCs."

Mitch watched for J.D.'s reaction and saw none. He wondered if that was because the Distinguished Flying Cross didn't matter to J.D. or if J.D. assumed Morton would talk the commander out of the recommendations.

Lawson continued, "That's the best BDA we've had since last spring. Everybody all the way up to Seventh must be overjoyed with you."

"There's always that ten percent who never gets the word," J.D. said.

Mitch got closer to a laugh.

Lawson looked confused by J.D.'s choice of clichés. "Keep up the good work, tigers."

"Yes, sir," Mitch said.

J.D. responded with a low growl.

Once outside, Mitch and J.D. started up the street leading toward the quarters. After walking a block, J.D. broke the silence. "I appreciate—"

Mitch whirled, glared at J.D., and said in a nasal mimic, "What can they do to me? Make me a forward air controller, give me an O-1, and send me to Vietnam?"

J.D. shrugged. "Maybe Vietnam won't be so bad."

Mitch grunted and started walking again. "I'll wait and see if I have to live in a tent and drink water out of rice paddies. Then I'll decide whether I'm going to kill you."

"Fair enough. But you flew more top cover for me with Morton than I deserved. I appreciate your taking more than your share of the heat."

"If I'd lost my visit with Elizabeth, I'd have really been pissed." Mitch paused. "You do understand I won't ever lie for you."

"I'd never expect you to. If lying was your only choice, I'd have whipped out the catsup and eaten a little crow. Anyway, if you'd reported how low I was flying, Mighty Mort might not've included you in—"

"I know *when* you hit the tree."

J.D. looked surprised. "Tree?"

"We earned this all-expenses-paid trip to sunny Nam because Colonel Morton has a pretty good idea, too."

J.D. blinked a couple of times with an expression looking very unlike James Dean.

Mitch almost laughed. Seldom had he been one-up on J.D. It was a pleasant change. Mitch could almost picture little gears working in J.D.'s head, trying to formulate questions that wouldn't confirm suspicions.

J.D. said, "Well, I mean, what can the colonel be sure of? This is the first time you—"

"He knows if you'd hit a tree near Foxtrot, we'd have been squawking on Guard to get a Jolly Green escort home."

"Well, maybe *you* would've—"

"Damn straight! I would've, and he knows it."

J.D. nodded.

"Ran a tank dry, didn't you?"

J.D. smiled.

"A guy's got to have a damned death wish to buzz buffalo without making sure his fuel selector's on the tank with the gas."

"Is that what the book says about buzzing buffalo?"

Mitch stayed serious. "A death wish!"

J.D. laughed. "How can anybody have a friggin' death wish in a Bird Dog? Jimmy Dean drove his Porsche faster than I can fly straight down at full throttle. If I had a death wish, I wouldn't have chosen Bird Dogs."

"You didn't."

J.D. shrugged. "I came anyway."

"You're too smart for dumb mistakes like running a tank dry at fifteen or twenty feet."

"I haven't studied the books like you have, Mister Wizard. Some—"

"Bullshit! You're a natural with airplanes. More than I'll ever be again if I memorize every word in the manuals. But you fly as if getting back to an airfield is optional."

"The most alive you'll ever feel is when adrenaline's pumping your blood so hard you can hear it. You'd enjoy your flights a lot more if—"

"We're not talking about me and my problem. We're talking about you and yours. They took you off the night program because you scared the crap out of Kirkland."

"Kirkland's a pussy. Flying with Kirkland's like flying with somebody's grandmother."

"Maybe he thinks flying with you's like flying with someone with a death wish."

"Maybe."

Mitch wondered if he'd broken through J.D.'s shell. "Maybe you have a death wish?"

"That's not what I said. Maybe flying with me is—"

"Maybe you ought to talk things over with somebody."

"I am talking things over with somebody—*doc*."

"I'm sure as hell not taking that kind of responsibility for you."

J.D. grinned. "Mighty Mort'll be so disappointed. But where there's life, there's hope."

"Reforming you's beyond my special talents." Mitch kicked a piece of gravel down the road.

"I'm not talking about reforming me. I'm talking about getting you to break a few rules."

"Right! In the morning, we could buzz Colonel Morton's hooch in a two-ship formation."

J.D. cocked his head as if considering the possibility. "Let's wait until we return from Nam. In the near term, I'd settle for you breaking one or two little rules."

Mitch smiled. "Maybe we can get you to follow a rule or two."

"Don't hold out for miracles." J.D. paused. "I wasn't flying that high."

"What?"

"Fifteen or twenty feet. Only a pussy would buzz buffalo at fifteen or twenty feet."

Mitch wished he had some of J.D.'s courage—maybe even some of his recklessness. Looking ahead, he noticed a cluster of Thais and Americans. "Wonder what's going on."

J.D. glanced at the group. "Maybe it's a nominating committee to draft Dauntless Dalton for base commander."

"I doubt your infamy has spread this quickly."

The crowd stood three deep around a young Thai with a dead snake.

J.D. raised onto tiptoes so he could see. "What kind is it?"

"A krait, sir," an airman said.

"A banded krait," a staff sergeant said.

J.D. asked, "Poisonous?"

"A two-stepper," a captain said. "Let one sink those fangs in you, and you won't walk more than two steps."

J.D. nodded. "Sounds like my ex-wife, the fang part, anyway."

Everyone who understood English laughed.

Mitch asked, "Where'd he find it?"

The captain pointed over the hill toward the quarters. "By the amphitheater."

"Great!" Mitch frowned, thinking of the hours he'd spent writing letters or reading books in the park-like setting.

"It's that time of year," the captain said. "Monsoons force snakes to higher ground."

"Things are looking up." Responding to Mitch's questioning look, J.D. added, "We aren't going to be here to worry about sharing this garden spot with the snakes."

"Nice try, but that doesn't get you off the hook." Mitch started to walk away but paused when J.D. didn't follow. "Going to the mail room?"

"No more mail for me. I couldn't take another night like last night."

"Not tonight!" Mitch's eyes widened, knowing he and J.D. were scheduled on dawn patrol before going on CTO. "You're not leaving me holding the bag again in the morning. Not tomorrow, of all days."

"No sweatski. I need to buy some sippin' whiskey to take on vacation."

Mitch nodded and started up the road.

J.D. called after him, "In case we're getting exiled to one of those places where the bars don't serve anything but panther piss."

Mitch turned and gave the most wicked glare he could muster.

After dinner, Mitch and J.D. packed for the trip. They were interrupted several times by other FACs who stopped to offer congratulations for the morning's victory.

Mitch worried about implications of what he'd learned about J.D.'s promotion folder. Mitch felt guilty about his excitement over seeing Elizabeth while J.D. had to feel so low. Wanting to go to bed early, Mitch went to the shower as soon as he finished packing. When he returned, J.D. sat with a cigarette dangling from his lips and his feet propped up.

J.D. said, "Wonder if the airlines are hiring."

Mitch sensed that was as close as J.D. would get to admitting his Air Force career faced a dead end. Mitch dried his hair with a fresh towel. "I sometimes suspect Elizabeth would prefer I give up the Air Force and go with the airlines."

J.D. stared at the ceiling. "Can you imagine me saying, 'This is your captain speaking'?"

"Yeah," Mitch said with a grin. Mimicking J.D., he added, "On this takeoff, would you all like to fly over the bridge or under the bridge?"

J.D. smiled. "I suppose I'd have to clean up my act a little."

Mitch nodded. "I've been curious about that haircut thing Colonel Morton mentioned."

J.D. ran his fingers through his hair. "That was at pilot training. I was a captain given a piss-ant lieutenant for an instructor. Lieutenant Greer loved to act like God where his students were concerned."

"I bet you accepted that gracefully." Mitch remembered instructors treating student pilots as if the students weren't full-fledged officers. He'd been a second lieutenant, so he'd been outranked anyway. However, he'd noticed lieutenant instructors acting as if they outranked captain students, and Mitch had never bought that attitude.

J.D. grinned. "Greer thought I wore my hair a little long."

"You do."

"I know. Anyway, one day Greer told me to get a haircut, so I did."

Mitch paused, waiting for the rest of the story.

"I went and got a hair . . . cut."

Mitch laughed. "Are you saying you got one—"

"Yeah." J.D. nodded. "Greer wanted to have me court martialed."

"You might've been smarter to humor him a little more."

"I stopped letting anyone treat me like that when I was fifteen."

J.D.'s bitter tone convinced Mitch it was time to change the subject.

"Well, we've got four great days ahead. I don't know if I can sleep, but I'm gonna try." Yawning, he stepped between the wardrobe lockers.

"I can understand you might have a little trouble dropping off tonight," J.D. said with an understanding look on his face.

"See you in the morning." Mitch pushed through the curtain.

"Pleasant dreams, roomie." J.D. turned toward the desk before Mitch could see if the expression matched a note of glee in J.D.'s voice.

In the shadowed part of the room, Mitch tossed his towel on the foot of the bed. Yanking back the blanket and upper sheet, he saw something dark under the edge of the pillow. With curiosity, but no caution, he grabbed the pillow. In about half a heartbeat, Mitch realized the oval-shaped mass beneath was a coiled snake.

Mitch screamed. The pillow flew away and glanced off the ceiling. Recoiling backward faster than his feet could catch up, he slammed against his locker. It shuddered, threatened to tumble over, then rocked into place. He bounced off and staggered into the opening between the lockers. His flailing arms tangled in the curtains, yanking them and the rod down around him. Beneath the glaring light, he came to a stop and tried to recover from having expelled every ounce of air he'd had inside.

J.D. was roaring with laughter.

After making sure the snake wasn't moving, Mitch glanced at J.D., who was doubled over the arm of his chair. Mitch's eyes jittered between the snake and his roommate.

J.D. tried to speak but couldn't. Instead, he howled again with laughter and leaned back so far he almost tipped over his chair.

Mitch shook the curtains free and flung them at J.D. "You crazy sonuva bitch!"

"Best twenty baht I ever spent," J.D. said, indicating the snake had cost a dollar. He grabbed the curtains and dabbed at tears glistening on his cheeks. "I thought you were going to—" Convulsions of laughter overwhelmed him, and he beat a fist on the desk.

"Very funny." Mitch looked at the snake. Without the curtain in the way, light splayed out beyond the lockers and gave more definition to the scaly mass. He saw dark bands interspersed between lighter ones around the snake's body. He recognized the snake from earlier in the day. "Getting nicked by a fang can kill you."

J.D. forced himself to stop laughing. "We buried the head."

Mitch grabbed the curtains and pulled them to one end of the rod. Inching forward, he imagined J.D. scaring him. "Stay put, or I swear I'll wrap this rod around your neck."

J.D. crossed his arms over his heaving stomach. "I couldn't move if I had to."

Mitch crept closer and poked the snake a couple of times with the rod. Slipping the rod underneath, he lifted part of the snake, confirming the head was missing and revealing a small stain of blood on the white sheet. "You got blood all over my bed."

"Probably nothing compared to what you did to your shorts."

"Very funny." Mitch suppressed a laugh as J.D. pounded the desk.

In a few moments Mitch had the snake draped over the rod. He stepped into the front of the room and dropped the body into the trash can. He tossed the curtains to J.D. "You can replace the friggin' curtains."

Mitch grabbed extra towels and spread them over the bloodstain. After retrieving his pillow, he stretched out on his bed with his fingers interlaced behind his head.

J.D. dragged his chair to the lockers, stepped up, and lifted the curtains into place. "You know, there's good news and bad news about snakes in Vietnam."

"I don't want to hear this."

"The bad news is even though Vietnam's known as the Land of Dragons, one hundred and thirty-three varieties of snakes live there."

"One hundred and thirty-three?"

"The good news is *two* kinds aren't poisonous."

"Go away!"

After minor adjustments, J.D. poked his head through the curtains. "Pleasant dreams."

"Screw you, Jimmy D." Mitch tried to look stern.

J.D. laughed as he jumped from the chair and dragged it to the desk. "Maybe I should take up fortune telling. I had a hunch you wouldn't drop right off to sleep."

"I'd think you'd be the one who's going to suffer a little insomnia."

J.D. peeked through the curtains. "I don't read you."

Mitch smiled. "Somewhere, sometime, somehow, I'll get even."

J.D. shrugged. "To fight the good fight, you've got to be willing to accept some losses."

Mitch gazed at the ceiling and the shadowy patterns on the walls from light seeping through the fabric of the curtains. He was glad J.D. could find humor on the day when the door to an Air Force career had been slammed in his face. Mitch also was glad that, God-willing, he would spend the next night with Elizabeth.

Chapter 19

At 0540 the following morning, Mitch drove the pickup on the return trip from the personal-equipment building to the flight line. J.D. whistled merrily in the passenger seat. His cheerfulness made Mitch feel uneasy. J.D. had been grumpy an hour earlier when they'd walked to the TUOC. Now he sounded like the one about to see his wife.

Mitch parked and got out to retrieve his gear from the bed of the pickup. J.D. crushed his cigarette in the ashtray, then hopped out the other door. He continued whistling as he slung his M-16 over his shoulder and grabbed his gear.

Mitch continued to suppress his excitement. Yesterday's reprimand had rekindled fears a last-minute snag could keep Elizabeth beyond his reach. His concerns centered on this remaining flight over Laos and on the possibility of the C-130 breaking down en route to Bangkok. He realized J.D.'s seemingly unjustified glee could signal preparation for a new stunt.

Walking between the rows of parked O-1s, Mitch decided he'd feel better if J.D. had remained grumpy—at least until they were airborne on the C-130. "You're whistling a happier tune than I expected."

"Why not? It's a beautiful day to be a flying officer in the United States Air Force." J.D. whistled the opening bars to the "Air Force Song."

Mitch's suspicions increased. "This isn't an either-or thing. Colonel Morton left no doubt we're in this canoe together. If you stand up—"

"Not to worry. You ain't gonna get dumped overboard."

"Not an *inch* below minimums!"

"Don't use up your stomach lining worrying about me. Mighty Mort's done scared hell out of me, and I was fearless."

Mitch remained unconvinced as he reached his aircraft. "Remember, if you hit the ground out there, I'll never get the paperwork done before the plane leaves for Bangkok."

"Would I do such a thing to my favorite roommate?" J.D. grinned, clicked his heels together, and attempted a deep bow. The sling on his M-16 slipped off his shoulder. He barely caught the rifle before it hit the PSP. "Besides, you'll be watching me like a hawk, or should I say like a falcon, for the next three hours."

"You can take that to the bank, *roomie*."

Whistling a cheery rendition of "Air Force Blue," J.D. strutted to his aircraft.

After getting airborne, Mitch had a new distraction. At four thousand feet, his O-1 shuddered through a turbulent wind shear. A few hundred feet higher, the turbulence calmed to a mild shaking. He seemed to be passing landmarks twice as fast as usual, so the forecast of strong, west winds was accurate. Crossing the muddy waters of the Xe Bangfai, he checked the clock. Four minutes later, he flew over a karst ridge ten miles east.

"We're doing a hundred and fifty knots." Amazement showed in

Mitch's voice.

"Kind of takes your breath away."

"So it's not Mach one-point-five in a Voodoo," Mitch said, referring to the supersonic F-101s J.D. had flown before pilot training, "but this is the first time in six months I've cruised faster than the takeoff and landing speeds of a C-141."

"Woopee-do, flash. If I were you, I'd be thinking about getting home. That is, unless I wanted to go to Vietnam today."

"No way," Mitch fired back, uncertain why J.D. would suggest bypassing Bangkok.

"Bucking a sixty-knot headwind goin' home could be an all-day job."

Now Mitch understood. A sixty-knot wind was more critical in an O-1 at less than one hundred knots than in jets cruising at five hundred. Returning to NKP at thirty-knots would take three hours—the length of a normal mission. "If we turn around when we reach the Trail, we'll be sucking fumes before we get home."

"No sweatski. We just drop to the treetops and get back—"

"Negative on the buzzing!"

"Operational necessity. Even Mighty Mort would understand."

"No way," Mitch said, but realized J.D. had the solution. Winds were much lighter beneath the wind shear. Once the O-1s left the AAA behind, he could descend to three thousand feet for the flight home.

Mitch was mission commander and flying the low O-1. Nevertheless, over the Trail, he looked for his wingman almost as often as when he flew as high man, whose main duty was to watch the other FAC. J.D. was always at the proper altitude. After fifty minutes of checking empty roads, Mitch turned for NKP. The flight across Laos was routine after dropping beneath the strong winds.

Near the river, J.D. said, "I'm gonna call for a precision approach."

"Today?" There would be little time after landing to debrief, pick up bags, and catch the C-130. "We don't have much time to waste."

"I need to log one before the end of the month. Unless they assign us to Danang, we'll probably be at an airstrip without a radar."

"Fine time to think about that." A real *Catch 22* situation, Mitch thought. J.D. could be grounded in the combat zone for not flying enough practice instrument approaches in an aircraft not authorized to fly in bad weather. "I can't imagine them grounding you in Vietnam because you're non-current for precision approaches in an O-1."

"Agreed, but you know old conscientious me. I'm only a simple aviator trying to follow regulations like my roomie does."

J.D.'s self-righteous tone increased Mitch's suspicions. "If you were like your roomie, you'd complete your requirements early, not on the last day, as my roomie does."

"But remember, I just learned you're supposed to be my hero."

"Colonel Morton'll be so proud. You aren't going to play screw around and get him all over us again, are you?"

"I won't fly an inch lower than I'm supposed to—*promise*."

"If you're late, don't expect me to hold the plane."

"Roger that, but how about you taking the debriefing solo and picking up our bags? I'll turn in our weapons and meet you at the pax terminal."

Mitch hesitated. Both pilots were supposed to debrief, and the radar approach wouldn't take much longer than a regular landing pattern. Nevertheless, Mitch thought with a grin, if he returned to their room before the maids emptied the trash, the dead snake would be his. Picking up J.D.'s bags had more appeal.

J.D. continued, "Don't worry about me missing the debriefing."

"I'm worrying about trouble you get into when I can't keep an eye on you."

"Would I, *a Mitchell McCall act-alike*, do anything non-regulation?"

"You're scaring me, J.D."

"Not to worry. What can he *really* do to us? Give us O-1s, make us FACs, and send—"

"If he doesn't send me to Bangkok first, I'll take care of your death wish for you."

"It's working."

"What's working?"

"I'm starting to rub off on you."

"Don't count on it, roomie," Mitch said, although he realized his determination would match any J.D. had ever shown.

"Relax. I promise not to do *anything* Mighty Mort told me not to."

"That leaves a million ways you can screw up."

Click-click.

Shiiiit. Mitch knew J.D. was planning something. Mitch reminded himself he wasn't J.D.'s keeper regardless of what Morton had said.

After turning north into the traffic pattern, Mitch looked toward the Mekong. J.D. flew parallel two miles east. Mitch stared at the other O-1 as if he could transmit a mental message: *Just let me have these four days with Elizabeth, and I don't care how much trouble you get us into afterward.*

Nearing the runway, Mitch encountered crosswinds but nothing compared to the wind high above. When he taxied off the runway, he relaxed. He'd already chosen the assessment for his log book: *damned good crosswind landing.* He smiled with confidence. He *had* come a long way as a pilot since that day in Oklahoma.

While an airman replaced safeties in the rockets, Mitch looked beyond the runway. J.D. was on final approach. Moments later, Mitch noticed J.D.'s aircraft level-off about three hundred feet above the trees. Mitch took a deep breath and hoped J.D. wasn't about to bid a personalized farewell by buzzing the parking ramps or the TUOC.

Mitch watched the O-1 continue a normal climb over the runway. He decided J.D. was flying a routine missed approach as if low clouds had kept him from seeing the runway. *Stop worrying.*

After parking, Mitch filled out the forms and asked the crew chief to keep an eye on his weapons until J.D. picked them up. As Mitch gathered his maps, he heard shouts and whoops of laughter. The most common phrase being yelled was "Look at that!" He saw scores of men gazing skyward. Several pointed. Men rushed out of the hangars.

Hoping J.D. wasn't about to roar overhead, Mitch hurried from beneath the wing. He looked up and saw an O-1 headed west and flying so high, he barely could hear the engine. Mitch didn't understand the uproar. Then, "Jesus, J.D.," escaped his lips without any conscious effort.

The O-1 was flying backward.

Mitch stared a few more seconds to be sure.

J.D. had extended full flaps, slowing to about fifty knots while flying into the sixty-knot headwind.

"Captain McCall, is that Captain Dalton?"

The voice didn't have the Texas accent of Colonel Morton, but Mitch felt a chill as if someone had splashed a cold Singha down his back. Turning, he discovered Chief Underwood.

"I'll never tell, Chief," he answered through a dry throat as he started toward Underwood. Mitch was relieved he didn't have to face Morton while J.D. was stunt flying. "I wouldn't bet the farm it's Colonel Morton's bird."

"The colonel's been airborne about an hour."

Good. They had a couple of hours for their getaway before Morton would learn of J.D.'s goodbye.

"Since you seem to be missing a wingman—"

"At this point, Chief, my best defense is denying I ever knew Captain Dalton."

Underwood seemed surprised. "Shoot, Captain, after this little fly-by, he'll be the most popular Cricket on the flight line."

"Not with everyone." However, Mitch again noticed the shouting and laughter. He looked around. Every face he saw was smiling.

"Those of you wearing flight suits see the bombs dropped, Captain, and you get your adrenaline flowing when those little fuckers shoot at you. The only excitement my two-stripers get in a long, miserable year is when me or Wellington or Marcum's riding their asses over something." Underwood looked at the O-1, which now was overhead. "I couldn't have come up with a morale booster like that if I'd thought for a month of Sundays."

"Me, neither." Mitch chose not to add that even if he'd thought of the idea, he wouldn't have had the guts to perform the stunt. "Captain Dalton'll be pleased to know his exhibition was appreciated."

After leaving NKP, the C-130 stopped at the big air bases at Ubon and Takhli. Nearing Bangkok, Mitch convinced himself to quit worrying. No place was left where the aircraft could break down. He began to accept he was minutes from seeing Elizabeth.

Still, as he listened to the drone of the engines, he repeatedly shifted his position in the side-facing, red canvas seat. His hands alternately rolled up and unrolled an end of the seatbelt. Occasionally out of habit, he reached to take hold of the tip of his mustache, which he'd shaved off after the wild flight to Mukdahan.

Sharing the bench-style seat, J.D. was slumped with an arm entwined in canvas straps above his head. He appeared asleep, but an eye popped open. "It's hard to get any beauty sleep while someone does calisthenics on the bed."

"Sorry."

J.D. stretched like a cat trying to decide whether to rise from a nap. "Enjoy the anticipation."

"What?" Mitch didn't understand J.D.'s point.

"An old Navy chief taught me that once when I had a case of the fidgets like you've got."

"I don't have—" Realizing J.D. was on target, Mitch dropped the end of the seatbelt and crossed his arms.

"The old chief said most events don't turn out nearly as good as we imagine. Sometimes they're downright disappointing."

"This visit won't be disappointing. I guarantee you!"

J.D. gazed at Mitch a couple of moments. "I hope you're won't force us to view any gushy PDA."

Mitch smiled. He'd been restricted from public displays of affection since his days at the academy when cadets weren't permitted even to hold hands when walking with girlfriends. "I won't do anything you wouldn't."

J.D. rolled his eyes upward. "That might get us all arrested. At least, try not to gross out the Thais," he said, reflecting that the Thai people were as uncomfortable with public displays of affection as the American military establishment was.

Mitch kept smiling. At last, J.D. was envious. "I have a favor to ask."

J.D. brightened. "I'm always glad to advise a guy who hasn't seen his wife in months. If you've forgotten how—"

"I'm asking for a favor, not advice. I don't want Elizabeth worrying about our TDY to Vietnam, so I'm not going to mention that right away. I'd appreciate it if you don't either."

J.D. nodded. "I suppose that's the least I can do."

Minutes later, the C-130 landed at Don Muang airport a few miles north of Bangkok. The pilot needed seven more minutes to reach the military terminal on the east side of the airfield. When the whine of the engines subsided, Mitch was the first person standing.

J.D. slowly donned his sunglasses, stood, and bellowed, "Your attention, please! For your safety, please heed the following warning."

Everyone paused and looked at J.D.

Gesturing at Mitch, J.D. continued, "Captain McCall's wife is waiting in the terminal. Blunder into his way, and you may end up with boot tracks on your back."

Other passengers applauded and whistled.

Mitch blushed. "So much for maintaining a low profile."

"What are friends for?" J.D. beamed, nodding at the door. The other passengers were clearing a path so Mitch could be first off.

Mitch hurried across the ramp in the glare of the afternoon sun. By contrast, the inside of the terminal was drab, except for one radiant spot that drew his eyes immediately. Elizabeth and Mandy wore matching white suits, which seemed luminescent against the background of dusty walls, wooden benches, luggage, and fatigue-clad airmen. Kneeling by Mandy, Elizabeth encouraged the little girl to wave at her father. Instead Mandy turned away, hiding her face behind a well-worn Raggedy Ann doll.

Mitch rushed toward them. Elizabeth stood, then raced with high heels clicking. She threw her arms around his neck and kissed him before he could put down his bags. He dropped them and pulled her off the ground into an embrace, crushing her tailored jacket against the metal zippers on his flight suit. She swayed rhythmically as if to find a way to cuddle closer. Her fingers reached into his hair, knocking his flight cap to the floor.

Mitch closed his eyes, luxuriating in the fragrance of perfume and of orchids in her hair. He loved the taste of her lipstick and the warm vibrancy of her body pressed against his. He was so happy to have her in his arms again that nothing else mattered.

Seconds passed—maybe ten or twenty or thirty. He wasn't paying attention, but finally he noticed rowdy cheering. He opened an eye and peered through strands of her auburn hair. Other men in the room were applauding, shouting, and smiling.

Mitch blushed and loosened his grip. This was his most flagrant violation ever of the rules against PDA, but he didn't really care. Elizabeth held on, keeping her lips eagerly on his. He closed his eyes and relaxed a few more seconds, then became more insistent. Hating the part of him that couldn't forsake someone else's rules even in such a special moment, he finally moved his lips to her ear. "Let's save something for the hotel."

"I love you, Mitch." She caressed his cheek with her lips as she spoke.

"We have an audience."

"I've missed you so much."

"I love you, too."

Elizabeth opened her eyes, gazed lovingly at Mitch a moment, then seemed to notice the noise. She gave Mitch an embarrassed smile and buried her face against his neck.

"Loosen up, roomie."

Mitch tried to turn enough to see J.D. "Say again."

"Don't look so uncomfortable, straight arrow. A hundred guys here would trade places with you in a heartbeat."

Mitch glanced around. With Elizabeth hanging on, he turned enough to see J.D. kneeling with Mandy perched on his knee. She had a firm grip on her doll and on J.D.'s sunglasses. Mitch flinched, jolted by an urge to rescue the sunglasses until he realized J.D. had the situation under control.

Mitch whispered, "Don't I have a daughter to get reacquainted with?"

"Oh, I forgot!" She started to spin away.

Mitch didn't let her. Instead, they knelt together.

"Hello, little sweetie." Mitch extended both arms.

"Come see Daddy," Elizabeth said.

Mandy hesitated, then released the sunglasses and rushed with short steps into Mitch's embrace. "Daddy." She encircled his neck.

Mitch stood, hugging his daughter for the first time in months. Tears burned his eyes. He nuzzled Mandy's soft, blonde curls and turned away so J.D. wouldn't see any sign of tears.

Elizabeth pressed against Mitch, and he enjoyed a three-way hug.

J.D. stood with his arms crossed and shook his head as if he didn't believe the scene before him. "Colonel Morton was right about one of us being pretty loose about following rules."

Mitch looked sheepish. "Elizabeth doesn't quite understand the rules on PDA."

"I understand," she said with a flirtatious smile. "I just didn't feel like following them." She kissed Mitch on the cheek.

Mitch said, "You've probably guessed this is J.D."

"You make a beautiful addition to the City of Angels," J.D. said in his James Dean drawl.

Her eyes sparkled in response to J.D.'s flattery. "Nice to meet you at last. Mitch mentions you often."

"I deny most of it."

Mandy dropped her doll, and J.D. retrieved it. "Here you go, little princess."

"Say, 'Thank you, Captain Dalton'," Elizabeth said when Mandy took the doll.

Mandy echoed the words, much to J.D.'s delight.

"Little princess," J.D. said, holding out his arms, "come to Uncle J.D."

Mandy went right to J.D.

Elizabeth asked, "How many children do you have, Jimmy?"

J.D. smiled. "Shows that much?"

"Definitely."

"J.D. Junior's almost six. My princess, Monica, is four."

While waiting for the baggage to reach the terminal, Elizabeth talked to J.D. about his children. After a forklift brought the baggage pallet inside, Mitch and J.D. gathered their bags.

"Give me a moment to put this away," J.D. said, indicating a small bag he'd carried on the C-130. He knelt and yanked open the zipper on a side compartment of his B-4 bag.

Mitch watched.

J.D. crammed the smaller bag into the larger one. The sound of crumpled paper seemed to cause him to hesitate. He moved his hand, shrieked, and scrambled backward. His sunglasses flew off as he tumbled across the bags of a sergeant and ended up on the floor. With eyes wider than Mitch had ever seen, J.D. yelled, "A snake's in—".

J.D. stopped when his eyes met Mitch's.

Mitch roared with laughter.

"You dirty—" J.D.'s expression changed to a perturbed smile.

When Mitch stopped laughing, he said, "Maybe I should take up fortune telling. I had a premonition you wouldn't unload that bag in one try."

J.D. peered into his bag, then reached in. He lifted out the newspaper, which had about three feet of banded krait dangling from each side.

The crowd claiming bags cleared a wide path to a nearby trash can.

Elizabeth was aghast, clinging to Mitch's arm. "Did you do that?"

"You don't know the half of it." When J.D. returned, Mitch added, "That's one tiny installment of payback for the snake in my bed."

Elizabeth looked more aghast. "In your bed?"

Mitch nodded but continued addressing J.D. "And for the water you drenched me with during Songkran."

Elizabeth shook her head and smiled. "Are you boys just over here to play games?"

"Mostly," J.D. said, "but we fly a little every now and then."

Mitch picked up his bags. "You might as well share our cab, J.D."

"Wouldn't want to impose," J.D. said while nodding his endorsement of the idea.

"There's plenty of room, Jimmy," Elizabeth said.

If we get a big cab. Mitch knew the luggage would be the biggest problem with all their gear for Vietnam.

Outside they were greeted by a chorus of, "Taxi! Best price. Only one hundred baht."

Numerous taxicabs waited for passengers who'd arrived on the C-130. Mitch headed for the first large cab in a line behind a black limousine idling in a no-parking zone.

The limousine's chauffeur, a Thai in a batik shirt, opened the trunk and hurried to the approaching Americans. He reached for Mitch's bags.

Mitch started to sidestep.

Elizabeth gestured at the limousine. "Darling, this is ours."

A quiet groan escaped Mitch's lips. J.D. looked surprised.

She added, "The ambassador said I could use it while I'm here."

J.D.'s expression changed to astonishment.

If Mitch hadn't felt so uneasy, he would've enjoyed J.D.'s reaction. "I can't accept it."

Her smile of pride softened. The look in her eyes suggested disappointment that he wasn't delighted with her surprise.

Guilt swept over Mitch. The visit wasn't starting the way he wanted.

Elizabeth said, "The car was offered to me, not to you."

Mitch recognized her tone from times she'd been angry but didn't choose to argue. Her expression had become what he called her *Mona Lisa with feisty eyes* look. He'd teased her about the look being from her southern-belle training, which included never arguing with her husband in public. When she flashed that look, he knew he'd better tread lightly.

In a more conciliatory manner, she added, "You shouldn't have to worry about it."

J.D. interrupted. "What's the mission here? I feel like I'm arriving while everyone's walking out of the briefing room."

"Wouldn't be the first time," Mitch said, distracted by implications of accepting special treatment from the embassy.

"Answer me one question," J.D. said. "Why's the ambassador sending a limo for us?"

"You can bet your last baht it wasn't Colonel Morton's idea." More of a sigh escaped than Mitch intended. "The embassy's attentive to Elizabeth because her father's a United States Senator."

J.D. bent forward, looking over the rims of his sunglasses. His eyes were as wide as when he'd found the snake. "I've bunked with you five months, and you've kept that big a secret?"

Mitch mimicked J.D.'s normal response. "You never established a sufficient need-to-know."

"Fair enough." J.D. gave a nodding smirk, suggesting he deserved the answer. He handed his bags to the chauffeur. "You know what I always say? Never look a gift limousine in the headlights."

Elizabeth laughed, then held back awaiting Mitch's reaction.

Mitch smiled, knowing there was no use making a big issue of it. He set his bags beside the limo, then put his arm around her. "Shouldn't hurt to ride to the hotel in style."

"I'm so relieved." J.D. wiped imaginary sweat from his brow. "For a minute, I thought Captain Straight Arrow was going to force us to take a kamikaze taxi."

"Well, Mister Fearless," Mitch said, hugging Elizabeth closer, "better start gathering your courage, because we're going to release the car and driver when we get to the hotel."

Once in the back of the limousine, Elizabeth turned to J.D. "Jimmy, did anyone ever tell you what a remarkable resemblance you have to—"

"John Wayne? All the time. Confidentially," he said, leaning closer, "he's a little taller."

Elizabeth laughed.

"Except when J.D. wears his cowboy boots with the three-inch heels." Mitch felt an unexpected need to compete for her attention.

By the time the limousine reached the main highway, J.D. was letting Mandy teach him how to play patty cake. Mitch pulled Elizabeth onto his lap and enjoyed the closeness.

About halfway to the hotel, Elizabeth said, "On the way over, I had the most marvelous idea." She slid a hand along Mitch's cheek. "I've decided Mandy and I are staying in Bangkok. I'm sure there'll be complications." She talked faster as she always did when trying to convince him. "I called father from Hong Kong, and the people at the embassy will be helpful, and we can take time this week to find somewhere to live. Today we rode around for a while, but I wanted us to look for a house together. Of course, you might want us in a city nearer your base so we could be together even more."

"No cities are near my base." His voice betrayed more uneasiness than he wanted it to. A kaleidoscope of thoughts swirled through his mind. Seeing her every month had overwhelming appeal, in spite of strong arguments against her and Mandy living in Thailand.

"Bangkok would be fine," she said. "We'd have four glorious days together every month."

"And nights," J.D. said with a lecherous wiggle of his eyebrows.

Mitch shot a silencing glance toward J.D., then turned to Elizabeth. "What'd your father say?"

She smiled nervously and rubbed lipstick from Mitch's cheek. "He was very senatorial."

"Didn't take a position?"

"You know Daddy. He needs time to get used to some ideas."

Mitch was certain her parents objected. They'd been unhappy when his assignment to California had taken her across the continent. That move produced a not-so-subtle campaign promoting jobs available in Washington, D.C., as soon as Mitch "finished his Air Force thing."

He still planned a career in the Air Force, so he'd tactfully ignored the pointed comments. Elizabeth had never pressed him. Before marriage, she'd understood that even though she was a senator's daughter, career decisions would be made by Mitch.

He was sure her parents had been pleased when he'd volunteered for Vietnam. He was just as certain their pleasure hadn't come from patriotic fervor. A son-in-law in the war zone made good press for the senator, and their daughter and granddaughter had settled in an apartment in Georgetown. Mitch knew his mother-in-law didn't want that changed.

When Mitch didn't respond, Elizabeth said, "Aren't you excited? I'd hoped you'd be as excited as I am."

"I'd love to have you close." Mitch struggled to find words that wouldn't crush her enthusiasm. These next four days were too important. "It's such a surprise, I haven't had time to think about it."

"In case you never noticed," J.D. said, "Captain Conservative's kind of stodgy in adjusting to new ideas."

"I never think of Mitch as stodgy." Elizabeth snuggled closer.

Mitch flashed a we-don't-need-your-help look at J.D., then turned to Elizabeth. "We have to consider several things. Should we expose Mandy for that long to all the terrible diseases? And if you stayed, the bureaucracy might not give me credit for an unaccompanied combat tour. The Air Force might send me right back to Vietnam."

"That wouldn't be fair. Daddy could have something to say."

Mitch frowned at the mention of her father's influence. "I'd worry about the two of you alone here." Mitch avoided his main concern. If he got shot down, he wanted her within minutes of her parents and not alone in Bangkok when the news arrived.

"We could make friends through the embassy."

"But," J.D. said, "since we're on our way to—"

"J.D.!" Mitch wasn't ready to break the news about Vietnam.

"The, uh, hotel," J.D. said, almost without missing a beat, "I think Mandy and I'd better concentrate on our patty cake."

"Good idea, roomie."

Elizabeth's expression suggested she knew something was happening between Mitch and J.D., but she didn't press the point. Instead she shrugged and seemed to have difficulty choosing her words. "I hoped you wouldn't be so eager to find reasons for us to go home."

Mitch saw her Mona Lisa expression had returned. Disappointment had replaced the feisty fire in her eyes. He hugged her closer. She stiffened but rested her head on his shoulder. "I'm not trying to find reasons, sweetheart—but there are reasons."

An awkward silence followed, which J.D. finally broke. "I'm glad I finally got to meet you, Elizabeth. My big question's answered at last."

She lifted her head to see J.D. "I don't understand."

"I'm afraid to hear this," Mitch said.

"Thailand's full of beautiful women, but Captain Straight Arrow never takes the slightest notice."

"Really?" Elizabeth perked up.

"Roger that. I was beginning to worry about sharing a room with him, but now that I've seen you, I understand."

"Thank you, Jimmy." Looking flattered, she squeezed Mitch tighter. "You never mentioned your roommate was so charming."

"Charming isn't a word that rushes to mind." Mitch studied her a moment, trying to interpret her sudden change in mood. The change was as if— "You hadn't been worried that I—"

She kissed him, cutting off the question. When she pulled back, she was smiling. "Promise me you'll at least think about us staying."

He hugged her. "Of course I will." He would—but the answer still would be no.

Elizabeth sat with her head on his shoulder and watched J.D. keep Mandy entertained. Suddenly she exhaled a ladylike sigh. "Pauline Schofield was in Washington last week. We had lunch."

Mitch nodded. Pauline and Elizabeth had been close friends while Mitch and Philip Schofield were in pilot training. Mitch turned away feeling guilty about his role in Phil's F-105 assignment. He now had been missing in North Vietnam more than four months. "How's she doing?"

Elizabeth shrugged. "She doesn't know what to do. She feels very guilty."

"She has no reason to feel guilty."

"Philip begged her to live in Bangkok while he flew at Korat. She was afraid to come over here." Elizabeth's lower lip quivered.

"I know you aren't afraid, and I love you even more for being willing."

"Of course, Philip flew over North Vietnam where there were lots of antiaircraft guns."

J.D. looked questioningly at Mitch.

Mitch ignored J.D. "For the next four days, I don't want to think about war. I want us to be a family enjoying Bangkok. Mandy, how would you like to go see elephants and monkeys tomorrow?"

"Monkeys!" Mandy clapped her hands with delight. "Can we, Daddy, can we?" Pointing at J.D., she added, "And can he come, too?"

Mitch wasn't ready to commit. "If he wants to."

"Sure, little princess. Monkeys are a big part of my life." In an aside to Mitch, J.D. said, "At least the one's who put together the daily frag at Seventh."

Elizabeth gave Mitch a questioning glance.

Mitch smiled. "Don't waste time trying to comprehend anything he says. Anyway, there's a park called Timland, which stands for Thailand in Miniature. They have pretty flowers and monkeys and elephants—"

"And snakes," J.D. said poking Mandy lightly in the ribs.

Mandy giggled but wrinkled her nose. "I don't like snakes."

Elizabeth cringed with extra exaggeration. "I've seen enough snakes to satisfy me."

J.D. grinned at Mandy. "Your daddy gets excited about snakes."

Mitch ignored the comment and went on to describe Timland with its displays of Thai history and culture. They made tentative plans to meet for breakfast in the hotel's restaurant before leaving for Timland.

"Sounds fun." Elizabeth kissed Mitch's cheek. "What's important is we'll be together."

The driver took them to the Siam Intercontinental where Elizabeth had checked in the day before.

Once inside, J.D. said, "Don't suppose you're going out for dinner?"

Elizabeth hugged Mitch. "Whatever Mitch wants."

Mitch gave a little growl of satisfaction. He wondered if J.D. expected to share dinner and Elizabeth's attention.

J.D. continued, "Thought you might need a baby sitter."

"How sweet of you to offer, Jimmy," Elizabeth said.

"Somehow," Mitch said, "I'd assumed you'd be finding another baby to sit with tonight."

"Possibly." J.D. nodded, as if considering the idea. "Nevertheless, I wanted you to know that being a good roomie, I'd be happy to play with the baby while you play with the baby's mother."

Elizabeth blushed.

"If you haven't noticed, J.D. doesn't take long to get acquainted." Mitch turned to J.D. "I assume this place has room service. If so, I don't expect to see this lobby again until breakfast."

"Tough duty, roomie. If you two run out of things to talk about, give me a call."

Mitch took Mandy from J.D., put an arm around Elizabeth, and started for the elevator. "Don't bother waiting by the phone— ex-roomie."

Chapter 20

The next morning Mitch sipped coffee and watched Elizabeth help Mandy finish breakfast. Sitting among a constant buzz of solicitous waiters, he decided the hotel must rate at least two-and-a-half stars higher than where he usually stayed on CTO. The service reminded him of his honeymoon in Bermuda, a wedding gift from Elizabeth's parents. The Siam Intercontinental and the Bermuda hotel were more expensive than he could ever afford on an Air Force salary.

He sometimes brooded over causing Elizabeth to lower her standard of living by marrying him. She never complained, but he felt guilty whenever he couldn't pay for something she wanted—except this morning. Sitting across the table from her, he was too happy to feel guilt because her parents' money made the visit possible.

The war seemed worlds away even though he'd flown over Laos the previous morning. He wondered if he would feel this serene each month if he could flee to her love for four days and nights.

Mitch was absorbed in enjoying her presence, so he almost missed a bellboy paging someone whose name began with an M-sound and ended with an L-sound. The result hardly sounded like McCall, but the room number sounded like a match. He accepted a folded piece of hotel stationery. The note seemed English. However, loops, flourishes, and accents made words look like the Thai lettering on street signs Mitch found so undecipherable. Ignoring the extra splashes of ink, he read: "Tell Captain McCall, please, to call squadron without delay. With warmest regards, Colonel Morton." Mitch assumed Thai courtesy, and not Colonel Morton, was the source of the *please* and the *warmest regards*.

Mitch wondered if something had forced a general recall. A knot formed in his stomach, and he struggled to avoid showing his alarm. He refolded the note and tapped the edge against the table. He didn't know how to call an American base from a Bangkok hotel.

Elizabeth touched his arm. "Anything wrong, honey?"

"I don't know. I doubt it." He tried to sound unconcerned.

They'd planned to leave in a few minutes, so he was sorry he'd noticed the bellboy. Perhaps, Mitch thought, he wouldn't call right away. What if he hadn't gotten the message until returning late in the afternoon? Colonel Morton surely would find another solution without messing up Elizabeth's visit. Mitch smiled, realizing he was starting to think like J.D. He checked his wristwatch and looked around for his missing roommate, who was to have met them for breakfast. If J.D. had received a similar message, a recall was a real possibility.

As Mitch, Elizabeth, and Mandy left the restaurant, J.D. sauntered toward the entryway.

"Hey, little princess," J.D. called out. He knelt, and Mandy rushed into his arms.

"We see monkeys today," she exclaimed.

I hope so. Mitch wondered if their trip to Timland was in jeopardy.

"I know, princess," J.D. said, "and I'm *soooo* excited."

Mandy hopped onto J.D.'s knee. "And tigers and elephants and *snakes*." She wrinkled her nose when she said snakes.

Mitch asked, "You get a message from Colonel Morton?"

J.D. looked as if the question caught him off-guard. "You mean, besides the one on Monday?"

Mitch held up the note. "He wants me to call."

J.D. turned to Elizabeth. "I told Mitch not to fly backward across the airfield."

Tilting her head, she gazed through long eyelashes. "Fly backward?"

Mitch focused on J.D. "This isn't a joke. Let's see if you have a message at the desk."

The desk clerk had nothing for J.D., so Mitch was even more mystified. J.D. suggested they stop at a hotel that included the billeting office for Air Force personnel newly arrived in Bangkok. Mitch realized that hotel would have a telephone tie-in to the Air Force's worldwide AUTOVON system.

Nearly an hour later, Mitch was in a spare office at the Bel Aire Courts waiting for an operator to get a call through.

When Morton came on the line, his tone was abrupt. "Have you been complaining about being sent to Vietnam, McCall?"

"Sir?" Mitch was baffled. "I don't think I under—"

"A congressional!" Morton used the term for inquiries from senators or congressmen about a constituent's complaint. "We received a query last night about your location, and we've been trying to find you ever since. Did you file a complaint with your senator?"

"No, sir. I haven't said—"

"Then why would Senator Nelson give a damn about your status?"

"Because I'm married to his daughter, sir."

"You're what? Why the hell am I just finding that out?"

Because my wife's none of your business. Mitch sat on the edge of the desk and watched Elizabeth playing with Mandy in the next room. "I didn't realize her parentage was important to the Air Force, sir."

"It's the type of thing we like to know about our people, Mitchell." Morton's tone was conciliatory. "I mean, if the senator ever came for a visit to the theater, or anything like that. Headquarters tells us he's on the appropriations committee."

Mitch shook his head. He was bothered that a request from his father-in-law had caused a discussion between the headquarters of two combat units.

Morton continued, "Why do you suppose Senator Nelson was asking about your status?"

Has you squirming a little, Mitch thought with satisfaction after the session on Monday. "I'm sure his call has to do with his daughter's visit to Bangkok."

"Of course. That makes sense." The hostility disappeared from Morton's voice. "Everything going okay, Mitchell?"

"Couldn't be better, sir."

"I don't mean to sound like I'm prying. Perhaps we should reconsider this TDY thing. Maybe there's no need for you to go to Vietnam."

"Do you mean Captain Dalton and I, both, sir?"

"That's a negative! A C-Forty-seven will pick up Dalton Saturday. Maybe I was hasty tarring you with the same brush."

The more Morton said, the angrier Mitch felt. He hadn't been offered a choice Monday, and he didn't want one now just because his father-in-law was an important senator. That wasn't a good reason to stick another FAC with the assignment to Vietnam. Mitch had a greater concern. If he chose not to go, he could never be sure the decision wasn't because he was afraid to go. That feeling of being chicken would gnaw at him for a long time—as the day of bad landings in Oklahoma had dogged him mercilessly.

Staying at NKP would make it more difficult to convince Elizabeth she shouldn't remain in Thailand. He looked at her and thought how wonderful it would be to see her four days out of every four weeks. He turned away knowing if he faltered now in his resolve to do his duty, she might convince him to let her stay. "I wouldn't want anyone else going in my place, sir."

"That wouldn't be a problem, Mitchell."

"No, sir," he said with determination but concealing his anger. Few people besides his grandmother ever called him Mitchell. "I've come this far, and I'd prefer to go all the way."

"That's what you'll tell Senator Nelson?"

"That's not what he's asking, sir." Mitch assumed Elizabeth's sudden desire to stay in Thailand had panicked her parents. Undoubtedly, the senator wanted Mitch to help change her mind. "He doesn't even know about my TDY to Vietnam unless the Air Force told him."

"We didn't." Morton laughed nervously. "We only said we're trying to locate you."

"I'd imagine the senator knows where Elizabeth's staying."

"Well, Mitchell, we've been told to have you contact the embassy and pass a message telling where the senator can reach you."

Mitch pictured how J.D. would respond and decided not to miss the opportunity. "It's a shame I didn't have the message yesterday. I could've dropped by the embassy in the car the ambassador provid—"

"You had a car from the ambassador?"

"Yes, sir. A limousine, actually." Mitch smiled.

"Good Lord."

Mitch enjoyed Morton's discomfort for a few silent moments. "Do you have details on our ride on Saturday, sir?" He was more interested in those arrangements than in discussing his personal life.

"Right," Morton said.

Pulling out a pen and a small notebook, Mitch felt triumphant.

"Your show time is twelve-thirty. That'll give a few extra hours with your wife."

Good. Mitch wanted Elizabeth and Mandy on their way home before he left Bangkok. "Will we be flying to Danang, sir?"

"A C-Forty-seven will take you to a detachment of the Twentieth TASS that's with the Marines at Khe Sanh. And—hold on a moment, Mitchell."

Mitch wasn't sure how to spell the name of the base, so he wrote Kay Son in his notebook. The name seemed familiar. He recalled meeting two Covey FACs from there in February. They were flying their O-1s out of Thailand because the monsoon rains in Vietnam had run them out of their base. He felt uneasy. His main recollection of the two young pilots was how thrilled they were with the living conditions at NKP.

Waiting for Morton, Mitch saw recent copies of *Pacific Stars and Stripes* scattered on a nearby coffee table. He picked up a newspaper dated the previous Thursday and headed by thick letters saying: "N. Viet Hopes Die on Hill 881." A quarter of the page was covered by a picture of Marines charging up a hill beyond the body of a comrade. The story told of the end of North Vietnamese dreams of a second Dien Bien Phu. He read of hundreds of casualties in a week-long attack on a "mountain stronghold in the northwest corner of South Vietnam about seven miles from the Laotian border." Suddenly his eyes were drawn back to the opening line: KHE SANH, Vietnam (UPI). That name would sound similar to what Morton had said.

Morton returned and asked if there were any questions.

Mitch had only one—the spelling of his destination. His spirits plummeted when Morton's response matched the name in the newspaper. Mitch looked at his wife and daughter. For an instant he wanted to bargain, to exchange the dangerous assignment with someone else, to take the easy way out—for once—instead of doing what was right and honorable. He sighed, ashamed for even considering such a course. If someone else went to Khe Sanh and died in his place—as Phil Schofield had probably died in Mitch's F-105—Mitch knew guilt would haunt him the rest of his life. "Is that it, sir?"

"Is Dalton there with you?"

J.D. had gone to buy film at a small store that was part of the hotel's military complex. Mitch looked and saw only Elizabeth and Mandy. "I don't see him, sir. Is there something I can pass on?"

"I wanted to talk about that damned stunt yesterday, but forget it. Just concentrate on showing Senator Nelson's daughter a good time."

"That's what I'm planning to do, sir."

Mitch was tempted to ask how Morton proposed to punish J.D.— make him a forward air controller, give him an O-1, and send him to Vietnam? But, the question would be more insubordinate than he could get away with, even as a senator's son-in-law.

Mitch hung up, drew a line through Kay Son, then replaced his guess with the actual name. He scanned the rest of the story about the battle but was too troubled to concentrate. No one was around to ask if he could take the newspaper. *Last week's news to everyone else.* Nevertheless, he tossed a dime onto the coffee table and put the paper in his bag. He was proud he hadn't shirked his duty even when Morton had encouraged him to. Yet when he watched Mandy playing with her mother, he had a more unsettling thought. If he got killed in Vietnam, he really blew it!

Mitch called the embassy and reached the action officer who had arranged for the car. Mitch had to reassure the embassy man twice that the car still wasn't necessary. When it finally was settled that the senator's daughter remained pleased with the support she'd received, Mitch was able to dictate his message. He provided the hotel name and room number and an estimate of when he would return for the evening. Then he added the information he assumed would satisfy his in-laws: Elizabeth and Mandy would return to Washington on schedule.

Mitch joined his three companions. "All taken care of."

"Now can we go see the monkeys, Daddy?"

"When you're ready, sweetie."

Elizabeth picked up Mandy. "We'd better stop by the powder room."

J.D. looked up from putting film in his camera and smiled. "You give Mighty Mort my regards?"

"He inquired about your well-being and asked me to pass on a couple of messages."

"I can't wait."

"First, he recommends you fly behind that whirly thing instead of in front."

J.D. shrugged and looked a little guilty. "Second?"

Mitch told J.D. about plans for flying to Vietnam on Saturday.

"Riding over on a C-Forty seven suits me fine." J.D.'s expression was non-committal, but he reached to his buttocks. "Every time I ride a C-One thirty, my ass takes two days to stop vibrating."

Mitch smiled and waited for J.D. to ask where they were going. Instead, J.D. returned attention to his camera. Mitch was relieved to keep their destination secret. He didn't want J.D. blurting out anything that would worry Elizabeth. Mitch didn't intend to show the *Pacific Stars and Stripes* to J.D. until after Elizabeth was on her way home.

The excursion to Timland filled the day. Timland was an oriental fantasy land that indeed was Thailand in Miniature. The foursome viewed the gamut from raucous Thai kick-boxing through traditional Thai dances performed in delicate costumes. Artisans worked hand-made miracles with silver, brass, wood, and silk. The snake charmers with their cobras were J.D.'s favorite, while Mandy couldn't get enough of the monkeys.

While J.D. and Mandy were in line to buy ice cream, Elizabeth bought Mitch a wallet. J.D. and Mandy joined them as Mitch was transferring money and pictures to his gift.

J.D. took notice. "New wallet?"

Mitch held it out, showing it off. "A present from Elizabeth."

J.D. nodded, appearing hesitant to touch it. "Elephant skin?"

"Right."

J.D. cautiously took the wallet. "You have to be careful with some of these, you know."

Elizabeth frowned. "Do they carry diseases?"

"Oh, no." J.D. held the wallet by the edges as if examining a photographic negative. He slowly opened it revealing a smiling picture of Elizabeth. J.D. rubbed his fingertips lightly over the words, Genuine Elephant Leather, stamped in gold opposite the picture.

Elizabeth leaned close to study J.D.'s movements. "Is it something besides elephant leather?"

"Nice picture," he said with a leering smile. He closed the wallet, rubbed his hand lightly over both sides, and handed it to Mitch. "This one won't give you any problems."

Mitch accepted the wallet, now regarding it differently than moments earlier. "What kind of problems were you concerned with?"

"When I first got to Bangkok, I bought one like that. Unfortunately, mine was made out of the foreskin of a large elephant."

Mitch looked skeptical. "What?"

A hint of a blush crossed Elizabeth's cheeks.

J.D. looked serious. "Rub the wallet a certain way, and it expanded into a two-suiter. I sat on mine wrong in a taxi once, and the damned thing nearly pushed me into the street."

Elizabeth blushed. "It didn't!"

Mitch shook his head. "I'm afraid you'll remember J.D. a long time."

"No doubt," she said smiling.

"It's a curse," J.D. said, "but I try to bear the burden gracefully."

Throughout the day, Mandy became enamored with J.D. and was almost always riding on his shoulders, sitting on his lap, or leading him by the hand to the next attraction. Mitch watched with a combination of envy and guilt—envious his daughter wasn't pestering him more; guilty he wasn't taking more of the father's role. Still he was so thrilled to be near Elizabeth, he was happy to let J.D. play baby sitter, an activity that seemed to fill as much of a void in J.D.'s life as Elizabeth's presence did for Mitch.

Mitch delighted in Elizabeth's soft laughter. He was so enthralled with her nearness, he accepted her gentle, persistent lobbying to stay. Many times he responded by smiling and kissing her on the tip of her nose. When he had his arm around her, which was much of the afternoon, he found himself hoping she would convince him to let her stay.

Chapter 21

On the morning of their last full day, J.D. was waiting in the lobby when Mitch, Elizabeth, and Mandy arrived for the tour to the Grand Palace. The three newcomers wore shorts. Mandy ran ahead and jumped into J.D.'s arms. When Mitch and Elizabeth got close enough that no one else would hear, J.D. let out a quiet wolf whistle.

"Down, boy," Mitch said, proud of how sensual Elizabeth looked in a blue silk sunsuit purchased the previous day.

Her smile was noncommittal, as if she didn't want to appear too appreciative.

J.D. looked serious as he addressed Elizabeth. "Mitch's knees are a little knobby, but I couldn't keep from whistling at him."

"You've *definitely* been here too long," Elizabeth said.

Mitch shook his head. "My roomie has trouble giving real compliments."

J.D. seemed to ignore the comment. "There's good news and bad news."

Mitch asked, "Besides the knobby knees?"

"The good news is I'm being treated to a look at the most beautiful legs in Thailand, and I don't mean yours, roomie."

Elizabeth looked pleased and stood a little taller.

"The bad news is I can't keep watching them because guards won't let you in the Grand Palace dressed like that."

She asked, "We can't wear shorts?"

J.D. shook his head. "Some Thai customs are a pain, but in Mitch's case, I'm with 'em on the long-pants thing. How about if little princess and I catch the bus to the Grand Palace?"

Looking outside, Mitch saw people getting into a bus. "We can change and catch a cab."

J.D. frowned, nodding as if to lead Mitch's eyes to Elizabeth. "Use some imagination."

Mitch smiled.

Elizabeth asked coyly, "What are you suggesting, Jimmy?"

"Make believe you're the senator's daughter who meets this intrepid aviator for a little fling. Tomorrow doesn't matter. Find a hotel renting rooms by the hour and be naughty."

Mitch protested, "But we already have a room here."

J.D. groaned. "Loosening up Mister Romance takes a little doing. Lord knows I've failed miserably."

Elizabeth smiled. "Are you sure Mandy wouldn't be too much trouble?"

"No sweatski." J.D. gave Mandy a little hug. "After the Grand Palace, little princess and I can go to the park and watch the kite fighting."

Mandy asked, "Mommy, can I go with Uncle J.D.?"

"If you want to, precious."

Mitch glanced at his wristwatch.

"Take your time," J.D. said. "When we run out of things to do, you'll find us out in the back yard."

Mitch smiled at J.D.'s reference to the hotel's beautifully landscaped grounds. "Better hurry, J.D., or you'll miss the bus."

As Elizabeth gave J.D. a bag with things for Mandy, Mitch pushed aside thoughts about entering the last twenty-four hours of his CTO.

Mitch and Elizabeth wandered through the bazaars, looking at trinkets and sampling food. When their flirting and playfulness became direct enough to make nearby Thais uneasy, Mitch said, "Pretty lady, I think it's time to take our act behind closed doors."

She lowered her gaze, then looked seductively through long eyelashes. "I've been ready since Mandy and Jimmy got on the bus."

After a short taxi ride, they checked into a hotel and made love until they were exhausted. For a long time afterward, Mitch enjoyed holding Elizabeth asleep in his arms. Finally he fell asleep, too.

Sometime later, he awoke with a start. Her arms tightened around him. She was pressed against his bare back, and he rolled over to face her. She appeared pale in the light filtered by curtains. He enjoyed seeing her natural beauty unadorned by lipstick and makeup worn off during lovemaking.

Elizabeth stretched. She raised a slender arm toward the ceiling, and the sheet fell away. "Let me stay. I'll make every month as good as this."

Mitch wanted to say yes. "I don't know what Eve said to Adam when she handed him the apple, but she couldn't have been more tempting."

Elizabeth took a long look into his eyes as if his answer would be there instead of in his words. She reached for him, then hesitated. Looking self-conscious, she pulled the sheet to her shoulders. "I guess I'm not very good at the seduction routine."

Mitch laughed. "You've never been more wrong. You make me want to give in, and I wish I could." Mitch pulled her to him, and they snuggled for a few moments.

She let out a dejected sigh. "I thought staying for you made so much sense."

"I'd worry a lot more if you were here."

Elizabeth looked disappointed. "I don't want to make things worse."

"You need to understand me in terms of me, not in terms of you."

Elizabeth stared at the window and spoke softly. "If you want me to understand you on your terms, you have to let me closer."

Mitch felt guilty. "There are so many things I don't want you worrying about."

"My imagination goes wild, not knowing the dangers you face. That's worse than knowing."

"Not always." Mitch remembered how his fears became more vivid after the terrifying flight through Mu Gia.

"What if your instructors didn't explain dangers because they didn't want you to worry?"

"That's different," Mitch said, although he saw her point.

"That wouldn't make sense, and this doesn't either. I'm your wife. We're supposed to share." She pulled herself to him, pressing her breasts against his bare chest. "Share the wonderful and the not-so-wonderful."

He took a deep breath, uncertain how much to open up to her. "Nothing would make me happier than spending every day like this. The main reason I can't even consider your staying is I don't want you here if—if something happened."

"But nothing's going to happen."

He put both hands lightly on her cheeks and raised her face toward his. "Do you want to face the dangers or ignore them?"

"I wish we could keep ignoring them."

"I'll let you, if that's best."

"I can't stop worrying even if I try. These last five months proved that."

Mitch nodded. "The day I got drunk and wrote that letter was the day a FAC in my squadron was shot down."

Her eyes widened, and she sat up. "I didn't know anyone was— Did he die?"

"I think so." He shrugged. "That's what I told the rescue people, anyway."

"You were there."

"That day was the worst of my life." He paused. "Since I've been here, anyway."

She gazed lovingly at him. "So that's what your letter was talking about."

Mitch smiled sheepishly. "I was too drunk to remember what I wrote, and I've been too embarrassed to ask."

"I'm the one embarrassed."

Mitch noticed brighter color in her cheeks. "What did I say? I'm sorry that—"

"It wasn't your fault, darling." She cuddled closer. "Your handwriting and a couple of the words convinced me you'd been drinking."

"I was upset and didn't know what to do."

"Something terrible had happened, and you were disappointed I wasn't there to comfort you. When I read that, I felt I'd really failed you." She turned away.

"That's a negative!" Mitch grasped her shoulders. "You've never failed me."

Elizabeth resisted, but he turned her to face him. She kept her eyes down. "You were disappointed you couldn't melt in my arms until I helped you forget what had happened."

"I'm sorry if I sounded like I was blaming you for not being there. It's my fault we were apart." Mitch realized she deserved to know why he'd volunteered.

"I know." She raised her face toward him. Teardrops slipped through her eyelashes. Reaching to wipe her cheek, she laughed nervously. "I feel like such a fool."

"Don't be ridiculous." Mitch placed a hand tenderly on her cheek. "I hadn't even told you about the dangers. You—"

"That's not why I feel foolish." She pulled his hand to her lips and kissed each finger. "I thought you'd gotten drunk and been with some—some Thai girl."

"What?" Mitch's mouth remained open, his expression frozen.

"I'm so sorry." Tears flowed, and she tried to turn away.

"Hey, there." He enveloped her in his arms. She seldom cried. Nevertheless, her tears always caused him to melt, even when he was angry—but he'd never told her that either. "None of that. I've never even—"

"I know." She continued through intermittent sobs, "I was so afraid I'd lose you, and when I finished the letter, I decided I was coming to you, and then I decided I had to stay here for you. And when you didn't want me to stay, I thought you didn't want me here because—" She couldn't finish.

"Sweetheart, sweetheart, sweetheart." He rocked her gently. "That's not why I don't want you in Bangkok. I—"

"I know I was wrong." A sob mixed with a laugh. "That silly roommate of yours. He made me so happy when he said you didn't even look at these beautiful Thai women. I could've kissed him right there in the limo, but I was afraid you wouldn't like that."

"No," Mitch said with a teasing smile, "but I'm sure J.D. would've."

Mitch kissed tears from her cheeks and eyelashes. *How had things gotten so screwed up?* He felt a little hurt she could suspect him of being unfaithful. He'd been so focused on subduing his fears and surviving one day after another, he'd never considered going to someone else for the special comfort only a lover could give. How many other things had she misunderstood because he'd forced her to guess why he did what he did? After a few quiet moments, he asked, "Do you want the real briefing?"

She leaned back to look him in the eyes. "I need to know."

Mitch sensed she was radiating more strength than he'd ever given her credit for. "I can't talk about what we're doing and where we're doing it."

"Daddy guessed you're flying over the Kingdom of Laos although he couldn't imagine what you could accomplish in a Cessna."

"Like I said, I can't say." A senator's daughter might be able to mention Laos in a Bangkok hotel, but he couldn't. "I don't want you here if something happens."

"Nothing will. It just can't."

"It can. Sometimes fliers at my base don't return, and I don't want you anywhere close to that. Last month, two pilots had their wives at NKP for a few of days."

Elizabeth looked surprised. "I could see your base, I mean, if I were to have stayed?"

"No way. Those wives had lunch with several pilots in their husbands' squadron. That night, two men the wives met were shot down over North Vietnam."

Her eyes widened, and she seemed at a loss for how to respond. "But those two wives didn't break like China figurines, did they?"

"I don't know."

"I bet they appreciated having their husbands still alive even more. Maybe they were determined to become even better wives."

"I don't know, but I made up my mind the next morning I'd never expose you to that."

She wasn't deterred. "When you were in pilot training, we wives talked a lot about someone getting killed. And it happened three times that year."

Mitch marveled at how the wives talked more about their men dying in plane crashes than the men said. "Unfortunately, death happens more often at NKP with about a fourth as many fliers as at pilot training."

Elizabeth looked as if trying to avoid showing how much that bothered her.

Mitch tried to be lighter. "If J.D. were here, he'd say the good news is you don't have to worry about that for the next month."

Elizabeth looked suspicious. "Knowing Jimmy, I'd say he was about to compare it to something worse."

"Maybe not worse." Mitch was uncertain how to describe the assignment to Vietnam. "J.D. and I are on our way to Vietnam." Feeling Elizabeth tremble at the mention of the word, he added, "Thailand's due for lousy weather, so most of us at NKP are going over to help out for a month or so."

"Will that be more dangerous?"

"Probably not." Mitch acted casual. He didn't want to say flying in Vietnam probably was safer and thereby cause her to worry when he returned. "So I don't know when I'll be in Bangkok again."

"Where will you be? Where will I write?"

He thought about the copy of *Pacific Stars and Stripes* hidden in his bags. "I'll let you know once I get settled."

Mitch could tell her mood had changed, and she seemed preoccupied with new worries. He decided to go all the way to try to get her mind off Vietnam. "You want to hear a silly story about why I volunteered to come here?"

She gave him a strange look, seemingly torn between what they were talking about and curiosity about what he meant. "I know why you volunteered. This is your career." Giving him a knowing look, she added, "Even if mother doesn't understand you're staying in the Air Force forever. You're here because you believe in fighting if your country needs you to."

"True, but I have a difficult confession."

Her eyes seemed even more alive, and he was confident he'd gotten Vietnam off her mind. He was nearly overwhelmed by a surge of embarrassment and a twinge of doubt about what she would think of him. "For a long time, I've had a fear of flying, well, landings anyway. I came here to get over my fears."

Her mouth dropped open. "You can't be serious!" She looked very unlike the Mona Lisa. "I mean, you? This is what you've always wanted to do. You were such a natural at flying from when I first met you. I mean, if you really didn't want to, you could've just—" She stopped as if remembering she'd never seen Mitch *just quit* anything. Finally she seemed to understand the enormity of what he'd said. "Oh, darling!"

"I told you it's silly. I scared myself one day in Oklahoma and have had trouble getting over it."

"Oh, darling." She pulled his head onto her bare shoulder. She stroked his hair as she would a small child needing comfort. "What happened? Or can you tell me?"

Mitch was beginning to think he should've told her long ago. He slowly told her of the wild afternoon in Oklahoma.

When he finished, Elizabeth looked angry and supportive. "Well, Captain Walker shouldn't have done that to you."

Mitch sighed. "Afterward there were times if I could've quit, I probably would've."

"That wouldn't have mattered to me, if that was what you wanted."

"Quitting wasn't what I wanted. I couldn't've quit and still lived with myself, let alone be a good husband. I never want you ashamed of me."

"I never could be, but your flying's one area where I don't know how to help." She looked compassionate. Tears sparkled in her eyes. Forcing a smile, she said, "If you had arachnophobia, I'd step on spiders for you."

He laughed, pulling her to him. "I don't deserve you."

"I'm glad it's not spiders. Has it worked? Coming over here, I mean."

"I don't know. I—I guess it's working. I've concentrated so much on landings that the grading column in my log has a lot more *Okays* and *Goods* than *Ughs*."

"I wish you'd told me before."

"I might've told you long ago, but there was nothing you could do."

He kissed her and felt more in love with her than at any time he could remember. He also felt better for having told her of his fears. His concerns that she would reject him for being so flawed had disappeared.

Elizabeth leaned across the pillows and stretched sensually. She glanced at the filtered sunlight creeping higher on the wall opposite the window. "I don't know what the clock says, but it must be time to relieve the baby sitter."

"He's tough." Mitch straddled her and lowered his lips to her ear. He was determined to hold onto these private moments for as long as possible. Nuzzling into the soft waves of her hair, he smelled the lingering fragrance of perfume.

She tried to slip from beneath him.

Mitch made no move to let her leave the bed. "J.D. owes me at least another hour."

Elizabeth looked surprised. "You didn't pay him money to baby sit, did you?"

"No, but I've put up with him five months. Another hour with you isn't too much to ask."

After a quick cab ride to the Siam Intercontinental, Mitch and Elizabeth headed for the terrace. She said, "You and Mandy should go out and spend an hour or two together."

"All three of us can take a walk through the gardens."

"That isn't what I mean. Your daughter needs time alone with her father."

"I need time with you."

"We'll have more time together this evening," she said as they reached the terrace.

Palm trees cast long shadows. She quickly located Mandy splashing in a decorative pool. J.D. sat alongside with his feet in the water.

"I've been swimming," Mandy squealed as she leaped out.

Mitch swept her into his arms and felt water soak into his shirt. "I can tell, sweetie."

"I trust you two had a pleasant day," J.D. said in a businesslike tone.

Elizabeth kissed J.D. on the cheek. "Thank you."

J.D. looked pleasantly startled. "I'm a great baby sitter, but I'd have settled for ten baht and a couple of pineapples."

"That was for being so sweet, Jimmy."

"If I'd known I was that good," J.D. said with lecherous wiggling of his eyebrows, "I'd have offered Mitch a couple of pineapples, and we—"

Elizabeth nestled sensually against Mitch. "You're good, Jimmy, but not *that* good."

J.D. groaned and clutched his chest. "Mayday, Cricket. Nail Three-six has been shot down over the Siam Intercontinental."

Mitch smiled. "Underestimate the defense, hot shot, and you're bound to take hits."

In their room, Elizabeth changed Mandy into dry clothes. Minutes later, Mitch and Mandy were in the lobby after Elizabeth had shooed them from the room.

"Do you know what, little sweetie? Day after tomorrow is Mother's Day." When Mandy didn't respond, he added, "We need to buy a present for you to give to mommy."

Her face sparkled with excitement. "Can we buy mommy a monkey? Please, Daddy."

Mitch hugged Mandy closer, then lifted her onto his shoulders. "We'll see, sweetie, but maybe we'll find something mommy would like even better than a monkey."

On Saturday morning, Mitch, Elizabeth, and Mandy took a cab to the airport. After checking in the luggage, the trio shared a quiet breakfast. Mitch and Elizabeth toyed with their food, and Mandy ate more than either of them. Mitch had kept aside a shopping bag. Once they settled in the departure lounge after breakfast, he pulled out a festively wrapped box.

After fussing about the pretty wrappings, Elizabeth said, "You didn't need to get me anything else. The jewelry was more than enough."

Mandy started pulling on the ribbons. "Mommy, can I open?"

Mitch said, "It's for Mother's Day."

"Do I have to wait?"

Mitch smiled. "It's from your daughter, and she seems ready."

"Okay, precious." Elizabeth helped Mandy slip the ribbons over the corners. Mandy ripped off most of the paper, and Elizabeth removed the lid. Moving tissue, she revealed black silk and lace. She found delicate straps and raised some material from the box. "A negligee? And a matching peignoir?"

Mandy danced around.

Elizabeth said to Mandy, "This is beautiful. Did you pick it out?"

"Daddy did. I wanted the monkey."

Elizabeth's eyes widened.

Mitch smiled. "When we were shopping yesterday, a cute little monkey got Mandy's vote. I had trouble convincing her this was better."

"Mommy, can we take a monkey with us? Please, Mommy, please?"

Elizabeth explained that they couldn't take a monkey on the airplane. When Mandy seemed satisfied, Elizabeth turned to Mitch. "Good choice, though not what I expected for Mother's Day from a precocious, almost three-year-old."

Mitch shrugged innocently. "It was black lace or a black monkey." Becoming more serious, he added, "I wanted to give you something special to wear when I get home."

She slipped her hands under the intricate lace and looked at him with a playful smile. "You want me to wear this to the airport when I pick you up?"

"The part of my brain that's starting to think like J.D. is shouting a big *yes*. The rest says I don't want to share you in that with anyone."

She kissed him. "I'll never wear this for anyone else."

He pulled her into an embrace. "When the months get long, and you wonder if I'm ever coming home, this is your reminder I *will* be back." His voice cracked on the last few words. He was angry for being unable to remain stoic.

He felt her nod against his cheek. Her arm around his shoulder pulled him closer.

A loudspeaker announced the boarding call for her flight.

Elizabeth pulled back and took a quick look to ensure Mandy hadn't wandered off. Turning to Mitch, she said, "I'm counting on you to keep your word, Captain."

While Elizabeth packed the present, Mitch gathered Mandy into his arms for a few private moments. Silently the three of them inched toward the departure gate.

As they neared the ticket agent who was checking boarding passes, Elizabeth pulled five envelopes from her purse. Each was from the hotel, was sealed, and had an imprint of lipstick across the flap.

She held the envelopes against her. "Yesterday while you were teaching your daughter how to shop for lingerie, I was writing letters."

"Five?" Mitch smiled, now understanding why she had hustled him from their room.

"It's going to be a while before I know where to write. I didn't want you without mail all that time. They're numbered, and if you promise to open a letter every other day, these will last a week and a half."

Mitch reached to accept them, but Elizabeth didn't offer the letters. "Promise?"

"Promise." After he had them in his hands, he added, "Of course, I didn't promise I won't open number one today."

"You're impossible!"

"And you're a real sweetheart." He pulled her close for a long kiss. She lingered in his arms with her head on his shoulder. Moving his lips against her ear, he whispered, "I love you, Elizabeth."

"And I'll always love you, Mitch."

Mitch swooped Mandy up for a final hug and kiss, then put her down, and she took her mother's hand. Mitch breathed deeply. He blinked at tears burning the edges of his eyes as he watched Elizabeth and Mandy walk beyond the ticket agent. At the doorway, Elizabeth lifted Mandy and helped her wave at her father.

Smiling bravely, Mitch waved.

Elizabeth's Mona Lisa look seemed to have moist eyes. She turned and disappeared with Mandy in the flow of passengers.

Mitch slipped the letters into a pocket, then went to huge windows overlooking the parking ramp. Feeling sadness ripping through him, he wished she'd talked him into letting her stay. He didn't move until the aircraft was pushed from the gate and taxied away.

On the ride to the hotel, he was hardly aware of anything beyond his thoughts of Elizabeth. The driver stopped and turned to collect. Mitch was surprised to discover a doorman from the hotel opening the door of the cab.

Mitch checked the time and concluded he and J.D. needed to leave for the airport in about thirty minutes. Mitch knocked on J.D.'s door and didn't get an immediate answer. He banged again and called loudly, "Are you awake in there, J.D.?"

"Come on in, roomie."

Mitch turned the handle and was surprised to find the door unlocked. He pushed through. "We've got about thir—" Mitch saw J.D. lying nude on the bed with the most beautiful young Eurasian woman Mitch had ever seen. Without breaking stride, he did an about face and headed out the door. "Pardon me."

"Wait," J.D. shouted. "I don't have anything you haven't seen, and she doesn't either."

"That's okay." Mitch stepped out.

"Come back. Give me the skinny on our schedule."

"We've got about thirty min—"

"It's hard to hear you. Get your ass in here."

"Not until you're decent." Mitch chuckled at his ridiculous phrasing.

"If you want to wait that long, we may miss the rest of the war."

Mitch pushed the door open and walked in. J.D. had pulled a sheet across covering himself and the woman from the waist down.

J.D. asked, "Any changes to the schedule?"

"Negative."

"Damn. I was hoping the airplane was broke, and Mighty Mort was ordering us to hold in position another forty-eight hours." He slipped his arm around his companion's shoulders and toyed with her hair.

She smiled, appearing much less concerned about Mitch's presence than Mitch was.

Mitch tried to maintain eye contact with J.D. but glanced occasionally at the woman. Her shiny black hair hung across her shoulders and partially concealed her bare breasts. Mitch felt he was somehow being disloyal to Elizabeth by even being in the room. "I'm catching a cab in thirty minutes. You better make the twelve-thirty show time at the pax terminal if you know what's good for you."

Wiggling his eyebrows, J.D. nodded at the woman. "I know what's good for me."

Mitch turned for the door. "Be there!"

"Don't rush off from the hotel. I'll be downstairs in thirty minutes."

Hurrying to his room, Mitch felt his last few special minutes with Elizabeth had been tainted by the encounter in J.D.'s room. He changed into his flight suit and finished packing. When his irritation subsided, he smiled: J.D. was only being J.D.

The perfume on Elizabeth's five envelopes evoked thoughts more pleasant. Mitch slipped the letters into a pocket on the thigh of his flight suit.

Twenty minutes later, Mitch sat in a big easy chair in the lobby. He was about to leave when J.D. emerged from the elevator. Mitch carried his bags near the door while J.D. checked out.

As J.D. pushed money into his wallet, he seemed to notice the silence. He put his wallet away, put his flight cap on, and grinned. "Seems to me, mom, if a man's about to go over to the big war and maybe get killed, he shouldn't have been flying solo on his last significant sexual experience."

"This isn't my day to take confession, my son."

J.D. leaned over to pick up his bags. "As Mighty Mort would say, go to Vietnam and sin no more." He stood, then tilted his head and sniffed like a deer checking a new scent. He leaned closer to Mitch and sniffed. "You wearing new perfume?"

Mitch patted his pocket. "Thanks to Elizabeth, I'm playing mailman."

"Perhaps you're related to the young lady in my room." In response to Mitch's questioning look, J.D. added in his drawl, "She came special delivery."

Mitch offered an obligatory smile and headed out the door. Inside he wasn't smiling. A deep sense of melancholy flooded his entire being. A long time likely would pass before he experienced anything as special as those last four days and nights with Elizabeth.

Chapter 22

Mid-afternoon over South Vietnam was dark as twilight.

Mitch listened to the C-47's droning engines and looked impatiently out a window at ghostly images of the wing and an engine. Dirty gray clouds swallowed everything else.

He glanced at his wristwatch. The pilot had lowered the wheels a few minutes earlier. Mitch's experience on jet transports told him the airplane should be below the overcast already and the airfield should be in sight. He looked toward the forward bulkhead where a young loadmaster wore a headset and monitored the intercom. Obviously unconcerned, the airman was absorbed in a copy of *Stars and Stripes*.

Across the cabin, J.D. appeared to doze. His hands were shoved into pockets of his flight jacket. Shifting restlessly in the side-facing seats, J.D. opened an eye and yelled above the noise of the engines, "You haven't taken to worrying about other people's landings, have you?"

"I'm not sure anyone can land in this weather. Maybe we'll have to return to Thailand."

J.D. closed his eye. "Another day, another two dollars and a dime."

Moments later, the C-47 slipped below the overcast. Mitch studied the darkened world beneath clouds four-miles thick. Lush vegetation covered a nearby mountain that formed a steep wall of a deep canyon. He saw a river on the canyon's floor a thousand feet below.

Mitch felt better knowing the clouds were that far above the ground. He wondered why the pilot had extended the landing gear so early. The wing edged forward, revealing the prettiest waterfall he'd ever seen. He searched for roads, villages, or even rice fields but saw no evidence of civilization.

"They're taking us into the boonies," Mitch said. "I don't—" Panic jolted him. The ground rushed up as if the C-47 were charging headlong at the canyon's other wall. Mitch was convinced they were going to crash.

Suddenly, the hill leveled off fewer than fifty feet beneath the aircraft. In quick succession, Mitch saw green foliage, concertina wire, reddish-brown mud with sand-bagged fox holes, and a mud-caked, metal runway.

The C-47 landed with a noisy thud and slowed, throwing both FACs against their seatbelts. The flight mechanic unstrapped. Making his way to the tail, he trailed a long cord linking his headset to the intercom. Passing Mitch and J.D., the airman said, "The major wants you offloaded ASAP. He's not shutting down." Apparently prodded by voices in his headset, the airman hurried on as if expecting the FACs to follow immediately.

"*Offloaded*," Mitch said to J.D., "is a term for cargo, not passengers."

"Probably the major's term," J.D. said, unbuckling his seatbelt.

Mitch didn't hurry to comply. Instead he kept his seatbelt buckled, according to the safety training he'd received. The aircraft swerved right. The airman staggered against luggage strapped down near the door.

J.D. picked up a bag carrying his beer and liquor, then followed, taking care not to bump his bottles. Mitch waited until the aircraft shuddered to a stop. Then he moved down the sloping floor toward the tail.

The airman opened the door. He didn't bother to put steps in place. Instead he turned to unbuckle the straps holding the luggage. Mitch and J.D. jumped down, and the airman tossed out the bags.

When everything was unloaded, the airman knelt in the doorway and shouted over the noise of the idling engines. "Sirs, the control tower says to tell you to look both ways before crossing the runway. The major says to stand clear and be sure you don't get in our way."

Mitch was confused, unsure what he'd heard was what was said. J.D. nodded vigorously and swung his arm forward as if to chase away the airplane. The airman spoke into his microphone, and the engines' roar increased. The C-47 edged forward, blasting a swirling mist of reddish-brown water from puddles in the holes in the steel planking.

Turning from the momentary storm, Mitch shouted, "Did he say—"

J.D. lunged at Mitch, knocking him to the muddy parking ramp. The big, horizontal stabilizer swung around, slicing through cool air and passing inches above.

"No Purple Heart for being run over by a Gooney Bird," J.D. said." Before Mitch could respond, the tailwheel snagged a B-4 bag and dragged it across the ramp. J.D. scrambled to his feet and chased the C-47. "Stop, you fainthearted sonuva bitch!" The bag broke clear. The C-47 rumbled toward the runway, leaving behind an angry J.D.'s obscene gesture.

"Welcome to Vietnam," Mitch said, as the roar faded.

J.D. whirled around. "Screw you, roomie." His scowl became a grin.

Mitch wiped mud from his hands. "He's in a hell of a hurry. Wonder what he knows that we don't know."

"He's damned lucky he didn't run over my goodie bag. If he'd busted those bottles, I'd shoot him down myself."

"Might be better if he'd spilled your booze. Survival around here might depend on staying very sober."

J.D. scrutinized the surroundings. "Looks to me like survival here could depend on staying very drunk."

With FAC-trained eyes, Mitch surveyed his new home. The base reminded him of backgrounds in clips where newsmen wore fatigues and reported on Marines in the field. One word came to mind. "Dreary."

The ramp was coated with red mud and was empty enough to make him worry about being an easy target for snipers. A half dozen troop-carrying helicopters, painted in dull camouflage, were parked in the distance. Much nearer, toward the opposite end of the runway, a single O-1 sat a few yards from an earthen work dike at the edge of the metal planks. The O-1's engine cowling was open, but Mitch didn't see anyone working on the airplane.

Most of the base was on the other side of the runway. Beneath the solid ceiling of sullen clouds, he saw a few men interspersed between bunkers, tents, shacks, and piles of supplies. No one scurried from one spot of cover to another, so Mitch tuned his imagination a notch lower.

He saw jungle-covered hills, some nearby, others more distant. Clouds hid the tops of hills rising more than five hundred feet above the runway.

J.D. placed the errant B-4 bag with the others, then turned a complete circle. "Remember when I said you shouldn't worry about landings because no one'd be shooting at you?"

"I sure do."

"We may need to talk that through one more time."

"I was afraid you were going to say that." Mitch noticed a mechanic now working on the O-1. "Wonder where he came from?"

"I don't know, but maybe he can point us to our tent."

Mitch groaned.

The mechanic explained the Air Force detachment operated out of two bunkers on the other side of the runway.

As the airman gave directions, Mitch wondered where the rest of the O-1s were. He assumed the unit had more than one, and the weather seemed too bad for flying. At least he hoped it wasn't routine flying weather. "Where do the O-1s park?"

The airman pointed at the dirt wall. "The rest are there, sir."

J.D. looked at the wall rising three feet above the ramp. "They musta shrunk in all the rain."

Mitch noticed the top of a whip antenna beyond the wall. He walked over and saw a long pit gouged from the earth. Walls of red and white barrels divided the pit into six sections. The first section of below-ground parking held an O-1 sitting on a square of metal planks. Mitch saw antennas of others beyond three of the next four walls. He assumed the barrels were filled with dirt to minimize damage from rocket and mortar attacks. The wall closest to the runway was a sloped ramp with a PSP path leading up to ground level.

J.D. said, "That'll be fun if they push us into parking like at NKP."

Mitch imagined sliding down the ramp backward in an O-1. Unwilling to joke about the new predicament, he gave J.D. a perturbed look. "Somehow I don't think we'll do anything here like we did at NKP."

The C-47 rumbled by on takeoff and eased up into the low clouds.

After gathering their bags, Mitch and J.D. crossed the runway and discovered more people. Most were Marines in fatigues. Here and there, Vietnamese workers were dressed in civilian clothes. Mitch eyed them suspiciously. "How do we tell the VC from the good Vietnamese?"

"If a guy kills you, he probably was a VC."

"Can't you ever be serious?"

"If I took this place serious, I'd get as goosey as you are."

The red mud reminded Mitch of NKP, but Khe Sanh had a different feel. A sickening odor, a little like burning chicken feathers, was part of the strangeness. He wondered if the smell was a residual stench of the battle discussed in *Stars and Stripes*. The thought nauseated him.

J.D. stopped a Marine at the next corner to ask directions.

While waiting, Mitch discovered the source of the odor. The Vietnamese were burning something pungent in cutoff barrels. He couldn't imagine what they'd be cooking that would cause so much smoke.

"Over there, sir." The Marine pointed at bunkers half a block away.

Walking through the smoke, Mitch held his breath. That didn't help. Finally he exhaled. "I miss NKP more with every breath."

"Roger that."

Two large concrete squares were half buried. The first bunker had several antennas. Dirt sloped up to the tar-paper-covered concrete roof with sandbags scattered over the top. The bunkers were the only solid structures in a neighborhood of tents, slit trenches, and shanties constructed from packing crates, sheet metal, tin, and whatever else Marines could scrounge.

J.D. paused at the first bunker. "I remember why I chose to be a pilot instead of a ground-pounder."

"Roger that."

J.D. started down the steps. "Guess we rate the penthouse."

"Penthouses aren't in the basement." Mitch followed.

The bunker was divided into several rooms with a cluttered hallway connecting them. Mitch was reminded of a basement that had accumulated a lifetime's worth of boxes and junk.

The ops center was crammed into a small room. Most space was taken by a table and desk littered with papers, maps, coffee cups, C-ration cans, a beat-up typewriter, and a conglomeration of radios that looked older than Mitch.

Staff Sergeant Espinosa sat on a tattered chair. When the newcomers stopped in the doorway, he looked up. "Can I help you, sir?"

"I believe your commander's expecting us," Mitch said. "We're from the Twenty-third TASS."

Espinosa shrugged. "I don't know about it, sir, and the commander's gone. Lieutenant Colonel Hale's our operations officer. He's due shortly to work tomorrow's schedule."

J.D. dropped his bags in the hall. "My dance card's empty." Responding to Espinosa's confused look, J.D. said, "We'll wait."

"Lucky you got in this afternoon," Espinosa said. "Weather's supposed to turn real dogshit."

Mitch said to J.D., "*Lucky* would be stuck in Bangkok."

J.D. put a cigarette between his lips. It bounced up and down as he spoke. "It was great beach weather out there when we landed, Sarge."

"Really?" Espinosa looked surprised. "When I was out several hours ago, it was—"

"Great beach weather—if you live in Maine." J.D. lit his cigarette.

Mitch smiled but Espinosa didn't seem to get the point. "Or Alaska."

"Oh, right." Espinosa turned to answer a radio call from a crew chief.

J.D. moved into the hallway. "Guess he ain't been to Maine."

Mitch joined him. "You been there?"

"Nah." J.D. sat against a wall. "But I saw a picture once."

Mitch piled up his bags, then sat beside them. "Hurry up and wait."

J.D. nodded and blew a series of smoke rings. He pulled three bullets from his pocket and began juggling them.

A few minutes later, Lieutenant Colonel Hale bounded down the steps. In spite of the cool weather, his sleeves were rolled up, revealing tanned forearms that matched his face. He looked questioningly at Mitch and J.D. Both rose and stood at attention.

Perhaps a dozen years older, Hale had a fatherly look. Mitch was encouraged by the tan, hoping it meant sunny weather was the norm.

"We're the two FACs sent over from NKP, Colonel," J.D. said.

Hale extended his hand. "NKP?"

"Thailand, sir," Mitch said. "We're TDY from the Twenty-Third."

"The boss didn't tell me you were coming."

Mitch frowned, wondering why he'd been rushed to Vietnam. "Colonel Morton said you wanted us here last Tuesday."

Hale ran his fingers through thinning black hair. "Tuesday, huh? The Marines had things pretty well mopped up by then."

"We weren't given specifics of why we were needed," Mitch said.

"We've only got a handful of FACs," Hale said. "Most fly two or three missions a day when weather lets us. Some could use a breather."

"We're eager to get into action," J.D. said.

Speak for yourself, John. Mitch wanted a sunny day to test Khe Sanh's skies.

Hale appeared pleased at J.D.'s enthusiasm. "Colonel Anderson's due from Elephant in an hour or so. He'll decide how to work you into the flying schedule. While you're waiting, I'll have Captain Lynch fix you up with a place to sleep next door."

Mitch wondered where Elephant was but didn't ask. He expected to have lots of time to learn more than he wanted to know about Khe Sanh.

Minutes later, Captain Lynch greeted Mitch and J.D., then led them outside onto the a walkway connecting the bunkers. The sidewalk was wooden pallets that had been shipping platforms for ammunition.

In front of the bunker, the walkway split. A branch leading to the entrance passed between rusty fins of old bombs, which stood like miniature columns. The second branch led to a strange wooden structure, which supported four red barrels above the edge of the bunker's roof.

Lynch said, "Our shower. It's cold unless the sun warms the water."

J.D. grinned. "Who says Uncle Sugar doesn't take care of his boys? So he sent us to the end of the earth with no women in sight. He made sure we can take plenty of cold showers."

Lynch's expression suggested he wasn't sure how to take J.D.

Mitch smiled. "J.D. takes getting used to. Stick with him a year or two, and you'll be as crazy as he is."

Nodding, Lynch led down steps beneath a hand-painted sign that said USAF Officers and a tail fin of a five-hundred-pound bomb.

The musty odor reminded Mitch of a cellar shut up a few months too long. Most of the bunker was one large room. A couch, several chairs, and two card tables were near the far wall, which opened into a lighted storage area. Blocking part of the entrance to the storeroom, a wooden bar had whiskey bottles, a reel-to-reel tape deck, and speakers on it. Two rows of double-deck bunks had footlockers at the ends.

After introducing Mitch and J.D. to four other FACs, Lynch pointed to a stack of beds. "These two are vacant."

J.D. vaulted onto the top bunk, stretched out, and wiggled around. "Home, musty home. Don't you just love it?"

"We'll see." Mitch was skeptical. "If you wake up dead, tell them to check your neck for my fingerprints instead of some VC's."

They spent a half hour settling in and getting acquainted. Lynch showed them that the storage area also served as a kitchen with a refrigerator and a hot plate. Pointing at cases of C-rations, he said, "The Marines give us all we can eat. They take good care of us so we'll be ready to fly when they need us." He went on to explain an unofficial mess hall was near the flight line. For a contribution of ten dollars a month, a FAC could eat three meals a day.

When Lynch asked for questions, J.D. said, "I need to find a latrine. Magellan, here, probably wants a map to memorize every hill and gully within a hundred miles."

"Maps are in ops." Lynch grabbed his hat. "For latrines, you have two choices: the barrel across the street or the six-holer at the corner."

Great, Mitch thought facetiously, unsure what the comment about the barrel meant. He'd gotten used to going down the walkway to the latrine at NKP, but he hadn't used an outhouse since his grandmother in Oklahoma had gotten indoor plumbing.

At the top of the steps, Lynch pointed across the street. Two Marines were urinating into a barrel half-buried in the ground. "Community urinal."

Mitch was surprised it was out in the open. "So much for modesty."

"Doesn't take long to get used to it," Lynch said.

Mitch remembered the story of James Dean urinating in front of a crowd. Trying to sound serious, he said to J.D., "I'll be upset if James Dean and Elizabeth Taylor pop to mind every time I stand at the barrel."

J.D. laughed. "Might solve that landing thing in no time."

Lynch pointed at a small structure near the Vietnamese and their smoking barrels. "That's the latrine. Stay out of the smoke. They use kerosene in the barrels to burn the shit."

Realizing Lynch was being literal, Mitch wished he'd received an earlier briefing about living with the troops in the field.

J.D. started down the walkway. "A trip to the barrel will satisfy my current needs."

Mitch followed J.D., and Lynch waited in the street.

J.D. began reciting as if addressing a school assembly. "As I stand in pain trying to piss, I think of the girl who gave me this." He gritted his teeth as if overcome by anger. "If I ever see her again when I get well— I'll get it again, sure as hell." J.D. cackled.

Lynch said, "Sounds like quite a woman."

Mitch zipped his flight suit and stepped away from the barrel.

"Funniest piece of graffiti I ever read," J.D. said, zipping his flight suit. "I'd stopped at a filling station north of Bakersfield and—"

A shock wave cut off the rest of the words.

A thunderous roar triggered Mitch's reflexes, and he almost dived for cover. At the same time he glanced at Lynch, who seemed unperturbed, and Mitch saw why. A block down the street, a puff of smoke boiled upward above a 105mm howitzer.

"Talk about timing," J.D. said, joining Mitch and Lynch in the street. "Ten seconds earlier and I'd have pissed all over my boots."

Lynch said, "No one told you about outbound artillery?"

Mitch wondered if his pounding heart could be heard beyond his flight suit. "Not so far."

"The One-oh-fives aren't bad," Lynch said, referring to howitzers that fired shells 105 millimeters in diameter. "When the Marines fire a One-fifty-five, you're going to jump no matter what you're doing."

"Or what you're holding," J.D. said with a Groucho Marx wiggle of his eyebrows.

Mitch ignored J.D. "How often do they fire these things?"

"A week ago when blood was flowing all over hills, guns fired so often we almost stopped noticing. Now the Marines conduct H & I fire."

Mitch asked, "H & I?"

"Harassment and interdiction."

J.D. lit a cigarette. "Who they harassing? Us or the VC?"

"After a few weeks, you'll get used to it."

"A few weeks," Mitch said, casting a deadly look at J.D.

"Better find Magellan a map 'fore he gets real mayhem in his heart."

After picking up maps, the FACs returned to the other bunker. Before going in, Lynch gave directions on how to find the mess hall.

J.D. and Lynch joined a low-stakes poker game.

Mitch had sworn off poker, so he grabbed a soft drink and settled on the couch. For a few minutes, he studied a map and tried to sense things that might save his life. The map covered an area about thirteen nautical miles square, which was almost equally divided between Laos and South Vietnam. Khe Sanh was near the right edge. A quick survey showed mountains in all quadrants, so the challenge was much greater than memorizing the location of a few hills. He decided he could get familiar with the dangerous terrain more quickly if higher hills were marked with colors besides the map's light greens and tan.

He borrowed marking pens and selected yellow, orange, brown, and dark blue for terrain with elevations above six hundred, seven hundred, eight hundred and nine hundred meters. The four colors would highlight all terrain at least five hundred feet higher than Khe Sanh.

He outlined the 900-meter contour lines with dark-blue. One peak two miles north towered more than fifteen hundred feet above the runway. A few miles beyond, a larger peak rose more than a thousand feet higher and was the highest mountain on the map. The only other dark blue was ten miles west where four peaks straddled the border with

Laos. They were too far to be an immediate threat, but a long ridge stretched from them almost to Khe Sanh. On that ridge Mitch discovered two hilltops labeled 881. He remembered the headline: "N. Viet Hopes Die on Hill 881." The closest Hill 881 was barely four miles off the west end of the runway.

Once higher terrain had been colored in dark blue, he started filling in between the 800-meter and 900-meter contour lines with brown.

J.D. went to the refrigerator to get a beer, then stopped by Mitch for a look. "Painting by numbers?"

"Something like that."

J.D. returned to the poker table.

Mitch realized the coloring might look like a childish way of passing time. Nevertheless, the colors were feeding his subconscious a view of terrain he hadn't seen. Nearly an hour passed before a sergeant came and said the commander was ready to see Mitch and J.D.

J.D. rose and joined Mitch, who was gathering his pens.

Mitch nodded at his marked-up map. "Interesting terrain."

J.D. studied the map. "You left out something." J.D. pulled out a ballpoint pen and drew a small oval northwest of the airfield.

Mitch couldn't imagine what J.D. had in mind.

Inking-in a circle within the oval, J.D. added five lines expanding like sun rays from above the oval. He stepped back and admired his handiwork.

"What did you put on my map?"

"The dragon's eye," J.D. said with a matter-of-fact look. "You forgot to give it one."

"What the hell are you talking about?"

J.D. pointed. "Isn't this your earth dragon friend coming over to gobble up Khe Sanh? There's the dragon's foot. There's his body stretching into Laos. Here's his head with the smoke rising above, and this orange, here, is the fire he's breathing." J.D. tapped the eye he'd added. "And here's his eye."

Mitch saw J.D.'s dragon. The yellows, oranges, and browns looked like a dragon charging across the border toward Khe Sanh. "If I dream about dragons or see any, I'm coming after you."

J.D. smiled heading for the steps. "Just helpin' you feel at home in the land of dragons."

Called into a small office, Mitch and J.D. saw Lieutenant Colonel Anderson behind a battered desk, which covered about half the floor. The colonel occupied so much of the rest of the room, Mitch wondered how the man fit into an O-1.

Mitch and J.D. edged in and saluted.

J.D. said, "Captains Dalton and McCall reporting as ordered, sir."

Anderson pulled an unlit cigar from his mouth and snapped a salute. "At ease. Now how about explaining how you've come about being here?" He leaned as far back as he could and chewed on the cigar.

"Sir," J.D. said, "Lieutenant Colonel Morton, the ops officer at—"

"I know who Mighty Mort is."

Mitch's eyes widened. He had no idea anyone other than J.D. used that nickname.

"Anyway, sir," J.D. continued, "Colonel Morton said you needed FACs."

"I didn't ask for help. Why didn't anyone tell me you were coming?"

Mitch was shocked. If Anderson hadn't requested augmentation, why were they there?

J.D. shrugged. "I have no idea why, sir."

Anderson removed the cigar and seemed to study the dry end. "You boys in trouble?"

Astonished, Mitch glanced at his boots and hoped J.D. would respond.

When neither answered immediately, Anderson continued, "If Mighty Mort was tasked to send people TDY, he isn't gonna give away any of his shiny pennies. He's gonna slip me the leader of his toad farm."

Mitch was aghast at the assessment.

"That's me, sir." J.D. smiled faintly. "Colonel Morton got upset because I did some flying lower than regs allow."

Before Anderson could respond, Mitch blurted, "By flying that low, sir, Captain Dalton located a truck park with forty-one trucks. All were destroyed or damaged."

Anderson looked Mitch over. "You can talk, huh?"

"Yes, sir." Standing ramrod straight, he wished he'd stayed quiet.

"Captain McCall directed strikes that killed nineteen trucks," J.D. said.

Anderson put the cigar in his mouth. "I said to be at ease, gentlemen." As if in deep thought, he looked at the condensation-stained ceiling. Finally he shifted the cigar. "If I was working for Mighty Mort, I'd probably be in his toad farm, too."

J.D. smiled. Mitch tried to relax.

Anderson continued, "Anyway the only break my pilots've had in a month is when the weather's too dogshit to fly. I'm overdue to spend time at headquarters, so I'm gonna take a couple of my FACs along for a little R and R at Danang. We'll be bugging out on the next Marine C-130 that comes through. Colonel Hale'll be in charge for the next few days."

"Yes, sir," J.D. said. "We're looking forward to getting into the air."

Mitch concealed that he was less eager.

"Don't bend any of my airplanes while I'm gone."

J.D. and Mitch responded simultaneously, "Yes, sir."

Mitch hoped his face hid his thoughts of J.D.'s encounter with the tree.

"You two getting settled in okay?"

"Yes, sir."

Anderson stood and maneuvered around the end of the desk. He extended his hand. "Welcome to Khe Sanh, gentlemen."

Khe Sanh and the canyon of the Rao Quan

Bird Dog in the pit at Khe Sanh

Chapter 23

When Mitch and J.D. got outside, a cold, light mist was in the air. The approaching night had turned the world beneath the clouds even more dismal.

J.D. looked around. "Suppose you can find our way to the mess hall, Magellan?"

"I couldn't care less where the mess hall is! You realize there's no reason for us to be here. If it hadn't been for—"

"You mind chewing me out on the way? I'm famished."

Mitch looked up and down the street. "This way, I think." He continued complaining about the predicament J.D. had gotten them into. Mitch was still talking when they passed two Marine captains.

One turned and shouted, "Is that Dauntless Dalton?"

J.D. spun around and gave an I-can't-believe-this shrug. "Jesus."

The Marine gave his M-14 to his companion and stalked toward J.D.

J.D. thrust his flight cap at Mitch. "Here. I need to teach this gyrene a lesson."

Mitch took the cap and stepped aside.

Like wrestlers beginning a match, J.D. and his adversary circled in the muddy street. Taunts became more challenging. Mitch wondered if they were enemies instead of friends.

The Marine was six inches taller and thirty pounds heavier. "Come on, shorty."

J.D. growled and charged.

They danced around with arms interlocked and fingers grasping the other man's uniform. J.D. stepped closer, twisted, and tried for a hip throw.

In that instant, Mitch was startled by a shock wave that put his senses on full alert. A thunderous roar from the nearby artillery battery followed. Mitch shuddered so much he was sure his boots must've risen from the mud.

J.D. flinched. In that unguarded moment, his opponent sidestepped the oncoming hip throw. J.D.'s boots slid, and the Marine slipped around and grabbed J.D. from behind. With longer arms entwining J.D. into a full-Nelson, the Marine forced J.D. onto his hands and knees with his face inches above the mud.

"Say it, J.D., or you'll never get all the mud out of that mustache."

J.D. struggled but couldn't get traction. Finally he said quietly, "The Snake Man rules."

The Marine forced J.D.'s face near the mud. "I can't hear you, Air Force."

J.D. strained against the hold one more time, then spoke louder, "The Snake Man rules."

"Now and forever." He released J.D. and stepped away as if expecting a counter attack.

J.D. got up slowly, surveying the mud on his hands and knees. He smiled, embraced the Marine, and wiped the mud from his hands on the back of the Marine's fatigues.

The Marine stepped back, looking J.D. over. "How the hell'd you end up here, J.D.?"

"Just lucky, I guess." J.D. took his cap from Mitch. "My roommate, Mitch McCall, can give you chapter and verse. Mitch, Snake Sheldon."

Mitch extended his hand. "Snake?"

J.D. said, "We gave him a choice. Snake or Sherry."

"You could still end up with mud in your mustache, J.D." Snake's expression suggested this wasn't the first time he'd had to explain J.D.'s explanation. Snake turned to Mitch. "First name's Sheridan. A family name."

J.D. gestured at scratches across Snake's face. "Your face looks like you have a wildcat for a girl friend."

Snake touched a long scab that looked tender. "In our piece of the war, we root through the weeds instead of flying over them."

"That's the part we want to learn all about," J.D. said.

"No, you don't," Snake said with conviction. "You guys had chow?"

"We're on our way to Club Ptomaine," J.D. said, "but the place may be too high-class to allow Marines in."

"Then come with me. Our mess hall has no standards, so I can probably get you in."

J.D. growled.

Snake winked at Mitch and started along the muddy street, "You may find this hard to believe, but Dauntless Dalton was a pretty fair wrestler in his time."

"Wait until you see the rematch, roomie."

During dinner, Mitch listened to J.D. and Snake top each other with stories of drinking and athletics in their college days. Mitch was surprised to learn J.D. was a conference champion wrestler and had earned an NCAA diving title.

When the meal was finished, J.D. said with a grin, "Now you're a Marine, are you still allowed to drink hard liquor?"

Snake smiled. "A drop or two has been known to pass my lips."

"I managed to import a couple of bottles of Jack Daniel's." J.D. stood. "If you want to accompany us to our suite at the Hilton, you and I can share a little Jack D., while Mister Clean, here, quaffs down a sarsaparilla."

Mitch grinned.

Snake's eyes widened in mock shock. "Do my ears deceive? After all these years, Dauntless Dalton's offering to buy a round?"

J.D. reddened. "Well, they give the stuff away in Thailand."

Snake stood and looked at his wristwatch. "I may have time for a round or two."

"Don't let us make you late for the opera."

Leading the two FACs to the exit, Snake said, "The opera was last night. Tomorrow evening I'm taking a patrol out in the boonies for a few days."

Mitch was impressed by how casually Snake talked of going into the jungle. "In this weather? We heard it's getting worse."

"Good. If Charlie's socked in, he can't get a good fix on where we're inserted."

Mitch's review of the map hadn't revealed karst to provide prominent fixes on the ground. "Doesn't one jungle-covered hill look pretty much like another at that altitude?"

"They all look alike, which means we don't always start where we think we are." Snake smiled. "Adds spice to the game."

When they reached the FAC bunker, Mitch grabbed a Pepsi. He'd planned to open Elizabeth's first letter, but he wanted to learn as much as possible about Khe Sanh.

Snake wanted to sample a Singha first, so he and J.D. started with beer. They headed for a quiet corner away from a noisy card game near the kitchen.

J.D. placed two canteen cups and an unopened bottle of Jack Daniel's on one of four ammunition boxes that served as a makeshift table. He plopped onto a chair and lifted his boots onto a box. Mitch and Snake joined him, and the story telling returned to college days. Whenever J.D. moved the conversation toward recent fighting, Snake steered away.

After taking a long pull on his second Singha, J.D. smiled. "You need to convince my roomie what a good deal this is."

Snake glanced around. "These *are* about the best living conditions on base."

Mitch said, "We lived in an air-conditioned room and had four days a month in Bangkok before Dauntless's stunt."

Snake looked at J.D. "Stunt?"

"Sometimes I think flying should be more fun than the Air For—"

"Sometimes!" Mitch tried to look stern.

"So, I made a slight miscalculation."

"J.D. has a heck of a resume. Under job skills, he lists omnipotence."

"Just like I remember," Snake said. "J.D. may not always be correct, but he was never in doubt."

J.D. smiled. "I used to tell Mister Regulations there wasn't much else they could do to us."

"What can they do," Mitch said, mimicking J.D.'s James Dean drawl, "make us Forward Air Controllers, give us O-1s, and send us to Vietnam?"

"There are worse jobs," Snake said, lightly fingering scabs on his cheek, "although most of my Marines think all Bird Dog pilots must be certifiably crazy."

Mitch took the words as a compliment. "I'm looking forward to directly helping troops on the ground."

"Right," J.D. said, "instead of just blowing away monkeys and turning teak logs into toothpicks. We finally have a chance to make this war more personal."

Snake exhaled deeply and looked troubled. "Be glad you can keep your distance. War's a lot uglier close up."

"But if a guy's going to earn the Medal of Honor, it'll be for saving a bunch of grunts and not for dueling thirty-seven millimeters in Mu Gia."

J.D. had seemed indifferent to whether he earned any medals. Mitch wondered about the change. He assumed that either chasing the medal was a manifestation of a death wish, or J.D. knew earning the top award for bravery was the only way to save his career.

"Here it's not a question of going home with a wheelbarrow full of medals." Snake drained his second beer. "It's a question of going home at all, and I'm not sure I'll ever be able to."

"Careful, Snake Man. Captain Freud'll accuse you of having a death wish."

Snake remained serious. "I might wish someone else dead."

Mitch couldn't hide his surprise.

Snake looked at his wristwatch, then grabbed a canteen cup. "Fill it about three-quarters with the J.D., J.D."

J.D. opened the Jack Daniel's.

Mitch tilted his chair against the wall and gave his full attention.

Snake sat a few moments. "Our first day on Eight eighty-one, my men and I were thrown into the battle, we got pushed off our landing zone right away. We left dead Marines behind." Snake accepted the cup and held it between both hands as if warming them on a hot cup of coffee. "Marines don't usually leave Marines behind, but we were companies and platoons against a dug-in regiment. The clouds were too low for gunships." He took a long drink.

Mitch was surprised. The news story had described an American victory.

Snake stared at the light in the kitchen. "Heat does bad things to bodies. Bloats 'em quicker. Deterioration and rigor set in faster, you know."

Mitch didn't *know*. He watched Snake and sensed he was hardly aware his surroundings were the bunker and not the deadly hills beyond the runway.

"We retook the ground late the next afternoon and recovered the dead. When we found Smitty, part of his head and most of his blonde hair were gone. With all the blood and mud, I wouldn't have recognized him without help from his dog tags." Snake stared the thousand-yard stare. "Funny, but we thought he was lucky to still have a head. Two bodies had been decapitated and burned."

Images of mutilated Marines sickened Mitch. He didn't know or understand this enemy nearly as well as he'd thought.

"Smitty was on his back with both hands in the air." Snake raised his hands almost as if showing the size of a fish that got away. Whiskey spilled from the cup and ran down his arm. He didn't seem to notice. "His arms were so stiff we couldn't move them, so we used two body bags to get him to the mortuary troops on the hospital ship.

Snake took a long drink, glanced into J.D.'s eyes, and Mitch's, then stared at the light bulb. "When they were preparing Smitty to go home, a corpsman discovered a wire looped around Smitty's thumb. Where do you suppose the other end went?"

Snake glanced at J.D., then looked Mitch in the eyes.

Mitch shook his head. "I—I don't know."

"The corpsman traced the wire into the sleeve, then found the other end coming out the neck of his shirt and disappearing into the bloody mess at the base of his skull." Snake looked away and drained the remaining whiskey.

Mitch'd heard more than he wanted to hear.

Snake wrapped both hands around the cup. "They'd wedged a live grenade in Smitty's skull. The wire was supposed to activate the damned thing when we pulled his arms down."

A whistle of amazement escaped J.D.'s lips.

Mitch was stunned by the barbarism. Fury pushed aside his revulsion.

J.D. said, "I can understand why you wouldn't have patience with freaks back home singing praises of the VC."

"Gets pretty damned personal—even if Smitty hadn't been my sister's husband. She only got to live with him four weeks before we shipped out." Snake crushed the cup inward. "If some asshole who's never been here tries to tell me we're the barbarians, I might tear him apart right on the spot."

Mitch considered, then rejected, mentioning news coverage he'd seen in the months before leaving his base near San Francisco. Evening newscasts had featured each day's antiwar demonstrations at the Berkeley campus of the University of California. Mitch had been bothered by them then, but he'd vowed to keep them from eroding his sense of duty.

Snake stood unsteadily. "I gotta get my gear together."

J.D. walked Snake out of the bunker, and Mitch settled onto his bed. He pulled out Elizabeth's first letter. Instead of ripping the envelope open, he slowly tapped it against his chest. Earlier he'd been so eager to read the letter and to relive the sensual experiences of her visit, but his mood had changed. He wasn't ready to intermingle her cheery words of love with details of Snake's story.

Mitch knew he'd never forget even if he wanted to. He felt an obligation to the brotherhood of American fighting men to ensure he would never forget. He was glad he'd chosen to be a pilot instead of a soldier on the ground. He fought his war at a distance, even though occasional nightmares of Goodwin spinning into the jungle still awakened him. *How much worse it would be to see friends blown apart or to come upon mutilated bodies.*

He wondered how he'd handle seeing people he'd killed. Men died in that blazing truck park west of Foxtrot. In the kill-or-be-killed moments—while tracers blazed across the sky—there wasn't time to consider that some of those men had little girls waiting for their daddies to return home. The distancing of intervening days helped him live through such thoughts, which had caught him in unguarded moments in Mandy's presence. He pitied Snake. Years might never provide enough distance from his piece of the war.

Mitch started a letter to Elizabeth. Words came slowly. The hours since she left had been crammed with interesting revelations but few he wanted to tell her. He needed an hour to finish a two-page letter. By then, he was weary enough to sleep in spite of the noisy poker game. Deciding to visit the latrine before going to bed, he pulled on his flight jacket and headed up the steps.

Emerging into the cold night air, he was surprised to find clouds on the ground. Misty air took on an eerie shimmer, reflecting light escaping cracks in huts and slit trenches. Mitch stood at the top of the steps, trying to decide if he really wanted to leave the safety of the bunker. Like dark apparitions, the few Marines on the street caused a ghostly blinking when they passed between Mitch and the lights.

Looking into the darkness, he could barely see the barrel half buried in the ground. Beyond, clouds and mist merged with the blackness. He couldn't see the barbed-wire perimeter fewer than forty yards away. He fingered the switch on his flashlight but was afraid the light could draw attention to him. His imagination began to overrun his need to go to the latrine. What if sappers had crept through the wire? What if he were the first American they ran into? He tried to suppress his fears, but the horrible tale Snake told wouldn't let him.

"You looking for dragons?"

Mitch jumped, startled by J.D.'s voice from behind. "No! I'm trying to decide if I want to walk all the way to the latrine." Mitch hoped it had been too dark for J.D. to notice how much he'd jumped.

J.D. stepped around Mitch and started down the wooden walkway. "When you gotta go, you gotta go."

Mitch followed. Trudging along the muddy road, he tried to divert his thoughts from fears that men who booby-trapped bodies might lurk in the darkness. "I had no idea you were a champion diver."

"Almost drowned once, a week before I started college."

"How?"

"Too many beers, too much water, not enough sense. Got me afraid of water."

Mitch was surprised—surprised J.D. would admit to any fear. "You're afraid of water, and you're a diving champion?"

"That's why I took up diving, kiddo. You can't let your fears ruin your friggin' life."

"I try not to."

"So you had a bad landing once, ace. You've been in and out of the pool more than enough times since then."

Chapter 24

Mitch awakened with a start, confused about where he was. He smelled coffee brewing in contrast to the sensation of a cold, musty cellar. The bulb in the kitchen cast angular splashes of light across one end of the bunker. Noticing a weak scent of perfume, he remembered placing Elizabeth's first letter inside the pillow case.

He retrieved the letter and pulled out his flashlight. Flourishes in her handwriting reassured him before he read her words. The letter reminded him a world of civil people existed beyond the horrors of war. She'd written many words of love, both cheery and poignant. She was embarrassed about having doubted his faithfulness. She would support his choice, with all her heart, whether he wanted to fly forever or stop before his next flight.

He smiled, feeling the warmth of her love even in his dank surroundings. Air Force wives required special qualities, and she had them. He felt unworthy. She was a better Air Force wife than he was an Air Force pilot. The letter closed with how much she already missed him and how much she wished they could be together forever.

Feeling guilty because his absence caused her unhappiness, Mitch was determined to be a man she could be proud of. Several other pilots were in the bunker, but he felt alone. He was huddled beneath the blankets, thinking about Bangkok when Captain Lynch came in.

"Morning missions are scrubbed," Lynch said to two Covey FACs making coffee in the kitchen. "Ceiling's at four hundred feet with no improvement expected all day."

Mitch was relieved. He didn't want to fly his first mission with clouds obscuring all those colorful hills on his map.

One FAC asked, "What's that do to the ceremony at Elephant?"

"Colonel Hale says we'll take three planes," Lynch said.

"What time?"

"Ten-hundred hours."

Mitch remembered the commander had been at Elephant the previous day. He wondered why it was important enough to launch ill-equipped aircraft in marginal weather.

Noticing Mitch, Lynch said, "The colonel said you and J.D. can ride in back. You won't get much of an area orientation, but at least you won't have to worry about getting lost."

"Where is Elephant?"

"Twenty clicks west."

Mitch converted the twenty kilometers to about eleven nautical miles, which left him confused. The Laotian border was nine miles west.

Seeing Mitch's questioning look, Lynch said, "Elephant's a Lao special forces camp."

"On the Laotian side of the border?"

"Sure."

"You're talking about landing airplanes in Laos?"

"Sure. We've been supporting a little civic-action project over there.

We scrounged materials for a village meeting house and market place. Today's the dedication."

Mitch was shocked. Treaties prohibited U.S. forces, other than the attachés assigned to the embassy, from being in Laos. "Interesting."

When Lynch went to the kitchen for coffee, Mitch got out of bed and slipped into his flight suit. He looked to see if J.D. was awake. His eyes were closed. When Mitch reached to shake him, an eye opened.

Mitch whispered, "Did you hear where we're going?"

"Uh-huh," J.D. said sleepily. "I also heard something about a takeoff at ten so why—"

"We can't go to Laos!"

J.D. gave Mitch a why-are-we-having-this-conversation look. "You've been going to Laos nearly every day for five months."

"He's talking about on the ground. It's supposed to be neutral with no foreign troops—"

"You realize how sappy you sound? The NVA has what, maybe a hundred-thousand troops in Laos, and you're conscience stricken about dropping by to dedicate a market place?"

"Two wrongs don't make a right." Mitch realized the massive violations by the North Vietnamese made his emphasis on living by the rules seem silly.

J.D. rolled his eyes toward the ceiling. "If we run into any Pathet Lao, I'll tell them you didn't want to come. If we run into any NVA, you explain the rules to them."

"Right." Mitch knew he'd be foolish to make an issue of his concerns.

J.D. sat up and dangled his feet over the side of the bed. He seemed to be trying to wipe sleep from his eyes. "This is Sunday, isn't it?"

Mitch nodded.

J.D. looked around. "Happy day all you mothers!"

Mitch had to dodge pillows flying at J.D. Digging out his shaving kit, Mitch was glad the weather was too bad for combat. Mother's Day didn't seem a day for killing. He hoped the clouds would cancel Snake's mission. Mother's Day wasn't a day for dying.

Two hours later Mitch, J.D., Lynch, and two other Coveys joined Lieutenant Colonel Hale in the operations bunker.

"With this weather," Hale said, "we won't dilly-dally en route. We'll buzz right over and get the birds on the ground."

Mitch was skeptical about even that, considering the low overcast he'd seen while walking from the other bunker. His only flight under clouds that low was to Mukdahan.

Hale continued, "You can't drink their water, so be sure your canteen's full. Most don't speak any English, so smile a lot. Spirits are a big item in their lives. Back off in a hurry if someone indicates you're getting crossways with any of their spirits." He paused. "The Bru and the Lao are proud of their children, so it's fine to take a complimentary interest in the kids. Be sure you don't pat them on the head."

"Evil spirits can enter through the top of the head," J.D. said to Mitch.

Hale said, "Let's be airborne in twenty minutes."

"Remember to eat whatever they give you," Lynch said with a mischievous smile, "but if you're smart, you won't ask any questions about what you're eating."

The Coveys laughed, J.D. grinned, and Mitch felt more skeptical.

After crossing the runway, Mitch followed Hale into a revetment. The walls of dirt-filled barrels combined with low clouds to give a sensation of being in a small hangar. Mitch was happy to be paired with Hale for this first foray into the forbidding skies above Khe Sanh.

Hale did a quick preflight, and Mitch squeezed into the back seat. He attached the removable control stick to fittings on the floor and adjusted the rudder pedals. The back seat was equipped with little else besides a throttle quadrant and a radio panel. The air was cool and damp, but he opened his windows. Plenty of air would help counter the claustrophobia. The only time he'd been sick in an airplane was in the back of an O-1.

Hale got in and kept a commentary going as he started the engine and taxied up the sloping PSP. No arming/dearming areas were at the ends of the runway, so the crew chief pulled safing pins from the rockets before the O-1 taxied for takeoff.

Mitch spread his map and tried to follow progress once the aircraft was airborne. He got a quick glimpse of the beautiful waterfall. Hale blocked the forward view, so Mitch saw little of where they were going. By looking beyond the wing struts on each side, he saw what they were passing. Hale skimmed in and out of clouds, then descended into a river valley etched through the jungle by the Xe Pon. They flew so low Mitch got only glimpses of huts, villages, roads, and water buffalo.

"If you go to Elephant on your own," Hale said, "stick close to the village and river on the east end of the runway. We sometimes pick up sniper fire from trees at the west end."

Great. Mitch wished Hale had saved that tidbit until after landing.

Ten minutes after takeoff, Hale deployed full flaps and dived toward the river.

Mitch watched nervously out the side windows. The river rushed up on both sides, and Mitch almost grabbed the control stick when a crash into the muddy water seemed imminent. At the last moment, Hale raised the nose. The river bank rushed by a few feet beneath. Seconds later, the aircraft landed on a dirt strip.

Hale turned around well before the west half of the short runway. "I hate coming here in the back seat."

"Understand, sir." He hoped this would be his only trip to Elephant.

Hale taxied into a grassy parking area. Another O-1 was there. Mitch saw the third diving toward the river.

A Lao major and several other officers met the Americans. After a short discussion, Hale turned to the other FACs. "After we're presented to the village chief, I'll stay with him. The captain'll show you around."

Walking the muddy path into the village, Mitch was surprised by the contrasts. A number of soldiers wore tiger suits, the camouflaged fatigues of the jungle fighters. Other men carrying automatic weapons wore little more than loincloths. Modern weapons looked out of place among huts with thatched roofs.

Children tagged along. Chickens, pigs, and monkeys roamed freely. Water buffalo were tethered under huts built on stilts.

Tall trees seemed to support the clouds. Mitch felt closed in, and his skin tingled. He imagined living his entire life in such a setting. As darkness smothered the jungle each evening, it would be easy to imagine spirits filled the earth and river and trees and sky. The spooky feeling made him wish he were loitering high in the sunny skies above Steel Tiger.

A sickening stench, which the villagers seemed oblivious to, made him long to be flying an O-1 with the windows open. The odor of excrement was worse than anything encountered in downtown NKP or the Philippines. Mitch wondered how long it took to get used to the smell. He said quietly to J.D., "I wish I'd brought a gas mask."

"I wish I'd brought a basketball."

"A basketball?" Mitch blurted out the words, then hoped he hadn't offended anyone. He whispered, "These people are hardly five feet tall."

"I know, sport. I haven't played center since fourth grade."

"Why do I have the feeling we should've left you in the bunker?"

"No guts, no glory."

The FACs were introduced to the village chief. In a short ceremony, white strings were tied around the right wrist of each FAC, as a sign of respect. Hale was invited into the chief's hut. The remaining pilots received a six-minute tour, finishing at the new meeting house. Mitch recognized pieces of shipping crates and parts of CONEX storage containers as sections of the building. Inside, women prepared for the feast.

J.D. checked the string on his wrist. "These have magical powers as far as the spirits are concerned. Wonder if I could get one for my other wrist."

"Why would you need two?"

J.D. raised his fist and moved it back and forth as if deflecting karate chops. "Maybe these deflect bullets like Wonder Woman's bracelets."

Mitch gave J.D. a mock frown. "I doubt it."

J.D. shrugged. "Maybe they'd deflect Mighty Mort."

"Too late, pal."

J.D. nodded, then gazed at children who kept their distance. Taking a boot lace from his personal survival kit, he made a loop, then started a series of simple tricks. The tricks, little more than those around a boy scout campfire, enthralled the children. J.D. sat on a log and was surrounded by laughing children. Mitch sat on the steps of the meeting house and watched, smiling at how smooth J.D. was even without a common language.

The more adventurous volunteers tried to duplicate J.D.'s intricate patterns. He mimicked great surprise when tangled messes resulted.

When J.D. reached toward a child, Mitch said, "Not the head, J.D.!"

"No sweatski." J.D. moved his fingers gently against the youngster's ear instead of the top of the head. "Abracadabra and Mighty Mort!" J.D. displayed a shiny quarter. After he gave the coin to the boy, fresh volunteers mobbed J.D.

He touched his hand to the ear of a cute little girl who'd forced her way in front. "What are the magic words?" He looked at the clouds as if stumped, then smiled. "J.D. is *soooo* tall." He pulled his hand away and displayed another quarter.

The little girl giggled and reached for the coin.

J.D. moved his hand back. "You say, 'J.D. is *soooo* tall'."

She looked confused.

J.D. repeated himself a couple of times, and another child shouted a reasonable version of the words. J.D. mimed great delight.

The little girl said something sounding like J.D. is *soooo* tall, and he gave her the quarter.

All around, little voices squealed various versions of the statement.

J.D. smiled at Mitch. "I'm glad you made me come along."

Soon, J.D. rushed over with thirty children in trail. "I need coins."

Mitch searched his breast pocket. "Where's your green hat and flute?"

J.D. looked stumped.

"Aren't you the Pied Piper?"

J.D. smiled. "Guess it looks that way."

Mitch dropped several coins into J.D.'s open hand.

"Thanks for your contribution to national defense."

"Is that all I get, Mister Tall?"

"I promise not to use the magic words 'Captain Mitch is a fink'."

J.D. had few coins left when Hale and the Lao major joined the other pilots. Hale announced they'd been invited to observe a few demonstrations before lunch.

The Laotians placed targets at the edge of the village. After impressive displays of marksmanship and knife throwing, a soldier, wearing little more than a loincloth, came forward. He carried a foot-long piece of horn from a water buffalo. The piece was from the pointed end and included part of the bend of the horn.

Mitch saw it was hollow. The horn was similar to a ram's horn his father had bought years earlier on a hunting trip to Montana.

The interpreter said, "Horn makes good signal."

The soldier raised the horn to his lips and pointed the open end upward. He blew into a tiny opening in the tip. A haunting, melodious tone filled the air. The sound reminded Mitch of a French horn. The soldier varied the pitch within a narrow range. Mitch could imagine the tone being an effective signal, carrying miles across quiet valleys of jungle.

The soldier gave the horn to Hale. The interpreter said, "Try, please."

"Glad to." After discretely wiping his hand across the mouthpiece, Hale raised the horn and blew. Most air escaped around the mouthpiece. He took in a deep breath, puffing out his cheeks, and blew harder. His face reddened. The horn offered increased resistance with the increased blowing. The sputtering sound had no resemblance to a French horn.

The Laotians showed mild amusement, but nothing to insult the honored guest. Hale offered the horn to the soldier, but he gestured for the other Americans to try.

Lynch and the other two Coveys were no more successful.

J.D. took the horn and pantomimed his preparations with exaggerated expressions directed at the children. He puffed out his cheeks, closed his eyes, and blew with an intensity that raised the veins over his temples. Children's laughter drowned out his hissing sputter. He hammed it up twice more, then turned to Mitch. "Here you go, hot lips."

Mitch took the horn and moistened his lips. He blew, softly at first but slowly increasing until the haunting tone came forth. He wondered if he'd made a mistake by upstaging the soldier. However, the soldier, interpreter, and most of their compatriots clapped and smiled.

"Number one," the interpreter said with delight.

After raising and lowering the tone a few times, Mitch handed the horn to the soldier.

J.D. shook his head. "Will you ever cease to amaze? I may start calling you Satchmo."

When the food was ready, the pilots were led inside. On the way in, Hale said to Mitch, "You and Captain Dalton are the hit of the party."

"I'm glad we got invited, sir. This beats sitting in the bunker."

The village chief, the elders, the Americans, and the Laotian military leaders sat in a large circle on the floor of the new meeting house. Rice, bread, fruits, and other foods were within the circle. Women moved in and out, bringing more food and serving those seated.

A few minutes into the meal, a steaming soup was dipped from a large cooking pot. When the server got to Mitch and J.D., the interpreter spoke. The server seemed to make a special effort in filling a bowl, then handed it to J.D.

Glancing at its contents, J.D. smiled broadly and accepted the bowl. Bowing to the server, J.D. said, "This one should honor my friend who makes noises on the buffalo horn." Maintaining his smile toward the server, J.D. thrust the bowl at Mitch.

Mitch grabbed it to save it from falling. He looked at the chief to see if J.D. had committed a social error. The interpreter raised his hands as if bringing a horn to his lips and spoke quickly. The chief smiled and nodded. Another bowl was dipped for J.D.

Mitch soon decided the bowl contained a pork stew. Although spicier than he liked, the stew was tasty.

J.D. tore off a chunk of bread and dipped it in his bowl. "An unforgettable taste treat."

Mitch frowned to signal J.D. to mind his manners. J.D. nodded toward the chief. Mitch saw bread-dipping was acceptable, so he soaked juice into a chunk of bread. He liked the combination since bread offset the spiciness. While soaking a third piece, he pushed aside a piece of meat, then froze. He had pushed aside an eyeball.

Fighting the urge to vomit, he turned to J.D., and their eyes locked.

J.D. seemed trying to look innocent. Even he couldn't pull it off.

"You knew!" Mitch realized his words were louder than intended.

"They're honoring us with the choice pieces." J.D. lowered his bowl so Mitch could see. "I've got *soup de pig snout.*"

"What are we gonna do?"

"*Bon appetit.*"

Mitch glared. "If we don't find a way out, you may cash in your death wish today."

"Smile, roomie. We may be on Candid Camera."

Mitch wished the answer were that simple, but he didn't expect Allen Funt to appear. Instead the chief and the interpreter smiled at Mitch. Mitch smiled wanly.

His left hand rose, reaching for the tip of the mustache that had been gone a month. He avoided looking into the bowl. Instead he chose a banana and slowly peeled it. He stalled several minutes, trying to think of an acceptable way to avoid finishing his soup. By then, he and J.D. were the only ones who still had soup bowls.

J.D. nudged Mitch's elbow. "The *maitre' d* has signaled the end of the soup course."

"I don't think I can eat this."

"Get your canteen ready to wash it down. Imagine it's a cherry, or a grape, or a—" J.D. snickered. "Or a mountain oyster."

Mitch glared. "Rub it in, buddy! Someday, somehow, sometime, I'll get even."

He put his canteen beside his bowl. Selecting a long strip of bread, he wrapped it around the eyeball. He took a quick drink of water, inhaled deeply, closed his eyes, and pushed the eyeball into his mouth. For the first few seconds, he couldn't swallow. During his fourth try, his eyes came open, and he saw J.D. trying to suppress a smile.

Mitch finally swallowed. The eyeball lodged in his throat, making him feel as if he were strangling. He forced the eyeball down but was afraid it would come back up. He raised the canteen to his lips but didn't dare take anything else in his mouth yet.

"How'd it taste?"

"I don't know."

In a few moments, he could drink. When he was pretty sure he wasn't going to vomit, he saw the attention had shifted to J.D.

J.D. had pulled out the snout and was rinsing it with water. Using a handkerchief, he blotted the snout, then inspected it from all angles. An emphatic nod suggested he was satisfied. He retrieved his extra bootlace. Ignoring his audience, he threaded the lace through the nostrils. Once the snout was secured, he tied the ends of the lace together.

"Here goes," J.D. said to Mitch. Holding the bootlace with both hands and letting the snout dangle, he turned to the chief. J.D. spoke slowly and clearly. "I am greatly honored to be selected for this charm. It will contain much luck for me. The spirits that guide my life will be pleased I wear it in honor of the friendship of this feast."

J.D. looped the bootlace over his head like a necklace. Continuing to smile, he watched the explanation to the chief. Hale appeared concerned.

Mitch was glad for something to think about besides the queasy feeling. "What a cockamamie line? These people take their spirits seriously."

J.D. spoke like a ventriloquist, "So do I. Jimmy Dean would be very pleased."

"I hope they make you eat the bootlace, too."

The chief seemed unconvinced. The interpreter reached inside the collar of his own shirt and pulled on strings looped around his neck. Out popped two carved Buddhas and another item Mitch couldn't identify.

The chief pulled on gold chains around his neck, nodded and spoke to the interpreter. Three gold images were among the chief's amulets.

The interpreter faced J.D. "The chief hopes you much luck and fertility."

J.D. bowed to the chief, raised the snout for everyone to see, then slipped it into his flight suit. He said to Mitch, "*Luck*, yes. *Fertility*, I can do without."

Mitch saw the chief showing off his amulets to Hale. The interpreter was explaining.

"If I didn't want more soup," J.D. said, "I'd turn in my bowl."

The mention of the soup caused Mitch's stomach to clinch. "No, thanks." He pushed the bowl where the servers would remove it.

J.D. said, "I can't wait to see what the next course is."

"I can," Mitch said meekly, fighting another wave of nausea that threatened to swamp him. He was upset at eating the eyeball destined for J.D. while J.D. emerged unscathed. "You're going to have to wear that stinky thing, you know."

J.D. shrugged. "Soak it in a little medicinal alcohol for a couple of days, and it'll smell better than my socks."

"How can you just declare that chunk of pig a lucky charm?"

"It's already brought me luck." J.D. maintained a Cheshire-cat smile toward the chief. "I was lucky enough to not have to eat the damned thing."

Chapter 25

On fifth day at Khe Sanh, the weather improved late in the afternoon. Mitch flew as wingman for Colonel Hale on a short mission west on Route 9. Flying over the area about halfway to Tchepone, Mitch found the roads of Tiger Hound much the same as those in Steel Tiger North.

The major contrast was the terrain around Khe Sanh compared to the level ground on NKP's side of the Mekong River. Jungle-covered hills and mountains surrounded Khe Sanh. A very dangerous place for a base, Mitch concluded, especially with no way to completely control the high ground. Remembering stories of the 1954 Viet Minh siege of the French outpost at Dien Bien Phu, he wondered if Khe Sanh were any less vulnerable.

Two mornings later, Mitch was on his bunk writing a letter when he heard J.D.'s familiar whistling from the entryway. With a look of enthusiasm, J.D. hurried in with a mayonnaise jar. Mitch strained to see if the bottle contained some exotic bug. The bottle was empty.

J.D. tossed the jar toward the ceiling, then caught the tumbling bottle. "No more Mister Nice Guy. I'm tired of being just another pretty target."

Mitch sat up. "Gonna bomb 'em with bottles?"

"Right." J.D. reached into a pocket and pulled out a hand grenade.

"Jesus, J.D."

Captain Young and Lieutenant Nance, two local FACs, came closer.

Putting his letter aside and feeling apprehensive, Mitch stood. He'd attended a short course on throwing grenades. Their kill radius was forty-five feet, and because they were so dense and heavy, he'd had trouble throwing a practice grenade that far. "I never got enthusiastic about grenades. Seems to me that if you can't toss the suckers at least fifteen yards, there's no sense throwing 'em at all."

"That's the beauty of the old grenade-in-the-mayo-bottle trick. Fly over the target, drop the bottle, and gravity does its thing." He smiled at Mitch. "Kill radius isn't a problem unless you fly below fifty feet."

"Right," Mitch said.

Moving the bottle as if it were falling, J.D. whistled like the scream of a plummeting bomb. "Keep four things in mind. First, be sure the bottle isn't too big. It'll ruin your whole day if the handle pops off inside."

Mitch grinned. "Unless you can throw the bottle forty-five feet."

Nodding, J.D. removed the lid and demonstrated the grenade would slide through the wide opening with little room to spare. Even if the safety pin were pulled, the glass would keep the safety handle from springing free.

J.D. slid the grenade out into his hand. "Second, which is tricky, is be sure the handle doesn't get away when you pull the pin."

"We'll take your word," Mitch said.

J.D. pushed the base of the bottle against his chest, held the grenade about halfway out, and pulled the safety pin. With a distinctive click, a spring pushed out on the handle, wedging it inside the bottle.

"Jesus, J.D.," Mitch repeated as everyone backed away. "You may not care whether you survive this war, but some of *us* want to."

"No sweatski." J.D. let the grenade slide inside. "See. Safe as with the pin in."

"Bullshit," Young said.

"Unless you dump it out." J.D. screwed on the lid and displayed the bottle. "The third worry is replacing the pin if you don't find a target."

"I vote you do that outside," Mitch said.

Young and Nance nodded.

"No sweatski." J.D. flipped the bottle toward the ceiling.

Young yelled, and Nance gasped.

A thumping in Mitch's chest rushed into his throat, choking off the curse he wanted to shout. He stepped forward, concentrating on the bottle that tumbled end-over-end. J.D.'s hand flashed out, bumping the bottle, and deflecting it. Mitch shot a hand out beneath and almost had the bottle before J.D.'s hand collided. The bottle hit the concrete and shattered. The handle sprang free and clattered across the floor. The grenade twirled slowly.

"Shit, shit, shit," J.D. screeched.

The other three pilots dived behind things that might stop shrapnel. Young yanked over a pair of bunk beds with a clanging crash.

What a dumb way to die! Mitch lunged across a bunk, rolled under the next, and kept rolling. Bumping against a foot locker, he clawed his way behind it. In a tight ball, he was surprised he'd had so much time.

He waited one second, two, three. Instead of the thunderous blast he expected, the only sound was the hum of the refrigerator.

"Damn it," J.D. said. "Now I've gotta find another friggin' bottle."

Hunched behind the locker, Mitch tried to make sense of J.D.'s words.

"The fourth thing to keep in mind," J.D. said, "is don't do this for real with grenades with little white squares painted on them. They don't have any boom."

Mitch saw J.D. smiling and showing off the practice grenade.

The other FACs gaped. Young seemed to have trouble getting enough moisture into his mouth to speak. "Wha—What if there'd been a mistake and that wasn't inert?"

J.D. shrugged. "Wouldn'ta been our day." He paused. "Or, in a sense, it woulda—"

"I'm gonna break your fuckin' neck," Young bellowed, struggling from beneath a bunk.

J.D.'s taunting laughter echoed as he ran to the exit. "Gettin' your adrenaline up once in a while keeps you ready for that big mission."

That afternoon, Mitch sat strapped into an O-1 in a revetment. The propeller whirred, and he enjoyed a few tranquil moments waiting for J.D. to call for taxi clearance. The sky was clear, and Mitch's O-1 was bathed in sunshine. Light streaming through overhead windows caused him to feel warm for the first time since arriving at Khe Sanh.

From a second O-1, J.D. asked, "Ready to do it to it?"

Mitch signaled his crew chief to remove the chocks. "Five-nine's ready to roll."

J.D. received clearance to taxi, and Mitch coaxed his O-1 up the ramp. Both aircraft taxied west on the runway. Mitch was distracted by the stark view ahead. Battle-scarred hills seemed close enough to touch. Reddish-brown soil seemed somehow different in the bright sun. Rugged lips of individual craters—more craters than he could count—reflected sunlight and gave a sense of depth Mitch hadn't seen before.

In spite of the sunshine, he felt a chill as he reminded himself those craters were unlike thousands he'd seen along the Trail. Many of these holes had been gouged among men fighting in close combat. He imagined hundreds of Marines and NVA soldiers battling for those hilltops. "Wonder which hill Snake fought for."

"Don't know," J.D. said on interplane.

An eerie shiver coursed down Mitch's arms as the war seemed more real than ever. At the end of the runway, he put the hills behind him and tried to do the same with his thoughts.

J.D. got takeoff clearance and looked over his shoulder. He raised a hand and circled with a pointed finger, making a visual signal to rev the engine. Mitch pointed a finger forward, then snapped his thumb down as if firing a pistol.

J.D. nodded, and his O-1 rolled forward.

Mitch released brakes when he saw the tailwheel on the lead aircraft raise from the runway. J.D.'s aircraft remained inches above the ground, and Mitch looked for a reason why J.D. wasn't climbing. Mitch was just airborne when he saw a sight that made him forget what he was doing.

J.D.'s O-1 pitched up, and the right wing dropped.

Watching J.D. roll upside down, then fall, Mitch gasped. He held his breath, expecting to see an explosion and cartwheeling debris. Instead the aircraft disappeared.

Mitch strained against his shoulder straps to see into the canyon. The thought of losing J.D. stirred a sick feeling.

"Wahooooo!" J.D.'s voice roared over the hiss of the interplane radio.

"What the hell?"

Passing beyond the runway, Mitch lowered a wing. To get a better view ahead and below, he cross-controlled with the rudder. His trained eyes spotted movement—J.D.'s O-1 was upside down and falling.

Mitch shouted on interplane, "Pull out, J.D.!"

J.D.'s O-1 continued like a corkscrew, rolling upright momentarily, then entering another roll. "Say again, roomie."

Mitch was amazed at J.D.'s cool. Mitch knew that if he were falling toward the Rao Quan, he'd be speaking in a high-pitched squeak—if he could speak at all. An instant later, he realized J.D. was flying barrel rolls. Fright turned to anger. "You crazy sonuva bitch."

"No sweatski. I've been waiting all week for an east wind. I mean, is there another airfield where you roll an O-1 on takeoff?"

Mitch watched J.D. finish the final roll and begin climbing. "You scared hell out of me,"

"Try a couple. They'd be good for what ails you."

"This isn't about what ails me! I don't need to prove anything by doing rolls on takeoff."

"Lighten up. I'm talking fun. We only pass this way once in life."

"Once with you's enough."

"This pig snout's probably got enough good luck for both of us." J.D. said with a hint of mischief in his voice. "We could takeoff with you on my wing. Then I could lead—"

"Forget it, Houdini." Mitch imagined two O-1s flying a barrel roll in formation. "Let's go let you can scare someone besides your wingman."

"Okaaayy!"

Mitch knew O-1s alone wouldn't scare anyone. Nevertheless he expected to witness real terror from the sky. In forty-seven minutes, an Arc Light strike—two cells of three B-52s each—would drop nearly 450,000 pounds of bombs on suspected truck parks. The targets were along a branch of the Ho Chi Minh Trail in the A Shau valley near the Laotian border. He and J.D. were to loiter nearby and assess damage.

Climbing in bright sunshine, Mitch got his best look yet at the surroundings. Straddling Route 9, the town of Khe Sanh seemed peaceful enough. Reflected sunlight glinted from tin-roofed buildings among groves of lush trees. Children played soccer beside a schoolhouse on a playground of red mud. A splash of bright yellow-orange caught Mitch's eye. He saw two monks in saffron robes walking along Route 9.

He looked beyond Khe Sanh to thatched huts in a montagnard village nearer the foothills. Coconut palms and a grove of green trees lined one edge of the village, but the huts were out in the open. Mitch marveled at how different these two neighboring settlements were. He could imagine one was mistakenly placed in the wrong valley—maybe even on the wrong continent or in the wrong century.

He studied the rolling hills stretching north from the Xe Pon. The jungle seemed pure and secure and inviting. How misleading it was in bright sunlight. He looked at the children on the playground. These seemingly carefree youngsters were within five miles of where Snake had spent three days in a cat-and-mouse game with the North Vietnamese. Mitch had never seen such a land of contrasts. He doubted he could ever sort them all out.

J.D. checked-in with Hillsboro. The airborne controller offered no new guidance, and J.D. didn't say why the O-1s were headed for A Shau.

The O-1s climbed to six thousand feet and flew over jungle-covered mountains. Clouds seemed to have fled from Southeast Asia, and Mitch could see the horizon in every direction. Forty miles east, the South China Sea paralleled his course. Ahead he got his first good look at rugged terrain along the border between Laos and South Vietnam. Rivers and streams were reddish-brown torrents, surging from recent rains. For twenty miles, he saw few signs of war. Then he spotted the upper end of A Shau and a hillside with more bomb craters than trees.

Flying closer, Mitch saw a road zigzagging through debris of hundreds of air strikes. He estimated the road dropped more than a thousand feet from the summit. "What a great target," Mitch said, knowing the road was more vulnerable than most in Steel Tiger. "How'd you like to drive an ammo truck down that in the dark?"

"Might get a real bang out of it."

"Baaaad."

Mitch imagined sitting in a truck at the top on a moonless night. His headlights, dimmed by tape or paint, would cast narrow slits of light illuminating little more than the mud just beyond the front bumper. There'd be no streetlights, no guardrails, no line painted on the center of the road, no reflective signs warning to use low gear the next three miles or to beware of low-flying aircraft. If intelligence reports were accurate, he'd be chained to his truck to keep him from bugging out when aircraft approached. He clamped the stick between his knees and focused his binoculars on the treacherous hill. He felt a dogged respect for men who drove that road.

"The road's open all the way from top to bottom," J.D. said.

Scanning the road to verify the assessment, Mitch realized how much his attitudes had changed. Before coming to NKP, he would've assumed the Air Force could keep such a vulnerable road closed. Now he believed the reverse. The North Vietnamese kept such roads open except for a few hours after successful air attacks.

J.D. said, "There are worse things than being a FAC with an O-1 in Nam."

Mitch thought again about riding down the hill. "Roger that, but that still doesn't get you off the hook." He followed J.D. to the east side of the valley, flying well clear of the hill, which undoubtedly was protected by scores of hidden guns.

The valley widened between peaks north and south towering nearly a mile above the floor. Mitch located the targets. The first was heavy jungle near a ford where a road branched east to the imperial capital of Hue. The second cell of B-52s would attack dense jungle a half mile north.

Putting his binoculars aside, he scanned the lush valley. Almost primeval, A Shau seemed remote, even though within twenty miles of Hue. Scattered rice paddies and the pockmarked road were the only signs people inhabited the valley. Still, Mitch didn't doubt that soldiers and workers—numbering in the thousands—were concealed in the jungle.

A few minutes later, J.D. announced on the strike frequency, "I'm going to take a look at this road branching toward Hue."

Mitch realized J.D. had made an excuse to loiter near the first target without raising suspicions. "I'll stay out of your way here on the west."

He wanted a good view, but he wasn't going to fly too near the targets. Waiting for an Arc Light on a clear day wasn't as quite eerie as waiting for bombs to plunge through an overcast. Guiding his O-1 over the west ridge, he checked the time. Fewer than three minutes remained until the first attack.

He looked south. White lines cut across the sky, like slashes across a canvas of cerulean blue. The contrails were clean and straight, not yet distorted by the swirling winds at the edge of the stratosphere. The B-52s were too far away for him to make out the individual airplanes. Nevertheless, he saw three individual contrails growing toward him.

J.D. asked, "You got me in sight, roomie?"

Banking toward the first target, Mitch couldn't find J.D. After searching above the valley for several seconds, he said, "Where you hiding?"

"You're probably looking too high."

Jesus! Mitch rolled into a steeper bank. Searching frantically, he couldn't imagine why J.D. would go low. An involuntary gasp escaped when he spotted J.D. gliding through steep S-turns above the first target. "What the hell are you doing?"

"You close enough to cover me?"

"Cover you? You begging to get shot down?" He chose not to add over the open frequency that if gunners didn't get him, bombs might.

"Where are you?" J.D.'s voice was more insistent.

"Southwest. Over the ridge."

"Turn toward me and scream if you see ground fire."

"Check your clock and get the hell out of there!" The B-52s' contrails were so close Mitch didn't want to fly over the valley, but his hands responded to J.D.'s plea. Adding power and aiming his O-1 on an intercept course ahead of J.D., Mitch felt he was getting swept into a suicide pact.

J.D. sounded more excited. "Won't be long now—one way or the other."

"You've got that right!"

Mitch saw the first cell of B-52s overhead. He assumed they already had unleashed maybe three hundred iron bombs. Somewhere above, hidden in the blue background, unseen bombs hurtled toward the ford.

"I should be getting a bite any mom—"

Guns flashed beneath J.D.

"Ground fire!" Mitch cried out the words, then held his breath. Vivid memories of the fatal February morning welled up.

"Mark 'em! Mark 'em! Mark the guns!" Maneuvering wildly, J.D. spat out words like bullets from a Gatling gun.

Mitch yanked the throttle back, banked right, and jammed the right rudder pedal against the stop. Swinging toward camouflaged guns near the edge of a clearing, he was so far away he needed to loft the rocket. He raised the nose above the point where the road dipped into the river.

A quick check showed J.D. clear, racing away at maybe ninety knots. Two miles above the retreating O-1, sixty antiaircraft shells detonated.

Mitch squeezed the trigger.

Ka-baam!

"Mark's away!"

Simultaneously he armed another rocket and glanced through the windows in the ceiling. He ruddered the nose left to put spacing between his marks and squeezed the trigger.

Ka-baam!

"Two's away! Why the hell didn't you say you were planning that stunt?"

"Just avoiding an argument, roomie."

The first rocket slammed into the trees, creating a plume of smoke north of the river.

"Great smoke," J.D. said. "You're maybe fifty meters from the guns."

A quarter of a mile south of the rising puff of white, the jungle erupted. A mixture of 500- and 750-pound bombs walked a deadly path toward the smoke.

Mitch watched with morbid fascination. Brilliant flashes—sparkling faster than he could count—blasted shock waves outward. The jungle blurred, like when waves of heat dance above a desert highway. New flashes marched north as old ones turned into geysers of dirt, trees, and whatever—or whomever—was hidden there. Each outburst of debris peaked, then collapsed into itself, swallowed by churning dust and dirty smoke.

A puff of smoke from the second rocket blossomed above the trees and was immediately overtaken by the rolling wave of bombs.

"Take that, you mothers!"

Mitch couldn't remember having heard so much excitement in J.D.'s voice. He spotted J.D. doing aileron rolls just beyond the targets.

The bombs stopped exploding as abruptly as they started. The hundreds of churning puffs of dust and smoke merged into a rectangular cloud obscuring the jungle, the river, and about a quarter of a mile of the main road. He spotted more flashes—secondary explosions of ammunition or fuel. Closing his eyes a moment, he pictured the scene before the bombs hit. One group of popcorn-like explosions seemed centered where the gunners had fired. He watched for more blasts and identified their coordinates.

J.D. sent a rocket crashing into the roadside a half-mile farther north. Seconds later, bombs obliterated his white smoke.

Mitch saw a repeat of the earlier spectacle. "You going to BDA the second target?"

"My pleasure, Five-nine."

Mitch flew closer, counting fires and watching for more explosions. He heard halting Vietnamese spoken on the interplane frequency. "Someone else is—" He stopped, realizing the words were spoken in a James Dean accent. "What the hell was that?"

"Snake taught me a few words after I learned we were assigned to baby sit the Buffs." He repeated the Vietnamese words on Hillsboro's frequency, then continued in English on interplane, "It's a new old Vietnamese proverb. 'Ho Chi Minh say, Shoot at the FAC, and you pay the price!'"

Mitch smiled.

Once the bomb-damage assessments were finished, J.D. asked Hillsboro, "Do you have any fighters available this afternoon?"

"Negative. With this weather, the big boys are up north. You guys got lots of gas?"

"Not enough to fly to Hawaii for R and R," J.D. said, "but we could stir up a couple of hours worth of trouble."

J.D.'s in a rare mood, Mitch thought, pressing the microphone button for interplane. "Lord help the NVA."

Click-click.

"I can't guarantee much excitement," Hillsboro said, "but the Marines've requested an airborne escort for a convoy headed out of Khe Sanh down Route Nine."

"Sounds like we're being forced to do a little legal buzzing," J.D. said on interplane, then imitated the taunting laughter that had characterized the hero of the radio program *The Shadow.*

"Lord help our truck drivers," Mitch answered.

J.D. turned northwest. "Hillsboro, tell the grunts the cavalry'll be riding to the rescue in about twenty minutes."

"You do understand, Nail," Hillsboro said, "there isn't any current problem? They'd just like you overhead in case you're needed."

"Roger that. We'll hold hands even if they won't kiss us goodnight."

After Hillsboro gave a frequency for the convoy commander, Mitch said on interplane, "You wouldn't confuse everyone so much if you used standard terminology once in a while."

"Say what?"

Mitch smiled. "Disregard."

Several miles from Route 9, Mitch spotted the convoy. The line stretched toward Khe Sanh as far as he could see. "There they are."

"Don't suppose you want the honor of taking the lead, roomie?"

Considering J.D.'s tone and his earlier comment about buzzing, Mitch assumed his answer should be no. "What do you have in mind?"

"One of us flies out front and makes a little racket so Charlie knows we're there." J.D.'s tone got more serious. "If there's an ambush, we need to trigger it."

"What does the other guy get to do?"

"Make a few runs to the back. The rest of the time, you can cover me. Just remind Mister Charles he has to get us both before he can open up for serious business."

"I can handle that. I'll stay above a thousand feet, so there's no chance of a midair."

"Somehow the possibility of colliding with you on this little gig never crossed my mind."

Mitch smiled. "Just keep your Bird Dog out of the trees."

"Just don't run into any B-Fifty twos up in the stratosphere." J.D. rolled inverted and dropped like a hawk.

Click-click.

J.D. repeated his imitation of the Shadow's laugh, then called the convoy commander on the FM radio.

Mitch thought about how he'd become such a veteran except around J.D. Descending, Mitch got his first good look at the road linking Khe

Sanh and military reinforcements from the coastal lowlands. Route 9 crossed the Rao Quan east of the town of Khe Sanh, then hugged the hillside above the river. Mitch could see the road stretching at least ten miles toward the coast, and there was no way for friendly forces to control the jungle-covered slopes above the road. "That's worse than I imagined. No wonder these guys want someone to mother hen them."

"Ambush city. That's why they called Southeast Asia's Finest FACs."

"Southeast Asia's craziest FAC, maybe."

"Whatever."

Mitch looked and found J.D. over the slope between the road and the river. J.D. was flying beside the convoy at the same level as the truckers. Mitch decided that if he were driving Route 9, he'd feel better with J. D. buzzing overhead.

After passing the lead armored personnel carrier, J. D. pulled up over the road, then raced ahead in a series of S-turns between trees on the hillside and the river below. Less than half a mile ahead, he coasted upward, banked through a tight, 180-degree turn, then sped toward the convoy as if playing chicken with the APC. At the last instant the O-1 soared up a few feet and buzzed the first twenty vehicles.

Most Marines Mitch could see through binoculars had an arm raised. "They waving or giving you the finger?"

"They're eating it up," J.D. said, climbing into another turn and doing his Shadow imitation again.

"I take that to mean you're enjoying your flight, Captain."

"Hog heaven. I love the feeling that every guy in the convoy's glad I'm up here. If I get knocked down, every Marine's gonna do his damndest to save me."

Mitch preferred not to think about J.D. being shot down. "If you put tire tracks on that APC, they're liable to shoot you down themselves."

"No sweatski."

Mitch thought about the mistake that had doomed them to their exile to Khe Sanh. "Keeping an eye on your gas?"

"You bet. I'm not putting up with the concrete Hilton simply to end up out of gas in some rice paddy."

"I hope not." Mitch saw J.D. pull up a few hundred feet, do a wingover, and swoop down as if strafing. Mitch watched longingly, remembering days in Oklahoma when he'd been his class's best pilot—when he'd been at least J.D.'s equal as a stick-and-rudder man.

Mitch turned toward Khe Sanh. Flying above the back half of the convoy, he wished he had J.D.'s guts and enthusiasm.

Chapter 26

"Those grunts oughta be safe enough now, roomie."

"Agreed." Mitch could see the remainder of the drive to Camp Carroll was over the open, flat coastal plain.

"Besides, I'm running a little short on petrol, and I don't need to log another touch-and-go in a buffalo herd."

"Roger that."

"No telling where Mighty Mort would send us next."

Click-click.

J.D. did a low roll over the last few vehicles passing the Marine fortress on the Rockpile, then pulled up and flew above Route 9 toward Khe Sanh.

Mitch followed well above J.D.'s zigzagging O-1, which buzzed each outpost along the road. Reaching the bridge over the Rao Quan, J.D. turned north, followed the canyon, and called the tower for landing clearance. Mitch watched J.D. swing from one wall of the canyon to the other. If the Viet Cong had troops on the cliffs, J.D. would be an easy target. However, even if they were there, they wouldn't be expecting an aircraft to fly by at their level—or below.

"Isn't it time you climbed a little, J.D.?"

"No sweatski. I've always wanted to climb up and land like on an aircraft carrier."

"Navy guys don't climb up to land on a carrier."

"Whatever."

J.D. made the final turn into the box canyon with the waterfall. "Remind me we need to ask Snake if his gyrenes own the waterfall."

Mitch became suspicious. "Why do *we* need to know?"

"In case we get a day off and want to go cliff diving."

"Right."

Although pleased J.D. was in such a good mood, Mitch wasn't going to be talked into hiking into the jungle to dive off the cliffs. He watched J.D. climb over the lip of the plateau. Guards dived into trenches when the O-1 appeared unexpectedly a few feet above them.

"If you took any bullet holes, they're probably from those Marines."

"Can't please everyone. Two hundred guys at Camp Carroll are probably sending me fan mail by now."

After filling out post-mission forms, Mitch discovered mail had arrived from NKP. His two letters from Elizabeth were postmarked before her visit. After handing a letter to J.D., Mitch headed out of the musty operations bunker into the warm sunshine. Instead of going into the other bunker, Mitch climbed the muddy slope and sat on the edge of the roof near the shower.

J.D. followed. He pulled out two photos and a letter from his envelope. After looking over the pictures, he put them aside.

Mitch was aware of J.D. but remained absorbed in Elizabeth's letters.

Moments later, J.D. shouted, "Bitch!" He crumpled the letter, rose, and stomped away.

Mitch called after him, "Something you'd like to talk about?"

"Negative!" J.D. spit out the word and took four more long strides before adding, "Never buy it when they purr they're gonna love you 'til the twelfth of never."

"What in the—" Mitch stopped when it was apparent he was being ignored. He decided J.D. was referring to a love song sung by Johnny Mathis a decade earlier when J.D. might have courted his wife. Mitch picked up the pictures. Both showed two children on a palomino pony. In one picture, a willowy blonde woman stood with her hand on the saddle horn. *Beautiful—and probably four inches taller than J.D.*"

Surprised at the intensity of J.D.'s reaction, Mitch watched him stomp across the muddy road, fling the letter into the barrel, and urinate. When J.D. turned toward the bunker, Mitch looked awkwardly at his letters.

J.D. was energetically whistling "When Johnny Comes Marching Home Again" when he returned. Pulling his knife from its sheath, he sliced off the part of the picture showing his wife.

Mitch said, "Sometimes talking helps."

J.D. acted as if he hadn't heard until Mitch turned to his letters. "She's marrying some damned eunuch in New York City."

"You weren't expecting to remarry her, were you?"

"Hell, no! But she wants her new husband to adopt J.D. Junior and princess."

"So? What if you don't consent?"

"I don't know." J.D. shoved the knife into the sheath, then stood. "But even if I don't, New York City? I'd never be assigned anywhere close."

Mitch was uncertain how to reply. At least J.D. was talking about life after the war. Nevertheless, if J.D. were passed over twice for promotion to major, the Air Force would release him from active duty. This wasn't the time, Mitch decided, to mention civilian jobs J.D. could get in New York City. "Maybe they won't live in New York."

"He's a damned stock broker. He ain't gonna commute from Peoria."

Mitch shrugged. "McGuire in New Jersey has a big MAC wing."

"Me, a MAC weenie flying many-motors? Neither of us'll live long enough to see that."

The insult stung. Mitch stood and didn't hide his anger. "Maybe it's time you recognized real life isn't James Dean running around insulting everyone in *Rebel Without a Cause* and *East of Eden*. A father's responsibility is to do what's best for his children."

"I wouldn't know about that." The tone was sharper than the edge on J.D.'s knife.

"Pardon me," Mitch said, confused by the answer.

"The last time my father and I yelled at each other was back in nineteen fifty-three."

"Your parents divorced then?"

"No! That's when I left home. My mother'd already died."

"You left home at fifteen? Did you go live somewhere else?"

"Of course I lived somewhere else—but not with anybody I knew."

Mitch couldn't imagine living on his own at fifteen. He realized how alone J.D. really was. "Maybe it's time you grew up and climbed down off your James Dean cross. Go tell your dad you've been a sonuva bitch as a son and say you love—"

J.D. whirled and swung, hitting Mitch square on the cheek.

Letters flew from Mitch's hand as he fell backward into the mud, barely missing the edge of the bunker. He was stunned for an instant but angered as soon as he felt a stinging above his cheekbone. He scrambled to his feet.

J.D. muttered something, took a couple of steps toward the walkway, then turned. Mitch slammed him with a shoulder-high tackle, and they tumbled down the slope toward the street. As they struggled to their feet, Mitch swung wildly. J.D. grabbed for a wrestling hold.

After stumbling across the wooden walkway, they lurched into the street. Several Marines scrambled out of the way.

J.D. stepped in and got a partial hip throw. Mitch grabbed hold of J.D., and they rolled into the ditch near the urinal.

Adapting a line from *Dr. Strangelove*, a Marine sergeant shouted, "You can't fight here. This is Khe Sanh."

Most bystanders laughed.

J.D. locked his arms around Mitch from behind. "Stop it! Are you ready to stop?"

"Hell, no!" Mitch rose to a knee in a twisting attempt to throw J.D.

"Quit, now!"

Mitch kicked the heel of his boot into one of J.D.'s shins.

J.D. yelped, then drove Mitch forward against the barrel and bent him over the rim.

The stench was nauseating. Mitch's struggles became frantic.

"Are you gonna quit? Say you're ready to quit."

Grappling for a better hold, Mitch saw his name tag slip from the holder on his flight suit. The tag landed in the barrel near J.D.'s letter.

Watching the tag, Mitch became angrier. Words from a judo instructor at the Academy came to mind. *If your best friend breaks your arm, it'll hurt as much as if your worst enemy broke it.* Mitch had a hand against the inside of one of J.D.'s knees. Swinging up along the thigh, he slammed his fist into J.D.'s groin.

J.D. groaned and crumpled beside the barrel.

Mitch threw himself backward, caught a foot, and plopped hard in the mud. He struggled to rid his nostrils of the terrible smell. Scrambling to a knee, he looked at J.D. to prepare for another attack.

J.D. grimaced with both hands between his legs. He shifted slightly and let out another groan. His eyes opened, and he stared at Mitch. "Progress at long last. I finally conned you into breaking a rule."

Mitch almost laughed but was afraid that might start the fight again. "I doubt Mighty Mort would approve."

"He doesn't understand about being a warrior."

Mitch looked at his name tag holder. "I lost my name tag in that damned barrel."

J.D. reached limply to the name tag above his breast pocket. "You can have mine, or if you wanta fish yours out, I'll hold your ankles."

"Which is worse, going back in that barrel or having people mistake me for J.D. Dalton?"

"Life's full of little dilemmas, sport." J.D. grabbed the barrel and pulled himself painfully to his feet. He looked at his mud-caked flight suit. "I need a shower."

"Roger that."

Mitch wrapped an arm around J.D. and helped him limp across the street. They took off their boots and emptied their pockets. With flight suits on, they stepped into the shower stall.

J.D. opened the valve to release water from the barrels. "Don't tell Mighty Mort we've started showering together."

"I won't if you don't tell Elizabeth."

Chilly water splashed on Mitch's head, sending muddy rivulets cascading from his eyebrows. The water stung his cheek, and he rubbed the spot where J.D. had hit him. "I didn't mean to pry. I just thought—"

"You're right about lots of things, but I can't fix 'em. My old man begged me to see him last year, but I was still playing Jimmy Dean." J.D. ran fingers through clotted hair. "A visit probably wouldn'ta made any difference."

"Maybe when you've finished your tour, you—"

"Doesn't matter now." J.D. bit his lip. "He went ahead and died, so we're never gonna settle things, this side of hell anyway."

"Sorry." Mitch wondered if tears were mingled in the water on J.D.'s cheeks. Losing family and career would be devastating, no matter how much bravado disguised the hurt. He pitied J.D.

J.D. leaned against a wall and stared at the hills of Laos. "If you have to finish your life as a captain, no sense dragging it out."

"Don't even talk like that."

J.D. flashed his James Dean grin. "It's so easy to get a rise out of you. I flip a little bait on the surface, and you jump clear out of the water."

"Suicide isn't something to joke about."

"You're the guy using the S-word. I'm just playing."

"You know exactly what we're talking about."

J.D. partially unzipped his flight suit and let water splash on his chest. "What would you do, roomie?"

"About what?"

"If Elizabeth wanted to marry someone else and have him raise Mandy as his daughter?"

"I don't know." Mitch had never considered Elizabeth might ever want to leave him. "I wouldn't like it."

"Damn straight! But if that's the reality, Mister Logic, what do you do to make the best of the bad situation? You were preaching about a father doing what's best for his kids. Having two dads is probably as confusing as not having one at all."

"I don't know. That's why I think you should talk to someone.

Maybe a chaplain."

J.D. laughed. "If I ever walk into a chapel, expect lightning to strike."

"Maybe you could talk to—"

"A shrink? You start talking to shrinks, you stop flying airplanes. That's not how I intend to end my flying career."

"You almost ended your flying career making mincemeat out of buffalo. You're too good a pilot to make a dumb mistake like forgetting your fuel."

"Even Jimmy Dean wasn't infallible."

"Maybe something inside that you don't even control kept you from switching tanks."

"If you'd been along, you wouldn't have seen anything slowing me down. I nearly ripped off the handle."

"I'm talking about before the engine quit. A shrink might sort tha—"

"You're just whistlin' Dixie in the dark if you think I'm gonna see a shrink."

Mitch didn't know what else to suggest.

"Seems to me," J.D. continued, "if someone else is gonna be father to your kids, the best thing you can give them to remember you by is that blue ribbon with the white stars."

Mitch recognized the description of the ribbon that was part of the Medal of Honor. "A little J.D. one upmanship?"

J.D. smiled. "I don't see a better answer, and maybe I could accomplish something important."

"I wish I could convince you there're better answers, but I'm not much of a psychologist."

"Pretty crappy." J.D. hit Mitch's shoulder lightly. "But you're a fair-to-middlin' friend."

"Thanks."

Mitch leaned forward, closed his eyes, and let water drench his forehead. He was haunted by the feeling that J.D. had a death wish. Mitch could think of nothing to change that—short of reporting his suspicions and taking the responsibility for causing J.D. to be barred from the skies he loved.

Chapter 27

Early the next morning, Mitch stirred toward wakefulness beneath a blanket he'd pulled over his head during the night. The faint odor of medicinal alcohol mingled with the smell of the wool blanket. He rolled onto his back, and something brushed his nose. Mitch stiffened, suddenly awake. Yanking the blanket away, he imagined snakes, spiders, and yet-to-be-identified species of exotic bugs.

A dark mass swung slowly above his face. Too close for his eyes to focus on, the object was outlined by dim light from the kitchen. He recalled tarantulas rushing like puffs of black fur across Oklahoma highways. A squeal escaped his lips as he slashed out and twisted away. Something seared his wrist before he hit whatever dangled above his pillow.

Bitten! He got a foot on the floor and pushed. The metal legs of the bed screeched on the concrete. He didn't stop scrambling until reaching the far end of his mattress.

Someone groaned a sleepy response to the commotion.

Mitch gasped for breath. His eyes searched frantically until he spotted the thing swinging wildly, like a large bug flying from one side of the upper bunk to the other. A sound of muffled laughter was slow to register. The erratic motion had something regular about it, moving at a fixed distance from a point directly above his pillow. The motion slowed as if a pendulum-run-wild were being tamed by gravity.

Suppressing his panic, he became more aware of the quiet laughter. He glanced behind, expecting to see J.D.'s grinning face. Instead he saw Captain Young watching from two bunks away. Young's hand was over his mouth to muffle the noise. The light in the kitchen reflected a smile in Young's eyes. Mitch reached beneath his bunk for his flashlight.

Young whispered, "J.D. said you needed its luck more than he did."

As light caught the object, Mitch realized he would see the pig snout. He sat up and was momentarily distracted by an ache in his jaw. He remembered his fight with J.D. Mitch's fingers explored the tenderness, and he winced touching the cut on his cheek. Flashing the light on his hand, he saw a red abrasion where the bootlace had scraped his wrist.

He brought the snout to a halt and thought about J.D.'s vow to wear the snout. J.D. had kept the promise—at least a few days. Nevertheless, Mitch believed a lengthier period had been implied. "Where's J.D.?"

"Went to fly."

"Fly?" He checked his wristwatch. J.D.'s boisterous drinking at last night's poker game was the main reason Mitch had pulled the blanket over his head. That had been near midnight, with drinking closer than appropriate for an early morning takeoff. "J.D. wasn't scheduled to fly until noon."

"The Marines needed cover for an inbound convoy. Weather's dogshit."

"The grunts made the right choice. How long's he been gone?"

Young angled his watch to the light. "Ten, maybe fifteen minutes."

"So he might not be airborne."

"I doubt it."

Mitch quickly dressed, then unfastened the bootlace and headed for the exit. When he emerged from the bunker, a dismal Sunday greeted him. A solid overcast was as low as on the day he'd arrived. This morning, however, clouds rushed eastward as if in a race from Laos to the South China Sea. Mitch jogged toward the runway. The wind penetrated his flight suit and threatened to snatch his flight cap from his head.

After crossing the main road, he slowed to listen for an O-1. Above the roar of the wind, he heard an airplane. Reaching the cleared area along the runway, he saw an O-1 about halfway to the east end. He moved closer, stopping near one of the portable lights scattered along the runway. Unsheltered from winds blowing full force off Hill 881, he had difficulty standing still. One moment he had to lean into a blast to avoid being pushed sideways; in the next, the gusty gale died, and he had to take a step to regain his balance.

He glanced at the control tower, half expecting to see signal lights motioning him to move back. However, the men he saw seemed unconcerned. He assumed the Marines figured his wearing a flight suit meant he knew enough to stay out of the way of airplanes.

How different this was from the strictly regulated life he'd lived at the Academy, during pilot training, and while assigned to C-141s. He remembered the contentment of being within the comfortable cocoon of the rigid regulations. Now, shivering beside a windswept runway on this dreary Sunday morning, he realized he could never settle for such unquestioning comfort again.

J.D. had been right emphasizing judgment over blind obedience. Standing unprotected within plain sight of enemy gunners, Mitch was more aware than ever that regulations and strict procedures had limits. J.D. had been more correct than Mitch had ever given him credit for.

The Bird Dog accelerated slowly into the wind. Mitch raised a clinched fist above his head. Dangling the pig snout from the bootlace, he twirled the combination like a bolo.

J.D.'s O-1 had nearly reached Mitch before lifting tentatively from the runway and bouncing in tricky winds. J.D. stuck a hand out the window, pointed his finger like a pistol at Mitch, then snapped his thumb down like a pistol's hammer. Jostling by on an invisible sea of rough air, J.D. raised his finger to his lips as if blowing smoke from a gun barrel.

Then he pulled into a steep, climbing turn.

Mitch stopped twirling the bootlace and grabbed the snout. He stared at it a moment. *Why the hell not wear it? Even metal dragons can use all the luck they can find.* Smiling, he looped the lace over his head and tucked the snout inside his flight suit.

Eager to get out of the wind, he turned and jogged toward the bunker. He looked forward to opening Elizabeth's fifth letter and to warm feelings her words of love would create on this cold, cheerless morning.

Passing a supply dump near the perimeter of the runway, Mitch sensed something was wrong. The O-1's engine whined as if protesting the throttle had been advanced too far.

Mitch whirled.

J.D. had completed the turn. Flying downwind, the O-1 seemed to be having trouble keeping up with wind-driven clouds. The nose was up as if J.D. had pulled into a steep climb. Nevertheless the aircraft wasn't getting closer to the dark clouds.

The O-1 rolled violently, then plunged into a spin.

Mitch stood frozen by an aviator's special fright. He wanted to believe this was another stunt like barrel rolls on takeoff. A shuddery sensation weakened his knees and argued this was no stunt.

He saw the rudder full left when the tail rotated toward him on the next spin. Moments later he saw the elevator was full down, indicating J.D. had the stick against its forward stop. He was making the right moves to recover from the spin—but the plummeting aircraft needed more altitude. The only hope was that J.D. was over the upper canyon of the Rao Quan, which ran parallel to the runway before dropping over the waterfall.

"Please, God," Mitch whispered.

Racing toward the runway, he sensed the rate of spin was slowing. The nose angled down even steeper. The rudder and elevator were becoming effective. Instead of falling uncontrollably in the spin, the O-1 was straining to fly.

It plunged behind tents and sandbagged bunkers beyond the runway.

Mitch hoped the O-1 was over the canyon. A flash backlit the bunkers. Black smoke spewed up and rushed east, swirling erratically in the wind.

Less than a second later, Mitch heard a metallic thud that sickened him. He kept running. Like a quick echo of the crash, the sound of the explosion reached him. In the horrifying shock of the moment, the only sense of reality came from of his boots thumping on the metal runway.

He saw silhouettes of Marines rise above lines of sandbags. Other men—mechanics near helicopters, riflemen, supply sergeants—scrambled away from what they were doing. Everyone faced the boiling black smoke. Mitch ran headlong past people, trenches, makeshift huts, and stacks of supplies. He zigzagged until he could see the flames—and another explosion. A fluttering flash of red and yellow rushed like an elevator up into the black smoke. *The second fuel tank.* Flames now were being fed by 250 pounds of avgas. He wondered about the marking rockets whose white phosphorous burned on contact with air. The lack of white smoke indicated the rockets had survived the crash with warheads intact.

The plateau ahead was a wide meadow, stretching a mile before being cut off by the Rao Quan's upper canyon. A stream meandered across the middle of the meadow. The O-1 was burning on the gentle downslope leading to the stream.

The only things separating Mitch from the burning airplane were the base's perimeter defenses and three hundred yards of open ground. He bolted toward the trenches, the sandbagged bunkers, the scores of curious Marines, and the barriers of wire beyond. Dodging around a bunker, he barged by a Marine who had to jump out of the way.

A voice shouted, "You can't go out there, Captain!"

Like extraneous words on the radios, the statement hardly registered. Reaching the wire, he stopped short, searching frantically for a way across. His breath came in rapid gasps with the cool air burning deeply in his lungs.

As a teenager hunting in Kansas, he'd crossed three-strand, barbed-wire fences and had been nicked by the barbs more than once. Nothing from his experiences, however, prepared him for the barrier separating him from J.D.

It made him think of the old three-strand fences mutated beyond imagination. From the top of metal posts, barbed wire angled down to rows of stakes parallel on both sides of the fence. The triangular frameworks supported ten or twelve more rows of barbed wire. The base of the resulting barrier was nearly twelve feet wide. Beyond the first fence, coils of interlinked concertina wire formed a six-foot wide obstacle. Seeing no way to go around the wire, Mitch decided to go over.

As he caught his breath, he took one more look at the burning O-1. "Please, God," he whispered again, hoping for a miracle.

He remembered an instructor at the Academy telling about crashing a jet trainer upside down immediately after takeoff. Trapped, the young pilot had been severely burned while waiting for the canopy to melt so he could escape. Then he nearly had been run over by a fire truck. The crash crews hadn't expected to find a survivor as they raced to the scene. That was the kind of miracle Mitch was praying for. He looked in vain, hoping to see J.D. hobbling from the burning aircraft.

Mitch sighed, then rushed forward. Stepping onto the second wire, he used the horizontal strands like steps on a flimsy ladder. The taut wire jittered beneath him. He heard shouting voices almost swallowed in the roaring wind. Words didn't matter. His entire being had a single focus, with distractions shut out. When he grasped the top strand of wire, a hand grabbed his boot. Someone else tackled him around the waist. All three men tumbled into the barbed-wire.

"You can't, Captain," one man shouted. "They're in the minefield!"

Mitch strained against the men and the wire until his mind allowed words to register. Stiffening, he shouted, "We've gotta do something!"

"We can't, sir!"

Mitch struggled a final time but discovered he was entangled in several strands of wire with barbs clinging tenaciously to his flight suit. He slumped on the wire, unwilling to accept defeat but unable to refute the men who held him. "Understand," he said softly, and the two men released him.

As he fought to free himself, sharp barbs ripped his arms and legs. Other Marines stepped in. Mitch waited passively while wires were clipped and pulled away.

He was helped to his feet, and someone handed him his flight cap. Reddish mud was smeared across his captain's bars, but he shoved the hat into a pocket. When everyone was clear of the wire, he saw a lieutenant and a sergeant had stopped him. Both had cuts on their faces and arms. Mitch shrugged in utter helplessness. "Sorry."

"That's okay, sir," the lieutenant said. "We wanted to go out, too."

Now Mitch noticed his surroundings. Scores of Marines lined the wire, and more ran from nearer the runway. In the background he heard the deep-throated groan of a fire truck accelerating in low gear. Its siren wailed a warning that mingled with the whine of a helicopter engine winding up. Closer he heard a static-laced voice on a field radio and realized a nearby captain was answering queries from the command post.

Mitch didn't want to watch the fire, but he couldn't keep his eyes away. Staring at the pulsating red flames, he could almost hear J.D.'s voice. *The one thing worse than crashing and burning and getting killed is crashing and burning and not getting killed.* Mitch was confused about what to pray for.

A bright flash shook the base of the smoke, and a marking rocket fishtailed out of the wreckage. The errant rocket headed toward the spectators but whooshed overhead almost before anyone could react.

An uncoordinated chorus of voices yelled, "Incoming!" Everyone scrambled for cover.

Mitch dropped flat on the ground and watched the rocket until it disappeared beyond the nearby tents that blocked his view of the runway. Moments later, a puff of white smoke rose in the wind beyond the southern perimeter of the base.

"He's carrying three more Willie Petes," Mitch shouted to the captain with the radio.

As if on cue, a second rocket skittered out of the red flames. It rushed into the air on a tongue of fire, making a dazzling contrast to the dreary setting beneath the clouds. The damaged propellant casing caused the rocket to swirl wildly, ricocheting off the brushy upslope leading toward the Rao Quan. On the third glancing impact, the warhead exploded. Chunks of burning phosphorous spiraled skyward while larger pieces of rocket corkscrewed through expanding wisps of white smoke.

Mitch watched in awe, then stood. Red mud caked his hands and flight suit. As he absentmindedly wiped mud from his hands, he noticed no one else nearby was standing. Most of the Marines, who undoubtedly had a healthy respect for the dangers of white phosphorous, rose to a knee or rushed closer to trenches. Frustrated that time was slipping away, he shouted, "Let's get on with it! We can't stand here all day."

Moments later, the fire truck and an ambulance stopped at the fence. Two Marines rushed forward, checked maps, then pointed into the minefield. Other men started cutting a path through the barriers of wire.

Lieutenant Colonel Hale, Captain Young, and two other FACs joined Mitch. He hardly took his eyes from the fire as he described the crash.

"I'm sorry, Captain," Hale said. After patting Mitch lightly on the shoulder, Hale hurried to the Marine with the radio.

Young asked a couple of questions, eliciting no more than shrugs from Mitch. When another FAC joined the small gathering and asked what had happened, Young herded the others away before answering.

Mitch was engrossed in the preparations to clear a path when a hand grasped his shoulder. Glancing around, he saw Snake Sheldon.

Snake looked grim. "What happened?"

Mitch tried to form words but only felt a shiver through his entire body. He could either tell Snake what had happened or concentrate on holding back a flood of tears, but he wasn't capable of both. He shrugged and turned toward the burning aircraft.

"J.D.?"

Mitch nodded without taking his eyes from the flames.

"Any chance he—"

"No," Mitch said quietly, shaking his head.

"Damn it all!"

Snake threw his helmet. It bounced, then rolled into a nearby group of Marines. A corporal retrieved the helmet and stood dutifully until Snake was ready to accept it.

An armed, UH-1 Huey rose from the nearby parking ramp, swooped low over the crowd and flew across the no-man's land.

A cold rain, made more bitter by the gusty wind, began to fall. Mitch hardly noticed. Marines scurried to bunkers and tents to get ponchos and shelter-halves. Someone draped a poncho over Mitch's shoulders.

Mitch ignored it, and the next gust of wind carried the poncho into the wire. He concentrated on the helicopter hovering over the burning wreckage. Two Marines, swinging unsteadily beneath the Huey, lowered themselves on ropes. Mitch turned to Snake. "What about the mines?"

"The crash is at least fifty yards beyond our minefields."

"Can you get me on a chopper?"

Snake seemed hesitant, then gestured at the captain with the radio. "We aren't in direct contact with the Huey, but clearing a path through the minefield won't take long."

Mitch faced the fire. "J.D. was too smart to make a mistake like that!"

Snake looked confused. "Like what?"

"Turning quickly out of a gusty headwind. He knew damned well what an O-1 takes to keep flying!"

"All week I've had a feeling J.D. was gonna buy the farm."

"I've felt that way for months." Self-recrimination filled his head. *What could he have done—what should he have done to yank J.D. from his path of self-destruction?*

Snake wiped away rain sliding down his forehead. "The other night I was cringing in the boonies with a platoon of NVA taking a break thirty meters away. But you know what? I kept thinking about J.D. I was certain his final exit'd be a Medal-of-Honor mission, not—"

"Some fuckin', senseless accident!" Mitch kicked the lowest strand of wire. A barb gouged a jagged line across the black leather of his boot.

"He made another dumb mistake before and should've had his wings clipped."

Mitch was struck by the irony. The wing of J.D.'s O-1 almost had been clipped. Guilt surged over him. What if he'd reported the O-1 had been damaged because J.D. violated regulations? Mitch knew he would have had trouble living with himself after playing tattletale, but J.D. might still be alive.

"J.D. didn't know how to live life at other than full throttle," Snake said, "and I'm not sure he could've survived without airplanes."

"J.D. needed help." Mitch had to clear his throat. "I just didn't know how to give it to him."

Cold rain dripped from his eyebrows into his eyelashes. Mitch turned his back to the windswept rain. His thoughts were interrupted by a radio message from the command post.

"Gunslinger reports one fatality and no signs of survivors."

Mitch closed his eyes. He hadn't expected a different answer, but the finality jolted him. He wanted to cry or to scream or to hit someone. Instead, he yanked down the zipper of his flight suit and grabbed the pig snout. Snatching it upward, he finally got the bootlace over his head, then threw the good-luck charm as far as he could across the wire barricades. "Damn you! Damn all your spirits!"

The Marine with the radio said, "Colonel Hale says only one person was aboard."

The voice from the command post asked, "What's your status?"

"We've got the wire down," the Marine said, scanning men working near the fire truck. "We'll start clearing a path in the next couple of minutes."

Hale looked grim as he joined Mitch and Snake. Hale studied Mitch a moment. "I know you and Dalton were close. I need to ask if you feel up to flying this afternoon."

Mitch's mind was almost blank. He couldn't remember even having seen the flying schedule. He forced himself to concentrate, pondering what day it was and whether it was early or late morning.

"All the other pilots are on the schedule for this afternoon," Hale said. "If you need to stand down the rest of the day, I'll see about canceling another mission."

"No—no, sir." Mitch shook his head. "I'd rather fly."

"Good man." Turning toward the runway, Hale said, "I need to call headquarters."

"Yes, sir." Mitch faced the wreckage and noticed the fire was starting to burn itself out.

"Give me your attention," a voice blared over a portable loudspeaker. A Marine major, standing on top of the fire truck, continued, "We're going to set off a few mines, so hunker down or get behind cover."

As Mitch knelt, he saw the major was accompanied on the fire truck by a husky Marine with an M-60 machine gun. Lowering the loudspeaker, the major referred to a map a few moments, then pointed into the minefield.

The other Marine fired a short burst at the ground about forty yards beyond the barriers. He adjusted his aim and fired. When the major was satisfied, the gunner concentrated his fire around the last aim point.

Moments later, an explosion blasted shrapnel and dirt around the first mine. Gray smoke, seemingly inconsequential compared to the column of black, quickly disappeared in the wind. The black smoke made Mitch wonder why, in spite of his fears, he'd persisted in being a pilot. The small puff of gray reminded him he was glad he wasn't an infantryman.

Within minutes, the bullets had detonated six more mines. Two men with portable mine detectors hurried through the wire and methodically checked a path about twice the width of the fire truck. Other Marines followed, marking each side of the pathway with long ribbons of day-glow orange. Finally, the team's leader shot a fist into the air and pumped downward a couple of times. The driver of the fire truck gunned the engine and maneuvered through the opening in the wire.

Mitch started to follow, but Snake grabbed his shoulder. "We don't want to go out there."

Mitch whirled, glaring at Snake. "You may not, but I do!"

"No, you don't. You never forget seeing friends in pieces."

Mitch groaned, then pulled away. "I owe it to J.D. to be with him."

"J.D. isn't there anymore. I keep picturing him somewhere, looking down and saying it's nicer there than he'd ever imagined."

Mitch reached with both hands and wiped rain from his face. Watching from behind the wire had been gruesome enough. He feared he'd never want to fly again if he got a look into the burned-out cockpit.

Snake stepped between Mitch and the pathway through the minefield. "You've got a million memories of J.D. better than ones you'd have after seeing that airplane up close."

"I wouldn't want him thinking I didn't care."

"J.D. knows." Snake put an arm around Mitch's shoulder. "Come on. I've got a new bottle of Jack Daniel's we can kill."

"I can't drink." Mitch retrieved his flight cap and wiped mud from the captain bars J.D. had given him. Turning toward the runway, he spoke with determination. "I've got three times as many missions to fly as I had before."

Chapter 28

That afternoon, Mitch moved like a zombie. He hardly lifted his boots from the metal planks as he shuffled around the O-1. Item-by-item, he went through a routine pre-flight check. He finished at the right landing gear, then ducked beneath the wing strut. Lieutenant Mark Taylor, a Marine observer assigned to the mission, blocked the doorway while putting gear in back.

Waiting on Taylor, Mitch looked at his checklist. His thumb was pressed beneath the last item of the exterior check. However, he couldn't remember seeing the dipstick for the oil. Thinking back, he couldn't recall specifics about what he had checked.

Snap out of it, dummy. Guys are killed every day. He found no solace in the words. Gazing at the checklist, he wondered if he'd missed anything. Since O-1s were so rugged, he doubted he'd skipped anything that'd kill them. Nevertheless, while Taylor strapped in, Mitch rechecked the oil.

He mechanically went through pre-takeoff checks, but his thoughts hardly left J.D. *What if their schedules had been reversed?* Would he now be dead instead of J.D.? *Would both be alive?*

A feeling of quiet determination had taken hold deep inside. He might need a day or two to recover, but he now had a special calling for the remainder of his combat tour—maybe for the rest of his life. He must help ensure America didn't lose the war J.D. died in so needlessly.

The morning's storm had passed leaving a steady wind of ten knots. After takeoff, Mitch waited until gaining an extra fifteen knots before banking into a wide, gentle turn. He stared at the blackened wreckage. Several men and two jeeps were near the scorched mud and twisted metal. Orange streamers still outlined a pathway through the minefield. Watching them flutter in the wind, Mitch thought about how in a single, careless act, one could blunder through the frail boundaries between life and death, never to exist again—except in the hearts of one's friends.

While mentally replaying moments before the crash, he realized Taylor was snapping pictures. Mitch wanted to lash out and grab the camera, but he said nothing. Instead he looked at the beauty of the waterfall. He would give anything if he and J.D. could make that trek to the waterfall. He pushed aside painful memories long enough to check-in with the Marine command post.

"Roger, Five-nine," the radio operator said. "Contact Thurston on Fox Mike Forty-three decimal three. He's about four thousand meters west."

As Mitch acknowledged, he banked west. He saw what he guessed was a reinforced company of Marines at the edge of the valley. The lead platoon was winding its way up the ridge known as Dong Dang. The rest of the men were in old rice paddies and stands of bamboo at the base of the hill. Mitch switched frequencies. "Thurston, Nail Five-nine's with you on Fox Mike. I have you visual."

"Roger, Nail. Thurston's tromping weeds. We'd appreciate a little cover until we settle in on top."

"No problem." Mitch welcomed an uncomplicated flight, something simple to occupy his mind and to help him endure the next few hours.

Checking his map, he saw Dong Dang also was known as Hill 689, because its crest was 689 meters above sea level. He leveled off about a thousand feet above the hilltop.

"Sure beats walking," Taylor said, as the Marines struggled with heavy loads.

Mitch pictured the wreckage of J.D.'s O-1. "Most of the time."

He saw an irregular pattern of trenches on the crest. The hilltop was clear of trees and underbrush for fifty yards around the trenches. He saw scattered clumps of foliage in the clearing and on the edge of the jungle, which covered most of a ridge stretching into Laos. Mitch remembered J.D.'s dragon. Dong Dang was the left foot, and the ridge was the dragon's leg.

Mitch asked, "Are those trenches ours?"

"Mostly, sir. Periodically we go up and send patrols into the boonies."

Mitch nodded. For the next few minutes, he let Taylor study the hilltop. Mitch simply rolled the O-1 one way, then the other, to keep from being a tempting target for enemy troops who might be watching. Unable to muster enthusiasm for anything, he moved like a robot.

"I'm not sure what, sir," Taylor said, "but something doesn't look right."

Mitch clamped the stick between his knees and steadied his binoculars. He saw the hilltop was etched with marks where the runoff from the heavy rains had rushed across the open areas and beneath clumps of vegetation. In a few places old foliage had accumulated like tumbleweeds along a fence row. He wasn't used to studying the ground from only a thousand feet, but nothing struck him as out of the ordinary. "What's your concern?"

"Some trenches don't look as deep, sir, like they've filled in a little."

Mitch saw what Taylor meant. "How long since we've been here?"

"Six weeks. Maybe two months."

"Perhaps we're simply seeing debris that's washed in. Weather's been pretty damned wet since I arrived."

He rolled the aircraft level a few seconds. Even though he wasn't flying above AAA along the Trail, he didn't want to fly predictably. Crossing the east slope, Mitch got a good look at the Marines. They were at least thirty minutes from the top.

"Rain didn't wash out much," Taylor said. "The walls seem intact."

Mitch saw the width of the trenches was uniform. The deep, vertical ditches showed no major erosion. "You're the expert."

"Could be trash. In the southeast trench, I recognize soggy cardboard. Probably discarded C-ration cases."

Mitch saw a lump of dark tan and wondered why the cardboard hadn't disintegrated in six weeks of rain. Adrenaline stirred in him.

For the next ten minutes, he flew above Dong Dang and studied the trenches. *What would J.D. do—have done?* Mitch knew the answer. He presumed the trash was nothing but trash—but J.D. would never leave it to Thurston to prove there was no danger. Mitch couldn't either—not anymore. "Would a closer look help—about deciding whether anyone's waiting on the hilltop, I mean?"

"If we take a closer look," Taylor said with bravado, "we'll find out, one way or the other."

"No guts, no glory."

Mitch tried to think like a commander of NVA troops waiting in ambush. He could allow the American plane to buzz the trenches unopposed only if he had total confidence in his camouflage. However, a low pass would make him suspect his concealment was flawed. "Khe Sanh, Nail Five-nine. Are you monitoring this freq?"

"Roger, Nail."

"We're curious about some trash in trenches on Six-eighty-nine." Since Khe Sanh was an active fire base, Mitch assumed its artillerymen knew the range and azimuth to the hilltop outpost, but he wanted to make sure. "Do you have guns registered on the top of the ridge?"

"That's affirmative, Nail."

"If we stir things up, Thurston'll need fire support."

"Give us a couple of minutes to alert our gunners."

Mitch had shaken off his lethargy and now wished he had something besides unsecure radios to coordinate a battle plan.

"Nail Five-nine, Thurston. What do you want us to do?"

"Hunker down a few minutes. Sound off if anyone shoots at us."

"Will do, Nail."

Mitch circled the ridge and watched the O-1's shadow. The distance between the airplane and the ground changed abruptly over the rugged terrain, so the shadow hesitated in some areas, then raced forward across the treetops. He checked how far southwest he was when the O-1's blurry image rippled across the trenches.

"I want the sun behind us when we go for the close-up," Mitch said on intercom. "We'll come in steep, and I'll level off abruptly at a hundred feet. Be ready to look out the right window."

"Got it, sir."

The radio operator said, "Khe Sanh's ready when you are, Nail."

"Standby." Mitch turned southwest. When he was satisfied with the shadow's progress, he pulled his lapbelt tighter. "Ready back there?"

Taylor stomped his boots on the floor. "*Semper Fi!*"

"Hold onto your cookies."

Mitch pulled up as if rolling in to mark. Seconds later the O-1 pointed at the trenches, with the airspeed increasing from little more than zero. Through the propeller's blur, he watched the shadow and trenches grow. A surge of excitement echoed J.D.'s normal enthusiasm. *This really was flying at its best.* He started a rolling pullout from the dive, and a wave of foreboding swept over him. He sensed movement in the foliage and the trenches.

Mitch wished he'd lowered the clear visor on his helmet to protect his face. His hand shot upward, reaching for the knob that locked the visor out of view above his forehead.

Flashes erupted from trenches, bushes, and piles of foliage.

Tracers converged on the O-1. Slugs slammed the aircraft even before he heard the *rat-a-tat-tats* of more AK-47s than he could count. His left ankle smashed against the side of the cockpit. Half the windshield disintegrated. Instinctively, Mitch leaned to evade jagged pieces of Plexiglas.

Taylor shouted, "Sheee-it!"

A 110-knot wind blasted through the broken windshield, slamming Mitch's face like a slap from brass knuckles. Dirt from every crevice became a biting cloud of dust. His eyes closed automatically. The last, blurry view warned him the O-1 was on its side with the wing slicing vertically toward the hilltop. He realized the unbalanced pressure of his right foot on the rudder pedal was accelerating the roll.

Thurston called, "You're getting ground fire, Nail."

Mitch twisted the knob on his helmet, jerking the visor in front of his face. When he could see again, he was hanging by his lapbelt and shoulder straps. The topsy-turvy scene was terrifying. The O-1 was inverted and only seconds from plowing upside-down into the top of Dong Dang. Ahead, a young soldier, draped by a cloak of mud-smeared canvas, knelt on the edge of a trench with his AK-47 pointed at Mitch. The wide-eyed gunner obviously was having second thoughts about holding his ground.

Mitch didn't have time to arm and fire a rocket, so he did the next best thing. He slammed the stick sideways to stop the roll and pushed the rudder to point the O-1 at the man with the AK-47. For the second time in his flying career, he had to fight natural instincts screaming that you always pulled back to pull out of a dive. Instead, he pushed the stick and throttle forward, decreasing the dive enough to raise the nose above the trenches.

The soldier hesitated, then dived headlong into the trench just before the O-1 roared overhead with its whip antenna nearly touching the ground.

The engine coughed, convincing Mitch he couldn't fly inverted much longer. The airplane flew beyond the crest, and the hillside dropped away. He rolled upright, and the damaged O-1 swooped a few feet above the Marines. Mitch shouted over the roar of the air rushing through the cockpit, "You okay, Lieutenant?"

"I think so. Well, not really. A bullet went through my leg, and I'm not sure where else."

Mitch wondered about his own injuries. With breaths coming in gasps, he couldn't tell how badly he was wounded. Blood seeped onto his eyebrow. He'd felt no discomfort until he pushed the left rudder pedal pulling out of the dive. A sharp pain sizzled up to above his knee. A squishiness in his boot said his leg was bleeding more than his head.

He slowed the O-1, leaned behind the remaining piece of windshield, and checked the airplane. The propeller spun as smoothly as before. The instrument panel showed no engine problems. Three lines of bullet holes were stitched across the wing. Halfway out to where the strut met the wing, fuel streamed through oval-shaped holes. He checked the fuel selector and verified the engine was being fed by the main tank in the left wing. The rugged little airplane was in better shape than he was.

An excited voice came over the radio. "Thurston's taking RPGs and automatic weapons fire from the top of the hill."

Turning away from the safety of the runway, Mitch said on intercom, "We've still got some flying to do, Lieutenant."

Mitch scanned Dong Dang. Among tracers spewing from AK-47s and heavier machine guns on the crest, he saw rocket-propelled grenades flash from the hilltop and fall toward the valley. They would hit well beyond Thurston's Marines, who were on the side returning fire. No direct line-of-fire existed between the NVA soldiers and the Marines, so everyone was wasting ammunition—except for keeping the enemies' heads down.

"Nail, Khe Sanh. Can you estimate the size of the enemy force?"

"Standby." Mitch tried to recall the number of streams of tracers from the hilltop. Perhaps two to three dozen, he thought.

"Thurston estimates nearly a company fired the initial volley."

"Sounds a little high," Mitch said on intercom.

Taylor said, "If I was on that hill, I'd have a higher estimate, too."

Mitch nodded, then said on the radio, "Five-nine's not sure there're that many, but I'm not sure there aren't."

"Can you clear us to fire from Khe Sanh base, Nail?"

"Standby, Khe Sanh." Mitch had two concerns. He had to stay out of the way of the artillery shells that would arc up several thousand feet before screaming to the earth. And, *short rounds* might fall on the company of unprotected Marines between the base and the target. "What's your situation, Thurston? Can we put a few rounds over you?"

"Affirmative, as long as you keep off this side of the hill."

Mitch was surprised to find his map still fluttering on a clip on his flight suit. He estimated the coordinates. As he wrote XD803409 on his clipboard, a drop of blood splashed inside his visor.

"Damn." He shook his head to dissipate the drop. The movement spattered blood on the visor and shot a pain across his forehead. *Dumb move. Wait till I tell J.D. ab—* He stopped in mid-thought, then focused on the hilltop. "Khe Sanh, Nail. Confirm coordinates X-Ray Delta eight-zero-three, four-zero-nine for the summit of Dong Dang."

"Roger, Nail. That's what we're registered on."

In spite of his eagerness to counterattack, Mitch wanted to verify the artillery's accuracy. "Give me a single smoke no farther east than eight-zero-three."

"Roger the single smoke, Nail. Also, be advised two Gunslingers will come off the pads in about four minutes."

"Gunslingers are our armed Hueys," Taylor said, indicating the call sign represented the UH-1 gunships.

"Roger. How you doing, Lieutenant?"

"Hanging in, sir. Keep going about your business."

Mitch remembered his father's words about men under pressure.

Taylor measured up fine. Mitch continued climbing and angled from the north toward the crest of Dong Dang. He saw a flash at the main base. "Marking round's on the way." He noticed firing on the hilltop had ceased. "The bastards must be running,"

"The gomers plan their escapes as carefully as their ambushes, sir" Taylor said. "Unless ordered to stand and fight at all costs, they're *de-deing* out on a pre-planned route."

"Roger that. They'll be hundreds of yards away when gunships arrive." The search area would expand geometrically in a jungle favoring hiders over seekers.

"At least we gave a bunch of Marines another sunset, Captain."

Mitch nodded, proud of the accomplishment but hounded by remorse for the life he'd failed to save. Watching the jungle, he felt a determination to carry on the fight for J.D. The quicker the escape routes were found, the better chance he had of destroying the NVA ambushers. J.D.'s words echoed through Mitch's thoughts. *Shoot at the FAC, and you pay the price!* Mitch shouted into the intercom. "We've got to find 'em."

"I can't see for shit with the air conditioner blowin' full blast, sir."

"Sorry about that, Marine," Mitch said. "I'm—"

The phosphorous shell burst on the west edge of the hilltop outpost, and a huge plume of white smoke billowed skyward. Mitch studied the impact of the first shell to decide how to adjust the artillery. Something he was seeing—or wasn't seeing—clashed with his memory of the last few seconds before the North Vietnamese had opened fire. The crest of Dong Dang looked different, but he couldn't pinpoint the change. He hoped his confusion wasn't due to shock and the loss of blood.

The radio operator asked, "How's that, Nail?"

"Shit hot," Taylor said on intercom.

"Sierra Hotel," Mitch said enthusiastically on the radio. He wanted to walk the artillery shells away from the Marines and into the ravine west of the trenches. "Give me a half dozen rounds for effect from there to a hundred meters west."

"Six rounds coming up."

He struggled to see his map. The blood on his visor added to the difficulty caused by the wind blast. Contour lines showed a ridge leading southwest from Dong Dang toward the Xe Pon. A dashed line, indicating a trail, traced the ridge where it descended into the river valley. The trail offered a way to flee the hilltop, unobserved by anyone watching from the Khe Sanh. Looking out the window, he picked out the ridge shown on the map. "The trail down the backside of that ridge looks like the easy way out."

"They don't take the easy way, Captain. They booby trap it for us."

Mitch nodded and studied the terrain for an alternative. From above the battlefield, he saw a better escape route. Dong Dang's main ridge led a mile northwest and joined the foothills of Dong Tam Ve, the large set of hills and ridges cresting beyond the border. Mitch decided if he were planning an ambush, then fleeing in the confusion afterward, he'd drop into the ravine west of the trenches. From there he could run under cover along the back of the main ridge all the way into Laos.

Blood dripped from his eyebrow and made seeing difficult. Nevertheless, Mitch felt more like the hunter than he'd ever felt before. He edged closer to the hilltop, studying the terrain on his hypothetical escape route. In his peripheral vision, he saw three flashes at the main base. A few seconds later, three more shells hurtled from the howitzers. Even before the shells arrived, Mitch neared the long ridge leading northwest.

Taylor asked nervously, "You are paying attention to the incoming, aren't you, Captain?"

"Of course." Mitch knew six shells were somewhere above, screaming down at the ridge. Glancing at the base, he confirmed that shells on target would plummet by, just south of the O-1. "Don't you have faith in your guys yanking the lanyards?"

"They'll hit the target as long as we don't get in their way."

"No sweatski." Mitch figured his biggest concern wasn't a four-inch-diameter shell hitting his O-1.

The first shell exploded on the hilltop. The other two blew away the upper edge of the ravine on the side opposite Khe Sanh. Mitch saw a bush-like figure thrown crazily through the air and disappear into the mushrooming clouds of pulverized rock, trees, and dirt. Three more blasts rocked the ravine, and he turned toward the hilltop.

The radio operator asked, "What do you want now, Nail?"

"Standby."

Mitch now had confidence in the gunners, so the next shells would block the enemy's retreat.

He rolled into a steep bank, pointing the left wing at the hilltop. A breeze moved dust away from six craters. Seeing two oblong clumps of foliage in the nearby grass, he realized the objects were most of two bodies, camouflaged heavily with vegetation. A quick look at the clearing around the trenches solved the mystery of what had changed. The bush-like clusters—which had been vegetation-covered soldiers—were gone. He was surprised at how bare the hilltop had become. Thurston may have been right about how many NVA soldiers had been lying in wait.

Looking for fleeing bushes, Mitch studied the ridge. A double-canopied jungle shielded most of the back side beyond the new craters. He checked gaps where ravines and outcrops of rocks kept taller trees from taking root. The closest gap was two hundred yards from the trenches. As he watched, a bush-like object scurried across. Then another, and another.

"Bingo!" Turning northwest, Mitch saw at least a dozen men moving through the trees on both sides of the opening. He checked farther ahead where the jungle canopy thinned considerably—no movement there yet. He looked at the base and estimated the angle of the original line of fire.

"Khe Sanh, Nail Five-nine'll take six more rounds. Add four-hundred meters and right two-hundred-and-fifty and disperse 'em a little."

"Understand, plus four-hundred, right two-fifty."

Mitch used left bank and opposite rudder to get a better look as the aircraft flew straight ahead. When he pushed the right pedal, the left came back against his wounded foot. He yanked his foot out of the way, and a sharp pain shot almost to his groin. He relaxed the leg, but pain persisted. Taking a moment to assess his wounds, he realized his head was throbbing and probably had been for a while.

He concentrated on the gap in the trees. Seconds passed without any sign of fleeing soldiers. The first shell flashed less than thirty meters away and kicked up a huge geyser of dirt. The other five shells exploded in quick succession. Mitch saw no soldiers, but he assumed the explosions had struck fear in the hearts of every man running from Dong Dang. He'd bracketed them and now would sweep a curtain of shrapnel back across the side of the ridge.

"Great shooting," Mitch said on the radio. "Let's back up from the last target. Give me a minus eighty and left fifty."

"Minus eighty and left fifty, Nail."

Mitch looked at smears of blood on the floor near his left boot. "We're going to have to turn this over to someone pretty quickly. Nail Five-nine has two wounded aboard."

"Understand, two wounded. Be advised Gunslinger Three-zero and Three-one are lifting off at this time."

"Good. I hope they're loaded for bear, because we've got targets."

"Roger that, Nail. We're scrambling four more gunships."

Mitch circled south for a good view of the back of the ridge. He checked his map for the coordinates of where the shells should fall. Using his grease pencil, he wrote XD798411 on the window.

He saw the first shell explode, then he was distracted by hundreds of flashes that sparkled between that explosion and the trenches. He couldn't figure out how artillery could cause such a crazy pattern. Then he saw hundreds of tracers arcing from the hillside.

"They're playing 'Kill the FAC'." Mitch jammed the throttle forward and banked violently away. "There must be—"

Hundreds of bullets zinged by. Scores slammed into the O-1. Two ripped the instrument panel. Others hit Mitch's right shoulder and arm. Another burned across his thigh. His right hand went limp and dropped away from the stick. He screamed and realized the sound seemed to echo from behind him.

Mitch wondered how badly Taylor was hit. He also wondered if he'd ever see Elizabeth again. He remembered the fifth letter, which remained unopened in his B-4 bag. After J.D.'s crash, Mitch had felt too hollow to face her bubbly enthusiasm.

"Nail, Khe Sanh. Your transmission was broken. Say again."

The engine cowling on the left side popped open. Slamming upward and restrained only by its hinges, the cowling shuddered violently. Oil from the engine splattered what was left of the windshield and swirled like a black mist into the cockpit.

"Nail Five-nine, Gunslinger Three-zero. Do you copy?"

Grabbing the stick with his left hand, Mitch accelerated the roll. He hoped to convince the NVA his aircraft was out of control as he put more distance between the O-1 and the gunners. He sensed the firing had decreased. After completing a roll, he kept the O-1 upright and flew beyond the effective range of the automatic weapons.

"They just kicked the shit out of us," Mitch said on the radio. "Maybe two companies are fleeing northwest on the southwest face of the ridge." That sounded so much like double talk, he wondered if anyone understood. "What was my last correction, Khe Sanh base?"

"Minus eighty, left fifty."

"Okay." The pain started to blur the numbers in his mind. "Give me, uh, minus one hundred and fifty and left one hundred, and fire for effect." He glanced at the number scrawled on the window. "They're concentrated about two hundred meters back toward Dong Dang from X-Ray Delta Seven-ninety-eight, four eleven."

"Khe Sanh Base copied."

"Gunslinger copied. We'll be with you shortly."

"We're running out of oil, blood, and ideas, so I'm about to RTB."

Gunslinger Thirty asked, "Can you give us a couple more minutes?"

Mitch asked on intercom, "What do you think, Lieutenant?"

"I'm not doing well."

"We can't wait, Gunslinger, but standby."

Mitch wanted to get rid of the rockets before landing his crippled O-1. Holding the stick with his knees, he reached up and clicked the four shackle-arming switches. Four green lights illuminated. After easing the throttle toward idle, he pulled the nose up short of a stall. Without warning, he whipped the stick left and aimed at the ridge. He squeezed the trigger and a pair of rockets blasted from each wing.

Pulling out of the dive and heading across the southern fringe of Dong Dang, Mitch called out on the radio, "Ho Chi Minh say: 'Shoot at the FAC, and you pay the price'."

Although unable to use J.D.'s Vietnamese phrasing, Mitch knew the message would get across to NVA monitors. More importantly, the message was about to be delivered to soldiers slamming fresh clips into their AK-47s while running breathlessly along the ridge.

The four flashes were simultaneous as the rockets slammed into jungle that had sparkled with gunfire moments earlier. Four plumes of pure white fought up through the trees.

"The gomers are dressed like bushes, Gunslinger, and you'll find 'em near my smoke."

"Good job, Nail. We'll shoot any bush that moves."

The jungle around the white smoke erupted. Artillery rained down as if his rockets had been for the artillery instead of for the helicopter. *J.D. would've loved of the timing.*

Once clear of Dong Dang, Mitch descended. His checklist was gone, so he reviewed a mental list of items. Changing switches was difficult with only one hand. He felt light-headed. *Hold on two more minutes for Elizabeth and Mandy.*

"Lock your shoulder harness," Mitch said before switching to tower. "Khe Sanh Tower, Nail Five-nine's two miles west with battle damage. Request immediate emergency landing on Runway Ten."

"Roger, Nail Five-nine, continue. Be advised Runway Two-eight is active with winds at two-seven-zero at twelve knots. Say intentions."

Mitch checked gauges on what remained of the instrument panel. The oil pressure gauge was shattered. The cylinder-head-temperature was pegged out well above the red-line. With most of the oil smeared on the windshield and in the cockpit, he wasn't surprised the engine was badly overheated. He didn't dare risk flying over the canyon to land from the east. "I'm on a right base leg for a downwind landing on Ten."

"Roger, Nail Five-nine cleared for emergency landing, Runway Ten."

Mitch had trouble seeing through the blood on his visor and the oil on the windshield. Soon, he could tell the O-1 was well above the normal glide path. His right arm was useless, so he clamped the stick between his knees. He yanked the throttle to idle and extended full flaps. Aiming at the end of the runway, he watched a few seconds to judge the rate and angle of descent. The tailwind blew the O-1 ever closer instead of pushing back as a headwind would. Grabbing the prop-control lever, he decreased the propeller's pitch to increase drag.

As the O-1 fell faster, Mitch was almost overcome by exhaustion and a hypnotic sense of well-being. He fought the temptation to lean back and close his eyes. Realizing he was about to black out, he stiffened his left leg against the rudder pedal. An excruciating pain shot from his foot to his waist. He groaned, but the pain cleared his head.

The O-1 was badly overshooting the end of the runway.

Jamming the right rudder pedal against the stop, he pulled the stick full left. Skidding through the air, the O-1 plummeted without gaining airspeed. He aimed a third of the way down the runway, which was the best he could hope for unless he circled to land from the opposite direction. He stared at the runway that seemed to rush up at him.

Cross-controlling at low altitude was dangerous, but he was determined not to run off the end and plunge into the canyon. He sensed it was time to neutralize the controls and recover from the steep plunge. Instead, he took a deep breath and counted quickly to five—assuming J.D. would've held on at least that much longer.

Mitch yanked his foot from the pedal, and the nose swung left. He used the stick to level the wings and to break the rapid descent. The O-1 wallowed a few times, then pointed down the runway. His movements were clumsy. He'd never made a left-handed landing in the O-1.

Everything looked pretty good, except he was nearing the control tower at mid-field, and the O-1 was twenty feet in the air. Easing the airplane lower, he remembered the day of wild landing attempts in Oklahoma. He sensed that in the overall scheme of life, that experience had been a necessary prelude to this moment.

With the wheels near the runway and airspeed bleeding off close to stall speed, Mitch pulled the stick back to his lap. He expected a quick stall. Instead, the O-1 floated on the tailwind and refused to quit flying.

A one-handed go-around on a bad engine was impossible, so Mitch hung on and waited. *The Lord is my shepherd.* To his right, jeeps, a fire truck, and hundreds of Marines seemed to rush by. To his left he saw helicopters on the parking ramp near the east end of the runway.

Mitch felt panic. Little runway remained, and he couldn't stop quickly using one brake.

He shouted, "Hang on, Lieutenant! This is gonna be close."

The tail wheel hit, and the main gear slammed hard on the runway. The O-1 skidded left, but he caught the skid with right rudder. He pushed lightly on the top of the pedal to apply the brake. *Nothing!* He pushed harder. *No resistance!* Hydraulic fluid undoubtedly had spewed from severed brake lines somewhere over Dong Dang.

Mitch peered beyond the spinning propeller. The end of the runway was coming up quickly. He yanked the mixture control to idle/cutoff, then twisted the ignition switch to off. The propeller slowed. Looking once more, he decided the O-1 wasn't going to stop on the runway. He feared the aircraft would skid across the mud and into the canyon.

"Hang on," he shouted without bothering to use the interphone.

He jammed the pedal against the stop. The tail swung around, and the O-1 skidded sideways. The tip of the wing dipped low and almost hit the planks. A tire blew, shredding rubber in large chunks The fuselage twisted, then snapped a few feet behind the cockpit.

The tail broke away clean, cartwheeled a half-dozen times, and bounced across the mud beyond the end of the runway.

Without the weight of the tail, the fuselage rotated forward. The nose and left wingtip slammed into the runway. The propeller gouged out two metal planks before breaking off. The airplane flipped in the air like a gymnast doing a somersault. The landing gear tore into the runway, and the battered airplane hit solidly on its nose and rocked forward. The O-1 balanced momentarily as if doing a headstand.

Mitch feared the airplane was going over onto its back. He was facing straight down when the seat ripped from the floor. He fell hard against the instrument panel. His helmet slammed into the compass, breaking it from its mounting and knocking him unconscious.

Becoming aware of his surroundings, he was unsure how long he had been out. The thudding of running boots convinced him only seconds had passed. His right arm refused to move, and his left was pinned beneath him, jammed against the instrument panel by the weight of his body and the seat.

Mitch smelled fuel and overheated oil. Fear of burning alive unleashed a surge of panic in place of the adrenaline that had kept him going. A trio of jolting booms frightened him, adding a new urgency to his struggles. Nevertheless he could do little to save himself.

Straining only produced a new wave of pain and left him with faint sensations of noises, smells, and feelings. As his mind tightroped at the edge of unconsciousness, he realized the thunder was from howitzers firing into the battle on Hill 689.

He heard voices—some soothing, some shouting commands. In the background, the whoosh of fire extinguishers blasted foam on the engine and over puddles of spilled fuel. Hands, firm but gentle, lifted and pulled. They carried him and the seat from the wreckage. The lapbelt and shoulder straps released their grip. Several people stripped off his parachute and eased him onto the runway.

Someone kept saying, "I'm okay, really."

Mitch realized he was hearing his voice.

A Marine removed the blood-spattered helmet. Mitch felt cold steel slip within the cuff of his right sleeve. He tried to say he still had feeling in his arm and didn't want to be cut. Before he could respond, the knife slit the sleeve from the wrist to the shoulder. With the bloody visor out of his way, Mitch saw a red cross on a Marine kneeling beside him.

"This'll help, Captain." The medic stabbed a needle into Mitch's arm. "Try to relax."

Mitch closed his eyes. He heard vehicles and more people converging. A voice asked for blood type. Before he could remember, he heard the metallic clatter of his dog tags being checked. A cool wet cloth told him someone was clearing blood from his forehead. Trembling, he suspected he was going into shock. Part of him said to let it happen—he'd earned it.

A callused hand took hold of his. Opening his eyes, Mitch saw Snake Sheldon.

"I thought we were gonna lose both you and J.D. the same day."

"J.D.?" Everything before the landing was hazy, but Mitch soon envisioned the burned-out O-1. "No. I have too much to do for J.D."

"*Semper Fi.*" Snake squeezed Mitch's hand.

Mitch thought he detected concern about how soon he could return to carry on for J.D. "How's Lieutenant Taylor?"

Snake looked at a cluster of Marines. "He's in at least as good a shape as you are."

"That's not saying much."

Two Marines rushed up with a stretcher, and several men gently lifted him onto it while medics continued treating him. Three jeeps clanked to a halt on nearby steel planks. Men nearer the jeeps snapped to attention.

"As you were," a voice roared. The source of the command was a gray-haired Marine who stepped from the second jeep. The newcomers stopped first to check Lieutenant Taylor.

Snake said, "That's Barnes, a visiting one-star. He was being shown around when you started your little heroics."

Mitch tried to nod, but only his eyes went up and down. The pain killer made him feel as if his body were in slow motion. Moments later Snake and others around Mitch, except for the medics, stood at attention. Mitch strained to sit up. Pain threatened him with a blackout, so he abandoned the effort.

General Barnes greeted Snake and the other Marines, then knelt beside Mitch. "That was a hell of a job of flying, son. One of the best I've seen in three wars."

"Someone had to do something." Mitch wished he could sit up to speak to the general. "I feel fortunate to have been there."

"Two hundred Marines are damned fortunate you were, Captain."

"Thank you, sir."

"When you stirred things up, I was about to depart for Danang to catch my flight to Washington. The first thing I'm going to do at the Pentagon is submit paperwork for the Medal of Honor you just earned."

Mitch was taken back by the unexpected words. "That's generous of you, sir." Mitch realized immediately his answer sounded ridiculous.

"Generosity has nothing to do with it, son. I know how to recognize when someone goes well above-and-beyond the call."

Mitch heard a Huey, hover-taxing from the parking area.

General Barnes glanced at the helicopter. "Looks like your ride's here to take you to a hospital. Before they whisk you away, Captain, I need a name for that citation."

The pain killers were working. Mitch felt mellow, but his mind was as clear as at any time since he'd gone to war. He remembered losing his name tag. He assumed the medic scanning for blood type hadn't bothered to check the name. He looked around. With all the Coveys flying, the only face he recognized was Snake's.

Mitch chose his words carefully to avoid a lie. "Sir, that name would be J.D., well actually, James D. Dalton."

Snake's eyes widened.

Mitch flashed a look at Snake to show the statement wasn't a mistake caused by delirium.

Snake hid most of a smile. His eyes rolled toward the clear sky.

"James D. Dalton," General Barnes repeated as his aide wrote the name. The general eased a meaty hand on Mitch's shoulder. "One hell of a job, Captain Dalton."

"Thank you, sir." Mitch assumed he could accept credit on J.D.'s behalf without his response being a lie.

After the general returned to his jeep, Snake knelt and took hold of Mitch's hand. He said nothing but smiled broadly and shook his head.

Mitch smiled weakly. Four Marines lifted the stretcher and carried him to the Huey.

Snake still held Mitch's hand as the stretcher was placed gently onto the floor of the helicopter. He leaned over and shouted above the noise of the rotors, "Now I understand why J.D. thought so much of you."

The words threatened to release the flood of tears Mitch had held back since J.D.'s crash. Instead he swallowed hard and forced a smile. "I wouldn't have done what needed to be done if there hadn't been a J.D. Anyway, I doubt it'll work, but what can they do to me—make me a forward air controller, give me an O-1, and send me to Vietnam?"

Snake stepped back, snapped to attention, and stood firmly against the downwash while the engine accelerated to takeoff power. When the skids lifted, Snake's hand popped up into a perfect salute, which he held until the helicopter was well out over the canyon of the Rao Quan.

PART TWO
The Vietnam War
Khammouan Province, Laos
December 1967

Cricket FAC in an O-2 Skymaster

The Ban Laboy Ford

Chapter 29

A heavy overcast blocked the sun as Colonel Le Van Do climbed into his jungle hammock. He couldn't remember the last time he'd slept more than a couple of hours. It hadn't been in the last two days and three nights.

Le pulled the mosquito net into place but left the outer cover open. Water gurgled in the nearby stream. High above, palm fronds rustled, and featherlike leaves of bilimbi trees swished in the breeze. He stretched out and listened. Over the years, morning sounds had become like a lullaby, helping him escape the unrelenting responsibilities of war.

Beyond the gentle noises, he heard the whine of trucks struggling up the long grade from the ford at Ban Laboy. In the midst of the dry season, he seldom heard trucks by the time he got into his hammock. Normally they were hidden away for the day. Trucks moved freely, however, when low overcasts shielded the roads from spotter planes.

Memories of nighttime actions mingled into a weariness that kept him from concentrating. In moments between wakefulness and deep sleep, a kaleidoscope of images flashed through his mind. Vivid impressions of his own war pushed aside fleeting thoughts of young Chinh near Hanoi and of Kiem somewhere in the south. Visions—red dirt roads, grotesquely shattered trees, rusted hulks of trucks, and battered fuel drums—faded in and out. Finally, the truck hulks seemed to regenerate, belching black smoke and hissing red flames. Giant airplanes swirled around towering columns of smoke. A small plane dived and zeroed in on Le. He tried to run, but thick mud clutched at his feet.

Engine noise increased to a roar. Le struggled in slow motion to free himself. While he searched in vain for his AK-47, the aircraft loomed larger. *Why hadn't the pilot fired a rocket?* Le kicked desperately to free himself before a rocket showered him with phosphorous. He smashed an arm against a bamboo pole supporting his hammock.

Le wakened as a twin-engine O-2 roared overhead. He tried to verify whether the aircraft was part of a dream. Trees blocked his view, but sounds convinced him the plane was real. Checking his wristwatch, he discovered he'd been asleep less than an hour.

The overcast was unchanged, so Le was mystified. The Americans had stopped flying low long ago. The new O-2s remained high, although they patrolled singly, instead of in pairs like before. *Did this flight signal a new tactic or a foolhardy pilot at the controls?* Remembering the voice he used to know as the unpredictable Nail Three-six, he smiled. That American would have pulled such a stunt.

The *pocketa-pocketa-pocketa* of antiaircraft fire sounded near the ford.

Le held his breath, listened, and heard two muffled thumps. An engine sputtered. Excited voices shouted near the headquarters cave and nearer the meadow. Le couldn't make out words, but the meaning was clear—the aircraft was coming down. Hearing familiar sounds of an aircraft death spiral, Le pulled on his boots. He swung out of the hammock and grabbed his helmet, field pack, and AK-47.

Sergeant Dinh yelled to the other guards.

Le jogged toward the headquarters cave while his bodyguards scrambled to catch up. Passing perimeter guards near the camouflaged entrance, he heard a renewed round of shouting—a parachute had been sighted. In the cave, Le paused to catch his breath.

Bent over the map table, Major Pham Duc Quan shouted commands to a soldier at a field telephone. The warbling wail of an emergency radio came from the communications room. Seeing Quan with things under control, Le went to the men monitoring the American radios. He focused on voices in spite of the irritating wail.

"Cricket, Crown," came from the loudspeaker. "Say location of the downed aircraft."

"Nail Four-seven was at Ban Laboy, so he's near NKP's zero-nine-six at eighty-six miles."

"Be advised Sandies from NKP should be overhead in thirty."

Le checked his wristwatch: nine ten.

"Roger, Crown. The Sandies may not be able to get under the clouds."

"Crown copied."

Le hurried to the map table.

Quan pointed at a dusty area near a crease in the faded map. "The aircraft crashed here, Colonel. The pilot's near the river, four kilometers north of the road. I've sent soldiers from camps six and nine to search."

"Good. Order all gunners in sectors four, five, and seven to their weapons. If we don't capture him before the weather improves, other Americans may be as foolish."

Le studied the map. His weariness had disappeared.

In the cargo compartment of a C-130, Captain Mitch McCall strained against a dirty canvas seat for what seemed like the thousandth time. He reached overhead with both hands and grabbed a bar supporting his row of side-facing seats. Bracing his feet against a pallet of cargo in the center of the aircraft, he raised his hips from the sagging red canvas. He tried to stretch stiffness from the leg wounded on his last combat mission.

Now the seven months since being shot down seemed almost a blur. Hospitalization and convalescent leave in Georgetown had filled most of the time. A short stint at Hurlbert Field in Florida had qualified him to fly the Cessna O-2s. He thought wistfully of the time spent with Elizabeth. Some days had been as glorious as those shared in Bangkok. Their relationship, however, had changed markedly when he told her he had decided to return to the war.

The C-130's landing gear extended, adding its babble to the engines' drone. With a landing minutes away, Mitch smiled. He was eager to get on the ground at NKP for the first time in seven months.

He glanced at Lieutenant Angelo Martines, a companion since they arrived in Saigon eight days earlier. Angelo was asleep as he'd been for most of the time since Bangkok. An arm was intertwined in the seat straps, and his head was nestled at an odd angle in the bend of his elbow. Angelo's last-night-in-civilization celebration obviously had taken a toll.

Loud clunking in the wheel wells startled Mitch. He realized the pilot was retracting the landing gear. The C-130 banked into a turn.

The crackling public address system indicated an announcement. Mitch heard a few words such as: holding pattern, battle damage, and emergency landing. He strained to see out a porthole-style window behind him. The canvas straps were in the way, and the window was crazed from many days under the hot, Asian sun. Giving up, he unbuckled his seatbelt as the C-130 rolled out of the turn. He walked by pallets of cargo until reaching a paratroop door.

Its window was streaked with dusty oil, but Mitch recognized the scene. Jagged karst jutted up from the Laotian plain beyond the Mekong River. His shoulders tingled. The sensation seemed to say he'd come home as if he'd only been away in Bangkok for a CTO. "Not true," he whispered. He was a different pilot than before—and J.D. would never come whistling along the walkway again.

He looked for the Cricket parking ramp, but hangars blocked his view. Seeing two rows of A-26s increased the stirring of excitement. As familiar as everything was, something was different. In a moment, the answer hit him—the Jolly Greens and Sandies were absent.

Mitch noticed flashing red lights near the runway. His adrenaline stepped up another notch as always when the lights flashed.

He scanned the approaches to the runway but saw no aircraft. He looked south of the karst peaks along the path he'd followed in Laos. A trail of black smoke was low over the river. Before he could pinpoint the aircraft, the C-130 banked. He crossed to the other door and waited for the pilot to roll out on the northerly leg of the holding pattern.

The smoke trail was nearer the airfield. Mitch identified the burning aircraft as an A-1. A Sandy, Mitch assumed, as he saw another flying in close formation. He remembered the two Nimrods lost east of the field in what seemed a lifetime ago. The closeness of the second A-1 assured Mitch the brotherhood hadn't changed.

The C-130 came abeam the runway as the burning A-1 passed the last section of jungle. Less than half a mile from the runway's south end, the Skyraider dipped a wing. Mitch shook his head, certain the crippled plane would overshoot. However, the A-1's nose swung around quickly as the pilot applied the big rudder. In seconds, the fighter cleared the trees, raced across the threshold, and landed within the first five-hundred feet of the runway. The second A-1 flew parallel about fifty feet above the ground.

"Superb," Mitch whispered.

The crippled Skyraider careened along the runway, and a fire truck slowly accelerated in pursuit. When the A-1 neared the mid-field taxiway, Mitch saw the left wing rise. The right wing dropped and spewed a fountain of sparks into the smoky trail. He stared wide-eyed and pressed his forehead against the window frame.

The A-1 slowed abruptly and swung into a ground loop.

Mitch's mind flashed to the vivid view he'd seen from his cockpit during the ground loop at Khe Sanh. His grip on the door frame tightened, causing his recently healed arm to quiver.

Metal cartwheeled into the air. He thought the A-1 was coming apart, then realized the rectangular pieces were planks gouged from the runway. The A-1 spun into the dirt, disappearing into a huge red cloud.

Fire trucks converged from three directions. Scores of fatigue-clad men ran across the parking ramp toward the burning A-1.

The brotherhood was alive and well.

The C-130 flew beyond the end of the runway. When the rim of the window eliminated his view, dust still obscured the A-1. He looked toward the horizon. His eyes focused on the karst of Laos. He envisioned, instead, the belching black smoke over J.D.'s burning O-1.

Mitch crossed to the other paratroop door and waited for the next turn. He wondered if they'd have to bypass NKP because of the damaged runway. He was eager to return to combat and to find out if Elizabeth had written. Their last few hours together left him uncertain whether he'd hear from her personally or through a divorce lawyer.

The aircraft banked into a turn, and the pilot reduced power. The loadmaster motioned for people to return to their seats. Mitch moved past the cargo pallets and slumped onto the canvas seat.

The loadmaster said something to each group of three or four passengers. Reaching Mitch, he said, "The pilot wants everyone to know we'll be making an assault landing, so don't get concerned, sir. There'll be a lot of noise and dust, and we'll stop pretty fast."

Mitch shouted, "Why's he doing that?"

"They're not going to have the entire runway open for a while. We can get in on one end without anyone being in our way."

Mitch nodded, surprised at the answer. He'd never landed before on a runway that wasn't completely open. He wished he were in the cockpit instead of strapped into a side-facing seat with no control over his destiny. He pulled the seat belt tighter.

Mitch followed the C-130's progress through the routine turns and noises of getting aligned on final approach with the landing gear extended. The nose dropped. He saw enough out the window to know the dive was much steeper than any approach he'd ever made in a C-141. He braced to keep from sliding onto Angelo, who stirred for the first time since leaving Ubon. His eyelids raised halfway.

Mitch smiled. "We're about to land!" He gestured downward.

Angelo grunted. A far-away look in his eyes disappeared behind heavy eyelids. He nodded and slumped against the canvas straps.

Seconds later, the engines screamed, and the nose tilted up rapidly.

A look outside revealed the C-130 was rapidly approaching the ground. Mitch told himself the maneuvering was normal and not the last desperate act of a pilot who'd badly misjudged a high-angle descent. But, adrenaline surged, and he braced for a crash.

Trees raced by. The cleared area along the runway flashed into view, and the C-130 slammed onto the metal planks.

Angelo's eyes snapped open.

Mitch was uncertain whether they'd landed or crashed. Engines roared into reverse, giving him his first hint things were under control. The propellers switched into high-drag. Everything not tied-down bounded forward. He saw passengers straining to stay in the seats to which their seat belts had them attached. Terrified looks glimmered in the eyes of the men not wearing flight suits.

With engines screaming and the aircraft groaning in protest, the C-130 decelerated. The air in the cabin took on a rose-colored hue.

Mitch feared the cargo compartment was filling with smoke. He twisted to look out his window and could see nothing. The C-130 was engulfed in a red dust storm churned up by the propellers in reverse. The engine noise faded to a dull roar, and the aircraft lurched forward.

Angelo shouted, "What the hell was that?"

"The loadmaster said we were going to do an assault landing."

"Why didn't somebody warn us?" He seemed to recognize his response didn't fit. "I mean, why didn't somebody wake us, sir?"

"Wake you? I've been wondering how we'd get you off the plane."

"I'm sure awake now, sir."

Mitch grinned. "Welcome to NKP."

"But," Angelo said with a devilish smile, "we'll return to Bangkok in twenty-four days."

"Maybe twenty-six or twenty-eight, depending on how soon you start flying. So all the ladies may have to wait a couple of extra days."

Angelo shrugged. "Fortunes of war."

After the C-130 parked, Mitch put on his sunglasses and stepped onto the parking ramp. Breathing in the humid air and taking in the sights and sounds of NKP, Mitch felt as if he'd never been away. He stood taller, a warrior returning to the place he belonged.

Striding to the tail where the baggage pallet was loaded, Mitch and Angelo saw the A-1 canted at an odd angle near the runway.

Angelo did a double-take, and his eyes widened. "Wow!"

"You missed the real excitement."

"When did that happen?"

"When you were in dreamland. I watched the landing, and I can tell you this base has at least one super pilot."

"Why thank you, Captain," Angelo said with a grin.

"And now NKP's obviously got an additional smart-assed lieutenant."

"I do my best, sir."

Mitch hesitated, then added with a melancholy smile, "My friend, J.D. Dalton, set a standard for smart-ass that you'll never get close to."

Chapter 30

Before Mitch and Angelo could board an awaiting bus, an olive-drab jeep clattered toward the C-130 and skidded to a halt. A sun-tanned captain yelled, "Anyone here assigned to the Twenty-third TASS?"

"Right here." Mitch walked toward the dusty jeep.

The driver extended his hand. "Welcome to NKP. I'm Bill Kesler."

"Mitch McCall," he said, shaking hands. "And this is—"

"You're *the* Captain McCall, sir?" Kesler's expression brightened.

Angelo seemed confused by one captain suddenly calling the other sir.

"I was a Cricket until May." Mitch tossed his bags into the jeep. So much for hopes of returning without fanfare.

"And, you were shot down at Khe Sanh, sir?"

Angelo's eyes widened.

Nodding to Kesler, Mitch climbed into the passenger seat. "Call me Mitch, Bill."

Kesler smiled. "Anyway, we've got a FAC down, and—"

"Where?" Mitch felt excitement stir.

"Near a big ford over by—"

"Ban Laboy?"

"Right. A rescue attempt's in progress. I'll take us to the squadron to listen on the radios, and we'll get you settled afterward."

Mitch was eager to get to the action. Seeing Angelo settled in the back of the jeep, Mitch said, "Let's do it."

Kesler swung a tight U-turn. Once clear of the C-130, he jammed the accelerator to the floor and aimed at a metal-clad pathway leading between maintenance buildings.

Mitch recognized the route as the taxiway he'd used when taxiing out for missions. Over the clatter of wheels thumping metal planks, he shouted, "Do we know where he is?"

Kesler nodded. "He spent most of the morning under an overcast. The weather broke about an hour ago, and there's been a helluva fight ever since."

"I watched the Sandy crash land."

"The gunners knocked down another A-1, but the pilot got far enough from the Trail for an easy rescue." Nodding for emphasis, he repeated, "A helluva fight."

Angelo asked, "This happen often, sir? I mean FACs shot down."

"Things were quiet when I got here in the rainy season. Gunners've been more active since mid-November, but we hadn't lost a bird until—"

Kesler hit the brakes and swung into a turn. Angelo slid down between two B-4 bags.

Mitch looked up and saw they'd been headed for an O-2's front propeller. "You weren't taught to drive by someone named J.D., were you?"

Kesler flashed a questioning look as he steered through a wide arc.

"Never mind," Mitch said, watching the O-2.

Everything had seemed eerily familiar until now. The strange-looking

O-2s—with one propeller in front, and another spinning behind the cockpit between twin booms leading to the tail—looked wrong on the ramp at NKP.

After qualifying in the new FAC aircraft in Florida, he had flown O-2s a few times en route at Binh Thuy. He liked having a second engine and fourteen rockets instead of four. The O-2 had modern radios including a TACAN, which allowed him to know where he was without having to rely on a map with a grid of inked-in lines and arcs.

Watching the O-2 rumble by, Mitch realized it would take longer than he'd anticipated to get used to the absence of O-1s and J.D.

Kesler stopped and made a thumbs-up gesture above the windshield.

The pilot in the O-2 nodded.

Using the delay to find a steadier position behind Mitch, Angelo leaned forward. "You didn't tell me about getting shot down, sir."

"You didn't ask."

After the O-2 passed, the jeep lurched forward into the propwash, which swirled eddies of dust up from the round holes in the PSP. Kesler steered to the yellow centerline of the taxiway between the buildings.

Mitch got a quick look at two lines of O-2s as Kesler breezed across the parking ramp Mitch had come to know so well. "Just doesn't look right with O-2s instead of O-1s."

Kesler braked to a screeching stop at the main road, which was lined with slow-moving traffic. Dust hung in the air like a reddish-brown fog.

"The dust's the same," Mitch added, although the number of construction vehicles made him suspect NKP no longer was a sleepy, out-of-the-way base.

Kesler's head swung back and forth as if watching a tennis volley. A rumbling forklift gave Kesler a small opening, and he swung the jeep into the northbound lane.

Mitch passed uncomfortably near the fender of a Thai truck. "Your driving reminds me of J.D., except he would've run the stop sign."

"Say again." Kesler sounded as if he'd just noticed he had passengers.

"Never mind."

In a couple of minutes, Kesler bounced the jeep to a halt on the gravel-covered parking area in front of the squadron headquarters. He switched off the ignition, swung out of the jeep, and bounded to the steps. At the doorway, he paused. "You can leave your bags in the jeep. Give a couple of sets of orders to the sergeant in admin, then join us in ops." He disappeared through the dust-covered screen door.

Getting out, Angelo said, "The captain's in a helluva hurry."

Mitch grabbed his briefcase. "You get that way when a friend's down." Walking up the steps reminded Mitch of his last visit to the headquarters when Colonel Morton had given Mitch the biggest chewing out of his career.

Once inside, Mitch and Angelo gave the clerk sets of orders and enough other information to get their paperwork started. Satisfied, the clerk led them to a door marked with signs declaring: Controlled Access Area. He knocked, and Mitch heard the click of a latch releasing.

Technical Sergeant Gamble opened the door and said, "Welcome back, Captain."

"Good to be here," Mitch said, eager to rejoin the camaraderie he'd missed while recuperating.

After a few more words, Gamble returned to his desk by the door.

One wall had a Plexiglas-covered map similar to that in the TUOC. Lieutenant O'Malley, still as hefty as Mitch remembered, was using a grease pencil on the Plexiglas. He stood on a chair to reach the area Mitch recognized as the Ban Laboy Ford. A captain with a handlebar mustache was alongside giving instructions.

File cabinets, four-drawer safes, and cluttered desks were arranged throughout the room. Status boards hung on the wall opposite the door.

Along the front wall, two sergeants wearing headsets manned radio consoles. Kesler stood with a dozen more officers around the radios. Most men stared at loudspeakers on the wall. Mitch recognized Major Reed Lawson as well as Lieutenant Pittman, who'd arrived that deadly February day with O'Malley and Ted Forrester.

During Mitch's convalescence, Ted had sent several notes, but the notes had stopped in September. Mitch wondered about Ted.

"Sandy Five, Crown. Say status of Jolly Three," came through a loudspeaker.

Another loudspeaker sounded. "Good hit, Packard Three. Okay, Four, mix your bombs north of Three's dust. The guns are within fifty meters."

Mitch recognized the voice of Ted Forrester.

"Crown, Sandy Five. Jolly Three will touch down in about fifteen seconds. She'll be on the crest of Phou Kho at NKP's zero-nine-five at seventy. Jolly Four's in position to evacuate the crew, if necessary."

"Nail Four-seven, Sandy Seven. Give me another ten-second count."

"More ground fire," Ted said. "You're picking up thirty-sevens from your target."

"Copied."

Angelo was wide-eyed. "You have a clue on what's happening, sir?"

Mitch nodded. "It's a bit busier than the training ranges in Florida."

"Yes, sir."

"Crown, be advised Jolly Three's on the ground. They're shutting her down and gonna check the damage."

"Crown copied, Sandy Five. Keep us informed."

Major Lawson noticed Mitch. Hurrying over, Lawson smiled. "Glad you made it back, Mitch. I was really sorry about J.D."

"Me, too. Thought you might be home by now, sir."

"Twenty-six days and a wake-up," Lawson said, then added with a grin, "but who's counting. I've been playing assistant ops. officer to Colonel Quinn over there."

Mitch saw a stocky lieutenant colonel sitting on the edge of a desk near the radio operators. "You mean I won't get any more briefings on air discipline from Colonel Mort—"

"Packard Four's off. Four thirty-sevens are camouflaged in the southern tree line, and each of those mothers is firing for all it's worth."

Lawson hesitated long enough for any response to come from the loudspeakers, then continued, "Mighty Mort went home in September. Probably three-quarters of the guys are new since you left."

"Things are busier than I remember, sir."

Lawson nodded. "Jolly Three took hits trying to get in over Nail Four-seven, Lieutenant Jim West, who's down. Jolly just landed on a mountain about ten miles away. The chopper should be safe until the crew can patch it enough to get home. One of our guys, Nail Six-eight—"

"Ted Forrester?"

"You've got a good memory for voices. Ted's directing Phantoms against guns that hit Jolly Three. Sandy Seven's homing in on Jim's—"

"Super, Four," Ted said. "Your bombs are right in the tree line. I think you're—Yeah—you're getting secondary explosions. Super! Okay, Packard, I'll have to pass your numbers later. Break, Sandy Seven, Nail Six-eight. That position shouldn't be active for a while."

"Roger, Six-eight. We're bringing in Jolly Five."

"Copied. Nail Six-eight's coming over the top at six thousand."

"That's approved, Nail. Okay, Sandy Eight, let's lay a little smoke."

Fitting in comments between messages over the loudspeakers, Lawson said, "Sandy Seven's the on-scene commander for the rescue. He and his wingman are about to lay smoke screens along the helicopter's approach. Jim's in a narrow river valley near the Ban Laboy Ford. Lots of guns there, so we wish he were a few miles away."

"I remember Ban Laboy," Mitch said.

Angelo looked overwhelmed. "How many aircraft are out there, sir?"

Lawson shrugged. "I've lost track. At least eight more fighters are holding there somewhere."

"Be advised," a voice barely audible said, "I hear rifle and automatic-weapons fire from my east and south."

"That's Jim," Lawson said.

"Sandy, Jolly Five's taking small arms and AW from the ridge at our eleven o'clock."

"Roger. Sandy Seven's rolling in, doubling back across your nose from your three o'clock."

"Roger. Break, Nail Four-seven. Pop a smoke if you have any left."

"This is my last one, so it's time to get this wrapped up."

"Jim's hanging in real well," Lawson said.

Mitch nodded. "I don't envy him."

"Thanks, Sandy," Jolly Green Five said. "We were getting peppered, but that stopped 'em. Break, Nail Four-seven, we've got red smoke."

Other than the radio operators listening through headsets, everyone looked at the loudspeakers. No one spoke. Hardly anyone moved.

"Penetrator's on the way down."

Mitch pictured the heavy mechanism descending on the end of a cable below the helicopter. He thought of the jungle penetrator as a cross between an anchor and an umbrella. Heavy and bullet-shaped to penetrate jungle canopies, the device had three spring-loaded seats. They opened like an umbrella for the ride up and made the penetrator look like an anchor.

Angelo asked, "Is he in a lot of jungle, sir?"

Lawson nodded.

"Being yanked through trees must be a tough ride," Angelo said.

"Beats hell out of the alternative," Mitch whispered.

More than a minute of silence passed.

"Survivor's on the penetrator and coming up."

Shouts and war whoops echoed off the walls. A tall major and a shorter captain embraced in a bear hug and jumped up and down. Kesler slung a handful of papers toward the ceiling. They separated, snowing rectangular flakes on the celebration.

Lawson grabbed Mitch. "After two years, we're finally bringing a FAC home from near the Trail!" He screeched a war whoop and joined the group near the radios.

Angelo asked, "What did he mean?"

"Being a Cricket FAC's a dangerous way to earn your combat pay."

Lieutenant Colonel Quinn shot a fist into the air. "Time to break out the bubbly. I need someone to pick up a case of champagne at the club."

Lieutenant O'Malley hopped down from the chair with a room-shaking thud and yanked out a flight cap. "You got it, sir."

"Bring it to the flight line, ASAP," Quinn said.

"Yes, sir," the captain with the handlebar mustache said as he and another captain joined O'Malley heading for the door.

"Crown, Jolly Five has Nail Four-seven aboard. We're swinging around northwest."

"Copied, Jolly. Do you have any battle damage?"

"Negative, Crown. Another routine day at the office."

Kesler caught Mitch's eye and pointed at the door. "You guys better get your bags. You can stash them here 'til we get you some quarters."

By the time Mitch and Angelo stepped onto the porch, the captains were in the jeep. O'Malley was in the back repositioning the bags.

"We'll take those," Mitch said, "before O'Malley crunches my B-Four bag down to a B-Zero."

"Good to see you, Captain," O'Malley said, hefting a B-4 bag as if it were no heavier than a shaving kit.

With a grin as wide as his handlebar mustache, the captain behind the wheel said, "Welcome. You guys are getting here on a great day!" He pounded a fist on the instrument panel, and dust flew up.

"Sure a lot better than the day we got here," O'Malley said.

Mitch shared the excitement, knowing how different this was from the day Goodwin died.

When the bags were out, the captain swung the jeep through a reverse U-turn. He jammed the accelerator to the floor, thrust a clenched fist high above him, and screeched a rebel yell into the humid air.

Spinning tires threw rooster-tails of dust and gravel as the jeep lurched into a line of traffic. The driver of a step-van jammed on his brakes to avoid hitting the jeep.

Mitch smiled. "This isn't a fighter unit, but you can be proud to be a Cricket."

"Things are going a little fast, sir," Angelo said, trying to close a zipper on his B-4 bag.

Mitch gathered his bags. "Long nights in Bangkok do that to you." Inside, he knocked on the door to the operations section.

Sergeant Gamble's face was ashen as he unlocked the door. He turned away as soon as Mitch stepped in.

Pushing awkwardly through with his bags, Mitch realized the atmosphere had changed. Most men seemed frozen, and few seemed to be breathing. The only sound was static from the loudspeakers.

"Uh, Crown," Ted said, "it, uh, looks like they went in, uhh, almost inverted."

"Roger, Six-eight. Do you think anyone got out?"

"Negative."

Lieutenant Pittman slumped in a chair. He crossed his arms on a desk and lowered his head like a chastened first-grader.

Hearing a knock on the door, Mitch opened it.

Angelo forced the door open and stumbled through. "Geez, it's dusty around he—"

"Knock it off!" Quinn didn't turn from the speaker as he shouted.

The harsh tone produced a startled expression. Angelo's eyes flashed with anger. Before he could respond, Mitch raised a hand signaling halt.

Ted said, "Thirty-sevens on the hilltop were firin' down from the time Jolly Five reached five-hundred feet. Flames were spewing out all the way down. Sandy Seven's going in to take a closer look." Ted paused. "It doesn't look good—no damn good at all."

Major Lawson yelled, "Damn it! Damn it! Damn it!" He kicked a trash can that spun through the air, spewing a trail of orange peels, pencil sharpenings, and wadded-up papers. The crumpled can hit the wall and ricocheted against Pittman's desk. Pittman didn't flinch.

Kesler shuffled over to Mitch. "God. It seems we never can win!" His eyes were blank, and he punctuated the monotone with a slow shake of his head. "Jim was my room mate."

"Crown, Sandy Seven. The whole area around the chopper's an inferno. I don't think anybody made it."

"Cricket, Nail Six-eight. Who've we got holding?"

"Boston's number one followed by Bear."

"Break, Boston Flight, Nail Six-eight. What're you carrying?"

"Boston's four Thuds with a standard load of six seven-fifties each."

Ted rushed through a pre-strike briefing with a tone of determination Mitch had never heard in his friend's voice.

"Nail Six-eight, Crown," the rescue controller said when Ted paused.

"Go, Crown."

"Six-eight, Crown. We'd like you to hold off on your strike until we have a better assessment of the crash site."

"Negative, Crown. This gun position overlooking the site has to be taken out before any more rescues."

"We still prefer you hold off. We don't want to lose anyone else."

"Crown, Nail's having trouble reading you. While I'm fixing my radio, I've got a gun position that needs taking out."

Crown paused. "Understand, Nail. Don't lose anyone else."

Click-click.

A quizzical look formed on Angelo's face.

Nodding in response to the unspoken question about what Ted had done, Mitch imagined how much J.D. would've approved.

Angelo's mouth dropped open. "What rank's Nail Six-eight?"

"He was a captain last time I saw him."

"Can you get away with things like that, as a captain, I mean?"

"Sometimes. We've got a rule about guns that shoot at FACs."

Mitch slumped into a chair and watched men adjusting to the tragedy. Lawson dropped his lanky frame into a swivel chair and raised his boots onto a desk. A noticeable *snap* sounded from a pencil shattering in Lawson's grip. Sergeant Gamble policed up the scattered trash, replacing it in the dented can. Quinn leaned against a file cabinet, with his head supported on a hand as if shading his eyes. Mitch noticed lip movements. Quinn was praying.

Feeling as if eavesdropping on private grief, Mitch turned away. He saw a roster of names and call signs. Fifty-nine was blank.

For the next few minutes, little was said while the loudspeakers carried the duel between Ted's fighters and the guns. By the time Boston and Bear had dropped eighteen tons of bombs, the guns weren't firing any more—but Ted called in more fighters.

Quinn nodded his approval, then picked up a notebook and headed for the door. "Unless I'm mistaken, gentlemen, we still have a war to fight tomorrow. I'll be at the TUOC." The door clicked shut behind Quinn, and everyone was silent a few moments.

Lawson stood and faced Kesler, "Better take care of our newcomers."

Kesler pulled out a checklist and joined Lawson with Mitch and Angelo. "We've got an empty room if you want to room together."

"Fine," Mitch said as Angelo nodded.

Kesler scanned a list of items necessary to get new FACs ready to fly. He checked the time. "Monday's a day the medics give their newcomer briefing. You can fill that square at fifteen-hundred today."

Mitch remembered the focus had been an explicit slide show on venereal diseases. "That's one I want to claim prior credit for."

Lawson said, "Since you've been through the whole drill before, Mitch, you can pick and choose what you want a refresher on."

"Thank you, sir. Who assigns the call signs?"

"You got a preference?"

"Five-nine looks available. I'd like it again."

"It's yours."

Mitch felt anticipation rising. He was eager to get into the air and continue his unfinished business.

Twenty minutes later, Kesler drove the jeep to the quadrangle near the TUOC and parked by the dispensary. "I'll wait here."

Mitch nodded, recalling how he'd wanted time alone while suffering through those first hours after J.D.'s death. "We won't be long."

Mitch led Angelo down the maze of walkways to the mail room. When an airman at the service window greeted them, Mitch said, "We've just arrived at the Twenty-third. Do you have any mail for Captain McCall and Lieutenant Martines?"

The airman's eyes brightened, and he stared at Angelo. "You're Lieutenant Martines?" He turned to a sergeant in a back room. "He's here."

Mitch was surprised. "If the FBI's posted your picture on the wall, I want an autographed copy."

Angelo smiled. "My sister said she'd post my picture at her sorority house. You know, lonely pilot in the war zone needs mail from home."

"Lonely? She must not know about Bangkok."

The airman brought over a box crammed with letters. "Here you are, Lieutenant. These include the dozen that came today."

Angelo's smile broadened. "What can I say?"

Inhaling the fragrance of perfume wafting from the letters, Mitch watched with a pensive smile. Obviously the letters were even more impressive to the airman than Mitch's background had been to Kesler.

"That's not all, sir." The airman hefted up another box, which included a half dozen smaller boxes. "I think you got cookies, too."

In a few moments, the airman glanced into Mitch's peering eyes. "Sorry, Captain. You've got a couple of letters."

Mitch reached for them. Hopeful anticipation rose, then fell when he saw both were from his mother. He faked a smile. "I guess my box of letters won't arrive until tomorrow."

The airman laughed and offered forms used to assign mailboxes.

Mitch made three errors he had to scratch out and mark over. His mind was on Elizabeth. En route he'd stopped at least a night in Hawaii, the Philippines, Saigon, Binh Thuy, and Bangkok. Enough time had passed for letters from her to reach NKP—if she'd sent any.

As the airman got the combinations for mailboxes, Angelo browsed through his letters. Mitch mentally browsed through letters Elizabeth had given him in Bangkok so long ago.

"Captain." A sergeant with letters in his hand came out of the back.

Mitch couldn't suppress his optimism as he eyed the letters.

"These came today for Lieutenant West, and I understand he was shot down this morning. Do you know who's assigned to handle his things?"

Mitch shook his head. "Sorry."

The sergeant shrugged. "Guess there's no rush."

Mitch leaned against the wall of mailboxes. *Sorry in more ways than one.* He closed his eyes and pictured Elizabeth waving sadly as he left California. He pictured the letters in the sergeant's hand. Mitch sighed. At least he was alive to receive her letters—if any ever came.

Chapter 31

Kesler drove Mitch and Angelo to the FAC quarters. Once the bags were in the room, Kesler hurried Angelo to the briefing at the dispensary. Mitch unpacked and settled in. Finally too hungry to wait for Angelo, Mitch headed along the walkway. He reached the street as a shuttle bus stopped by the quarters. Angelo, Ted, and four other FACs got out.

Ted looked twenty pounds lighter than Mitch remembered. Angelo looked airsick.

"Well, friend," Mitch said, extending his hand to Ted, "listening to you on the radio made me think you must be J.D.'s prize pupil."

"J.D. taught us all some lessons," Ted said, along with a warm handshake. "I couldn't believe how he died."

Mitch shrugged. "Musta been his time—just like he'd say today was the time for everyone on the Jolly Green."

Ted looked skeptical. "I learned a lot from J.D., but he didn't make me a James Dean."

The other FACs, except Angelo, had headed to their rooms. Gesturing at Angelo, Mitch asked Ted, "You met my new roomie?"

"Briefly."

"Then I suppose you've heard of his non-stop exploits in Bangkok."

"Not quite, sir," Angelo said, his dark good looks now pallid.

"Then you can keep Captain Forrester entertained over dinner."

"Sounds good," Ted said, as he and Mitch started up the hill.

"I don't know if I can eat yet," Angelo said, tagging along.

"If you can't handle the C-130 shuttle," Ted said, winking at Mitch, "you'll miss out on the monthly visit to Bangkok."

Mitch added, "The ladies'll be *soooo* disappointed."

"I may never go to Bangkok again."

Mitch grinned. "Who are you, anyway? The Lieutenant Martines I rode up with—"

"You didn't have to see all those VD pictures. I mean, they were—I didn't even think about—I could already be . . . ."

Mitch grinned.

Ted sounded professorial. "You know what our old friend, J.D., would advise?" He paused, obviously stifling a laugh. "Use it while you still can?" He broke out in laughter.

"Before it falls off, as J.D. would've said," Mitch said, snickering.

Angelo stopped. "You two didn't see those abominable pictures. This is serious."

Ted and Mitch stopped.

"It's good to give it some worry time, Lieutenant," Ted said, his tone solemn. "However, *real* serious is thirty-seven millimeters and ZPUs and losing friends over the Trail."

"Just keep your hormones in check," Mitch said. "Come on, I'll buy you both a Singha. We'll see if that puts color back in your cheeks."

When Mitch walked into the bar of the new officers club, he found the atmosphere subdued. This wasn't a day for celebrating, he thought, as the three FACs sat at a table and ordered drinks.

Mitch gazed at a wall with wooden plaques of insignias of NKP's units. Two stood out. Bands of black cloth angled across plaques of the FAC and rescue squadrons. "Sure different from the little hole-in-the-wall where I had my promotion party."

Ted nodded. "The headquarters weenies are trying to civilize us."

Mitch shook his head. "Kinda takes away from the immediacy of winning the war. We've gotta whip the guys across the river, not settle-in all comfortable and hope to outlast 'em."

Ted raised his Singha to Mitch and took a drink. "I thought you were set stateside with a million-dollar wound."

"I can still push a rudder pedal, but when the weather acts up, I walk like J.D.'s James Dean shuffle."

"People were surprised you got the Air Force Cross instead of the Medal of Honor."

Angelo's eyes widened, and he almost choked on his beer. "You didn't say anything about that, sir." Turning to Ted, he added, "We've been together a week."

Mitch winked. "The lieutenant didn't have the need-to-know. Anyway, I committed the mortal sin of embarrassing a few Washington bureaucrats. Paperwork with J.D.'s name went quite a ways through the system before they discovered I wasn't J.D."

"J.D." Ted was wide-eyed as well. "How did that get so snafu'd?"

"While I was lying on the runway at Khe Sanh, I told a general to use J.D.'s name."

Ted smiled in obvious admiration. "You could've claimed delirium."

"I could have, but that wasn't how it happened."

"Oh." Ted shook his head. "I heard your father-in-law's a U.S. Senator. Couldn't you have gotten him to—"

"I could, but that blue-and-white ribbon was J.D.'s goal, not mine."

Ted nodded as if he shouldn't have needed reminders of what his friend was like. "You still haven't said why you're back so soon."

"Did my convalescence in Washington, so I was awarded my medals at the Pentagon. When the chief of staff asks where you'd like to go for your next assignment, it doesn't take long for orders to come through."

"That's the *how*. What's the *why*?"

"That's almost as simple," Mitch said, although the conflict between love and duty made the decision far from simple. "While I was laid up this summer, I kept seeing war reports in the newspaper and on the evening news totally opposite from what I'd seen with my own eyes. And I got a first-hand look at all the posturing by politicians. I finally understood how we end up with truces that help the enemy win the war."

Ted nodded. "I remember all those trucks in Mu Gia during TET."

"Exactly. What really topped things off was press coverage of the so-called Bertrand Russell War Crimes Trials in Sweden."

"And we were the war criminals," Ted said.

"Right."

"I remember something about that," Angelo said.

Mitch turned to Angelo. "If you bought the claims about the Ho Chi Minh Trail being a few footpaths, you're in for the surprise of your life."

Ted's mouth dropped open. "They really denied trucks were on the Trail? Our Trail?"

Mitch nodded. "The first thing I wanted to do was load Mister Russell in an O-1 and give him a guided tour. I remembered J.D.'s comments about dying by accident in a war we lost, so I knew I had to come back."

"I don't think we're losing," Ted said softly, "but I don't think we're winning either."

Remembering Ted's arrival in February, Mitch said, "I guess you'll be going home on us in a few weeks."

Ted sipped his beer and looked away. "I extended my tour six months." He paused. "I spent September and half of October stateside."

"Were you wounded, too?"

"No. Emergency leave." Ted paused and cleared his throat. "My wife and two sons died in a car wreck on Labor Day."

The words jolted Mitch. He remembered the obvious love with which Ted had discussed valentines from his wife. Mitch was horrified for his friend and understood why Ted had lost so much weight. Mitch also imagined how horrible it would be if Elizabeth and Mandy died while he was off on his somewhat quixotic quest. "I'm sorry, Ted. I don't know what to say."

Ted shrugged. "Nothin' to say. In ways, I suppose being in SAC helped me adjust."

Mitch wasn't sure what that meant. "You mean having to spend so much time apart?"

"That, too." Ted lifted his Singha and seemed to study the label. "There's a lot of pride when you qualify to stand nuclear alert. You know your willingness to be there means the Russians are a lot less likely to use their big ones on America."

Angelo nodded.

Mitch said, "I'm not sure I understand the adjustment."

"I've run to a B-Fifty-two a hundred times with the klaxon screaming in my ears. Most were practices or operational readiness inspections, but I remember a pretty serious alert during the Cuban missile crisis. You never knew if it were the last time the klaxon would ever sound, so you had to make some kind of adjustment." He paused. "How else could you do your duty knowing fifteen minutes after you got airborne, a ballistic missile might vaporize your house with your family in it."

Mitch had never thought of it that way.

"The last afternoon Sharon and I were together, she told me something I'd never known. Each time she heard the alert force thunder into the air, she gathered the boys in a big rocker. Whether they were asleep or awake, she told 'em stories for the next fifteen minutes." Ted bit his lip and gazed at the insignias on the far wall. "Seems like that kind of bravery deserved a medal."

Mitch nodded. He thought of Pauline Schofield. Phil had been missing in action a year, and she still didn't know if she were a wife or a widow. "I suppose if we had to define *worse* beforehand in 'for better or for worse,' we might never find women willing to marry us."

Ted shrugged. "After Sharon told me about the rocking chair, she said she would've married me anyway. She understood we sometimes have a higher calling." He tapped the bottle against the table. "But I wish I could've found a more equal balance for her."

The words stabbed at Mitch, and he felt even more confused. He wished Elizabeth had the understanding Sharon had had. And, looking at the lines etched deeper in Ted's face, Mitch hoped he'd never experience the grief and second-guessing Ted faced.

Ted took a long drink of Singha. "I don't take everything in life so seriously anymore."

"We heard that today on the radios," Angelo said.

Ted looked confused.

"Your *radio failure*," Mitch said, "when you put Boston on the guns."

"I'd seen it in movies, sir," Angelo said, "but I'd never have the guts to do that for real."

"If you stay around this Air Force long enough, Lieutenant," Ted said, "you'll learn you sometimes have to choose between doing things right and doing the right thing. Besides," Ted said, imitating J.D.'s drawl, "what can they do to me? Make me a forward air controller, give me an O-2, and send me to Vietnam?"

Mitch smiled. "We stopped kidding about that after we were dumped on the ramp at Khe Sanh."

Angelo didn't show any understanding of the joke. "Even if that radio-failure ploy was the right thing, sir, don't you have worry about angering someone who could keep you from making major?"

"Not any more." Ted sipped his beer. "Besides I got to wear major's rank a couple of months."

Mitch guessed. "Spot promotion in SAC?"

Ted nodded.

Mitch wasn't surprised Ted had earned that honor. Mitch's question from the first day remained. "I guess I've always wondered—"

"A lot of people do." Referring to the overall rating on an Officer Effectiveness Report, Ted said, "Once you get a One on an OER—"

"A One?" Mitch had seen many OERs during a year spent helping out in squadron administration. He'd routinely seen Eights, Nines, and Tens, which corresponded to Very Fine, Exceptionally Fine, and Outstanding. He'd never seen a Five for Effective and Competent, let alone a One, which equated to Unsatisfactory. "I can't imagine anyone rating you a One. J.D., maybe, but not you."

"J.D.'d call it fate. Right place at the wrong time." Ted turned to Angelo. "With a One in your promotion folder, the odds of making major are markedly less than of Ho Chi Minh joining us for dinner."

Mitch waited for Ted to continue.

Ted finished his beer. "The story's gonna cost you another Singha."

"You got it," Mitch said, raising a hand to order another round.

Once Ted had a fresh beer, he leaned his chair against the wall. "I'd worked up to instructor in B-52s and got sent along to spruce up a crew on airborne nuclear alert. The first sixteen hours were routine. I finally settled down for a nap, and the crew was supposed to wake me a couple of hours before landing." He took a long drink.

Mitch asked, "Didn't they?"

"We never got that far. While I was asleep, our mission got extended four hours and headquarters scheduled an extra refueling." Using the slang for aerial refueling, he added in an ironic tone, "When the crew hit the tanker, they *hit* the tanker."

Mitch hesitated. "A mid-air?"

Ted nodded. "The aircraft commander was hurt pretty bad. I fought to keep it flying, but we never had a chance. We all ended up in the water for a couple of hours. Our load wasn't where it could be recovered."

Mitch realized Ted was talking about the loss of nuclear bombs.

Angelo asked, "Where'd all this happen?"

"I reckon that's still classified."

Mitch was astounded. "But you weren't the aircraft commander, and you weren't at the controls. They shouldn't have hung you—"

"Fate," Ted said.

"Punishing you like that sounds damned unfair, sir," Angelo said.

"Too bad you weren't on the evaluation board." Ted shrugged and studied his Singha. "Losin' a nuke's serious business, even more serious than thirty-seven millimeters. At least they let me keep flying."

"But you were asleep," Angelo said. "If you can never be promoted again, I don't see why you're risking your neck over here."

Ted looked as if he'd never heard a dumber comment. "So I got the shaft from a few individuals in the Air Force. That doesn't wipe out patriotism. My country said it needs me here, so I'm here."

Angelo's eyes widened. "Wow!"

Mitch detected even more determination in Ted's tone than during the afternoon attack on the guns. "Well said, friend."

Finishing his Singha, Ted seemed uneasy at the admiration. He said quietly, "I'm like J.D. The Air Force is the only real family I have left."

The day's battle had kept Le awake until mid-afternoon. When he finally got to sleep, he hardly stirred until well after dark. The evening's operations were in full swing when he entered the headquarters cave. He was in his office scanning a log of American radio calls when he heard a loud voice.

"Colonel Le Van Do. I am most pleased to find you in your headquarters at last."

Le looked up and saw a familiar half-smile he'd learned to hate during the last two summers in Hanoi. In all his years of soldiering, he'd learned to despise—but tolerate—the ideologues who made up the political cadre. None stirred Le's anger to boiling quicker than the man standing in the flickering light beside Major Quan.

Le sounded respectful. "Lieutenant Colonel Tran Van Hoa, hero of Peking and Paris. This must be the season of bitter weather in France."

"I returned to Hanoi several weeks ago." Hoa took a more erect military stance. "The most honorable Chairman Ho wants me to help bring about the final victory over the imperialists."

Le let his expression show skepticism. He knew Hoa was a primary boot-licker of Commissar Dung but believed even Ho Chi Minh would have trouble tolerating Hoa's verve for the ridiculous. "It's welcome news to hear you're on your way to the front." Le wished Hoa were going all the way South, but instincts said Hoa had stopped for a reason.

"My important mission is to solve problems here in the Central Region. Some of the—"

"We always need truck drivers. Is the institute in Moscow training—"

"Colonel Do, the Chairman didn't send me to drive trucks!" Hoa's face darkened.

"Perhaps you can repair damage. We never have enough mechanics."

Hoa bristled. "I was selected for more important duties. The cadre in the Central Region does not receive enough cooperation in scheduling party lectures. I am sure you are aware, as is Commissar Dung."

"Scheduling party lectures would be easier if I scheduled the attacks by the Americans." Actually, Le knew he sometimes had influenced attacks. He assumed the time to exert that influence would come within twenty-four hours. He hoped the spirits would keep clear weather for the duration of Hoa's visit.

"Some failures here, Colonel Do, come from your failure to allow all patriotic comrades to be inspired to new heights. The final glorious victory approaches. We must all increase efforts to hasten that glorious day when the people's victory drives the Americans from our lands."

It's starting. Le seethed as he always did when babbling rhetoric flowed from Hoa and cadre members like him. "Have you told the Americans our victory is so near? Those who fly our skies seem unaware of your important mission!"

"The Americans are only paper tigers, and the falseness of their position was shown today. This morning we dealt a grievous blow within sight of this headquarters!"

We? Le crossed his arms and bit back the devastating response he wanted to make.

"Two airplanes now lie nearby on the scrap heap of doomed imperialism. They likely lost many others. Those aircraft are lost forever to the forces of oppression." Hoa was growing more animated. "Five American air pirates will no longer carry out criminal attacks on our heroic forces."

Hoa thrust out a hand and dangled three blackened sets of American identification tags. The dull slices of blackened metal contrasted with stubby, well-manicured fingers.

Le noticed the sweet smell of burned flesh, and his patience vanished. "Since you helped bring victory, maybe you can give Major Quan's report on sacrifices our forces made to overcome the Americans."

Hoa withdrew the tags and dropped them into an envelope, which he put into a pocket of his well-kept field uniform. "I didn't visit the battlefield until this afternoon. I will be preparing a full report of the victory."

Le turned to Quan. "Perhaps you can tell us the victory's costs."

"Colonel Do," Quan said, "losses in the ammunition storage area near camp nine are still unknown. Much danger from exploding shells remains. We lost nine thirty-seven millimeter guns and six ZPU machine guns. Two trucks near the guns were destroyed."

"Casualties? Surely we did not lose guns without losing gunners."

"Forty-seven men known dead, sixty-two wounded, and eighteen missing." After a pause, Quan added, "The missing are young and inexperienced. Perhaps some will return to camp when they get hungry."

"Even so," Hoa said, "the victory has been great. Chairman Ho teaches we must willingly sacrifice to bring total victory. The Americans grow weaker each time we shoot down one of the pirates."

Le bristled at Hoa's arrogant stupidity but kept his tone unemotional. "I've seen many planes shot down. Yet, more flood our skies than before the monsoon. Americans easily replace their losses. How soon will I get fifteen more antiaircraft guns?"

"The docks in Haiphong overflow with guns, trucks and ammunition and other comradely assistance. More arrive each day."

"How old will the boys be who replace my men who died today?"

"The streets of Hanoi overflow with patriots eager to join—"

"My son, Chinh, is thirteen. Will he be among the replacements?"

"Surely the son of the most honored Colonel Do would not shirk—"

"My son, Kiem, has seen more combat than your shiny uniform'll ever see!" Le's eyes narrowed, and his face hardened.

Quan stepped forward, ready to intervene.

Hoa turned from Le's piercing stare. "I'm sure he serves heroically."

"Do you have other duties here besides reporting our victories?"

"Your soldiers have been lax in attending self-criticism sessions."

"Military duties often take fifteen to twenty hours a day."

"That leaves many hours for vital training. I'll be here until everyone in your headquarters and nearby units has been given the opportunity—"

"Do you want to start this evening?"

"No, Colonel. Tomorrow will be sufficient. You do have meeting areas nearby where two hundred can be brought together?"

Le nodded. When permanent camps were established, facilities for cadre meetings had to be set up almost before bunkers were in place. "One is within a fifteen-minute walk."

"I will start the first of three morning sessions at eight."

Le turned to Quan. "See to the scheduling."

"Yes, Colonel."

"Now," Hoa said, "with your permission, Colonel, I must work on the report of today's victory."

"I, too, have important duties that demand attention," Le said, convinced he'd wasted more time than Hoa deserved.

Hoa's expression returned to the half-smile he often wore as a mark of the cadre's superiority. He headed to the administrative area.

Quan shrugged, giving Le the look of obedient tolerance necessary when dealing with the political cadre.

Le walked over and stood close enough to Quan so no one could overhear. "Gravel supplies in this sector are running low."

Quan looked surprised. "I'll check, but I've heard no such reports."

"I'm *sure* we need *more* gravel, Major." Le's tone was one his deputy was well familiar with. "I'd put out barrels at the old gravel pit."

Quan smiled. "Yes, Colonel."

"That will be far enough from the meeting area?"

"Yes, Colonel."

Le smiled. He'd learned long ago that all he needed to do to produce gravel was to leave fuel drums in the open beside a prominent karst that could contain caves. Americans usually bombed the karst within hours.

"I want the barrels in place by seven."

"Yes, Colonel."

If the spirits were favorable—and the spirits certainly should be when he was in conflict with cadre, Le thought—bombs would fall nearby before Lieutenant Colonel Hoa could waste much time of men who had little free time to waste. Perhaps if bombs fell close enough, Hoa would be on his way to Hanoi before he wasted more of everyone's time.

Karst

Chapter 32

Eight days later, Le sat at his desk at just after three in the morning.

Major Quan brought a sealed envelope. "This arrived from Hanoi, Colonel. The courier left Hanoi only two days ago!"

A chill rippled through Le's shoulders. "Two days? Nothing gets here from Hanoi in two days." Le ripped open the rough envelope and removed a sheet of paper. He hoped this didn't involve either General Giap's secret road or Hoa's hasty departure fewer than twenty-four hours after coming to Laos. Le adjusted his glasses and held the paper so it caught the light.

"The Americans will stop bombing Vietnam for their holiday of Christmas. The twenty-four-hour ceasefire begins at 1800 hours, December 24th. Move all category-one trucks from the Lao Central Region into North Vietnam by 0700 hours that day. Prepare for maximum-effort southbound movement through Central Region immediately after the truce ends on the evening of the 25th.   Giap"

Le reread the message. He was pleased to find no connection with Giap's road-building scheme nor a complaint relayed from Commissar Dung. Nevertheless, the message placed an enormous burden on his already burdened forces. Le handed the message to Quan.

"Not much time to put together an operation of that size." With so little in the jungle to distinguish one day from another, Le was uncertain of the current date. "Do we have six days?"

Quan glanced at papers on his clipboard. "Five, Colonel. We have to move trucks across the border five days from this morning."

"And move hundreds south again thirty-six hours later. Ridiculous."

Quan shrugged.

Le took the message and put a match to it. When the flame burned out, he crushed the crumpled black ash into the dirt of the floor. He glanced at his wristwatch. "Assemble the staff in thirty minutes."

On the fifth morning, Le listened to the loudspeakers and paced the dusty floor of the communications room. Aided by an almost moonless night, convoys of up to fifty trucks each had leapfrogged from one wooded area to the next throughout the Central Region. Like a final barrier to the border, however, American planes had spent much of the night over the Ban Laboy Ford and Harley's Valley. Le still had more than two hundred trucks hidden around the upper valley, and more than one hundred and fifty remained in the twenty kilometers southwest of the ford.

"Alley Cat, Nail Four-six. If you don't have anything else, we're about to head on home."

"Alley Cat copied. Nimrod Three-two's trying to find a couple of trucks south of Mu Gia. I don't have anything more in Sector Twelve."

Le clenched a fist in anticipation and checked the time. If the first FAC of the day didn't come to Sector 12, Le might yet get all the trucks across the border.

"Nothing's moving, Alley. They must be taking an early holiday."
Le smiled.

"Understand, Nail. You folks have a Merry Christmas."

"Humbug! I'll be back tonight trying to stay out of Santa Claus's way."

"Understand. Most of us'll be out here tonight, too."

"Roger, Alley. We'll call crossin' the fence."

A report over a field telephone said the 0-2 had circled the Ban Laboy Ford and headed west instead of following Route 912 southwest.

Knowing it was time to risk the all-out push, Le sat on the edge of a table. "To all sectors: Yellow Moon Rising."

"Yes, Colonel," the sergeant in charge of communications said.

Le imagined results of the message going out by field telephones, flare guns, flashlights, lanterns, and rifle fire. He pictured truck parks and side roads surging to life with scores of big Soviet, Czech, and Polish trucks groaning forward. Within minutes, he received his first report. Trucks were splashing through the Ban Laboy Ford at a rate of one every fifteen to twenty seconds.

"In forty minutes," Quan said, "only stragglers will be south of the ford."

"If we're lucky," Le said. "But all trucks won't be across the border before daybreak."

"A heavy overcast is reported beyond the ridge. Perhaps clouds will come over our roads. If the spirits help us with clouds, it'll matter little that a few trucks are late."

Le couldn't count on clouds keeping Americans from seeing trucks on his roads. The northeast monsoon brought rainy weather daily to the Vietnamese side of the mountains, but clouds seldom crossed to the west side. "Anyway, unless Colonel Khanh's taken care of the hundreds of trucks we've sent across, he can't complain that a few are late."

Quan smiled.

The operation continued with precision for twenty minutes. The first hint of trouble came in on a field telephone. "Colonel Do, a truck has stalled and is blocking the road!"

"Location?" Le quickly took a position behind the operator.

"Two-hundred meters north of the ford. The road's too narrow for trucks to pass."

Le did not need a map to know the situation was serious. The long northbound grade from the Nam Ta Le crossing was the steepest in the Central Region and the most demanding on his trucks.

"The transmission's broken," the operator said. "Nearly ninety trucks are behind it!"

"Push the truck over the side immediately."

Le paced for the next five minutes.

The telephone operator finally smiled. "Trucks are moving, Colonel."

The small group of men nearby cheered.

Le remained solemn. "Good, but sunrise is an hour away, and we've lost time that cannot be made up." He went to the sergeant monitoring the American control frequencies. "Have day FACs reported in?"

"No, Colonel. Nail Four-six just crossed the Mekong to land."

"Tell me as soon as any pilot calls in, no matter which sector he's headed for."

"Yes, Colonel."

Le took a few sips from a cup of hot tea, then resumed pacing.

"Colonel Do!"

The tone sent a shiver through Le even before he turned to see who'd called his name.

The corporal, who monitored the crude network of observation points scattered across Laos, looked nervous. "Colonel, an aircraft crossed the Mekong, flying east."

Le turned to the sergeant monitoring the radio. "What sector?"

The sergeant flinched. "I have no reports to Alley Cat, Colonel."

Le was surprised. American pilots usually called their airborne commanders at least ten minutes before his ground observers reported contact.

"Keep listening and turn on the loudspeaker." Le turned to the corporal, "Verify that report. I need to be sure it wasn't the aircraft returning to its base. If it's coming our way, find out when the aircraft was discovered."

"Yes, Colonel."

Le checked his wristwatch and said to Quan, "He's early. If there's no mistake, the American could be over the ford at daybreak."

"Our gunners are ready, Colonel," Quan said in an encouraging tone.

"But not our trucks."

The corporal turned to Le. "There's no mistake, Colonel. The post south of Thakhek is certain the aircraft flies toward us. The aircraft flew into Laos eleven minutes ago."

"Eleven minutes!" Le had few trucks to work with and no time to waste. "Order all trucks remaining between Mu Gia and Tchepone onto the road immediately."

The directive produced looks of astonishment.

"Yes, Col—"

"Tell the commanders to scatter trucks on open sections of the road. Push them into the open, if necessary. And they should use lights, anything to get the pilot's attention."

"Yes, Colonel," the sergeant said.

"Oh." Quan's quizzical expression changed to admiration.

"All gunners are cleared to fire," Le said. "Shoot down the aircraft."

"Yes, Colonel."

"We probably can't stop him. But if guns shoot the aircraft down, the attention of many Americans would be diverted."

"Long enough for all trucks to move under clouds across the border," Quan said, completing Le's thought.

"Colonel," the corporal said, "the post at Ban Phahoy reports the aircraft passed just south a minute ago."

Le looked at a map spread on a table in the center of the room. He projected the flight path forward and found the intersection of Routes 911 and 912. "Looks like it's headed for the intersection."

Quan nodded. "Perhaps the pilot isn't coming to the ford."

"If the spirits favor us." Le knew, however, that pilots often flew to the intersection, then followed Route 912 to the ford.

Quan scanned the map. "The American should take thirteen more minutes—fifteen at the most—to reach the intersection."

Le had made the same estimate. Turning to the operator in charge of the field telephone for Le's command net, he said, "Tell Major Nguyen he must get trucks on the road north and south of Ban Loumpoum within five minutes. He must get the pilot's attention."

Le paced, trying to think of anything else he could do. He exchanged a glance with Quan. There was nothing to do but wait. His tea was cold by the time he took another sip.

A telephone operator said, "The last ten trucks are at the ford."

"Good," Quan said.

Le glanced at his wristwatch. "Progress has been steady." He felt more positive. The trucks were near the relative safety of the upper valley where numerous truck parks, now empty, could provide hiding places.

Finally the loudspeaker crackled out the radio call Le had hoped for.

"Alley Cat, Alley Cat. This is Nail Five-nine, north of Alpha. I've got a mover in sight, so I need ordnance."

For the first time in his life, Le found himself hoping attack aircraft were available. In his relief that a truck had gotten the pilot's attention, Le realized the voice sounded familiar. The call sign, which he hadn't heard for months, also triggered memories. *Had Metal Dragon returned?*

Not bad! Mitch was surprised to have spotted a truck on only his ninth mission. He assumed the problem would be finding attack aircraft during the transition time between night missions and day missions.

"Is that Nail Five-nine calling Alley Cat? Say again your location."

Mitch smiled, recognizing a tone of confusion. The controller obviously expected the first call at the Mekong, a good thirty minutes before FACs were in position to find a truck. When Mitch had vowed to return to the war, he also had vowed to fight smarter than before.

"Roger, Alley. I crossed the fence a few minutes ago. I *am* at Alpha."

"Standby, Nail. Nimrod Three-two's about to RTB from Sector Six. He might have a bomb or two left."

"Great, Alley, but I'll need him in a hurry. The truck's heading into cover on a spur road north of Alpha."

Le slammed his fist on the map table. "Tell Major Nguyen to keep that truck in the open until the other aircraft arrives. He must keep the FAC in the area."

"Yes, Colonel," said the operator on the field net.

"Roger, Nail," came through the loudspeaker. "Nimrod Three-two's five minutes north. He'll meet you on Two-thirty-nine-point-six."

"Copied, Alley. Be advised, I picked up ground fire east of Alpha."

"Roger, Nail. Say type and number of rounds."

"Probably thirty rounds from a pair of thirty-sevens. I'm going Two-thirty-nine-six."

"Roger, Nail."

Le watched to ensure the radio operator set in that frequency.

While talking to the Nimrod, Mitch crossed Route 911 and studied the area where the truck had disappeared. The spur road crossed a quarter-mile-wide band of jungle stretching north and south. Hidden roads might carry the truck miles from where Mitch saw it enter the trees.

"I'll mark where I saw the truck," Mitch said. "Mix your bombs in those trees, Nimrod."

"Copied. I've got you in sight, Nail. Nimrod Three-two's about two minutes out."

"I'll mark in about—" Mitch was stopped by the sight of the truck moving out of the trees. "The truck's passed through the cover and is moving farther east on the spur. Wait. It's stopped."

Even in the dim light, Mitch saw a figure jump from the truck and run into the trees.

"Mark any time, Nail."

"I'll mark the truck on the second segment of a spur east of Nine-eleven." Pulling into the marking pass, Mitch tried to figure out why he had seen what he had seen. "Something's strange, Nimrod. The driver pulled into the open and abandoned his truck. Don't take chances."

"Copied."

With the glowing hint of dawn behind him, he dived at the truck. The rocket sparkled in the semi-darkness and was answered by flashes from four AAA sites near Route 911.

Tracers—brighter than Mitch'd ever seen in daylight—rushed at him. He rolled hard left, maneuvering away from both major roads.

"You're clear, Nail," Nimrod said. "I've got your smoke."

In a steep climbing turn, Mitch looked through the overhead windows. "My smoke's by the spur where it exits the trees. The truck's forty meters east. I think they've set us up."

"Is Nimrod cleared in hot?"

Mitch looked north of the smoke and couldn't see the camouflaged A-26 against the dark jungle. Under night rules, the FAC never saw the attack aircraft and depended on altitude separation to avoid mid-airs. "I'm coming up through six thou' southeast of the target. You're cleared if you have me or can stay below six."

"Nimrod Three-two's crossed Nine-twelve on the deck. We'll stay well below you."

"Three-two's cleared hot. Let's count on one pass."

"Roger."

"Smoke's drifting almost over the truck."

"Roger."

Mitch looked for movement between his smoke and Route 912.

Nothing—until flashes of the Nimrod's eight .50 caliber guns spit tracers at the truck. The gunfire ceased almost as soon as it started, but he saw the dark apparition streak southward. White smoke from his rocket boiled wildly as the A-26 raced through. Hundreds of sparkling bursts engulfed the truck.

Fragmentation bombs or CBU. Mitch turned to check for damage. The flickering ceased, leaving an oval-shaped blur of smoke. He saw a flash as if a bomb had detonated late. Flames backlit the blur, and the cab of the truck burned fiercely.

"Got him, Nimrod." Mitch was excited to have gotten a truck after so few missions.

"We've got more fifty-cal, Nail, but the sky's gettin' kinda bright."

"Let's leave well enough alone." He still sensed they'd been led into a trap. "Whatever that was all about, I'll give you a truck destroyed."

"Thanks for the target, Nail. We're headed for the barn."

"Roger. I'll have your numbers in a minute."

Le listened to the post-strike report. *The delay might be enough.* He paced, hoping Metal Dragon would discover another truck.

"Colonel," the operator on the field net said. His expression was solemn. "The American is flying northeast over Route Nine-Twelve."

Le nodded. *The delay hadn't been enough.*

Approaching Ban Laboy, Mitch aimed his binoculars at the long grade leading to Harley's Valley. He was surprised to spot a truck on the bank of the river well below the road. Fresh gouges on the hillside suggested the truck had wrecked during the night.

He estimated the coordinates and wanted to report them to Alley Cat. However, Alley Cat was briefing Cricket's incoming controller, who would supervise day operations in Steel Tiger. Mitch smiled. J.D. had called it the Ho Chi Minh briefing, figuring the North Vietnamese benefited more from the daily summary than Americans did.

Mitch started to circle. He focused on the truck, but something drew his eyes to Harley's Valley. The road didn't look right. Halfway up the valley, the reddish ribbon of road was marred by dark blotches—many, many dark blotches.

Looking toward the ford, he scanned for ground fire and wondered if a B-52 strike had torn up Route 912. But craters would be reddish-brown, not dark, evenly spaced marks. He rolled onto the other wing, putting Harley's Valley in the center of the windshield.

Adrenaline stirred. Trucks stretched from the middle of the valley to where the road disappeared. Now he understood the abandoned truck. He headed for karst bordering the valley on the north. He wanted to call Alley Cat, but the frequency still was tied up.

Mitch raced toward the border to estimate how extensive the target was. He saw too many trucks to waste time counting. They were spaced about a truck-length apart, so he decided to see how long the convoy was and to make estimates later. Listening to Alley Cat chattering, Mitch mentally urged, *Get off the radio!*

Approaching the border, he noticed a potential problem. Low clouds covered everything from the first ford in North Vietnam to well beyond the coast forty miles away. He was too excited to worry about consequences the clouds might portend. Wherever the road peeked through the jungle, he saw trucks grinding forward, a truck-length apart. Just beyond the ford in North Vietnam, trucks were lumbering up the grade and slipping under the clouds—still at truck-length intervals.

Mitch was astounded. He had a line of trucks at least four-miles long. *How many per mile? Sixty? One hundred?* He'd never seen a more significant target. Maybe this was the big mission. He switched his radio to Guard. "Alley Cat and Cricket, Nail Five-nine on UHF Guard. I've got more than a hundred trucks in Harley's Valley, and I need bombs."

The chatter on the control frequency ceased.

"Five-nine, Alley Cat, say again."

"I've got at least four miles of trucks stretching to under the overcast in North Vietnam. I don't know what the clouds are gonna do, so I need fighters as soon as you can get 'em."

"Standby, Nail. The cupboard's bare at the moment. May be about thirty minutes before we've got ordnance."

Damn! "It'll depend on the weather. If the clouds go east, we've got a potential turkey shoot."

"Understand. You'll get everything we can send."

"Roger. I'm crossing the border to check the weather."

"Approved."

Right. Mitch was going—with or without approval. He paralleled the road to the first ford. Watching truck after truck slip beneath the clouds, he imagined the relief he'd feel if driving one that reached cover. Overhead in an O-2, however, he hoped the morning sun would burn away the clouds. He considered praying for the clouds to go away but stuck with hoping. He'd never felt right about praying for advantages to help kill the enemy.

Nevertheless, he hoped to destroy as many trucks as possible. Perhaps a rocket mark near the ford would panic drivers into fearing a strike was imminent. A few minutes of confusion could leave more trucks at risk.

Mitch launched a rocket. Maneuvering away, he saw fire from 37mm guns. The shells weren't close, but he drifted farther away anyway.

His rocket exploded beside the ford. Smoke blossomed and blew west. He watched the trucks splashing through the ford. None hesitated. He'd learned something disturbing. If the sun didn't burn away the clouds, surface winds were likely to carry clouds into Laos.

Impatient, he flew farther into North Vietnam. He hoped to find the clouds thinning. Reaching a large hole in the undercast, he was shocked. The hole was over the road, and trucks were passing—still at truck-length intervals. Looking toward the border, he estimated the first ford was three miles away. His line of trucks was at least seven-miles long.

Turning toward the border, Mitch called, "Alley Cat, Nail Five-nine, how we coming on the ordnance?"

"Cricket's taken over, Five-nine," Cricket said. "We've lined up four flights. The first birds are about twenty minutes out."

Mitch reached the ford and found clouds over it and lapping at the edges of the truck-covered road leading from the border. "We're running out of time, Cricket. The clouds are moving west."

Discouragement swept over Mitch just as the clouds were sweeping over the target he'd wanted to destroy on J.D.'s behalf. Mitch had imagined a day-long series of strikes that would've made headlines in the states. Today would've been his personal answer to those who denied the existence of trucks on the Ho Chi Minh Trail. He also would've had a defensible answer for Elizabeth's questioning of why his return mattered. Looking toward the sunrise now bringing brightness to the cloudless sky above, Mitch said quietly, "Well, roomie, if you've got any pull up there, you need to pull those clouds toward the sea."

In ten minutes the clouds had reached the middle of Harley's Valley, and Mitch didn't have a truck in sight.

In a dejected tone, Mitch said, "Cricket, Five-nine, I'm afraid we've lost the trucks to the clouds. Recommend you Skyspot the road between the border and Quang Khe. If you cut the road, we might strand some trucks until the clouds burn off."

"Roger, Nail. We'll look into that."

Mitch flew near Ban Laboy, looking at the wrecked truck. His quiet contemplation was broken by an unexpected voice on the radio.

"The spirits are against you, Metal Dragon."

The words sent chills through Mitch.

"You should go away and stay away. You don't belong here."

"Neither do you, Earth Dragon. It's well past time your people left South Vietnam in peace."

"Go home, Metal Dragon."

"I tried that already. Now I've come back to finish the job."

After the trucks were safe in Colonel Khanh's region, Le settled behind his desk. He was amused he could feel so elated and so weary at the same time. Five exhausting days of preparation had produced a triumph he'd not believed possible. He was proud of his men. His exhilaration, however, was tempered. When the trucks returned to Laos in fewer than thirty-six hours, he would face another task almost as gargantuan.

Quan approached with a solemn expression clouding his face.

"Cheer up," Le said. "The spirits are with us."

Quan sighed and looked at his feet. "One of the straggler trucks brought wounded from the southern war. Outside—"

"My son?" Le rose from his chair. He was excited at the possibility of seeing Kiem but fearful of how bad the wounds might be.

"No." Quan didn't look up. "Outside is a friend from his unit."

"And?"

Quan shuffled his feet. "The friend begs permission to talk to you."

Le grabbed his AK-47 and field pack. "He has a message?"

"Yes, Colonel."

Le slowed, assuming Quan's lack of enthusiasm meant the message was bad. Le pulled his pack on, straightening each strap with a deliberate motion. Pausing, he stared at papers cluttering his desk. He gathered the papers, aligning them into a neat stack.

Looking up, Le asked, "Where?"

"Just outside the main entrance, Colonel."

Gesturing at the papers, Le said, "Take care of these."

"Yes, Colonel."

Le walked away. He appreciated Quan's understanding that there was nothing to take care of.

Sergeant Dinh and Corporal Cung followed Le outside. Dinh yelled, "Make way."

Le saw a litter surrounded by several men. One held a cigarette for the wounded soldier, whose body was covered by a ragged blanket.

Pushing through, Le saw bandages over the soldier's forehead and one eye. The blanket was slack where the right leg should be. Kneeling, Le said, "You know Kiem?"

The soldier nodded, grimacing at the movement. His lips twitched but didn't form words.

Le hesitated a few moments. "And Kiem has died?"

The soldier gazed at Le and nodded. Tears flooded into the visible eye.

Le fought the finality he'd feared moments earlier. Realizing he was the center of attention, Le cleared his throat. "I hope his death was honorable."

"We were in attack," the soldier said, his voice clearer than Le expected. "American bombers came too soon. Kiem was brave."

"Good," Le said, taking little comfort but knowing that was the only comfort he'd ever have. "You have been brave."

Le almost continued with words about glorious victories over the imperialists. However, he had no glorious feelings, and such words would only make him sound like Lieutenant Colonel Hoa. Le put a hand softly on the soldier's shoulder, then stood.

"I have something from Kiem," the soldier said. An arm moved beneath the blanket.

Le knelt, pulled the blanket aside and saw something dark clasped in a bandaged hand. Pulling the item free, Le needed a moment to recognize Kiem's flute, now charred darker than the light color Le remembered.

"Thank you." Le gently tucked the blanket in place, then stood. "Get him a new blanket, and see that he's taken care of. Put him on a homebound truck as soon as he's well enough."

"Yes, Colonel," a corporal said.

Le turned away wondering if the young soldier would be alive when more trucks went north. His gaze rose along the karst mountain that housed the headquarters cave. The solid overcast obscured the crest. Lower down, a mist of clouds drifted into the trees. Slowly, but relentlessly, wispy white overwhelmed dark green.

The clouds were like spirits on a march that couldn't be turned back. He wanted to feel Kiem was there in spirit along with Le's brothers who'd died fighting the French. Watching clouds swallow trees, he was jolted by the notion that perhaps the trees represented his brothers and Kiem and everyone else being swallowed inexorably by a war that had no end.

He hurried along a path. Dinh and Cung followed.

Reaching a trail leading up to observation posts , Le said, "Wait here." Sergeant Dinh looked hesitant. "I grieve with you, Colonel."

Le nodded, fearful words couldn't come without tears. He moved quickly up the trail.

After minutes of hard climbing, Le stopped on a rocky ledge. As he struggled to catch his breath, the only other sounds were birds chattering, the breeze swishing through treetops, and the first splatters of rain. He had a commanding view of the valley. Even with dense showers moving in from the east, the road seemed hauntingly serene. Le found it difficult to imagine more than six hundred trucks had rumbled through in the last twelve hours.

He recalled his earlier pride, which now seemed hollow. Perhaps the magnificent accomplishment would help win the war—though not in time to save Kiem. Looking over the thousands of bomb craters marring the tranquil scene, he knew he must find a way to end the war before Chinh had to make the long march south. He remembered General Giap's road-building scheme and wished somehow it could end the war.

A shiver coursed through Le. His legs quivered, and he felt too exhausted to stand. He leaned against a boulder and slid down until he was sitting. Clouds crept in through the trees engulfing Le in white darkness. Sprinkles gave way to a pounding downpour.

Le pulled out Kiem's flute, held it against his chest, and wept.

The walkways near the mail room were crowded with Christmas-eve hopefuls. After a short wait, Mitch knelt and found a bright red envelope addressed in Elizabeth's handwriting. Excitement of receiving her first letter pushed aside even the frustration of losing all the trucks hours earlier. He hadn't heard from her since their final words nearly a month ago. Unsure what to expect, he wanted some privacy. He tucked away the envelope and headed for the Harley-Smith-Wolfe Amphitheater.

Walking down the wooded slope toward the abandoned stage, he pictured how different the setting had been the previous week. Bob Hope and his entertainers had been on stage while most of NKP's population filled the benches and surrounding hillside. Mitch had made himself hoarse during more than two hours of cheering from the second row.

Now, the hillside was deserted except for an occasional passerby on a shortcut between the quarters and work areas. Leaves rustled softly. The setting had an almost religious sense about it as Mitch settled on a bench in the back row.

The envelope included a cheery Christmas card with a scrawl from

Mandy and with Elizabeth's name in her delicate script. Mitch noticed the absence of the word love. He found a short note on a separate card.

"Mitch, I'm sorry you have to spend Christmas alone again this year. I'm even sorrier Mandy's spending a second Christmas—out of only four—without her Daddy. I don't have a good answer each time she asks why you can't be with us. After Christmas, she and I are going to father's place in Nassau. I need to find some answers for myself. Mandy and I wish you a good Christmas and a safe new year.   Elizabeth"

Mitch ripped the note in two, then pieced it together. He was torn by anger and guilt as he reread the words. *Why couldn't she understand?* A man sometimes was driven by obligations more important than self—more important than family. It wasn't as if she hadn't met J.D. Mitch was angry at her for not understanding. He also felt guilty because trying to live up to his commitments caused her such pain.

Pushing the note and the card into the envelope, Mitch felt sorry for himself. He needed loving support in the loneliness of another Christmas eve at NKP. He didn't want to spend Christmas worrying whether or not his family would be there when he returned. He thought of Ted Forrester. Mitch decided his own uncertainty was infinitely better than the finality Ted faced in what should have been a joyous holiday season.

Mitch stretched out on the bench and looked at green leaves swaying in the breeze. There'd be no white Christmas, but the rhythmic swaying of the leaves was calming, almost mesmerizing. He tried to imagine Ted's final hours with his wife and how the undercurrent of concern would've been on concerns about his survival instead of hers. He hoped their parting had been more loving than his final hours with Elizabeth.

Mitch sighed and closed his eyes to reminisce. Mandy hadn't come to California. Trying to make their day in San Francisco like Bangkok, Mitch and Elizabeth agreed to a truce since arguing about his decision wouldn't change the reality. They did tourist things—cable cars, Fisherman's Wharf, a drink at the Top of the Mark while fog crept through streets far below.

Window shopping after dinner, Elizabeth was drawn to an expensive pair of earrings. Mitch knew she wanted them because she made an effort to hide her interest.

Over her protests, he paid more than $220. Once outside, she hugged him, kissing him like their final kiss in the airport in Bangkok. When she drew back from him, lights sparkled from the diamonds, and tears glistened in her eyes. Mitch and Elizabeth knew he'd never have spent that much money if what he faced wasn't so dangerous.

They walked in silence. The laughter and the light mood never returned.

That night she came to him wearing only the earrings.

They got up early the next morning to drive to Travis Air Force Base. Elizabeth said very little. Mitch attributed her silence to being tired after only a couple of hours sleep. On the way, he stopped the car at an overlook near Sausalito while the sunrise painted clouds above hills across the bay. His memories remained vivid. He had pulled her to him, and she seemed resistant. He leaned to kiss her. She turned. His kiss ended up on her cheek.

She slipped away. "I don't know if you should plan on seeing me when you come back."

Mitch was jolted by her words and the look of determination in her eyes. "You can't mean that." Shock gave way to anger.

"If Mandy and I mean so little to you for you to leave without having to, I'm not sure we can be there when you finally end your quest."

"It's not a quest!"

"No one in Washington gives a damn about the war. Why should you?"

"It's not a quest!" He held back angrier words. "We already talked this over."

"And you could've changed it then. I don't know what else I can say now." She moved against the car door and faced her window.

Watching her, he wished she'd say she wanted to be there when he returned. He wished even more she'd say she wanted him to return.

Putting the car in gear, Mitch floored the accelerator. The car roared out of the overlook and earned a blast of an airhorn on a truck he cut in front of. He hardly saw anything but the road ahead until he pulled up to the passenger terminal at Travis. Neither spoke throughout the ride nor during a half hour in the terminal.

When his flight was called, they stood.

Mitch said, "I have to go."

Elizabeth didn't even look up at him.

Mitch didn't know whether to shake her or kiss her, so he ended up doing neither. He turned without a final touch and walked to the line. His guts were churning, but he faced forward until a sergeant at the exit checked Mitch's name on a roster.

Mitch paused in the doorway and turned. His eyes met Elizabeth's. Her cheeks glistened, and she was biting down on her lip. He didn't know if her expression meant "I'm so confused," or "Goodbye forever."

Elizabeth held his gaze a few seconds until the next person passed the sergeant. She shrugged, raised her hand waist high, turned her palm toward him, and waved.

Her wave made Mitch think of an insecure little girl. He wanted to rush to comfort her. Instead he nodded, turned, and walked away.

Now, almost a month later, Mitch drifted off to sleep on the bench beneath the swaying leaves. He awakened later when an O-2 flew over.

The sun was lower, glinting off the three names of Cricket FACs on the blue-and-white sign above the stage. A Christmas carol carried from a radio of someone walking across the hillside. Sitting up, Mitch tried to decide what would get him through Christmas and the rest of his combat tour without Elizabeth's loving support. Keeping busy was the answer.

Mitch stood and checked the time. He decided to recruit Ted Forrester to help the chaplain prepare for Christmas Eve services. Mitch would also tell the schedulers to keep him flying through his CTOs. Those four extra missions a month would be J.D.'s.

Chapter 33

Le sat on the hood of his GAZ-69 and watched flares sparkle beneath small parachutes. An A-26 was attacking a convoy farther up Route 912 near Ban Laboy. Intermittent flashes and the rumble of secondary explosions told Le this Nimrod had found targets.

Tracers raced skyward, announcing the next run of the unseen attacker. The stuttering orange flares cast a surreal glow on everything in reach. Watching such a battle from a distance reminded Le of badly dubbed movies where the voices and lips weren't synchronized. He saw flashes of bomb explosions just before he heard the antiaircraft guns that had fired before the bombs were even dropped. Then he heard the howl of the attacking A-26 from when the aircraft had been beyond the target.

Seconds later he heard the bombs explode. This time, the drone of the aircraft increased, suggesting the A-26 wasn't circling for another attack. The flares drifted into the trees. Except for a crimson glow from the target, darkness reclaimed the jungle.

Le tried to spot the A-26 against a background of stars. The bomber's roar reached a crescendo. He sensed, more than saw, a dark shadow race across north of him. He heard scuffling among his bodyguards as a couple scrambled for cover. His companions' unwarranted fears made him chuckle. Satisfied the A-26 wouldn't return, Le slid off the hood. "Corporal Cung! Private Kiet!"

"They're right here, Colonel," Sergeant Dinh said from beside the rear bumper.

"Good." Le swung into the front seat. "I didn't want to search all the way to Tchepone for them. Let's check the damage. No lights!"

When the GAZ reached two burning trucks, salvage crews were on scene. Le saw six trucks disabled. The odor of spilled fuel and the stench of burning rubber filled the air. He looked at his wristwatch. Daybreak was fifteen minutes away. Turning to Cung, who was driving, Le said, "Let me off here and stay with the vehicle."

"Yes, Colonel," Cung said, braking the GAZ to a stop.

Le shouted at scores of men swarming around the trucks, "Hurry. The sun comes soon." He hoped the first day FAC wasn't coming to Sector 12.

Fifty miles west, Mitch guided his O-2 by the Pathet Lao strong point of Mahaxai. Still upset over losing all the trucks to the weather three mornings ago, he'd gotten airborne thirty minutes ahead of schedule. Once again, he hadn't told Alley Cat—and enemy soldiers who monitored the frequency—he was well into Laos. Instead he listened to Nimrod Thirty-one report leaving two trucks burning and four possibly destroyed. Mitch copied the coordinates and checked his map.

He turned toward the Ban Laboy Ford.

Half an hour later, Le stood on the dusty road. Four trucks had been towed two hundred meters down a camouflaged spur that angled away from Route 912 between where the fourth and fifth trucks had been hit.

Le was disappointed that two burned-out hulks still smoldered on the main road. He took pride in confounding the Americans by removing as much evidence as possible of any aerial successes. Still, those hulks—now covered by hundreds of fresh cuttings—would be difficult to distinguish from overhanging trees.

Across the valley, sunlight had crept halfway down a massive karst peak. Le looked at the peak to estimate how soon direct sun would reach the hidden trucks. The sun glinted off something higher. "Aircraft! Approaching from the west!"

Mitch aimed his binoculars at a ribbon of road southwest of Ban Laboy. Movement caught his attention. "Alley Cat, Nail Five-nine's got troops. Do you have any ordnance?"

"Say location, Five-nine."

"Sector Twelve, where Nimrod Three-one killed his trucks. These guys are scattering."

Mitch widened his scan. He noticed two large clumps of foliage tucked beneath trees overhanging Route 912. "Bingo," he said without transmitting.

Mitch thought about the debacle on Christmas eve. Whether the clouds had been propelled by spirits, fate, or unseasonably strong upslope winds, he remained frustrated over missing the greatest mission of his life. He pressed the microphone button. "If you're somewhere listening, Earth Dragon, the Metal Dragon's back."

"Aircraft calling Alley Cat, say again."

"Disregard."

"Nail Five-nine, Alley Cat has Honda, a flight of F-Fours weathered out of Dong Hoi. We were about to Skyspot 'em, but you can have them on Two thirty-seven eight. Honda should be almost overhead."

Great. Mitch wrote 237.8 on the window. "Switching."

When Le reached the closest truck on the spur road, he stopped to catch his breath. Looking around, he was pleased to see the sprint had caused Sergeant Dinh and Private Kiet—and scores of other younger soldiers—to be at least as winded. He struggled to stop panting so he might hear the aircraft. The Americans would dictate his next move. He hoped the aircraft had flown by, thereby allowing him to continue to his headquarters. If the O-2 circled, Le would wait to see if armed aircraft came.

Le noticed the strong odor of fuel leaking from a shrapnel-laced tank on the truck. The draining fuel had cut a tiny gully into the nearby ditch, but the flow had slowed to a steady drip. He walked beyond the front of the truck to where fumes weren't so strong.

Le heard the buzz of the O-2 drifting farther east near the main road. He noticed something more ominous—the deep roar of circling jets.

"The bombers are here quicker than I expected," he called to Dinh, who still was bent over with hands on knees. If the hulks on the road became the target, Le wanted to be farther away. "Dinh. Kiet. We're too close." He turned and started up the spur road.

A hissing whistle howled in from overhead.

Le tensed, dropped to a knee, and raised his AK-47. A rocket flashed through upper foliage and exploded against the trunk of a large teak. A bright flash disintegrated into hundreds of tiny, white-tailed comets arcing outward toward everything. Le was so mesmerized by the brilliant spectacle, the noise of the detonation didn't register. Smoky trails through the air led to at least a dozen men. Sound didn't seem to exist until men showered with burning phosphorous screamed.

Acrid, white smoke belched from a thousand pieces. Before Le fully comprehended what had happened, a flash set fire to the fuel-soaked ditch, to the air above, and to Dinh, who had started across. He transformed into a human torch.

Horrified, Le dropped his AK-47 and yanked off his ammunition pouches. He raced forward, uncertain what to do.

Dinh staggered from the ditch and dropped to his knees in burning grass. His face twisted into a grimace, and his wide-eyes locked on Le's. Dinh's head shook side-to-side as he pushed the muzzle of his AK-47 beneath his chin. Five rounds popped from the weapon before Dinh's finger slipped off the trigger.

Le froze mid-stride and stumbled to a knee as Dinh slumped. Watching in disbelief, Le felt intense pain in his forearm. He gazed down and discovered smoke spewing through a hole in his sleeve. He yanked at his cuff, and the button catapulted away. He slapped the glowing phosphorous and dislodged it from a hole cauterized into his forearm. He bunched the sleeve over the wound and pushed as hard as he could.

Air, saturated with smoke and the sickeningly sweet stench of burning flesh, assaulted Le's nostrils. Staggering to his feet, he coughed at the choking smoke and reeled backward toward his abandoned weapon. He knelt and grabbed the AK-47 and ammunition pouches. A soldier burst out of the smoke and smashed into Le. Both men fell hard. The soldier rolled to his feet and disappeared into the smoke.

The contact jarred Le's thinking. Part of him mourned Sergeant Dinh. Experience and instinct overruled. Le jumped to his feet. "Clear out. Get far away."

He ran, weaving by the trucks on the spur road. A jittery feeling in his chest spread outward. The rocket was a harbinger. Bombs would follow in seconds. In all his years of soldiering, he'd never encountered the panic engulfing him on this steamy, smoky jungle morning. He dropped his ammo pouches, something he'd never done while on the run.

Mitch watched the growing cloud of smoke emerge from trees at least two-hundred meters from his aim point. "Sorry about that mark, Honda. I couldn't hit a bull in the ass with a bass fiddle this morning." Mitch wondered where that phrasing had come from. "Anyway the target's on the road. Come north from my smoke to the closest spot on the road and hit fifty meters east. The two camouflaged trucks are under over-hanging trees."

Honda Lead asked, "Is that the trees opposite the L-shaped meadow north of the road?"

Mitch looked. "Affirmative. Honda Lead, you're cleared in hot. FAC'll hold south."

"Lead'll be in position in about thirty seconds."

A hundred meters beyond the trucks, Le saw two soldiers cowering along the spur road. He tried to yell, "Keep moving," but the words lodged in his throat. He gave a half-hearted wave of his arm but didn't bother looking to see if they followed.

Beyond a bend in the road, Le had to stop. He pulled up by a large durian tree and tried to catch his breath. Adrenaline and aching lungs blanked out pain in his arm. Listening for aircraft, he heard an O-2 buzzing overhead, but the jet noises had faded. He assumed the bombers had climbed and were awaiting the command to plummet toward the smoke.

When Le could hold his breath a few seconds, he heard it—the increasing scream of a diving jet. He darted around the tree and flung himself headlong into the undergrowth. A vine tripped Le. The AK-47 cartwheeled forward and disappeared into the bushes. Struggling to his feet, he heard an even more fearful noise—the shrill whistle of plummet-ing bombs. The jungle possessed no comparable sound.

Le dived between two large trees and burrowed under decaying leaves and stalks of fallen bamboo. The deep-throated roar of a jet clawing for altitude drowned out the bombs' whistling. He felt a quick sequence of earth-jolting explosions near the main road. Le sensed the rippling pressure waves, but the bombs had hit several hundred meters away. His feeling of panic began to subside. His noticed the throbbing in his arm.

Assuming he had at least forty-five seconds before the next bombs hurtled into the jungle, Le decided to retrieve his weapon. The AK-47 was nearby, but Le found the barrel clogged with dirt. He tapped the muzzle against his hand as he returned to his hiding place. Experience convinced him to stay put.

The second string of bombs hit close to the first. Le heard screaming and yelling. From that distance, the jungle air carried the suggestion of sounds, but not the words. Sitting against the biggest tree, he tried to regain his composure. He wondered where Private Kiet was.

Trying to rub away some of the searing pain in his forearm, he heard noises of the next attack. The bomber's roar masked the whistle for several critical seconds. Then, Le realized the whistling was more intense than the first two. He covered his ears, opened his mouth, and burrowed deeper into the leaves.

The roar and the jarring concussion hit Le almost simultaneously. Dust, leaves, and branches showered down. A painful ringing in his ears didn't keep him from hearing falling trees and shrill, frightened cries of jungle animals. *Had the bombs fallen on the spur road?* Overwhelming panic hit him. The Americans could be working bombs down the road. *The next bombs would fall even closer*. He must get away from the road!

In an adrenaline-charged frenzy, Le vaulted up and flailed through vines and bamboo.

"I'm afraid Three was about as far off as my rocket." Mitch thought of the old days. J.D. would've commented on interplane about some headquarters-staff weenie flying number three. Mitch smiled as he could hear J.D. saying *Maybe we oughta give him a bass fiddle and see if he can hit anything with that.* "Four, I need you closer to lead's hit. He was right on two trucks on the main road."

Clawing, struggling, and twisting, Le lunged against clutching vegetation. He'd moved a few meters farther when he heard the telltale scream of the fourth bomber. He tripped and fell hard in a thrashing tangle of bamboo, passion vines, and wild fig vines. The sword-shaped leaf of a pandamus tree sliced across his forehead and cheek, leaving a burning sensation. Le ignored the slow ooze of blood as the piercing whistle of bombs increased his struggles. Flinging himself to his feet, he noticed a vine slither away.

A few steps later, Le dived between two trees. He realized he'd lost his AK-47.

The fourth string of bombs hit by the main road.

Shooting a fist skyward, Le cursed the third pilot for his lack of skill. Le also was angered by the inaccurate marking rocket, but in a way, he shared the blame. His gunners forced the spotter planes higher, and the pilots were less accurate with rockets.

Le tried to stand, but dry heaves racked his body. After violent retching, he rolled onto his back and felt drained of energy. He listened for more jets, but he heard only the O-2 circling the main road. Minutes later, the aircraft drifted toward the border.

Normal caution discouraged Le from rushing back into a target area. If the FAC decided to restrike, more fighters would be overhead soon. Experience let him rationalize his reluctance to return. The cold sweats and the gut-wrenching feeling in his stomach, however, belied the rationalization. Gazing at peaceful foliage, he knew he wasn't hurrying back because he did not *want* to go back. He couldn't recall having been overcome by such fear since hearing bullets whiz by in early skirmishes with French Legionnaires. He'd been so young then. Now Le felt so old.

Closing his eyes, he saw a fiery white octopus extending sizzling tentacles from the tree. He vividly pictured the last expression on Sergeant Dinh's face before bullets ripped his head. Le opened his eyes but feared he'd be sick again. Staring at small patches of blue sky visible through the tall trees helped defend against images he didn't want to see again—ever again.

For a few minutes, Le didn't move. Then he decided he should find his weapon. His AK-47 was near the pandamus tree. Picking up his weapon, he cursed himself. Never since his youth—when he'd first earned the right and responsibility to carry a single-shot rifle against the French—had he lost his weapon.

Backtracking, he was surprised to discover he hadn't moved even fifty meters from the shelter used during the first three attacks. Trudging along the spur, he grieved for his son, Kiem, and for Sergeant Dinh. Le wondered if he'd been at war longer than should be expected of any man.

When Le reached his headquarters two hours later, Major Quan limped over with a quizzical look on his face. "We've gotten another strange message I can't decipher, Colonel."

Le frowned. "I suppose they want me to feed some damned buffalo."

Quan's eyes widened. "Exactly, Colonel."

Adrenaline jolted Le. Expectations of sleep disappeared.

"Also, Colonel Khanh wants to know why you're taking his bulldozers and graders." Quan paused. "He was very excited."

"How many days until Tet?"

Quan looked taken aback by the question. He shuffled through papers in his hand. "Thirty-two, Colonel. But I haven't seen plans for activities during Tet. Last year—"

"I may have."

Giap had wanted trucks on the proposed road twenty-eight days after sending the coded message Le had just received. That twenty-eighth night and two more would cover a convoy's movement over the length of the road and leave maybe two nights at the southern end to prepare. *Prepare for what?* Giap had been so tight-lipped, Le's only clue was that the mystery road led to the vicinity of the U.S. Marine base at Khe Sanh.

"Assemble the staff. We have another impossible job to do."

Quan nodded. "Yes, Colonel. Is there any message for Colonel Khanh?"

After the morning's bloody experience, Le was in no mood for anyone's whining, include complaining from his counterpart across the border. "Tell him he should send the machines quietly. And, tell him if he doesn't send them in good working order, he will wish he had."

With a sardonic smile, Le wished he could exchange his problems with those Khanh had east of the mountains. For Chinh's benefit, however, Le was willing to do whatever it might take to end the war.

Chapter 34

Le's next twelve days merged into a continuous blur. From Mu Gia in the north to beyond Tchepone in the south, he pulled his most experienced people to match with the raw manpower Giap promised. He dispatched a pair of trucks to blaze the new trail through the jungle. Trellises went up over the first half of the route. Raft segments bridged the closest rivers when needed, then were moored nearby beneath overhanging trees. Cliffs were blasted. Graders and bulldozers pushed aside residue and carved the road wider. In spite of the progress, there were setbacks, especially where the road had to be cut from faces of cliffs.

All this went on while American aircraft bombed the main roads of the Trail daily and attacked convoys every night. Le made sure the Trail stayed open, but the new road took most of his time.

During two nights he personally oversaw how the new road would connect with Route 912. He wanted to ensure that if Americans spotted trucks turning off the main road, attacks would be in nearby truck parks instead of following the new road. By the end of the second night he was satisfied. The new spur doubled back and paralleled Route 912 for two thousand meters before angling southeast into a valley leading to the assembly area.

His men designed roads and turns to accommodate ZIL-157s, the six-wheel workhorses that carried most cargo in the Central Region. Still, questions were asked about how the road would be used and about the numbers of trucks at stopover points. Le had no answers. In exasperation, he coded a simple message to Giap. "I must know more about the buffalo."

Two days later Le was ordered to be at Quang Khe an hour after dark. That evening Le and Giap were in the bunker where they'd met before the rainy season.

Once settled, with guards outside the door, Giap said, "Before you ask about buffalo, I have a question. Will my convoys reach the south end of my road in seventeen days?"

"We're about two days behind schedule, General."

"We can't afford to lose two days."

"When we blow up cliffs in the dark, General, sometimes boulders don't fall the way we expect. We have camouflage in place by daybreak, but we can't detonate again until dark."

Giap sipped tea. "Before we finish, we'll talk about what you need to get on schedule."

"Yes, General." Le doubted the delay could be held to two days.

Giap handed Le a cup of tea. "What are your questions?"

"Numbers, General. I can't plan truck parks without knowing the size of convoys."

Raising his hands, Giap touched his index fingers to his lips. After a pause, he said, "Plan on a hundred and fifty."

"One hundred and fifty? At once, General?" Le knew the road had great significance, but he hadn't expected that many trucks in a short period on such a basic road.

Giap nodded. "Maybe a few more."

"Four convoys of thirty-five to forty," Le said, thinking aloud. "Now that I know, I can clear enough space in stopover areas."

"Can't you park on the road?"

"They make better targets that way, General. That's why I—"

"They only become targets if the Americans can discover the road."

"Yes, General."

Giap sipped his tea. "More than a hundred trucks will be towing antiaircraft guns."

Le's eyes widened, surprised at the extraordinary number of weapons. Much more parking space would be required. He was dismissing that as of no significance when another thought jolted him. "Some sections of road may not handle the added length of trucks towing trailers or guns."

"What?" Giap put his cup down hard enough to splash out tea. "You were to build a road to take any truck you handle in Battlefield C."

Le remembered Giap's earlier guidance was the new road should handle the types of trucks being used on the main roads. That's why he'd focused on the ZIL-157s. Yet, those two-lane roads through reasonable terrain could handle almost any vehicle including tanker trucks. "You weren't expecting a two-lane road, were you, General?"

"No, but I wasn't expecting to limit vehicles traveling south. The trucks can return on normal roads."

"Some mountains force hairpin turns, or we have to carve the road from solid rock. On some turns, trailers would scrape against the cliff or fall over the edge."

Giap looked worried.

"We could station men at the sharpest turns, detach the gun trailers, and move them by hand. That'll take extra time, but we can do it just as we moved artillery by hand to Dien Bien Phu." Le hoped the solution would satisfy Giap, but the look in the general's eyes didn't change.

"Gun trailers aren't the only problem." Giap leaned back against the wall and crossed his arms. "I'm going to tell you more than I planned. You will have to act on this information without passing it to anyone."

"Yes, General."

"Those in Hanoi who called for a massive offensive have won favor with Ho Chi Minh. They have more faith than I that the people will rise and throw out the Americans."

Le remembered Giap mentioning that major point of difference the last time they'd been in the bunker.

"If the people don't rise up," Giap said, "the People's Liberation Army will be decimated in many areas. Years would be needed to recover. Therefore, I have decided on a separate offensive by our North Vietnamese divisions. We will capture the base at Khe Sanh."

Le nodded at the confirmation of his suspicions. "And capturing thousands of soldiers will cause the Americans to quit."

Giap smiled. "It worked with the French. The soldiers helping build your road are part of the force that will overwhelm the base. However, we must hold off American bombers long enough for our victory."

"And that's why trucks will tow guns. Does that mean many trucks will carry ammunition, General?" Le would need to space ammunition trucks farther apart.

Giap nodded. "And many will carry additional antiaircraft machine guns, but those and the towed guns don't reach high enough to hit American B-52s." He paused. "I've committed to remove a regiment of surface-to-air missiles from defenses around Hanoi."

Le was stunned. He'd seen such missiles during rainy seasons spent in Hanoi. "Missiles have never been this far south. The transporters must be twenty meters long."

"Yes. The regiment has radar vans and eighteen missiles, and I hope to add spare missiles. None of those trailers can be moved by hand."

No doubt. Le studied the map. "Could you send missile transporters on regular roads, General? Route Nine's within kilometers of the target."

"Too open. If Americans discover even one transporter, we'll never get them through."

"Will you have problems getting them from Hanoi to the border?" Le wished the SAMs would have to be eliminated so his job would be easier.

"Jet fighters over Viet Nam at night can't find targets. Even if transporters are caught under flares, the pilots would have trouble identifying them. The problem in your region is those little spotter planes."

Le nodded and thought through the road's sharpest turns. Missile transporters wouldn't stay on the road on at least a dozen. Perhaps more blasting might straighten some hairpin turns enough. Others could be eased with more fill. In some cases, he'd have to select a different route. Le sighed, angry he'd gone so far without knowing of the missiles. "We'll have to do much more blasting and grading, General."

"And that will take more time."

"Yes, General. A third of the way down, a ten-kilometer stretch crosses the most rugged terrain. If we're going to move SAM transporters, we'll still be moving rock when the convoys are gathering."

"So even if I take another grader and bulldozer from Colonel Khanh, making up two days isn't possible?"

Le nodded. "Even traveling in daylight, we can't make up two days. Trucks kick up much dust, particularly near the end of the journey."

Giap sighed. "The Russians tell me the American Army's Mohawk airplanes have electronics or radars that sometimes detect moving trucks. We can't afford that." He sipped his tea and seemed to study the ceiling.

"Can the attack be delayed until the guns are deployed?"

"Everything is set for the darkness of the new moon on the first night of Tet. A delay couldn't be more than one night." He paused. "I'm not sure we could get messages to all units deploying throughout the South."

"One night won't be enough, General."

"Perhaps the opening days of the offensive will be as successful as its champions in Hanoi believe. If so, we could delay our attack on Khe

Sanh until the American reserves are committed. When can the convoys reach the objective area?"

Le had studied the calendar on the journey to Quang Khe. "I believe the earliest would be the second night of Tet, General."

Giap closed his eyes and rubbed his forehead. Finally, he shrugged and looked at Le. "We can still win if you are there the second night." Giap stood. "I must talk to Khanh, and you must return to your work."

Le stood along with Giap. "Yes, General."

Giap reached the door, then hesitated before opening it. "I forgot to mention that I will send along one shoulder-fired, antiaircraft missile. Save it for the later battle unless your convoy is threatened."

"Thank you, General."

"So many antiaircraft weapons are being taken from protection of the fatherland, most won't arrive until the night before you leave."

"We'll be ready to accept trucks and transporters when they arrive."

Giap put a hand on Le's shoulder. "You've been given the most important job in the war. You're the only man who could possibly succeed under the impossible schedule I gave you."

"Thank you, General."

Walking to his GAZ, Le appreciated the words of confidence, but he wished there had been someone else to give the job to. Then he pictured Chinh and Kiem. Le hoped the spirits would look favorably on this difficult effort to end the war.

Seventeen nights later, Le and Quan stood in the assembly area just before sunset. Listening to the first convoy of twenty trucks approach, Le was more optimistic than at any time since being ordered to build the road. He'd just learned that a regular ZIL-157 had encountered few problems in running the entire route. Crews working around the clock in the most difficult terrain should have the road ready for SAM transporters within the next forty-eight hours—if the spirits remained favorable.

As trucks parked, Le noticed these ZIL-157s were towing twin-barrel, 37mm guns, which were double the firepower of most of his guns. When men stepped down from the cabs, Le heard Quan utter something under his breath. "What was that?"

"Perhaps the spirits have turned against us, Colonel. Isn't that Lieutenant Colonel Hoa getting out of the first truck?"

The name jolted Le. Anger rose in him as he recognized Hoa. The sycophant would be in the way, but Le knew from experience he didn't have a choice of whether Hoa went along. Le shrugged, then grinned at Quan. "Perhaps the spirits sent him as a good sign."

"A good sign?" Quan looked incredulous.

"The cadre in Hanoi must believe a glorious victory is likely."

Quan nodded. "Lieutenant Colonel Hoa wouldn't come all this way unless there was great credit to claim."

Le started toward the convoy commander. "In this case, let's hope Hoa returns to Hanoi a hero."

Chapter 35

Mitch smelled perfume when Angelo entered their room.

"Got a couple of real winners to add to the collection," Angelo said, dropping letters on the desk. Singing the opening lines of *California Girls*, he pulled pictures from three envelopes.

Amused and a touch heartsick, Mitch watched Angelo tape new pictures near more than twenty decorating the wall by Angelo's locker. Mitch was happy Angelo was receiving so much attention. Nevertheless, Angelo's regular haul of letters highlighted that Elizabeth had written only twice since Christmas, and those were merely notes accompanying Mandy's drawings.

Angelo stepped back to admire the collection. "I think it's time to visit my sister."

"NKP's dreary," Mitch said, "but seven weeks and a day doesn't qualify for a trip home."

"Just wishin'. What if this Tet-truce becomes the real thing? Maybe we'd—"

"Maybe we'd just surrender and go home!" Anger stirred within Mitch. He remembered last year's Tet truce, which had put the war on hold in Vietnam after Goodwin's death.

Angelo looked confused. "That's not what I meant."

"I know. Anyway, the Viet Cong violated this truce so much in the first few hours, General Westmoreland pulled American forces out of the truce late this morning."

"Really? I still don't see why we do the truces the way we do."

"Because we're stupid! Politicians in Washington don't have a—"

A loud knock interrupted. Even before Angelo opened the door, Mitch had recognized the short-long-short pattern as Ted Forrester's trademark knock.

Ted burst into the room. He radiated the can-do enthusiasm Mitch found invigorating.

"As you were, gentlemen," Ted boomed in an official-sounding voice. "No need to stand, Captain."

"Hadn't planned to, Forrest Man," Mitch said with a smile.

Ted stepped to Angelo's photo gallery. "Not bad— for a non-Aggie."

Sitting on the desk, Angelo said, "Sir, maybe after tonight's mission, we might misread the compass a little and fly east to California instead of west to NKP. I'll put in a good word for you with my sister."

"Even though you're an Aggie," Mitch added.

"Mere children," Ted said, turning away from the wall, "but very attractive children. Speaking of tonight's mission, Ops called. They want us at the TUOC by three. We're—"

"Three!" Angelo stood. "Takeoff's at six."

Mitch was surprised, too. "A mid-afternoon takeoff in a black O-2 doesn't make sense."

Ted said, "We're playing delivery boy to Khe Sanh."

"Khe Sanh?" Angelo turned to Mitch. "Isn't that where—"

"Yep." He felt as if every hair on his arms had stood at the mention of the Marine base.

Ted winked at Angelo. "Don't expect to earn a Medal-of-Honor nomination like—"

Mitch growled a response to the teasing. "It may be shooting-gallery time at Khe Sanh. This morning, the VC attacked Kontum, Pleiku, Nha Trang, Danang, and a bunch of other places."

"Really? That must be why Seventh's hot to divert us. A broken O-2's stuck at Khe Sanh, and we've got the one part in Southeast Asia that'll get the bird in the air."

"And," Mitch said, "since you were going in the general direction—"

"Right. Ops figured we could swing by and still make our regular on-station time."

"Makes sense." Mitch grinned toward Angelo. "Your FAC training's incomplete until you've had a visit to Khe Sanh."

Angelo gave a questioning look. Ted smiled.

Mitch continued. "Khe Sanh'll make you appreciate how good you have it here at NKP."

"That'll be the day, sir." Angelo opened the door to his locker and removed a flight suit.

"I'd plan to be out of there by dark," Mitch said with a serious tone.

"No argument from me." Ted opened the door. "I'll be ready in fifteen."

"Fly safe," Mitch said, as Ted stepped onto the walkway.

That evening Ted taxied onto the runway at Khe Sanh. The last vestiges of day had disappeared along with the new moon that had set moments earlier. Stars were almost as bright as snippets of light escaping from various tents, lean-tos, and slit trenches.

"Captain McCall was right," Angelo said from the right seat.

"Say again," Ted said, as he finished the instrument checks on the taxiing checklist.

"He was right about me appreciating NKP. This place is spooky."

"Roger that." Ted swung the O-2 into the wind and hurried through the checklist.

"Nail Six-eight, winds are zero-eight-zero at eight. You're cleared for takeoff."

"Six-eight's rolling." Ted punched the timer and pushed the throttles forward. On intercom, he added, "Log us off at one-two. Once we're airborne, tell Alley Cat we're inbound to Steel Tiger."

Angelo nodded and wrote the time on his kneeboard. When the O-2 was in a sweeping turn toward the Laotian border, he called on the UHF radio. "Alley Cat, Nail Six-eight."

"Six-eight, Alley. Go."

"Six-eight's airborne from Khe Sanh at one-two, en route for a normal mission in Sector Twelve. Should be on station in about twenty."

"Copied, Six-eight."

"Khe Sanh Tower, Nail Six-eight," Ted said. "Thanks for your help.

We're switching to en route frequency."

"Six-eight, command post wants a call on Fox-Mike Forty-one three."

"Forty-one three." Ted exchanged a questioning look with Angelo while clicking the frequency into the FM radio. "Command Post, Nail Six-eight."

"Roger, Six-eight. Are you carrying a starlight scope?"

"That's affirmative."

"Request you contact ZULU-MIKE west of the base and checkout lights they spotted."

"We can give them ten or fifteen minutes."

"Great. Make contact on Forty-one decimal nine."

"Forty-one nine. Switching."

Twenty-five minutes later, the black O-2 cruised west of the DMZ. "Talk about dark," Ted said. "It's like not a living soul's anywhere."

Angelo leaned on the window frame with the starlight scope extended into the airflow. "I can't even find a campfire."

"This is Sector Sixteen. Mitch ever tell you about our mission out here last spring? I've never flown through so much rain and lightning—"

"There aren't any roads out here, are there?"

"Negative. We're at least—"

"I think I see a convoy," Angelo said, his voice higher.

"Not out here." Ted glanced at the TACAN to verify his location. "We're at least twenty-five miles east of Nine-eleven."

"I saw lights strung out like a convoy. And I see more, about a klick farther north."

Banking, Ted strained against his seat belt to see over the instrument panel. Much to his surprise, he saw lights twinkling through trees.

Corporal Cung had maneuvered the GAZ-69 by seventeen trucks of the first convoy and crossed the intervening thousand meters to where the eighteenth was stalled with a broken axle. Le jumped out even before Cung shut off the engine. As Le feared, the truck was on a narrow ledge, blocking the trailing twenty-two trucks—and the three trailing convoys.

Le studied the problem in dim light cast by torches and taped-over headlights. The obvious answer was to unload the ammunition, disconnect the gun being towed, and push the truck over the side. Le was so absorbed that rifle-shot signals didn't register into his consciousness until men around him started shouting and extinguishing lights.

"What's going on?" He listened. "Shut off the engine!"

The truck *chug-chugged* to silence.

Even over the grumble of trucks farther up the hill, Le recognized the buzz of an O-2. "I can't believe this," he said as he crept closer to the edge to get a better look through overhanging foliage. He assumed the command was superfluous, but he shouted anyway, "Total darkness!"

When the final truck in the convoy went silent, tracking the aircraft noise became easier. Still, he saw nothing but blackness and stars of a deep night sky. He couldn't believe a FAC had found his lead convoy in a darkened jungle unmarked by well-traveled roads.

"The spirits are against us," someone said in the darkness.

Le wondered why the spirits should help violate Tet? He had no good answer as he looked in vain for the aircraft. Even with his doubts about the spirits, he reassured himself. His blacked-out trucks should be more difficult for the Americans to find than the circling O-2 was for him to pick out against the background of stars. That is, he thought, unless the spirits have chosen the side of the Americans just to teach a lesson.

Lieutenant Colonel Tran Van Hoa stood in the darkness beside the lead truck. The convoy's abrupt halt, coupled with shouts about an aircraft, had awakened him into a state of terror and confusion. The pounding of his heart almost overwhelmed the drone of the aircraft, which in turn threatened the visions of the glory he expected to claim. A sense of impending doom shook him. He braced his legs against the fender to keep his knees from knocking together. He looked into the darkness, wondering which way to run if bombs rained down. He shouted, "Where's Colonel Do?"

A sergeant in the truck said, "At the back of the convoy, Colonel."

The revelation sent a ripple of fright through Hoa. Although he was political cadre, he was the most senior officer present. "What are we to do to defend ourselves?"

"No movement and no lights are our best defense, Colonel," the sergeant said. "And, Corporal Linh has a *Strela* missile ready."

"Where?"

"Here, Colonel," Corporal Linh said from darkness near the truck.

Hoa was encouraged. While studying in Russia, he'd witnessed a demonstration of the killing power of the shoulder-fired missile. But, he knew he must act before the aircraft reported the convoy's location. His throat went dry as he envisioned Colonel Do's fury if attacking the aircraft was the wrong decision. Nevertheless, even General Giap would be impressed if a masterful decision saved the convoys.

Hoa swallowed hard, trying to get enough moisture in his throat to speak. "Fire!"

"I can't see the target," Corporal Linh said.

"Activate the seeker." Panic swept chills into Hoa's spine. *What if the aircraft couldn't be shot down in the dark?* He considered ordering drivers to make a run for it, but he didn't know where to tell them to go.

The corporal swung the *Strela*'s launch tube in small circles in the direction of the noise from the aircraft. In a few moments the indicator light flashed on and remained steady.

Seeker acquisition, Hoa thought with extreme relief. "Fire!"

The corporal hesitated.

The sergeant in the cab said, "But, Colonel Do might—"

"Now!" Hoa screamed the word so loud, he wondered if it would carry all the way to Colonel Do, wherever he was.

Angelo said, "They shut off all the lights."

"I can't explain what you could've seen way out here." Ted was suspicious, however, about the lights disappearing.

He jotted down the distance and radial from NKP. The winds had been from the west, so he assumed the O-2 was upwind of whatever Angelo had spotted. He armed the flare rack.

"Wish we had a moon," Angelo said.

"I'm gonna drop a flare."

"Might help. I can't see any kind of a road through the scope."

"Doesn't surprise me. We've never found a road in Sector Sixteen in the daytime." Ted pressed the trigger on the yoke. A flare dropped from beneath the wing. "Alley Cat, be advised—"

A flash on the ground beyond the right wing sizzled a hole in the center of his night vision. Ted blinked at the unexpected intrusion. He saw the flash rising on a short tail of fire.

Leaning away from the starlight scope, which had blanked out from the overload of light, Angelo shouted, "What the hell?"

"Holy shit! SAM!"

Ted's iron-fisted grip had kept the mic switch pressed as he twisted the control wheel to turn away from the missile.

"No! No! No!" Le screamed at the shimmering ball of fire racing upward. "Some fool confirmed our position." He immediately pictured Lieutenant Colonel Hoa.

The fireball veered west.

Le watched in morbid fascination, never having seen a shoulder-fired missile race at an airborne prey. He tried to decide how to counter this ominous development. Even if the last 142 vehicles weren't blocked, he was at least another night away from the deployment area west of Khe Sanh. Making a run for it in daylight—

A bright flash lit the sky as two-and-a-half kilograms of explosives hurled jagged shrapnel.

Le saw the black O-2 outlined against the burst of light. Trying to recapture his night vision, he closed his eyes. Still he saw the explosion with the blurry aircraft centered in the image. The *bang* of the missile's detonation reached him. He opened his eyes to darkness that lingered only a moment.

A parachute flare flickered to a yellow-tinged brightness of 2,000,000 candlepower, casting an eerie glow across the jungle.

A hundred miles southwest, Captain Wade Davis sat in a command-and-control module in the back of an EC-130. He'd been pouring coffee from his thermos when words in his headset sent a chill through his shoulders. Using his boot, he pressed the microphone button on the floor. "Nail aircraft calling Alley Cat. You were broken. Say again."

Awaiting a response he feared wouldn't come, Davis scanned his logs. Nail Forty-four had been on the radio ten minutes earlier from south of Mu Gia. Davis checked a few lines higher and noticed the entry for Nail

Sixty-eight, who had called in from Khe Sanh nearly half an hour ago.

Le raised a hand to shield his eyes. He thought he saw the hint of flame higher and to the side. He was unsure, because the glimmer of red disappeared into the lingering effects of his flash-blindness when he tried to look at the fire in the sky.

A bright explosion dwarfed the stars, making Le's previous vision difficulties irrelevant. Mesmerized, he watched four burning chunks of aircraft cartwheel downward amid cheers. Hoping to salvage his secret mission, Le shouted, "Shoot down the flare!"

He knew flares burned for three minutes, and the sooner the jungle swallowed this flare, the better. Yanking his AK-47 from his shoulder, he aimed at the shimmering light. The others seemed hesitant, so he was the first to fire. The muzzle flashes, the smell of gunpowder, the solid thumping against his shoulder, and the rapid popping of the shots invigorated Le. By the time he'd blasted thirty rounds skyward in short bursts, others up the line were firing. Tracers converged on the flare with no effect. Finally the flare jittered, then plummeted as the white parachute fluttered east on the wind.

Cheers erupted. Several voices claimed credit for separating the flare from its chute.

Darkness chased the flare downward. The circle of lighted jungle raced inward, converging to black when the flare plunged into trees. The scene looked as before except for tumbling debris leaving spooky trails of luminescent smoke.

Le pulled out an emergency radio, turned it on, and was greeted by the weak sizzle of static. The lack of a beeper suggested no one had bailed out. His trucks might yet avoid the swarm of aircraft that converged on calls for help from downed Americans.

Captain Davis jammed the plug into the thermos. "Nail Four-four, Alley Cat. You still with me?"

"Roger that. Do you have any ordnance yet?"

Despite being distracted by the earlier call, Davis checked recent log entries. "Nimrod Three-two crossed the fence a few minutes ago. If you find anything big, I could send him your way."

"Thanks, Cat."

"Nail Six-eight, Alley Cat. Have you reached Sector Twelve?" Davis paused a few seconds. "Nail Six-eight, Alley Cat on Three thirty-two two."

Davis felt a familiar knot twist his gut. The sickening feeling appeared every time he lost an aircraft. With one hand, he set his radio to transmit on Guard. With his other, he made a new log entry, trying to write words he'd heard in the incomplete transmissions. "Nail Six-eight, Alley Cat on Guard. If you read, come up Three thirty-two two or Guard."

He heard only static-laced silence.

Davis repeated his call.

"Nail Six-eight," Le repeated after hearing faint transmissions.

Watching the first piece of flaming debris reach the jungle, he thought about how he almost knew several of these Americans. Except for Metal Dragon, however, he knew them only by number. He wished he were at his headquarters where radios would tell more about what the Americans knew. Here in the darkness he had only the captured emergency radio, and he was afraid its battery wouldn't last.

Davis heard a voice on the second control frequency he monitored. "Alley Cat, Nimrod Three-two. You having trouble locating a Nail?"

"Affirmative."

"We saw something, Alley, but we're not sure what."

"Go ahead."

"John noticed a flicker on our eastern horizon. Maybe five seconds later, we saw a bright flash. We couldn't tell what it was."

Davis knew. He waved his arm to get the attention of the senior officer in charge. "Nimrod, can you estimate the location?"

"Uh, maybe at the Chokes. Distance is hard to estimate."

"Okay, Nimrod. Alley Cat requests you head for the Chokes and see if you locate any wreckage. We may've lost Nail Six-eight."

Le put a clip into his AK-47. "Disconnect the gun! Unload the truck."

Men accustomed to working in darkness sprang into action. In minutes they'd pulled the gun to a wide place in the road and had formed a human chain, passing along crates of Soviet-made antiaircraft shells.

When the truck was empty, Le said, "Over the side."

He watched the next truck push until the dark hulk of the crippled truck disappeared over the cliff. He listened to the truck smash downward, pause, then grind through more trees. Finally, the crashing ceased, and the silence of the jungle returned.

Le slid into his GAZ and said to the sergeant in charge of the recovery team, "Have the wreckage camouflaged by sunrise."

"Yes, Colonel."

Le turned to Corporal Cung. "Get us to the front of the convoy."

The GAZ bumped forward in darkness parted by slits of light squinting through partially covered headlights. Le wondered if the Americans knew enough to locate his four convoys. Destroying the aircraft either saved his secret mission or doomed it. In either case, Le wanted to make such decisions. Speaking loud enough so both could hear, Le said, "We'll never let Lieutenant Colonel Hoa out of our sight again. One of you will always be with him."

"But, Colonel," Cung said, "our duty is to—"

"If Hoa's blunders destroy these convoys, my life's not worth saving." Le paused, cradling his AK-47 against his chest and pressing a cheek against the barrel. The metal was warm, and the weapon had a reassuring smell. "We'll be in the objective area in thirty hours. If Hoa does anything to jeopardize our mission before we get there, kill him!"

Le looked at his bodyguards. Kiet sat as a dark form. His cigarette didn't give off enough light for Le to see even his eyes. The muted lights on the instrument panel lit Cung, whose eyes seemed focused on the road ahead.

"That's my order!"

"Yes, Colonel," both men answered simultaneously.

Mitch was finishing dinner in the officers club when he saw Lieutenant O'Malley lumber through the doorway. Mitch watched the lieutenant scan the crowd until spotting the two tables surrounded by Crickets. O'Malley charged across the room, bumping chairs and people as he homed in on the FACs. Mitch knew something was wrong—very wrong.

"We've got a bird down," O'Malley blurted.

All nearby conversation ceased.

"Who?" Mitch got to his feet, knowing few O-2s were up.

Tears glistened in O'Malley's eyes. He stammered, then bit on his lip. Mitch bolted to door before O'Malley regained his voice.

After convincing the schedulers to put him on a search mission at 0530, Mitch spent the evening at the TUOC. He sat in on the debriefing of the crew on Nimrod Thirty-two, but they hadn't found anything at the Chokes. He collected the times of all contacts with Nail Sixty-eight and marked a map with the range of course lines from Khe Sanh to any point in Sector 12.

Near midnight, he knew he could do nothing more. On the long walk to his quarters, he pictured happier times with Angelo, Ted, and J.D. He also thought of Elizabeth and Mandy, and how his dedication to J.D. had put unfair burdens on the two people he loved most.

In the quiet of his room, Mitch scanned Angelo's gallery of bright faces. At that moment in California, he decided, many of those young women would be smiling and cheerful, preparing to attend morning classes. Later in the day, some would talk to Angelo's sister and learn the war had reached out and touched them from thousands of miles away.

Envelopes remained scattered on the desk where Angelo had left them. Mitch made a single pile against the wall as if awaiting Angelo's review the next morning. After getting into bed, Mitch stared at the dark ceiling. He felt a bone-deep certainty Angelo would never touch those letters again.

Mitch's thoughts were a cycling jumble of airspeeds, times, distances, and azimuths, along with the locations of Khe Sanh, the Chokes, and the Nimrod. He dozed off about three a.m.

His alarm jolted him awake at three fifty-nine.

Chapter 36

Mitch's spirits remained low as he trudged to the TUOC. When he neared the chapel, a C-130 roared into the air. Watching the dark apparition fly across a star-studded background, he was curious about whether it had delivered mail. Shortly after Christmas, he'd abandoned his ritual of checking his mailbox before each flight. This morning, however, instincts detoured him by the mail room.

He was encouraged when he found the building lighted and someone working inside. He knelt at his mailbox and discovered a letter from Elizabeth. Optimism swelled within him, but he kept it in check. Her words could be as sterile as before. At least, he thought while slipping the letter into his pocket, he'd have drawings from Mandy.

Mitch was surprised to see Thai guards posted outside the fence surrounding the TUOC. They hadn't been there when he left five hours earlier. Glancing toward the flight line beyond, he saw a jeep with USAF security police parked near the Jolly Greens.

He asked the guards, "What's going on?"

One saluted, flashing a nervous smile. The other opened the gate and stood at attention.

Mitch returned the salute and offered the all-purpose Thai greeting. "*Sawat dee.*"

When he walked inside, he sensed an air of commotion. Even in the entry hallway, he heard the buzz of voices and the clatter of teletype machines. The offices and the big room in the administrative section were alive with more members of the Intelligence staff than he'd ever seen at once—let alone at four twenty-five in the morning.

Lieutenant Scott barged out of an office and ran into Mitch. Scott, a briefer who'd replaced Winters while Mitch was gone, looked surprised. "Sorry, sir. What are you doing here so early?"

"I'm scheduled for a briefing in five minutes."

"Really." Scott's eyes went to the wall clock. "Is that clock right? It can't be four-thirty."

"Time flies when you're having fun, Lieutenant."

"I can't believe it. The entire staff was recalled at one-thirty. A huge VC offensive is underway."

"Damn!" Mitch wondered if the offensive would affect his mission.

Scott dangled a long teletype listing. "Every major base and provincial capital in South Vietnam must be under attack."

"Damn," Mitch repeated, shocked at the scope of this year's Tet surprise. With thousands dying in the South, a missing O-2 wouldn't be a high priority for anyone beyond NKP. Looking around, he realized even in NKP's nerve center, the loss of Ted and Angelo had become less significant in the last five hours.

"Sir," Scott said, "I'll need a minute to get your briefing ready."

"Take your time, Lieutenant."

After pouring a cup of coffee and retrieving the map he'd marked with notes the previous evening, Mitch went to the FAC briefing room.

In the relative solitude, he sipped his coffee and gazed at the map covering the front wall. On a whim, he focused his eyes short of the wall. Roads, interdiction points, antiaircraft sites, and karst mountains fused into the blurry green background. He closed his eyes and moved his head around a few moments. His eyes flashed open, and he hoped they somehow would be drawn to the spot where Ted and Angelo were waiting. The map came into focus, but his eyes knew not where to look. Deep, deep down Mitch knew he needed a miracle—but miracles were beyond his power to create. He'd learned that lesson eight months earlier on a cold, gusty morning at Khe Sanh.

One hundred and fourteen miles east, Le sat in his GAZ. The vehicle was parked crossways on the new road, which had been packed down by seventy-nine heavy trucks of the first two convoys. He tried to think of anything else he could do to keep the trucks safe for one more night.

"I still think stopping here is ridiculous, Colonel," Hoa protested.

"You don't even know where 'here' is." Le didn't bother to conceal his disdain.

"We're wasting too much darkness, Colonel. Surely I don't need to remind you we're three nights behind the original schedule."

No. Le had been reminded by Hoa of the delay about ten times a day. Le could press on nearly another hour. Nevertheless, the objective area was less than a night's travel away. He preferred using the next hour to ensure everything was well camouflaged before daylight.

"Yesterday morning," Hoa continued, "we drove until after five-thirty. Now, it's—"

"We hadn't had our position marked by some fool firing a SAM."

"We'd already been found. I only—"

"This morning there are defenses to set up. Camouflage must be perfect, and—" Le stopped on hearing the roar of a truck approaching in the darkness.

"These weapons are critical to victory," Hoa said, "and they should not be delayed."

"Go to sleep," Le said, stepping from the GAZ.

"My duties are not to sleep, Colonel." Hoa climbed out the back.

Le waited until Hoa was alongside, then stepped nose-to-nose. In a tone that couldn't be misinterpreted even in the dark, Le said, "I have operational orders to issue. Don't get in my way!" Le couldn't see Hoa's face but knew the message had gotten across.

Le, Hoa, and Private Kiet stood in the middle of the road. The lead truck of the third convoy stopped a few meters away. Le heard others in the line braking to a stop. A captain in charge of the convoy got out of the lead truck. He was followed by the lieutenant colonel who commanded the SAM regiment making up much of the convoy.

"Because of the incident last night," Le said, "we're gathering into two convoys. You and the fourth convoy will settle in from here to the hill a thousand meters down the road."

"Yes, Colonel," the captain said.

"The lead convoys are setting up about five thousand meters farther, beyond the ridge. I want fresh camouflage on the tops of all vehicles. Any guns in the open will be covered."

"Yes, Colonel."

Le turned to the lieutenant colonel. "This morning I want defenses set up. Two batteries of thirty-sevens near the front and two near the rear and a dozen ZPU-fours scattered throughout. Do not fire unless you're certain we've been located."

"Yes, Colonel."

Mitch reached into his pocket and pulled out the envelope he'd placed there minutes earlier. Instead of drawings from his daughter, Mitch found one of Elizabeth's monogrammed note cards. He read the following in her delicate script:

"Dearest Mitch, I've spent enough time without you in my life to know I don't want you out of my life, darling. I just don't know what I can do to have more of you. Anyway I am eagerly waiting for you to finish with this dreadful war and to complete whatever you have to for J.D. Hurry home, sweetheart. I love you. By the way, I'm pregnant. Elizabeth"

Mitch wished he had time to read the letter over and over. Its news made him happier than he imagined he could be on this grim morning. He wanted to go to his room and write her how pleased he was and how much he loved her. Letter writing would have to wait a few hours, he thought, staring at the last sentence. He was encouraged that she'd come through with her sense of humor intact.

He slipped the letter into its envelope. Along with the letter, he tried to tuck away the euphoria coursing through his body. He felt renewed, ready to face the mission he wished wasn't necessary.

He saw the weather briefer in the hall. "Let's get on with it, Sarge." As expected, the weather forecast was like the day before and the day before that.

After the sergeant finished, Scott entered. The young Intelligence officer bit on his lower lip as if that would help him select the right words. "Sir, there have been no contacts with either Captain Forrester or Lieutenant Martines." He paused. "They could be having trouble with their emergency radios."

Mitch shook his head. "We carry two on our survival vests, and an automatic beeper is in risers on each parachute. Odds are all six wouldn't malfunction."

"Yes, sir."

"But," Mitch said, in a more encouraging tone, "they might wait until daylight so a call wouldn't give away their location before a rescue's possible." That rationalization didn't explain why no one had reported a beeper from either parachute.

"That's part of why your mission was added on, sir."

Right. And also because he'd finally used the clout that comes with earning an Air Force Cross. He'd demanded the schedulers put him over the Trail at first light to set up a rescue—if one were possible. "Has Seventh checked all airfields?"

Scott nodded. "Things are confused due to all the attacks in South Vietnam. There could be holes in the reporting—"

"Captain Forrester would've called in last night to let us know where he is—if he could have." The last phrase came out unintended.

Moving to the map on the front wall, Scott circled the tip of his pointer over the three interdiction points marked Alpha, Bravo, and Charlie. "We recommend you begin your search at the Chokes."

Mitch glanced at the map he'd prepared the previous evening. One line of grease-pencil connected Khe Sanh and the Chokes. "Can you think of a reason why they flew to the Chokes at the west end of Sector Twelve? I mean, we start there when we fly from NKP."

Scott looked at the map and didn't offer an immediate answer.

"Anything special in the briefing last night that would've sent them there?"

"Negative, sir. They briefed in the middle of the afternoon. We wouldn't have had any specifics yet. Maybe they learned something at Khe Sanh."

Mitch shook his head. "No one at Khe Sanh knows the Chokes from Mu Gia. But if I'd flown from there, I'd have headed for Ban Laboy where truck hunting's better."

"Anyway, our best assessment is something around the Chokes caught their attention. They probably spent time checking that out or perhaps drifting north to the intersection of Nine-eleven and Nine-twelve." The pointer moved to the junction of the two major roads above Alpha.

"They didn't spend much time there."

Scott looked confused. "Say again, sir."

"They checked in with Alley Cat thirty minutes before being declared missing. Right?"

Scott began to search through his papers.

"That's right," Mitch continued. "Khe Sanh's fifty nautical miles from Alpha. In an O-2 averaging about two miles a minute—minus a bit for a westerly wind and a little time to climb to cruise altitude—they used something over twenty-five of those thirty minutes to reach the Trail. So whatever happened, happened pretty damned quick."

"You've given this some thought, haven't you, sir?"

Mitch looked Scott in the eyes. "They were like brothers."

"Do you have any questions I might be able to answer, sir?"

"Not unless you know anything new that came in after I left at eleven-thirty last night."

Nearly six hours later, Mitch lowered his binoculars and tried to stretch stiffness from his back and his old wounds. He'd reached the Chokes before dawn. In the intervening hours, he'd searched both sides of Routes 911 and 912 from south of the Chokes to the North Vietnamese border. His eyes burned from looking for the flash of a signal mirror or for the dull black of the missing O-2. The physical discomfort of being strapped into the pilot's seat for five hours didn't compare to the hurt ripping at his soul.

He checked the time and the fuel. A feeling of defeat surged over him, and he slammed his fist down on the glare shield. He couldn't give up on Ted and Angelo.

Looking at his map, he tried to find something overlooked in estimating their route from Khe Sanh. Perhaps someone at Khe Sanh *did* know something. "Cricket, Nail Five-nine."

"Go, Five-nine."

"Would you ask Hillsboro if the airfield at Khe Sanh is normal operations this morning?"

"Standby. Hillsboro's had his hands full trying to plug all the holes in the dike."

Mitch let his O-2 drift east away from the guns along Route 912. He wished he'd paid more attention to the major offensive underway in South Vietnam. He looked southeast almost expecting to see towering columns of smoke hundreds of miles away.

"Nail Five-nine," Cricket said, "Hillsboro says Khe Sanh is Ops Normal, but major defensive operations are in progress from the DMZ for as far south as he has coverage."

"Roger, Cricket. I want to continue my search. Please advise Khe Sanh I'll drop in for gas and maybe talk to a few people about our Nail bird lost out of there last night."

"Copied. Give me a call when you're airborne again. Sorry about your buddies."

A fullness in Mitch's throat threatened to choke off any response. He double-clicked his microphone button.

Minutes later, Mitch spiraled down toward the runway. Seeing Dong Dang, Mitch felt twinges in scars on his arm and legs. From altitude, he saw the ridge he'd once colored with marking pens on a map. On this cloudless day, J.D.'s analogy of a dragon bounding in from Laos to consume the Marine base seemed very real.

Khe Sanh looked much the same. He saw more scars on nearby hills and more crowding in the perimeter. Craters marred the area where the ammunition dump had been. Looking toward the canyon of the Rao Quan, he spotted a darkened scar almost overgrown by foliage. He was surprised by the jolt of despair he felt from seeing J.D.'s crash site again.

After landing, Mitch taxied to the parking ramp and felt a little naked with no other aircraft in sight. Maybe diverting to Khe Sanh hadn't been such a good idea, he thought, as a sergeant guided him to a stop near the revetments.

He shut down the engines and stepped out. "Fill 'er up, Sarge."

The sergeant nodded. "I don't have information on you, sir. How long are you staying?"

Mitch shrugged. "Long enough to refuel and ask a few questions. I want to see what the command post knows about the bird we lost out of here last night."

"All our pilots are flying, sir. There's a big shootout down at Hue."

Striding across the runway, Mitch saw a Marine approaching.

"Mitch," Captain Snake Sheldon called out. "I saw your name on a message and figured there couldn't be another Captain McCall crazy enough to fly in here on a day like today."

"I'm no J.D., but some of his craziness rubbed off." They embraced. Mitch felt as if he were greeting a brother he'd never expected to see again. "What're you doing here? I figured you'd be holding down some posh Marine job in the states."

"Posh Marine job," Snake repeated with a snicker.

"Oxymoron?"

"You're a lot more like J.D. than I'd imagined." Turning somber, Snake added, "After J.D. bought the farm, I decided to extend my tour."

"J.D. had that effect on people."

"I spent the last four months on the coast. But, Charlie's cooking up something big for Khe Sanh, so I returned a couple of weeks ago."

"Sounds like Charlie's busier along the coast."

"Our turn's coming. A week and a half ago, incoming blew away fifteen hundred tons of our stockpiled ammo. An NVA lieutenant told us we'd be part of the action two nights ago."

"Maybe he was giving disinformation."

"I don't think so. I listened in on the interrogation at Regimental Intel." Snake nodded toward the east as they moved away from the runway. "Back on the twentieth, he came walking up to the runway with an AK-47 and a white flag. He was pissed off, so he came in willing to spill his guts. That night Hill Eight sixty-one was attacked as he predicted."

"Why was he so helpful?"

Snake smiled. "He'd gotten passed over for captain."

Mitch thought of Ted being passed over for major.

"He commanded an antiaircraft company in the Three twenty-five C Division, which is out there in the hills. He'd been in fourteen years, and they'd just promoted guys he felt were incompetent."

"I've got a friend who didn't make major. His response was different. Anyway, he was on the black O-Two we lost out of here last night."

"I heard the bird was Thai-based. We appreciate their help."

"Right." Mitch was surprised Snake would know Ted had come to bring a part for an Air Force aircraft. "But, losing one aircraft just to fix another is a damn poor tradeoff."

A confused look flashed across Snake's face. "I'm talking about them helping us. They checked out some enemy activities for us."

Mitch took four more steps, then stopped abruptly as if his boot were stuck to the red dirt. "Are you saying they flew around here before going to Steel Tiger?"

"I'm sure they did. I was in our command post. Nail Sixty-eight, I believe."

"Right."

"Our observers spotted lights in gomer country just after dark. Your guys had a starlight scope, so we asked 'em to take a look. When they found some action, we dropped in a couple of rounds of artil—"

"What time? They reported in to Alley Cat at eleven-fourteen Zulu."

"That would be nineteen-fourteen local, which is just about full dark. I don't believe Nail Sixty-eight left that soon."

"Can I find out exactly when they left?"

Snake hesitated. "Command post logs show when the artillery—"

"Can you take me there?"

"You got it!"

In the bunker, Snake read from the log, "The first artillery went out at two-seven. Your Nails adjusted, and the second round went out at two-nine."

"Two-nine!" Mitch's shoulders tingled. "They hung around at least fifteen minutes after checking in with Alley Cat?"

Snake nodded. "That's about the size of it."

"Alley Cat declared them possibly missing at four-four." Mitch wished he hadn't left his map of Steel Tiger in the airplane. Closing his eyes, he pictured the lines marking routes from Khe Sanh to Sector 12. He projected the O-2 fifteen minutes closer to Khe Sanh. *Sector 16.* "That makes no sense."

Snake offered the log. "The numbers are here in black and white, and sunset—"

"They weren't within shooting distance of the Trail." Mitch shook his head as part of him denied the implications. An even smaller part deep inside said maybe the glint of a signal mirror awaited him in Sector 16. "I've gotta get airborne! I spent all morning in the wrong place."

In fewer than ten minutes, Mitch held the O-2 just above the runway as the landing gear retracted. He rolled into a forty-five degree bank and skimmed across startled Marines as the O-2 reversed course within the perimeter of the base. Letting the aircraft coast skyward, he pointed the nose at Hill 881 to reach the starting point Ted and Angelo had used.

Mitch folded his map to show the area between Khe Sanh and Sector 12, then attached the map to his clipboard. He measured thirty nautical miles back along his grease-pencil line connecting the Chokes and Khe Sanh. He felt even more confused by what the map was telling him. "Middle of nowhere!"

When the trenches of Hill 881 slipped beneath the nose, Mitch punched the timer button on the clock, then turned toward the Chokes.

His senses jumped to a higher state of alert. Whatever the key to the mystery was, he decided, he now was within fourteen minutes of that answer—if he had the skill to find it among the millions of trees spread out ahead of him.

"Cricket, Nail Five-nine's airborne out of Khe Sanh."

"Say intentions, Five-nine."

"I'm going to search for Nail Six-eight about fifteen minutes closer to Khe Sanh."

"What does that mean?"

"It means Six-eight never reached the Trail. My initial starting point's about X-Ray Delta Five-zero six-zero."

The controller repeated the coordinates in a tone suggesting he expected to be corrected.

"Affirmative."

"According to my maps, there's never been much out there to get you guys' interest."

"Middle of nowhere," Mitch repeated, reflecting his uncertainty.

"Getting shot down in that area makes no sense unless they flew over a bunch of troops headed south to reinforce the offensive."

"Regular troops wouldn't see a black O-2 in the dark, let alone hit one at the altitude he should've been flying." Mitch paused a moment to shift his focus from his missing friends. *What would it take to shoot down an O-2 fifteen minutes east of the Trail?* "If I find something that could've shot 'em down, I'll need ordnance."

"Be cautious. Alley Cat said Six-eight might've mentioned SAMs, although ELINT during the night didn't detect any electronic signals."

Mitch glanced at his map. "I don't consider that SAM country, but I'm gonna find out."

Droning northwest, Mitch sensed he had missed something. Looking at the map between Khe Sanh and the Chokes didn't give him any ideas. Perhaps, he thought, the nagging feeling was due to waiting at the TUOC until Nimrod Thirty-two returned, then being unable to sleep the rest— "Nimrod!"

Mitch ripped the map from the clipboard and unfolded the map to show NKP—and his line between the Chokes and the Nimrods' location when they'd seen the explosion.

He extended the line east of the Chokes, all the way to the Vietnamese border. Obviously, Nail Sixty-eight could've been anywhere on that line and still have appeared to be in the direction of the Chokes. He studied the map a moment, then drew a line between Khe Sanh and the Ban Laboy Ford. The two new lines intersected just west of the Demilitarized Zone. *Even more remote!* Mitch estimated the distance between the new intersection and Khe Sanh. He guessed an O-2 would fly about that far in the time between when Ted finished adjusting artillery and when Nimrod saw the flash.

The lines crossed in an area that made no sense. Studying the map, he made a discovery that jolted him. The North Vietnamese might have concealed a road that detoured around the west end of the DMZ. Such a road into Laos offered a shortcut for supplies for the ongoing offensive. For the first time since O'Malley had lumbered into the bar with his tragic news, Mitch felt as if he'd found something that might explain where Nail Sixty-eight had been shot down—and why.

Chapter 37

Le was in a sleep so deep he hadn't moved in four hours. Suddenly, he was wide awake and wasn't sure why. He stretched and looked at his wristwatch. At that instant, he realized he heard the buzz of an O-2.

He rolled over but couldn't determine which direction the sound had come from. The engine noise was drowned out by the grinding of antiaircraft guns being cranked around. He'd chosen to sleep near the command battery set up to defend the lead convoy. Those four 37mm guns were concealed beneath camouflaged netting and a blanket of fresh foliage in a clearing by a stream. No other guns around these seventy-nine trucks were to fire unless the command battery fired.

Le jumped to his feet and ran. In moments, he was in the open. The O-2 seemed to be coming out of the sun. His heart thudded as he feared the pilot was making a rocket pass. He relaxed when the plane emerged from the fiery sun. The O-2 was only a couple of miles south but headed northwest.

The battery commander asked, "Are we cleared to fire, Colonel?"

"Not yet!"

Le was afraid the pilot had seen something the camouflage had failed to conceal. Perhaps a windshield reflected the glaring sun that had obscured the aircraft. Nevertheless, the O-2 was beyond the effective range of the ZPUs and 37mm AAA deployed around the lead convoy. Holding his breath, Le crouched lower and watched the O-2.

"Are we cleared to fire, Colonel?"

"No. Stand by!"

He wished Hoa hadn't wasted the shoulder-fired missile. Le wasn't yet prepared to attack, but if he had to, this wasn't a shot he could afford to miss.

The buzz from the O-2 increased, but its heading remained steady.

Le watched and waited and waited. "Stand by."

The O-2 passed a mile away without varying the heading.

Le held his breath and listened. He hoped no one in the second convoy would fire at the aircraft passing almost overhead of the other eighty trucks.

Without knowing what brought Ted and Angelo down, Mitch stayed high. Within three miles of where the two lines crossed on his map, he tightened his seat belt and maneuvered as if approaching Route 911. The lines crossed in a confluence of rugged valleys, with a four-thousand-foot peak to the north and thirty-five-hundred foot peaks west and south. Just beyond, mountains angled from northwest to southeast, defining part of the border.

He flew big, lazy circles to give Ted and Angelo opportunities to flash signals with their mirrors. He switched to Guard to repeat a call made throughout the morning. "Nail Six-eight, Nail Six-eight, Nail Five-nine. If you read, come up on Guard." He waited. This wait proved as futile as those after each previous call.

Flying through the first large circle, Mitch saw no roads and no Stars-of-David—the characteristic outline of a battery of six SAM launchers—etched into the ground. The green carpet of trees was unmarred by bomb craters. He saw nothing that would've drawn his interest on a routine mission.

While circling, he decided his earlier theory didn't make sense, now that he'd seen the terrain. A road through the mountains around the west end of the DMZ would be harder to build than one down from Ban Laboy along the west side of the mountains.

He saw no blazing flashes of reflected sunlight. Discouragement swept over him. The exhaustion of being awake twenty-nine hours out of the last thirty weighed him farther down in the seat cushion.

Passing on the west side for the second time, he saw something different—something white tucked high in a tree. He yanked up his binoculars, which he hadn't used while scanning for mirror flashes. Locating the white through the binoculars, he shouted, "A chute!" He hoped to see glimpses of orange mingled with white, signifying a parachute like that in his backpack. No orange—at least, not from this distance.

Flying closer, he saw only white caught in the treetop. *Only a flare chute.* "Damn!" He almost flung the binoculars across the cockpit but chose instead to slam a fist onto the glare shield.

Drifting away, he scanned for anything of interest near the chute. *Nothing.* He thought about the roads of Steel Tiger where hundreds of flare chutes dotted the trees. He looked toward the horizon, scanning as much of the jungle as he could see. There wasn't another man-made object in sight.

He looked at the chute. *Someone had dropped a single flare to see something in the middle of nowhere.* Cargo planes, such as Blindbat with its three-hundred flares, would've dropped three or four. A shiver coursed through his arms. *Ted couldn't afford to drop more than one of his six flares at the beginning of a mission.*

Mitch estimated the chute's coordinates, then wrote them on the window.

Everything looked like virgin jungle until he saw splintered trees on a steep hill east of the chute. Damage looked fresh, and a black smudge caught his attention. He entered an orbit about a thousand feet above the hills and focused his binoculars on the black spot. A large rock glistened in the sun as if covered with a film of oil.

Mitch felt his heart beat faster.

His eyes followed the path of broken trees downward. A clump of foliage stood out from the rest of the jungle at the bottom of the hill. The clump was the size of a truck. He looked upward from the oil-covered rock. *Dust!* Green foliage was trimmed in reddish-brown. Not a lot, but enough to suggest recent truck traffic. Between some trees, the open sections also had foliage. He saw telltale traces of squared-off frames—trellises intertwined with camouflage.

Mitch maneuvered more violently, realizing he was well within range of AAA deployed to protect the road. He flew beyond the hill top, then reversed in a wingover, and dived at the valley. Skimming above trees on the face of the hill, he looked from the side beneath the foliage. "Bingo!"

He jammed the throttles forward, pulled out of the dive, and let his airspeed carry him just over the treetops on the higher hills northeast. When he reached terrain too steep for roads, he soared upward to return to a safer altitude.

"Cricket, Nail Five-nine. I've found a new road!"

"Where, Five-nine?"

"Just west of the DMZ. About X-Ray Delta—" He glanced at the coordinates written on the window, added about five-hundred meters to the east-west component to account for the distance from the flare chute, and gave that number to Cricket. "I'm guessing Nail Six-eight went down somewhere in this vicinity."

Cricket read back the coordinates. "You certain?"

"Roger that. I pulled a J.D. and went down for a look."

"Say again."

"There's a road there. Mark it on your map and take it to the bank."

When Mitch reached a safer altitude, he located the oil-covered rock and the hillside above. Other than the oil and splintered trees, nothing indicated a road was carved through the jungle. Even the foliage-covered trellises blended in. With binoculars, he studied the hillside both ways. *Nothing.*

Switching to the flare chute, he expanded his search outward. He looked for dull black metal, the flash of a mirror, or someone waving.

"Nail Five-nine, Cricket with a request."

"Go, Cricket."

"Seventh requests more information. They want to send out an RF-Four for pictures and need information on where the road goes."

"The road's concealed. RF pilots won't see it unless they get out and walk."

"The photo interpreters might do some good if you can put the RF in the right place. Also, a road there would be significant enough that I'm sure Seventh will send in Ranch Hand to defoliate."

"I'm still looking for Nail Six-eight."

"Maybe you can do both."

Mitch checked his fuel. He could stay four more hours before heading for NKP. Besides, he thought with a new determination, he needed to finish whatever Ted had started with the single flare. "I'll take a look, Cricket. But if I find whatever Six-eight discovered last night, I'll need more than an RF-Four to join the party."

"The weather over Hanoi isn't too pure. If you find anything, I should be able to break loose some ordnance."

"Count on it, Cricket."

Mitch looked at the empty right seat and thought how J.D. would've loved this mission. Anger stirred within—anger that this war had taken such good men, such good friends—the brothers he'd never had as a child.

He decided to follow the road south, as convoys would to support the ongoing offensive. He dived to treetop level over the northeast mountains. Punching the timer on the clock, he swooped alongside the camouflaged road much as J.D. had flown level with the Marine convoy in what seemed another lifetime.

Trees rushed by in a blur, reminding him of his terrifying ride through Mu Gia. This time, however, anticipation—not fear—coursed through his veins. His weariness had vanished, pushed aside by keen concentration required to keep the road in sight and to fly within feet of the treetops. When possible, he glanced at his map and tried to match contour lines with ridges and valleys. Dust and trellises helped him stay with the road. Twice, however, he missed abrupt turns, pulled through a tight circle, and picked up the new direction.

Two impressions struck him in contrast to what he'd expected. The road wasn't graded. Instead its base seemed to be crushed underbrush packed solid by the wheels of many, many vehicles. And, Mitch concluded with no reasonable explanation, the road seemed deserted.

Glancing at the timer, he was shocked and amused. He felt as if he should be half way to Khe Sanh, but only three minutes and twenty seconds had passed. He'd flown no more than seven miles and probably was fewer than five from the oil-covered rock.

He looked up from the clock and spotted a huge clump of foliage on the road—and another and another.

A single line of tracers flashed across inches above the propeller.

Jesus!

He heard the distinctive bark of an AK-47—and another and another. Part of Mitch screamed to climb away from the guns. A quieter part repeated J.D.'s warning about never-never air above the masking cover of the jungle. He must fly low until beyond the convoy but he didn't need to keep quiet.

"Cricket, Cricket, Nail Five-nine's taking ground fire in the middle of a convoy."

"Say location, Five-nine."

Mitch couldn't afford a look at his map. "Five to six miles—"

A back window shattered.

"Uh, miles southeast of the earlier coordinates." Mitch glanced at the electronics rack in the back of the cockpit but saw no smoke or sparks.

"Can you identify the type of fire?"

"Small arms, so far."

"Small arms?"

"I'm on the deck trying to follow the friggin' road."

"Copied."

Mitch tried to count vehicles but gave up. He couldn't even keep up with the various types. He saw regular cargo trucks, massive vans, tankers, semis with trailers with foliage-covered radar dishes, and semis with long, canvas-covered trailers. Even regular trucks had foliage-covered trailers.

Away from the road in a clearing off his right wing, a ZPU spit four distinct streams of tracers. They weren't leading him enough, Mitch decided. Nevertheless, the bullets narrowed the gap as he flew behind a solitary outcropping of karst rising from the jungle near the middle of the convoy.

Le was wavering between asleep and awake when he heard distant gunfire. A dream tried to form around the sounds. He forced his eyes open. The noise didn't disappear. He feared someone was panic firing instead of letting camouflage provide protection. "No!"

He glanced at where Hoa had been sleeping earlier. Hoa was snoring. The noise of battle intensified as more guns joined in. Le hurried to the command battery.

Mitch maneuvered constantly above the road. Even with air hissing in the broken window, he heard gunfire grow to a constant din. He imagined J.D. shouting, "So much for this being-a-target shit!"

Mitch's hand reached for the armament panel even before he made up his mind. Without looking he twisted the switches for the two rocket pods, then flipped up the Armament Master Switch. Maybe he was going to blow himself out of the sky, but—he tapped the trigger. A rocket flashed from beneath each wing and skimmed above the treetops. Assuming he wasn't going to need the remaining twelve—one way or another—he hit the trigger again. Two more rockets raced ahead as the first two exploded.

White puffs billowed from the flashes. The O-2 burst through the white smoke and crisscrossing tracers. Seeing the other rockets detonate, he pushed closer to treetops and the growing clouds of white smoke.

A glance at the timer showed he'd been over the convoy for at least a mile. Other camouflaged vehicles remained ahead.

"Cricket, Five-nine's got more than a mile's worth of trucks cornered. I need all the ordnance you can get."

"Can you give me a DME and radial?"

"Negative. Send them just southwest of the DMZ."

Ahead, ZPUs opened up on both sides of the road. Streams of red blazed an X a few feet above the trees.

"Five-nine's taking ZPU fire."

"Copied. Keep us advised."

"Nail, Five-nine, Crown," an air-rescue controller said.

Mitch hunched down in his seat, and the O-2 skimmed through leaves of a tree below the center of the X. Tracers chased him, but the road ahead was clear of vehicles. He glanced at the timer for a reference on when to pull up.

"Five-nine, Crown. Do you copy?"

"Standby, Crown."

Mitch gulped several breaths. Chills turned into trembling. Not as bad as after flying through Mu Gia, he thought. His excitement was as much from anticipation as from delayed fear. This convoy had more trucks than J.D. had found west of Foxtrot.

Mitch tried to recall what he'd seen. The vehicles were camouflaged with foliage and netting arranged to conceal from prying eyes high above. At treetop level, he'd seen more than the North Vietnamese had expected.

Something his eyes had taken in—and his brain hadn't interpreted—nagged him as he guided the O-2 toward a jungle-covered ridge. His thoughts went to the long trailers with canvas-covered cargoes and to the big trucks pulling them. He'd seen that combination before, and he didn't think it had been in Southeast Asia. In a moment, he had the answer. Newscasts had shown such trucks in formation, five abreast—in Red Square during Moscow's May Day parades. Then, however, cargoes weren't covered by canvas. He felt a shiver. He'd flown over transporters for SA-2s.

"Cricket, Five-nine. Be advised this convoy's got at least a dozen SAM transporters."

"Are you positive?"

"Pretty sure. I also saw radar antennas, big vans, and a bunch of things we don't see in routine convoys."

"If you're sure, we'll divert a chunk of the Strike Force from Hanoi."

"Send 'em to me!"

"Cricket, Crown. I'm concerned about strikes in the area where Nail Six-eight may be down."

"Crown, Nail Five-nine," Mitch interrupted. "I'm at least five miles from where Six-eight probably was shot down."

"But we can't be sure. You didn't spot wreckage, did you?"

"No," Mitch said, with an edge to his voice. "And I didn't see parachutes either."

"We don't normally strike where we don't know the position of possible survivors."

Until I told you different, you thought Six-eight was near the Chokes.

"Break, Cricket, Crown. We need to talk this over off-line."

Mitch recognized Crown wanted to influence Cricket on a private frequency. He was angry because he couldn't listen, but Le Van Do's people likely could. "Cricket, I've had a windshield-to-windshield look. This convoy's packing more firepower than we've ever seen this far south, and I'm spitting distance from Khe Sanh. My friends'd be willing to duck bombs if that keeps the Marines from looking down the barrel of another Dien Bien Phu."

"Let's not let ourselves get carried away, Five-nine," Crown said.

"I'm trying to not get blown away! Break, Cricket. This isn't ring-around-the-rosie time. If this convoy gets where it's going, a lot of men'll die. I need bombs."

"Standby, Nail. You'll have the first flights in about twenty minutes."

"I'll be waitin'."

Mitch checked his timer and decided he was at least two miles from the convoy. Approaching the ridge, he soared into a climbing turn toward the mountains. He saw the karst he'd ducked behind to avoid the first ZPUs. Four puffs of smoke were merging into a white haze just south of the karst.

"There!" The commander of the lead AAA battery pointed above trees blocking the view to the north.

Crewmen cranked furiously, turning 37mm guns toward the O-2 rising above those trees.

Beyond effective range, Le thought, standing near the guns. Nevertheless, the aircraft was near his defenses at the northern end of the convoy—but those guns were holding fire. Le tried to decide as he watched the aircraft climb. Guns in the other convoy had gone silent, but the convoy had been discovered. If he shot down the FAC, others would come looking. If he didn't, the FAC would attack that convoy.

With the bottom of the aircraft facing his guns, Le decided his gunners had a chance. "The aircraft must be shot down."

The commander looked at Le.

Le nodded and covered his ears with his hands.

"Fire!"

Four guns blasted shells skyward.

Other guns protecting the convoy sounded like echoes.

Mitch saw nothing hinting at a road. He spread his map across his lap and searched contour lines for the karst in the middle of the convoy.

Pop-pa-pop.

Mitch's head jerked up. Tracers sparkled just beyond the left wing. Twisting the yoke to roll out of the turn, he saw a flash.

An explosion peppered the rocket pod and fuselage with hot metal. Smoke and fire belched from the pod. Fuel streamed from the bottom of the wing and became a shimmering mist inches from the flames. The fire-warning horn for the rear engine screeched. Smoke spewed from the cowling around the front engine.

Panic welled up. Mitch wasn't sure he had *even* seconds to get rid of the burning rocket motor packed in with four others. His hand shot to the armament panel, twisted the control switch to DROP, and armed the panel. He squeezed the trigger.

Latches released. Propelled by fire escaping the side, the pod whirled wildly, bounced off the wing strut, cartwheeled beneath the fuselage, and disappeared. He now had a clearer view of damage. A crumpled aileron was jammed upward at a strange angle.

Mitch saw other tracers race by—well clear. The yoke was stiff, but he ruddered the aircraft over enough to see the jungle south of the ridge. Three sets of guns sparkled. He eased off the rudder allowing the jammed aileron to turn the aircraft away.

Checking engine instruments, he confirmed the fire-warning horn wasn't lying. His hands raced through items in the Engine Fire/Inflight checklist. Finishing, he noticed the oil pressure on the front engine. *Zero!* Dark smoke swishing over the windshield likely was from oil—the front engine's life's blood—spraying onto the hot engine. Temperatures had climbed well beyond normal.

"You're about to become a glider, babe." His voice was so calm, it hardly seemed his.

A hand dropped and unlatched his shoulder harness and seatbelt. "Mayday, Cricket. Nail Five-nine's hit bad and losing both engines!"

"Say location, Five Nine."

Mitch glanced at his map. "I'm bailing out near NKP's one-oh-eight at one-ten."

Four lines of tracers raced by.

Mitch tightened the turn to avoid them, then noticed the O-2 was pointed toward the gunners. He armed the other pod, raised the nose to loft the rockets, and rippled the remaining five at the jungle south of the ridge. "Shoot at the FAC, and you pay the price," he said quietly, knowing rockets from a burning O-2 would do little to scare those celebrating.

"Nail Five-nine, Crown. Confirm you are abandoning your aircraft."

"Roger that. Break, Cricket, keep that ordnance inbound. I'll see if I can get bombs on target from down in the cheap seats."

"Good luck, Five Nine."

Click, click.

Throwing off his shoulder harness, he rolled the wings as level as possible and trimmed the nose up into a gentle climb. He grabbed his M-16 and jerked the rifle free from bungee cords holding it against the side. Climbing across onto the right seat, he yanked on the jettison handle to release the door. Nothing happened.

Le listened to thundering antiaircraft artillery and cheering men. Those sounds and the smoke trailing the aircraft were like a tonic to his warrior spirit. Moments earlier, worries about his convoys being discovered had added crushing weight to the exhaustion of the last few days. Now he felt invigorated, ready to do battle with the consequences of this latest encounter with an American FAC. His gunners now were two for two. Maybe the spirits were smiling on his desperate undertaking to end the war.

He half-saw, half-sensed a streaking rocket an instant before it disappeared into the trees and detonated. He dropped into a crouch as four more rockets slammed into the jungle.

His heart pounded. His mind replayed the sight and smell of the white octopus of phosphorous enveloping Sergeant Dinh in flames. These clouds of smoke were much farther away. Le decided two shots had gone wild. Three were somewhere in the convoy.

He scanned for other aircraft but found none. He hoped none were close enough to see the five plumes of smoke.

The front engine shuddered, shaking the O-2. *Death rattle.* The engine gave up the lawnmower-like sound that had been so reassuring.

Pop-pa-pop-pop-pop.

He froze, watching tracers rush by aft of the wing. When the shells disappeared from sight, his thoughts returned to getting rid of the door.

He remembered that the flight manual said to push the door open before trying to release it. He unlatched it and pushed—and the airflow pushed back.

Mitch leaned farther to get more leverage and pushed hard with the hand holding the sling of the M-16. The door edged open, and he pulled the jettison handle with his free hand.

Air rushing by caught the door, and it plunged away as if sucked from the aircraft.

Mitch lurched into the gaping hole where the door had been. The radio cord pulled taut and separated at the plug. The free end recoiled and slapped across his face—but he hardly noticed.

Air screaming by seized the M-16. It bucked wildly, jerking against his grip on the sling. Fear stabbed deeply, terrorizing him with the possibility of being thrown against the wing strut—or even into the rear propeller. Clawing fingertips grasped the jettison handle. He tried to hook his legs on the seat. The canteen on his pistol belt snagged the frame of the door.

The M-16 whipped in wide arcs, banging off the fuselage and pulling him farther into the airflow. The sling wrenched his wrist and fingers back, pulling his fingers straight. The M-16 whirled away like a bottle thrown from a speeding car.

With his hand free, he grabbed the door frame and halted his slide. Panting, he looked at the scene below. The O-2 was in a large circle, now heading toward the karst and the convoy he'd overflown.

After pulling himself in, he positioned his boots on the lower frame and held both sides. He pictured Elizabeth waving goodbye at the airport. Wondering if he'd ever see her again, he dived from the O-2.

Tumbling out of control, he grappled for the D-ring that would release his parachute. He extended his legs and other arm to stabilize, then yanked.

Silk streamed out between his legs. Risers pulled taut with a jolt that flipped him. His eyes closed, and he didn't see whatever gyrations he went through. When he opened his eyes, he was swaying under an orange-and-white parachute. He looked up to make the post-opening check. The four risers from his harness were untangled. They branched into scores of shroud lines connected to the canopy, which looked perfect. *So far, so good—all things considered.*

Looking down, he saw five clouds of white smoke along with flashes from four batteries of ZPU and 37mm AAA south of the ridge. He picked out two clearings and a meandering stream to help locate what must be another convoy. The O-2 had drifted nearer the first convoy and drew more fire from 37mm AAA south of the karst. The aircraft was descending in a spiral tighter than the original sweeping circle.

Le saw the parachute as he'd seen so many others. This time, however, he shouted an order he'd never uttered before. "Shoot at the parachute!"

The battery commander looked surprised, but nodded. "Yes,

Colonel."

Le watched as if transfixed by the blot of orange and white against a limitless azure sky. He doubted anyone could hit the parachute. Yet he felt duty bound to try anything to stop the pilot from guiding others to the hidden convoys. If his mission to end the war required the sacrifice of another American pilot, so be it.

Mitch straightened his legs and looked beyond his boots to determine drift and see where he was likely to land. He was over the ridge, but the wind was carrying him north, closer to the convoy he'd overflown. Looking in that direction, he searched for a place to land. The obvious candidate was a large meadow a mile east of the road he'd overflown. The triangular meadow sloped upward toward the higher mountains. The upper end was wider but too steep for his first parachute landing. He chose the lower half with its gentle slope, then reached to the risers to change the direction of drift.

Pop-pa-pop— Passing shells were so numerous, they merged into a popping howl.

He hunched into as small a target as he could and looked for the shells. Four streams were passing to the side, seemingly close enough to touch. They were above him almost before he could be frightened. He strained to look over his shoulder at the guns south of the ridge. Two other groups of tracers were rising toward him.

He yelled as loud as he could. "Bastards!"

He was facing the meadow he'd picked moments earlier, so he reached high on the two front risers. He grabbed the coarse straps and pulled as if doing a chin-up. In actuality, he pulled the risers down against his chest and air spilled from the back of the canopy. He looked between his boots and saw he was drifting toward the meadow.

More shells raced by but not as close as those before.

Mitch strained to keep the risers against his chest. Soon, his arms quivered, and he gritted his teeth trying to maintain the position. He looked around for the gunners and his airplane—anything to keep his mind off the risers pulling on his fists.

He was pleased by what he discovered. His O-2 was in a faster, steeper, tighter spiral that seemed centered near the gunners south of the ridge. Those guns were spitting tracers at the aircraft. If the O-2 kept the gunners attention much longer, trees on the ridge would screen him. The aircraft appeared to be making a final attempt to save him in this land where spirits ruled. Even in the hot Asian afternoon, thoughts about spirits guiding airplanes produced a chill that raised every hair on his forearms.

Le watched in morbid fascination while tracers converged on the O-2. A ZPU-4 near the center of the convoy pumped scores of shells into the aircraft, which was almost overhead. Le saw silvery pieces flutter away and flames trail a wing.

Seeing the battery commander preparing to fire, Le put his hands over his ears. The four 37mm guns thundered sixty shells skyward. Five slammed into the O-2 and exploded in staccato flashes that brought cheers from around him.

A larger flash engulfed the aircraft, and a wing broke off. A new round of cheering overwhelmed the sound of the explosion.

The burning fuselage tumbled out of control.

Cheers changed to shrieks. Soldiers scrambled in every direction.

Le guessed the airplane would crash north of where he stood, but he ran anyway. He dived under the closest truck and listened to the scream of the falling aircraft. He looked across the clearing and saw a soldier stumble over Hoa. Hoa yelled. The soldier leaped up and kept running. Hoa sat up bleary-eyed and pulled off a padded tanker's helmet and removed a plug of cotton from his ear.

Ba-boom.

The O-2 hit a few hundred meters away. Anguished cries replaced sounds of battle.

"Cung! Kiet! Get the vehicle." The two bodyguards scrambled toward the GAZ. Le turned to Hoa. "Come on, Hoa. We're going to check for damage."

The battery commander asked, "Any instructions, Colonel?"

"I hope we stay concealed until dark. Hold fire unless they attack."

"Yes, Colonel."

The GAZ rumbled from the trees, and Le jumped in. "Get over here!"

Le hoped his words would hurry Hoa. Waiting, he activated the radio tuned to the Americans' emergency frequency. The radio barely hissed. He pressed the small speaker to his ear. He heard the faint warble of an emergency beeper. Conversations wavered in and out, too indistinct for Le to decipher. Switching off the radio, he said, "Perhaps the radio will pick up words when aircraft are overhead."

Hoa barely got in through the opening in the canvas covering the back.

Le glanced at Hoa, then shouted to Cung, "Go!"

"Good hit!"

Mitch felt sad at the loss of his aircraft, but he was certain it crashed within the area the antiaircraft guns were trying to protect. Watching the column of smoke, he assumed his O-2 had frightened more people than his five rockets had.

His aching biceps returned his attention to more immediate problems. The risers had pulled his arms almost straight. He unwrapped his cramped fingers from the rough straps and hung in the harness. While massaging his arms, he looked beyond his boots. He was much nearer the ground, and the winds weren't carrying him north anymore. He was descending toward thick jungle on the ridge. Panic stirred again. Unless he intervened—and quickly—he wouldn't reach the clearing.

He grabbed the risers and pulled. Closing his eyes, he grimaced and grunted against pain threatening to rip muscle from bone. This time he didn't have enough strength to pull his fists to his chest. Nevertheless, air dumping out the back of the canopy moved him toward the clearing.

Snap.

His eyes flashed open. *Were shroud lines breaking?* He looked up, and everything appeared normal. Although curious, he decided to ignore the sound and focus on landing preparations.

Snap. Snap.

When he checked the canopy, he noticed two small tears near the center. Still confused, he realized the snaps correlated with delayed pops.

Someone was shooting at him!

Hunching his shoulders, as if that would make a difference, he looked toward popping. Two soldiers stood in a small clearing beyond the big meadow. Mitch saw a rifle flash, and he felt helpless. Training pushed aside shivers of panic. He decided to focus on things he had some control over and looked at the jungle.

The meadow, which had appeared smooth from a thousand feet higher, now showed rugged rocks and clumps of trees. The slope also was steeper. He knew a safe landing and a quick rescue were more likely if he reached the clearing.

Trees raced at him. He checked the drift and realized he wasn't going to make it beyond the jungle. Gritting his teeth, he pulled in desperation.

Mitch searched for places where the jungle was less solid—and was horrified by what he saw. Beneath him, squared-off frames of trellises held interwoven foliage.

He was over the road!

Glancing west along the ridge that extended into the jungle-covered valley, he realized an ascending road along the side was the easiest way to cross the ridge.

Seconds from the treetops, he had no time to worry about his mistake. Letting the risers extend almost to full length, he tried to kill the drift but still ease himself over the last stand of trees. His frantic efforts accomplished neither. Plunging into trees as tall as twenty-story buildings, he clamped his legs together and crossed his forearms to shield his face.

The parachute was still drifting when the canopy snagged. The jolt swung him like a pendulum. The strap on his helmet popped open. When his boots were as high as his chest, the collapsing chute and limbs gave way. His helmet flew off and disappeared.

Time seemed to slip into slow motion. He fell backward, flailing, trying to catch something. Orange-and-white cloth strained to hold, then failed. Mitch felt himself falling from at least fifty feet above the jungle floor. He closed his eyes and stiffened his body.

The tattered canopy snagged again and jerked him through another pendulum swing. He opened his eyes in time to see a horizontal branch rushing at him. Twisting, he tried to protect the arm wounded in May. He took most of the blow below his left shoulder. The branch and his upper arm shattered each other. A flash of pain gave way to blackness.

Chapter 38

A vision of Elizabeth shimmered. She waved sadly. Mitch tried to call to her but couldn't force words. He reached. Excruciating pain stabbed his shoulder.

Mitch's eyes flashed open, but he saw only blurred images of browns and greens. He tried to blink the intrusions away, then closed his eyes. Elizabeth was gone. The pain remained.

Wavering near unconsciousness, he became aware of trying to focus on a strange tree. He had no idea what had happened—until he looked up. Risers led to the parachute, which now was a tattered mess. Most of the chute was entangled on two large limbs. A couple of panels had ripped away on branches at least a hundred feet higher. Memories of bailing out returned.

How long had he hung there? Minutes? Hours? He was bewildered about time. *Was this another bad dream like those after the deaths of Goodwin and J.D.?* Perhaps he'd awaken, caught in sweat-soaked sheets. Throbbing in his shoulder suggested otherwise.

Mitch saw the jungle floor maybe four feet beneath his boots. He listened for soldiers thrashing through the underbrush. He heard birds, a light breeze rustling through treetops, and a quiet squeaking as the parachute twisted on the supporting branches. Thoughts of Elizabeth stirred his will to survive.

Hearing no aircraft, he felt frighteningly alone. He vaguely remembered a Mayday message. Cricket must've sent aircraft. What if he'd been unconscious for hours? Or days?—and the brotherhood had given up on him being alive. He started to look at his wristwatch, but the movement triggered overwhelming pain. Broken arm or shoulder, he decided, as he hung limp and panted for a few moments.

Struggling to free a radio from a pouch on his survival vest, his fingers cramped. *A good sign.* Little time had passed since his hand had wrapped around the risers.

Mitch held the radio to his ear and clicked the switch on with minimum volume. The jungle was too quiet to risk a loud voice roaring over the radio. A gentle hiss gave him encouragement. He increased volume. The warble of an emergency locator beacon blared from the tiny speaker. Discouraged, he twisted the volume control. If someone else had been shot down trying to find him, his rescue could be delayed.

Confused about what to do, he remembered lecturing Lieutenant Scott about the emergency radios on parachute risers. "Dummy," he whispered, looking up and seeing a canvas-covered bulge on a riser.

He needed to turn off the transmitter so its continuous warble wouldn't make talking to rescuers difficult. Working with only one hand was exhausting. He was sweating profusely by the time he disabled the transmitter. The closed-in feeling of the humid jungle was taking its toll, and Mitch suspected he was going into shock. He took a long drink from his canteen and poured a few drops over his forehead.

He tried his emergency radio again. After transmitting the warbling tone five seconds, he selected *voice*, and touched the radio to his lips. "Any aircraft, this is Nail Five-nine broadcasting on Guard. Do you copy?" He held the radio against his ear.

Several transmissions blocked each other until all but one stopped.

"Five-nine, this is Nail Three-four. Do you copy?"

"Roger, Three-four." Recognizing Captain Kesler's voice and call sign, Mitch felt less alone.

"Three-four's a few minutes out. What's your status?"

"I've had better days. I'm a little beat up."

"Hang in there, Mitch. Jolly Greens are launching from NKP."

"Great." But, they'd have to find him, and he knew how difficult spotting men in the jungle could be. He looked up and confirmed most of the chute was below the treetops. It would be of little help—except, perhaps, to North Vietnamese searchers. "I may have to shut down a few minutes while I get away from my chute. Once I hear you, I'll call."

"Call me back in five in any case."

"Right."

Mitch returned the radio to its pouch on his survival vest. Keeping as quiet as possible, he listened for soldiers. He heard nothing louder than birds. The ground looked close enough to reach using his good arm—if he could get unstrapped from the harness.

He unbuckled the chest strap and tried to ease his injured arm clear of the shoulder strap. Teeth-gritting pain countered every effort. Frustrated, he reached through and grabbed his hand. He took a deep breath, bit hard on his lip, bent his left arm at the elbow, and yanked his arm through. Bone splinters stabbed torn flesh. Nausea surged into his throat. His vision blurred, and he fought to avoid blacking out.

The most excruciating pain subsided after a few seconds, and he swallowed the taste of bile. He wiped at his mouth and discovered blood where he'd bitten his lip.

Loosening both leg straps, he released one buckle, leaving his weight supported by the other strap and the harness beneath his good arm. With misgivings, he pressed his good arm against his chest, trying to trap the harness while he released the leg strap.

The buckle opened, and the harness swayed, oscillating crazily as he started falling. Frantically trying to regain balance, Mitch grabbed the harness. For an instant he held, then slipped free, hit the ground, and toppled backward into bamboo stalks and banana leaves.

The jolts caused bone fragments to tear again at raw flesh. He blacked out in a vivid flash of stars. Coming to, he noticed his fitful gasps for air contrasted with peaceful green foliage trimmed in tatters of orange and white. The pain seemed to drain all energy. Part of him demanded to give up and remain where he'd fallen—but he couldn't do that to Elizabeth. She mustn't be left wondering if he'd gotten her last letter.

When his breathing calmed, he listened for soldiers drawn by his noise. He heard normal jungle sounds and a truck in the distance. *Trucks!* He remembered camouflaged trucks whipping by just beyond his wingtips. He remembered talking to Cricket and arguing with Crown. A great deal more than his life was at stake on these Laotian hillsides.

He grabbed the trunk of a litchi tree and pulled himself to his feet. A billowing blackness crowded his vision and weakened his knees. He leaned on the tree.

When he felt stronger, he headed in the direction the sun suggested would be north. He couldn't move forward without fighting through underbrush, so he stopped worrying about leaving a trail. He struggled for distance instead. If he couldn't quickly reach a place where the Sandies could cover him, the size of the trail he left wouldn't matter.

He ran, staggered, and stumbled through a seemingly endless maze of vines, bamboo, and trees. Soon a cottony dryness in his mouth contrasted with the wet flight suit, which felt pasted on his arms and legs. His lungs ached, but he pushed forward, refusing to take the break his body demanded.

After a few minutes, he was confused about why he hadn't reached the clearing. He divided his attention between watching for soldiers and selecting a path. While looking over his shoulder, he stepped on a fallen stalk of bamboo that was sloped up on a rock. His feet shot sideways as if on an inclined sheet of ice. He fell hard, and the jolt forced air from his lungs.

New waves of pain and shock pinned him to the crumpled underbrush. Thoughts of the comfort of death flooded over his determination to continue. His eyelids felt heavy and blinked closed longer and longer. Hallucinations flowed from the pain and exhaustion.

He saw Elizabeth shimmering in the darkness, shadowy at first, then in sharp focus. He tried to tell her what was happening but couldn't form words. She drifted, ever smiling. He reached, but she floated just beyond his grasp, then faded. Blackness swirled inward, then was pushed aside by an image of J.D. saying "Get your ass moving, tiger."

Mitch opened his eyes. He pulled himself to a sitting position and drank water while his head cleared. Listening for pursuers, he decided he needed to tell Three-four about the trucks. "Nail Three-four. Five-nine on Guard."

"Roger. Three-four's about five minutes out. I see smoke near your last reported location. Could that be your aircraft?"

"I don't—" He remembered smoke curling up from his O-2. "Could be. My bird crashed in the middle of a convoy."

"You know where you are from your aircraft?"

"A couple of miles northeast."

"The Sandies and Jolly Greens are airborne."

Pride swelling in his throat choked at his words. The brotherhood was coming, but it sometimes had a higher calling. "Getting me out's not number one right now. Did Cricket tell you about a road filled with trucks?"

"They said you'd made some astounding claims."

Memories of the last few minutes flooded back. "There's more than I got the chance to tell Cricket. Stay high. It looks safe, but there are a bunch of camouflaged thirty-sevens and ZPUs. You have ordnance?"

"Roger that. Redneck's inbound. Four Fox-fours loaded for flak-suppression."

"Any CBU-24?" Mitch knew the big cluster bombs with hundreds of large ball bearings would be the easiest way to find camouflaged trucks.

"Roger that."

"Okay." Mitch closed his eyes and envisioned the terrain where his O-2 had crashed. "My bird's south of an east-west ridge that leads out of higher mountains on the border just south of the DMZ. Find my bird and have Redneck lay CBU-24 north-south across it."

"I need to locate you first."

"Negative. Jolly Greens can't help until I reach clearer ground. Instead of pinpointing me for the bad guys, give 'em something to think about besides me."

"We'll see."

"No 'we'll see' about it! You've got to get these trucks before they move. I'm shutting down so I can get moving."

"Call me every five," Kesler said.

Pulling a compass from his survival vest, he found he'd been moving more northeast than north. He looked north. The clearing could be beyond a tangle of vines and underbrush.

After two more swallows of water, he stood unsteadily and staggered to the wall of foliage. He lunged forward to avoid retracing hard-fought steps. Vines held firm, then gave way. He pushed through, and in less than a minute, the meadow spread before him. Mitch looked for soldiers and for a hiding place. He was high enough on the ridge to see into the valley. The karst he'd flown by earlier was visible three to four miles northwest.

The clearing, maybe three-quarters of a mile long, stretched wider above him and was much steeper near the upper end. Studying the lower section, his eyes were drawn into the trees. Orange and white winked through foliage moving in the breeze. He was shocked by how close he still was to his parachute—and to the road he'd drifted over in those final seconds. His struggles had taken him fewer than a hundred yards.

Feeling discouraged, he studied the clearing dotted by outcrops of rocks and scattered clumps of durian, gnetum, loquat, and carambola trees. Groups of wild banana plants were more frequent. A layer of rock jutted from the steeper terrain, forming boulder-laden cliffs across the upper end. The cliffs were at least five times farther than he'd walked, but Mitch made them his goal. After checking the clearing for soldiers, he pushed out of the underbrush and headed for the cliffs.

Grasses were knee-high to waist-high, so Mitch made better progress in the meadow. He'd covered about half the distance, when a fatigue-clad soldier came around a stand of trees fewer than a hundred yards to Mitch's left. Carrying an AK-47 at the ready, the soldier moved with cautious steps, angling up across the clearing.

Mitch froze, wishing he'd stayed closer to the jungle instead of moving on a direct line toward the rocks. He also wished he had more than a pistol and one good arm.

His eyes darted between the soldier and nearby vegetation. Ahead, banana trees grew around the trunk of a downed durian tree. Ten steps and a dive would put him behind cover. Then, he'd keep the tree between him and the soldier while crawling to the jungle.

Mitch heard the buzz of an O-2.

High and a couple of miles west, the aircraft also drew the soldier's attention. He dropped to a half-crouch and faced the approaching aircraft.

Mitch raced forward and dived. Rolling in mid-air, he stretched out to land on his right side. He watched the soldier until the durian came between them. Only then did Mitch notice a large snake coiled by the tree.

"Jesus!" His uncontrollable half-shout was in unison with the hissing of the snake.

The snake was recoiling when Mitch's face flashed by inches away. Mitch hit the ground, and the snake struck his chest. He envisioned needle-sharp fangs stabbing bare skin. The impact felt like a jab over his heart, and Mitch hardly noticed pain from hitting the ground.

The snake flailed like a bullwhip, slicing off stalks and sending leaves and bananas flying.

Mitch kicked his feet and clawed with his good hand in a frenzied attempt to get away. Even in his panic, however, he was certain his efforts wouldn't matter. The snake was a banded krait—and an even larger version than the one J.D. had put in the bed. Mitch wondered if the soldier heard either the cry or the thrashing of the snake. Even sprinting the hundred yards, the soldier wouldn't beat the effects of the venom.

Mitch assumed the soldier didn't matter—until Mitch looked toward his chest. Two tiny holes oozed venom from the canvas over one of the radios. The snake's head and fangs were entangled in webbing of the survival vest. The long body added momentum to the twisting head. Mitch knew the krait wouldn't stay hung up much longer. He had to throw the snake out of striking range.

Rising to his knees, Mitch grasped the snake just behind its head. When he yanked the hissing head away, the agile body coiled around his arm. Instead of being able to throw the snake, Mitch found himself looking into a pair of angry, unblinking eyes.

The snake squeezed tighter, trying to escape Mitch's stranglehold. Incredible pressure caused numbness in his arm. The snake would not be denied for long.

Mitch glanced over the trunk of the durian and saw the soldier stalking forward, now higher on the hill. The distance separating them was fewer than seventy yards.

The snake hissed and squeezed and twisted.

Mitch's grip weakened. Panic flooded over him. With the struggling snake slowly pulling free, he panted animal-like gasps. Searching wild-eyed, he saw a flat rock near the tree. He shuffled on his knees, then raised a boot onto the rock.

Flailing stronger and hissing louder, the snake seemed to sense the danger.

Mustering his remaining strength, Mitch thrust his snake-encircled arm at the rock, and slid the head under his boot. Grunting, he forced as much of his 175 pounds as possible onto the head of the squirming snake.

Snake and man struggled in a final, straining effort.

Bones crunched under the hard cleats of Mitch's jungle boot. He rotated his foot back and forth. The snake shuddered and its grip loosened. Mitch twisted out of the first few coils.

Bursts of gunfire from an AK-47 echoed across the clearing.

Mitch dropped lower before realizing the bullets were aimed at his parachute. Peering over the tree, he saw the soldier reloading his AK-47. Mitch tossed the snake away.

While flexing feeling into his hand, he unsnapped the cover on his holster. Gripping the .357 magnum, he hugged the pistol to his chest to mute the click of cocking the hammer.

Banana trees had overgrown most of the fallen tree. Mitch edged up against the log and found an opening in the leaves where he could watch the soldier. Resting his forearm on the trunk, he struggled to control his breathing and to shake off numbness tingling in his arm. Blinking off sweat from the corners of his eyes, he aimed at the soldier's chest.

In the jungle quiet, he heard the O-2, closer now but farther south than before. He couldn't risk a look, but he assumed Kesler was checking smoke from the downed O-2.

The soldier continued toward the parachute, taking a route that would pass very close to the downed durian.

Mitch became more unnerved as the distance decreased. Perhaps he'd already been spotted. *Would the young soldier suddenly empty a full clip into the foliage around the durian?* Mitch was afraid to wait for the answer since searchers might be hurrying toward the noise of the earlier firing. Mitch was tempted to gamble. On Air Force firing ranges, he'd put one shot after another into the bullseye. Still, the Laotian jungles were not a practice range, and he might get one shot against thirty from the AK-47. He decided to wait.

The deep-throated scream of jets echoed across the valley. *Redneck.* Even if the brotherhood were too late to save him, he was proud his information could destroy at least one convoy. He wished he'd mentioned the second to Kesler.

The soldier crouched to watch the F-4s, then continued his advance.

Mitch heard Phantoms circling, but he didn't look up. Instead, he alternated his focus between the pistol's front sight and the soldier's chest. He wanted to shake sweat from his eyebrow but feared making even that motion.

The distance narrowed.

The soldier's face and uniform became clearer. Mitch guessed the soldier was about twenty. Soft facial features and small stature made him appear much younger. The AK-47 made him seem older.

Mitch's throat was dry. His legs quivered in protest to holding their position, and his shoulder throbbed constantly. He minimized his breathing. Nevertheless, blood rushing through his temples pounded out a drumbeat that surely his adversary could hear.

The soldier moved within fifteen yards and stopped. Seeming to sense someone watching, he turned slowly toward the durian. He eased up his AK-47. His eyes met Mitch's.

The soldier dropped to a knee and aimed.

Mitch's pistol shattered the jungle quiet.

Bluish-gray smoke blurred Mitch's view. Fearing his shot had been high, he rushed to focus again on his target.

The smoke thinned, and he saw the soldier seemingly frozen in mid-motion. By the time the soldier's cry registered into Mitch's consciousness, Mitch had cocked the pistol. He refocused on the front sight, aligning its clear image on the blurry mass a few yards beyond. He squeezed off a second round.

The soldier staggered backward. His AK-47 flew from his grasp. He collapsed before Mitch could shoot again.

Mitch stood. His breath was more difficult to catch than before the shooting. Sweat trickled from his forehead and dripped from his hair, forming tiny rivulets on his neck. When he looked at the body sprawled in the weeds, nausea swept into his throat. *Tough it out.* He tightened his left fist sending mind-jarring pain up his arm.

He listened for soldiers rushing toward the gunfire. If the earlier firing of the AK-47 hadn't gotten the attention of everyone close enough to hear, two unanswered pistol shots would. Searchers would know the American had been flushed from cover—and had come out fighting. Mitch hurried around the tree. One glance told him their fight was over.

Mitch avoided looking at the anguished features of the young soldier while pulling the bloody ammunition belt from the his waist. The belt had three clips. Mitch draped the belt over his head and good arm, reloaded his pistol, jammed it into his holster, and grabbed the AK-47. He wanted to talk to Kesler but decided to get away from the body and move to a more defensible position before other soldiers arrived.

He believed he'd scarcely seen the contorted face. Yet as he struggled up the hill, a clear image of the face kept intruding in his thoughts. Mitch moved closer to the clearing's edge instead of heading at the cliffs. He stayed close enough to trees to hide if other soldiers appeared. Trudging forward, he pulled out the radio. "Nail Three-four, Nail Five-nine."

"Go, Five-nine."

"Have you found my aircraft?"

"I'm above the wreckage, but where are you?"

Mitch looked over his shoulder. "I'm midway up a triangular clearing at your eight o'clock, about two miles."

"I'll come your way."

"Negative, Three-four. Start laying CBU on that target, and I've got another by the karst north of you."

"Crown's hesitant about us bombing until I confirm your location."

Mitch paused to catch his breath. He was high enough to see over trees on the ridge. He saw smoke rising in the area where his O-2 had crashed. "Drop the bombs, Three-four. Tell them I'm acting as a ground FAC."

"I don't see signs of a road or motorable trail."

"I've seen the road," Mitch said, knowing his words implied more than the road he'd flown over two miles to the north. J.D. would have approved. "There's an active thirty-seven-millimeter site and ZPU within a hundred meters of my O-2."

"You sure?"

"Do it!"

"You gonna be okay another twenty minutes until Sandies arrive?"

"Do it—for Ted and Angelo and J.D.! I'll call when I get set up."

Mitch pushed harder than before. Within a hundred yards of his goal, he noticed a change in the sounds from the O-2. He looked toward the noise and saw the aircraft diving.

A rocket flashed from the O-2.

Excitement stirred in Mitch. He hadn't watched from the ground since on practice ranges in Florida. Then, he'd hardly understood what was happening until the strike was over. Now he understood everything—and the bombs and targets were real.

Tracers spewed upward.

Mitch held his breath until the antiaircraft shells raced above Kesler. Watching the target, Mitch saw the flash of the marking rocket near his burning O-2. He also saw the leading F-4 high in the northwest sky with three others strung out in trail.

The rocket detonated a hundred meters south of Le. Foliage blocked his view of the airborne O-2 but not of the one that had crashed across the ravine from him. He wished the wreckage were in the trees instead of almost in the open. His men had been unable to extinguish burning fuel or to smother the resulting brush fire.

"We're too late," he said, not letting Hoa hear the acknowledgment of impending doom. Turning to the captain in charge of putting out the fire, Le said, "Tell the men to take cover."

"Yes, Colonel."

"Private Kiet, tell Corporal Cung to move the GAZ two-hundred meters north of where we left him." He glanced at his wristwatch. "Hurry."

"Yes, Colonel," Kiet said, then raced up a trail to the road.

Le looked at Hoa, whose eyes no longer glistened with the smug assurance of a political officer. Tightening the straps on his flak vest, Le said, "You're about to see the costs of your shooting at one of those little airplanes." And, Le thought, we're about to pay the price for not building truck shelters. He headed for a fallen teak he'd picked out earlier.

The F-4 plummeted, reminding Mitch of a hawk diving on a field mouse. The Phantom's deep-throated scream sent a shiver of excitement through him.

Seven batteries of ZPUs and 37mm guns blasted shells toward the northern sky.

The F-4 plunged through tracers and released two canisters of CBU-24. Afterburners lit off with double booms that vibrated across the valley.

"Yes!" Mitch restricted his shout of excitement to a whisper as shivers ran through him. The odds no longer were many to one.

He told himself to get moving but paused to watch scores of shimmering reflections. Each glimmer came from a grapefruit-sized bomblet, now spinning and armed to explode on contact. He hoped ground fire hadn't ruined the pilot's aim. If the pilot had targeted the guns, Mitch predicted fewer than seven batteries would fire on Redneck Two.

Mesmerized, Mitch watched the metallic mist swoop into the jungle. A few flickers revealed bomblets detonating in the treetops. Redneck One was on target, Mitch thought, seeing the tiny explosions near his O-2.

Two seconds later, an ammunition truck exploded.

The deafening explosion filled Le's ears, overwhelming the zinging of ball bearings, which sounded like a thousand angry hornets. Dust, leaves, and flaming debris rippled out in an ever-expanding circle. A chain reaction of explosions ripped into at least five or six more trucks—Le couldn't be sure because of ringing that echoed through his head.

Amid continuing explosions, anguished screams, and choking dust and smoke, Le clawed deeper beneath the log.

The earlier sequence repeated: antiaircraft guns roared, fewer this time; the scream of afterburners, less noticeable because of continuing explosions; and the whistling of bomblets reaching a shrill crescendo vibrating fear throughout his body. This time—among the smell and sounds of death—the staccato popping of bomblets reminded Le of the French snare drums at executions he'd witnessed in his teens.

Explosions, muted by jungle and distance, fed an irregular drumbeat Mitch felt in the air. Nearing the layer of cliffs and boulders, he watched Redneck Three roar down the chute, then break abruptly to the west. He knew this wouldn't be happening if gunners hadn't shot at Ted and Angelo. He whispered, "Shoot at the FAC, and you pay the price."

Reaching the cliffs that stretched more than a hundred yards across the hill, Mitch had a choice of three positions defensible against an attack from below. He picked the middle one, then poked around with a stick to check for snakes. Satisfied, he settled into a little niche offering good cover and separate firing positions on each side of a large boulder. He had a full view of the meadow below—and of towering columns of smoke and flame. The fourth Phantom angled upward, maneuvering near a single grouping of tracers.

His makeshift fortress was at least as good as he'd imagined from a distance. Rock ledges overhanging above offered some protection from soldiers in the jungle above the clearing. He hoped the Sandies would arrive before NVA soldiers discovered how vulnerable he was.

In all his years of fighting, Le had never felt so vulnerable. Still, he had to find out if the convoy could be saved. When the initial attack was over, he assumed he had at least two minutes before another flight struck. He bounded to his feet into air heavy with smoke, dust, and cries of the wounded.

"What are we going to do, Colonel?"

Le turned toward the wailing voice and saw Hoa rise from beneath another part of the log. Le cast a look of hatred at Hoa, then started for the trail.

"What are we to do?"

"Die, most likely."

No longer interested in watching over Hoa, Le raced up the trail. The carnage was worse than he'd imagined. Bright points shimmered red in dense black smoke. The larger fires were trucks. He saw smaller fires— supplies, spilled fuel, crates of antiaircraft ammunition, trees, bushes, and bodies. The growling hiss of flames was as loud as some secondary explosions. Blazing camouflage fell from trellises. The profusion of sparkling embers caused Le to feel as if everything around him were burning.

Le tried to think of a way to save what wasn't already lost. Without shelters, antiaircraft revetments, stores of water, and the hundreds of extra men he could call out, he had no options to save this convoy.

Nothing looked real, and he was confused about his location. "Corporal Cung! Private Kiet!" Smoke seemed to swallow his words and choke deep into his throat.

He bent forward to cough. An explosion behind him threw 37mm shells clattering all around. Someone lurched against him. Le turned, saw Hoa's eyes above a scarf stretched across his nose and mouth.

Le shoved Hoa away, then hurried opposite the way the trucks were pointed. The GAZ, if it survived, should be farther back in the convoy. He tied his neck scarf across the lower part of his face and lifted it periodically to call out for Cung and Kiet.

Le hadn't found them when he heard the scream of an F-105 pulling out of a dive. He scrambled off the road into a tangle of trees knocked down by an earlier explosion. Hearing the whine of plummeting bombs, he hunched into as small a ball as possible, opened his mouth wide, and put his hands over his ears. The whine became blood-curdlingly shrill.

Le wondered if these finally were the bombs he wouldn't survive.

Mitch watched the first F-105 zoom out of a column of smoke. The thunder of the afterburner set the pace of his heart up a notch or two. Even if he didn't survive, he was seeing the air show of a lifetime.

Exhausted, he stretched out with his radio and the AK-47 on rocks in front of him. He couldn't find a position where the hurting in his shoulder was less than a dull throb. His wallet, which he carried in the zippered pocket over his left bicep, pressed against his injuries. He struggled and finally freed the wallet in spite of more stabbing pain.

The elephant-skin leather was sticky with blood. He smiled, remembering J.D.'s solemn expression while explaining the wallet's potential dangers.

Opening to Elizabeth's picture, he accidentally smeared a bloody fingerprint across the plastic covering her Miss Texas smile. He pulled out his soggy handkerchief to wipe away the blood. She deserved better than the worry and anguish she'd put up with over the last year. He wondered if he'd ever get the opportunity to tell her. He wondered if he would ever see the second child she now carried.

Excited shouts interrupted his thoughts. He saw a man at the downed durian. Another soldier ran over from the jungle. Mitch couldn't understand the words, but the tone made the message clear. His pursuers had discovered their dead comrade.

While one man peered warily up the hill, the other moved around looking down. In moments he pointed at what Mitch assumed was a trail left by his jungle boots. The two men separated, then raced forward from rocks to bushes to trees.

Mitch put the wallet into his breast pocket and grasped the AK-47.

The last three jets had struck nearer the front of the convoy. Nevertheless, burning leaves fell in smoke swirling around Le's hiding place. After he heard bombs from the fourth F-105 explode, he picked his way out of the shattered trees.

"Cung. Kiet," he called out, weaving between downed trees and damaged trucks.

Le heard an engine, and the GAZ-69 appeared like a dark apparition in the smoke. He stepped toward the passenger side and grabbed at the door handle. The GAZ rolled by and clanged into a tree.

Hurrying around the GAZ, Le noticed it appeared unscathed.

The door opened, and Corporal Cung toppled out. The truck shuddered as the engine died when his foot came off the clutch. Blood oozed from Cung's mouth. Looking up with glazed eyes, Cung said, "Private Kiet is dead."

Le knelt.

Cung coughed. "And so am I." A bloody arm shook. His head rolled back, and his eyes stared into the smoke.

"And so, I'm afraid, are we all." Le pulled Cung's body to a protected area near the tree, then returned to the GAZ.

Hoa was in the passenger seat.

Le glared at the political sycophant but got behind the steering wheel without speaking. Le maneuvered between trailing vehicles, then reached the road leading to his eighty trucks in the second convoy.

Mitch had paralleled the treeline, so the soldiers weren't moving at him. Nevertheless, they needed little time to reach where he'd angled toward the outcropping. Both men paused and looked at the cliffs.

"Nail Five-nine, Three-four, radio check." The radio sounded while the breeze was calm, no jets roared nearby, and no explosions drove away the quiet.

Both soldiers aimed, and one fired a burst.

Mitch flinched down. Bullets blasted rocks and trees to his left. Two ricochets shattered rocks behind him and peppered him with chips. He edged up to look through the foliage. One soldier was replacing a clip. The other knelt by a boulder just above the front sight of Mitch's AK-47.

Mitch aimed and fired.

Bullets struck the boulder and the soldier.

Mitch swung the AK-47 sideways.

The second soldier disappeared into knee-high grass.

"Nail Five-nine, Three-four. You still with me?"

Mitch strained to locate the soldier and to calm shudders of nervous energy. He shook at drops of sweat sliding from eyelids into eyelashes, then wiped his face across his sleeve. The sodden flight suit didn't dry anything but blotted enough to clear his vision.

Grass dipped out of sight a few feet from where the soldier had disappeared. Mitch fired again. Seconds later the sequence repeated. This time, his firing was answered by a screech of pain. He squeezed the trigger again. The AK-47 fired two bullets, then went silent.

Empty!

Mitch fumbled with the release. The clip clattered against the rock.

The soldier staggered to his feet, fired wildly, turned, and ran.

Mitch slipped a wooden peg from the loop holding a canvas flap over a clip in the ammunition belt. He pushed the canvas out of the way but had trouble pulling the clip free.

Glancing up, he guessed the soldier was more than a hundred yards away. Blood darkened the man's shirt. Mitch shoved the clip in, chambered the first cartridge, and looked up to aim.

The soldier had disappeared.

Mitch studied the clearing but saw no movement.

"Nail Five-nine, Three-four on Guard!"

"Go, Three-four."

"You found a hell of a target. I count more than forty trucks burning or blown up."

"Do you have more ordnance?"

"Four flights, and the promise of more."

"Another big target's around the single karst a couple of miles north."

"I think I've got the karst, but I don't see anything obvious."

"Dump some CBU-24 north-south over it. You'll see."

"The next flight has more CBU. Once I finish with Crossbow, I'll take Cobra to the karst. Hang tough, Mitch."

Click-click.

Slipping the radio inside his survival vest, Mitch closed his eyes, and tried to relax. He thought of his father's words about true character coming out when a man was pressured by fear. Mitch didn't know how this day would play out, but he knew his father would've been proud. That conclusion helped him relax.

Between the muffled chatter of distant explosions, he heard an engine. A truck was on the road somewhere beyond the ridge. More troops, he thought, as he released flaps over the two remaining clips. Listening a few moments, he concluded the truck, and whoever it carried, was getting closer. He drew the AK-47 to him, prepared to face whatever came.

Le raced the GAZ along the road. Hoa's white-knuckle grip on the seat and door frame caused Le to smile deep within. He feared the day would leave nothing to smile about, but he tried to be optimistic. Eighty vehicles, including a full regiment of surface-to-air missiles remained unscathed. If they weren't undetected before sunset, he might get them close to Khe Sanh during the night. Crossing the ridge, he was absorbed in thoughts about how to salvage his mission and help end the war.

A figure staggered out of shadows in the subdued light beneath the triple canopy.

Le hit the brakes, swerved, and barely missed what he now recognized as a bloody soldier dragging an AK-47. Surprised to find a wounded soldier between convoys, Le jumped out.

The soldier reeled toward the GAZ and grasped at the canvas covering. He slumped to the ground, leaning against the rear bumper and leaving a reddish-brown blot on the canvas.

Hoa came around from his side.

Le heard the thunderous roar of an F-105 climbing to the east. Kneeling, he saw fatigues blood-soaked from the waist to below the knees. The soldier was so pale, he looked almost American.

The soldier gestured with his eyes. "He's up there."

Hoa asked, "Who?"

Le looked at a thinning in the jungle northeast of the road. He saw a clearing beyond. Something drew his attention upward. He saw orange and white panels flutter in the trees.

"The American!" The soldier gulped air. "The top of the clearing."

Le looked, but trees obscured the upper end.

Hoa picked up the AK-47. "We can get the man who led them to us." His tone carried more than his usual bravado.

"You led them to us."

"And I might have succeeded if I'd had authority to act sooner."

The soldier coughed up blood. "He's got a radio."

Of course, Le thought, nodding. "They always carry—" *No!* He realized the upper part of the clearing was high enough on the ridge to look down on both convoys.

"The American's directing the killing. We must stop him!" Hoa knelt and grabbed at extra clips in the ammunition pouches strapped to the wounded soldier.

The soldier flinched.

"Easy," Le said. Like talons of an eagle, his fingers stabbed around Hoa's hand.

The soldier coughed up more blood. He shuddered, lapsing into unconsciousness or death.

Fire blazed in Hoa's eyes. He yanked, trying to escape Le's grip. "Do you want Commissar Dung telling General Giap you kept me from saving the last eighty trucks?"

Le glared at Hoa. The parasite was less interested in saving the convoy than in being able to claim he'd saved it. Yet, the American must be silenced—and quickly—if the trucks were to be saved. Deciding the soldier was beyond feeling pain, Le released Hoa's hand.

Hoa pushed the small wooden pegs through the loops on the covers and yanked the two clips from their pouches. He jammed them into his pockets and hurried toward the clearing. He seemed in a race.

Le grabbed his AK-47 from the GAZ. Picking up his ammunition vest, he noticed the survival radio. Perhaps he was close enough to the downed American to hear at least his words. Le pushed the radio inside his shirt as he ran around the GAZ.

The soldier raised an arm and got Le's attention. In a raspy whisper, he said, "He's got a Kalashnikov."

"I know." Dropping to put a reassuring hand on a shoulder, Le assumed the delirious soldier was explaining his AK-47 had been taken.

"The American. He has a Kal—" He shuddered and went limp.

Le laid the soldier gently onto the ground. Thinking about how much the young soldier looked like Kiem, Le reached down and closed the eyes. Standing, he took a final look. Le realized he was beginning to see Kiem in all the young soldiers.

Appreciative of what could be life-saving information, Le caught up with Hoa crouched near the clearing. Le stood over Hoa. "I thought you'd have the American by now."

Hoa's eyes had lost their enthusiasm. "The clearing's very big with many hiding places."

"I don't suppose they teach such problems in Moscow or Paris."

"Finding the enemy's not the cadre's job."

"Today it is." Pushing forward into the meadow, Le tried to appear less wary than he was. "Now get moving."

Hoa stood tentatively. "But we will become the American's target."

"The sooner we tempt him to reveal his location, the better."

Hoa's eyes widened, and he leaned away.

"If we don't silence him quickly, silencing him won't matter." Le leveled his AK-47 at Hoa. "Now get moving before I shoot you myself."

Uncertainty clouded Hoa's expression as he stepped into the clearing.

Le moved about fifty meters from the trees and started uphill. He ordered Hoa out half as far and added commands that kept Hoa from taking advantage of clumps of natural cover.

Away from the jungle, Le got his first view of the O-2 controlling the strike. The plane was well north of the columns of smoke. Le returned his attention to the area ahead. He stalked forward a few more steps before a frightening conclusion jolted him. *The O-2 might have flown north because the downed pilot was guiding the aircraft to the other convoy.*

Increasing his pace, Le shouted, "Hurry!" He reached in his shirt and turned on the radio, producing no more than a faint hiss. Either the battery was too weak or no Americans were talking on the frequency.

Mitch peered above sights of his AK-47 and watched the two soldiers. He had no doubt they would find him before the Sandies arrived.

The soldier nearer the trees surprised Mitch with an apparent lack of tracking skill. That man seemed oblivious to the fact that several times, he'd crossed the path followed by Mitch and his earlier pursuers. The other man looked more savvy. As both got closer, Mitch decided he'd go first for the man straight ahead.

Mitch saw an O-2 climbing away from a rocket pass. He glanced at the closest soldier, then at the karst in the middle of the convoy. He saw a flash. White smoke mushroomed from the top of the karst.

"Go get 'em, Three-four," Mitch whispered to himself.

Mitch aligned his sights on his first target but had a difficult time keeping them there. The man continually weaved and bobbed. Mitch glanced at the other soldier. Both men were approaching reasonable distance for Mitch to open fire. His breathing speeded up, and he tried to decide how long to wait.

The soldier straight ahead hesitated near an outcropping of rocks and banana trees. The man didn't stand still, but his eyes seemed to zero in on Mitch's hiding place.

Mitch noticed the barrel of his own AK-47 was in a patch of sun. *Was his weapon reflecting sunlight?* He tried to keep it from moving.

The soldier's AK-47 swung upward, and he lunged toward the rocks.

Mitch fired a burst. The soldier disappeared, and Mitch had no idea whether he'd hit the man or not. Swinging the AK-47 left, he saw the other man dive toward a nearby clump of trees. Mitch fired a short burst at the movement. Leaves fluttered, and the man screamed.

Mitch kept his AK-47 aimed at the trees and looked for movement.

An AK-47 roared in front of Mitch. Bullets splintered branches, shattered rocks, and clipped off leaves all around him. He dropped lower behind the larger boulder and clawed his way to his second firing position. He edged around but couldn't see either soldier. His heart pounded so hard he wasn't sure he'd hear the next burst from the soldier's AK-47.

Explosions rumbled in the distance. Mitch looked at the karst and saw additional explosions, which he assumed were more trucks in response to an onslaught of CBU-24.

Mitch returned his attention to the clearing. He saw no motion straight ahead, but grass was moving at the edge of the jungle beyond trees where the second soldier had disappeared.

"Five-nine, Three-four," Kesler said. "You've put us on another great target."

Mitch nodded without taking his eyes off the clearing.

Le was trying to stop bleeding from his left bicep when he realized exploding bombs were in a different direction. He froze, holding his breath to determine that direction. The most prominent sound he heard was Hoa thrashing through the grass far to the side.

A sense of foreboding told Le all now was lost. He stretched to see the second convoy without revealing himself to the pilot on the ledge. Sunlight glinted off an F-4 diving out of the western sky. Projecting the aircraft forward, Le knew its target was the SAM Regiment that represented the only possibility of saving General Giap's plan.

In near collapse, Le leaned against the rocks. His will to continue drained away. Silencing the downed pilot no longer mattered.

In the quiet of the moment, he heard a voice from the radio tucked in his shirt.

"Three-four, Nail Five-nine. How close are the Sandies?"

"Nail Five-nine!" Le blurted the words so loud, he wondered if they were heard on the ledge above. He paused to listen for an answer but heard nothing from the radio. *Nail Five-nine.* Le laughed a quiet laugh.

After the FAC answered, Le listened a couple of minutes but heard nothing from higher in the clearing or the direction Hoa had disappeared. The thump of more bombs produced rumbling detonations that continued without pause. He saw huge columns of smoke from his second convoy.

Le rolled over and crawled to foliage offering a good view of the ledge above. He confirmed the clip in his AK-47 was more than half full.

After waiting at least another minute, he assumed Hoa had fled well beyond hearing range. Le took a deep breath and yelled, "Is that you, Metal Dragon?"

The shout made Mitch jump. With his senses at full alert, his mind processed what the words had said. Even then, he was uncertain he could trust his conclusion.

"Nail Five-nine," Le called. "You have become a matter of my very special concern."

Mitch zeroed in on the voice but didn't see anyone. "You are far, far from Hanoi, Earth Dragon." After shouting the words, Mitch crawled to the other side of the boulder.

"Surrender, Metal Dragon. This is not a good day to die."

"No chance, Colonel. Today I'd more likely die in your trucks than on this hillside."

"Very true."

"Today makes up for the last time we talked when I missed hundreds of your trucks."

"Those trucks were insignificant. Today you stopped me from ending this war."

The charge shook Mitch before he understood its meaning. "We're not the French. We won't let you have another Dien Bien Phu."

"You'll still lose on the streets of America as the French lost on the streets of Paris."

Mitch bristled. "Not because of these trucks getting through."

"You've made my future uncertain. Failure is not easily forgiven by my government."

"I could take you with me when the helicopters come. That might be preferable to reporting your losses."

"Tempting, but I think not. I would enjoy another of your picnics, but I really do have a son I can't leave behind."

Mitch remembered a discussion of two children. "You said your two sons were dead."

"That wasn't true."

Mitch wondered whether the missing second son had been real or fictitious. "I'm going to have another child. Anyway I hope I'll be there for the birth."

"An earth monkey to go with your little wood dragon."

"The wood dragon was a girl, as you predicted."

"Expect the new child to be impatient with a streak of independence."

Mitch sensed the conversation was becoming a distraction, so he stayed alert for a sudden attack.

Le continued, "You should've stayed in America with your family."

"Maybe, but I lost two of my best friends here last night. That's why I'm here today."

"They flew where they shouldn't have. I wanted to leave them alone, but—" His voice trailed off. "I did have a second son. This war has taken much from all of—"

A rock clattered off an upper ledge and skittered across the path Mitch had used.

Mitch saw a soldier regaining his balance and raising an AK-47. *The talk was just a diversion!* He felt deceived and stupid, knowing he'd never swing his weapon around in time.

An AK-47 roared.

Mitch flinched but saw no flashes from the soldier's weapon. Instead tracers converged, shattering rocks and glancing off the soldier's AK-47.

The soldier grunted and staggered against the rocks beside him.

Mitch squeezed the trigger. A dozen bullets stitched upward from the ledge the man stood on. Mitch was sure some hit their target. Nevertheless, the man already was tumbling forward. He fell, landing with a sickening thud on the trail fifteen feet below.

"Good shot, Metal Dragon," Le shouted.

Mitch was almost too shaken to move, but he looked over the rock in time to see Le flip an empty clip into the air. After taking a moment to get enough saliva into his mouth to speak, Mitch yelled, "But, I—"

"Must have been your bullets," Le said. "We have rules against the killing of the political cadre. If we didn't. . . ."

"He wasn't a member-in-good-standing of your brotherhood?"

"I do not understand."

Mitch was beginning to understand more than ever before. "Thanks, Earth Dragon."

"The cadre officer caused the deaths of your two friends."

The phrasing shook Mitch with sadness.

"And, many who die today would live still if someone had killed him a few days ago. I—"

From the northwest, the dull grumble of propeller-driven A-1s filled in the intervals of quiet between distant explosions.

Mitch's radio hissed. "Nail Five-nine, Sandy One. Do you copy?"

"I must go, Comrade," Le called from below.

Mitch pulled the radio from his vest. "Standby, Sandy." Getting to his feet, he shouted, "Wait! Come with me, Colonel. What you just did will convince my people."

"But not mine in the South." Le stood, raising his AK-47 high. A bloodstained arm hung limply at his side. "My men need me—and I can't abandon my son." He stabbed the AK-47 toward the sky. "Go home, Metal Dragon. Be done with this war, or it'll take everything you have."

"Nail Five-nine, Sandy One."

Mitch didn't know what to say to Le. "Godspeed, Colonel."

Le turned and sprinted a zigzag course toward the jungle.

Mitch lingered the grip on the AK-47. Did he dare let an enemy of Le's importance fade into the jungle? Mitch recognized Le's answer in the zigzag path. He glanced at the lieutenant colonel's body sprawled a few yards away. It somehow represented the answer to a larger question Mitch didn't even know how to phrase.

Breathing in air heavy with the smell of burning vehicles, fuel, and ammunition, Mitch gazed at the two conflagrations pumping dense smoke into the cloudless sky. Whichever direction Le chose, he might not survive until dark. But, Mitch thought as he watched the running figure grow smaller, Le Van Do's death would not be at his hands.

"This'll have to be our little secret, J.D.," Mitch said quietly. He sighed and raised the radio to his lips. "Sandy One, Five-nine, go."

"Sandy One and Two are a couple of minutes out. Give me a ten-second tone."

"Roger." Mitch kept the button depressed and counted to ten. Watching the underbrush, he saw movement farther down the hill. He released the button and tried to repeat, Godspeed. The word hung in his throat.

"We got a solid cut on you, Nail. We're coming in from the north."

Mitch spotted two specks above trees northeast of the karst. His FAC instincts pushed aside the confusion lingering from the last few minutes. "Sandy, ahead, you'll see a long ridge jutting out like a finger pointed between the strikes."

"I've got it."

"I'm in the upper end of a clearing on your side of that ridge. Inverted triangular shape."

"I may have it. I'll know when we get closer."

Mitch looked but saw no more indication of Le.

Mitch guided the A-1s to him. "Ready . . . Ready." The air around him vibrated from the power of the huge engines. The biggest shiver yet coursed through his arms. "Ready, mark!"

The Skyraiders roared over menacingly at treetop level.

"You've got a great, front-row seat, Five-nine," Sandy One said, "but the Jolly Greens'll be here in about ten to take you away from all this excitement."

"I'll be waiting."

Mitch felt exhilaration, exhaustion, relief, and a dull throb in his shoulder. Tears of elation swelled in his eyes, then spilled over. He rubbed his face to ensure no lines were etched through the sweat-caked dust on his cheeks.

"The hill's pretty steep, Nail," Sandy One said. "If you're up to it, Jolly'll hover and pull you out on the penetrator."

"Roger."

Mitch explained where the road was, then rested while the A-1s wheeled and dived and soared and swung. Thinking about what would come next, Mitch pulled a smoke flare from his survival vest. He removed the safety cap from one end exposing a ring attached to the activating lanyard. Studying the device a moment, he questioned how he could use one hand to set off the smoke signal. He decided it couldn't be any more of a challenge than the snake had been.

Sandy Two swooped across the lower end of the clearing. "I've got a vehicle beneath trees near the parachute."

Sandy One asked, "Any threat?"

"Negative. Looks like a utility vehicle, somewhat bigger than a jeep."

The sounds of both aircraft faded with distance, and Mitch heard the truck engine start. "Is it kind of an ugly crossbreed between a jeep and an old three-quarter-ton truck?"

"Sounds accurate," Sandy Two said. "I can get it on my next pass."

"Negative!" Mitch spoke before he had any idea how to explain.

"Say again, Five-nine," Sandy One said.

"I think, uh, only one guy's left of those who came after me. I'd rather give him a chance to bug out than force him to stay and maybe take pot-shots when I'm being pulled out." *Not a lie, but certainly not the whole truth.*

"That's your call, Nail," Sandy One said. "Let us know if you think he's a threat."

Click-click.

When both A-1s were at a distance, Mitch listened to the truck continue toward the convoy under attack. A huge flash near the karst was followed by a rumbling explosion. Mitch watched in awe and wondered what had exploded.

"I've never seen so many fireworks on one mission," Sandy Two said.

"I've seen almost this many a couple of times," Sandy One said. "It's nice they're ours for a change instead of the bad guys aiming 'em at us."

"This is a mission to remember," Sandy Two said.

Mitch hoped at debriefing time, Sandy Two would remember the fireworks and the clouds of black smoke and the rescue—and not the ugly little crossbreed truck. If the truck were mentioned, Mitch assumed someone in Intel would recognize its significance and ask why it wasn't attacked. He doubted his answer would satisfy anyone. "You're right, J.D.," Mitch said. "Things aren't always black or white."

Within minutes, Mitch heard the thumping of helicopter rotors and the drone of more A-1s. The lead Jolly Green Giant swooped low over the jungle-covered hill above the clearing. "We're ready when you are, Sandy," Jolly Green One said.

"Copied," Sandy One said. "Break. Go to it, Two."

"Inbound," Sandy Two said.

Mitch watched Sandy Two scream in and fly diagonally across the clearing. The A-1's flight path paralleled Mitch's estimate of the road. Seeing four quick flashes behind and below the A-1, Mitch almost called a ground-fire warning. Each flash, however, spewed phosphorous downward like long tentacles of a huge, white jellyfish. Mitch was mesmerized as more flashes produced more jellyfish at intervals behind the A-1. The smoke spread into a white wall blocking the view of anyone near the road.

"Okay, Nail," Jolly Green One said, "pop a smoke for us."

"Standby," Mitch said.

Rising to a knee, he held the smoke grenade between his other foot and a rock. The increasing thunder of rotors beat the air above and behind him. He took a deep breath, yanked the lanyard, and grabbed the cylinder as fuming red smoke hissed from the open end. Smoke enveloped him before he threw the cylinder over the boulders to the grassy slope below. He grabbed his AK-47 and stumbled into clearer air. Below, smoke belched from the cylinder and drifted up over the ledge.

Coughing and trying to fan clearer air in front of his face, Mitch saw the red smoke sucked upward in an enormous spiral. A roaring shadow glided over him. Leaves, dirt, gravel, and every loose bit of dust swirled around in a biting, gritty cloud.

Mitch tried to shield his face from the helicopter's downwash but found nowhere to turn to escape the blinding cloud.

The penetrator clanked against rocks below the ledge, thereby dissipating static electricity built up by the helicopter. Then, the penetrator bounced slowly up the hill.

Mitch staggered through swirling dust to the bright orange penetrator. He unsnapped a safety strap, turned once to wrap the strap around his torso, then clicked the strap into place. He pulled down on a spring-loaded panel, straddled it, and hunched against the penetrator. Raising his good arm toward the helicopter, he jerked his wrist through two thumbs-up signals, then hugged the penetrator. The roar of the engines, and the vibrations in the pulsating air changed. The cable went taut, lifting Mitch a few feet above the ledge.

"Talk to me, Sandy," Jolly One said. "We're coming out."

"Down across the clearing," Sandy One said. "A right climb out when you have speed."

Mitch heard an A-1 roar overhead. He felt himself jerked forward and upward as if on a thrill ride at a carnival. Racing across the clearing, the helicopter gained speed and altitude, then turned toward the jungle-covered hills.

As the winch reeled in the cable, the penetrator rotated slowly, giving Mitch a panoramic view. Turning through the east, he saw jungle so pristine that a nearby war seemed unthinkable. A half a turn away, he saw smoke churning upward from hundreds of fires.

High above the thinning screen of white smoke, Mitch looked at the jungle concealing the road. Each time his view took in that sector, he searched for the road and the truck. He should intentionally forget every detail of this final encounter with Colonel Le Van Do. Mitch knew, however, those few minutes had revealed an aspect of the brotherhood that would stay with him the rest of his life.

The End

Sandy—guardian angel in green-and-brown camouflage

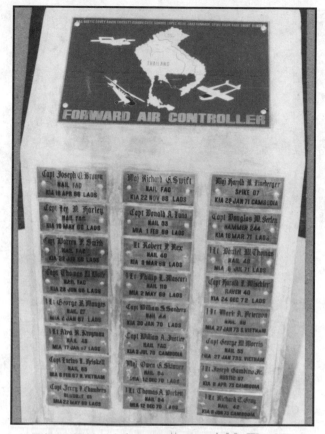

FAC Memorial—Hurlburt Field, Florida

Nineteen of the twenty-four nameplates
on the front of the memorial honor U.S. Air Force
pilots who flew as Nail FACs.

On each side of the road there are heaps of scrap metal, pieces of aircraft, the containers of antipersonnel bombs, empty munitions casings, 37-mm cannon shells, detonated antipersonnel mines. . . . At certain points, it is impossible to walk on the sides of the roads. You sink up to your knees in an impalpable dust, the earth having become dust under the impact of the bombs and incendiary weapons. . . . When the monsoon comes, that dust turns to mud and slides onto the roads. . . . Nothing lives in this dust, not even crickets.

**Observations of a French news correspondent
made during the height of the battle for
control of the Ho Chi Minh Trail.**

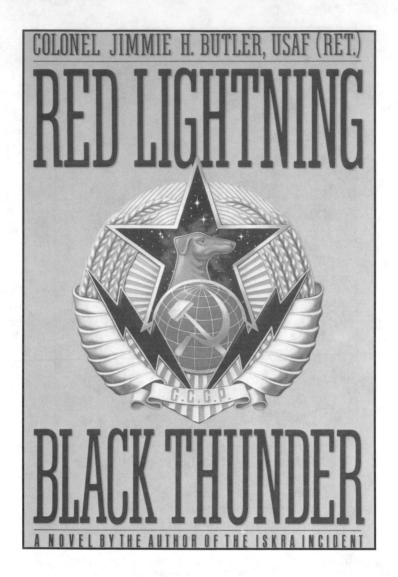

COLONEL JIMMIE H. BUTLER, USAF (RET.)

RED LIGHTNING

C.C.C.P.

BLACK THUNDER

A NOVEL BY THE AUTHOR OF THE ISKRA INCIDENT

The action never stops as Chisholm and his crew match wits and skills with terrorists, MiGs and laser beams, all on their way to the final confrontation with Red Lightning..

—*Publishers Weekly*

This novel rockets off the launch pad in the race to militarize space.

—*Library Journal*

A supercharged thriller set on the fringes of outer space.

—*Rave Reviews*

Red Lightning—Black Thunder
(Dutton, 1991)

The President orders the launch of America's first armed satellite. The high-tech marvel is the first in a purely defensive constellation whose objective is to protect against accidental missile launches and nuclear blackmail by third-world tyrants. The Soviet President views Defender I in more ominous terms and summons charismatic General-Major Peter Novikov to the Kremlin. Within hours, the first of a secret force of Russian attack satellites lifts off.

In the Pentagon Air Force Colonel Michael Chisholm is intrigued by pictures of two powerful Soviet ICBMs on pads used to launch satellites. Piecing together reports of unprecedented Soviet launches, he begins to suspect that the Soviets are preparing to destroy Defender I. But can he convince a skeptical Washington that a superpower face-off in space may be only days—even hours away?

Both scary and immensely readable. *Red Lightning—Black Thunder* projects a scenario where the Soviets make a desperate grab for the ultimate military high ground—space. . . . Several factors make this novel rewarding. One is Butler's intimate grasp of space technology and his ability to break down these dauntingly complex issues into easily understandable form. Another is his portrayal of women in the Air Force and their growing role in the combat arms of the United States. . . . Butler skillfully moves the reader in a complex and chilling chess game. It is a topnotch performance.

> —Harry Crumpacker
> Navy Veteran & Military Historian, *The Tampa Tribune-Times*

A wealth of technical detail, an interesting and believable Air Force romance, and a hair-raising climax over the South Pole are just a few of the high points of this breathtaking thriller. . . . Once the action starts, there are thrills, tension, and terror all the way to the gripping climax. Don't miss this original and groundbreaking thriller by this former chief of staff of the Air Force Space Division.

> —**Marc A. Cerasini**, *Rave Reviews*

With just enough technical jargon to inform but not confuse the lay reader, Butler describes the very plausible could-be scenario of the Soviet response to a planned U.S. first-launch defensive satellite. Alternating chapters between opposing camps, he lets the tension build with final-countdown accuracy. The two major protagonists, both aging veterans of their respective services, approach their tasks with a healthy cynicism not often found in current technothrillers.

> —**David Lee Poremba**, *Library Journal*

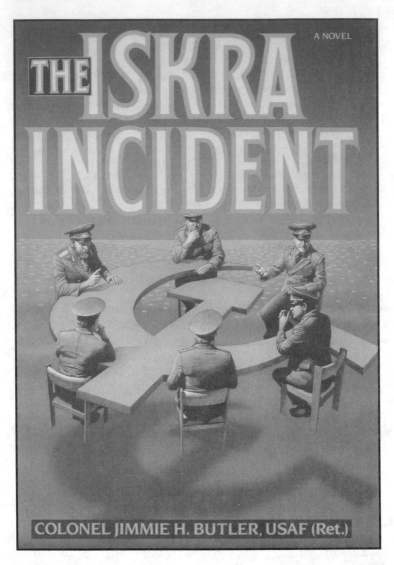

A NOVEL

THE ISKRA INCIDENT

COLONEL JIMMIE H. BUTLER, USAF (Ret.)

"Fast, hot, and straight as an incoming ICBM. . . . techno-thriller fans rejoice!"

—Stephen Coonts

"Fantastic. . . . exciting twists and turns, realistic action, and memorable characters."
—Dale Brown

"A first-rate story. . . . Even the most critical readers will relish the adventure."

—Publishers Weekly

"An entertaining, lickety-split thriller!"
—Booklist